Frances Galleymore's first novel was published to brilliant reviews when she was in her early twenties. She then became an award-winning writer of television drama. *Widow Maker* is her fifth novel.

WIDOW MAKER

Zoe Maker's husband, Charlie, made her a widow at the age of thirty-eight when he tumbled off Suicide Bridge. Zoe knew that he didn't jump, he wasn't the type. He left her a triple legacy — his security company to run, his teenage daughter to raise, his death to avenge — if she can hunt down his killer . . . Who did Charlie meet that night? Would a competitor kill for the patent to his brilliant new project? Zoe's number-one ally, private investigator Alison Seely, is keeping secrets. She disappears. So does Zoe's daughter. What the hell does Zoe do next?

FRANCES GALLEYMORE

WIDOW MAKER

Complete and Unabridged

ULVERSCROFT
Leicester

First published in Great Britain in 1999 by
Orion
London

First Large Print Edition
published 2000

by arrangement with
Orion Publishing Group Limited

The moral right of the author has been asserted

The characters in this novel are fictitious.
Any resemblance to real persons, living or dead,

British Library CIP Data

Galleymore, Frances
Widow Maker.—Large print ed.—
Ulverscroft large print series: mystery
1. Widows—Fiction
2. Suspense fiction
3. Large type books
I. Title
823.9′14 [F]

ISBN 0–7089–4280–6

Published by
F. A. Thorpe (Publishing)
Anstey, Leicestershire

Set by Words & Graphics Ltd.
Anstey, Leicestershire
Printed and bound in Great Britain by
T. J. International Ltd., Padstow, Cornwall

This book is printed on acid-free paper

For Sophie and Elizabeth,
and in loving memory of John

Acknowledgements

The author would like to thank the companies, institutions and many individuals who gave helpful information, expertise and advice. Among them are Andrew Simmen, Maurizio Casiraghi, the British Security Industry Association, Classix Alarm Intruder Systems, Chris Guscott and Masco Security Systems, Nicholas Pole and Sly Fox.

1

In the small hours of the night, our minds play tricks.

I was falling, falling. Something was tugging at me through layers of darkness. A quiet scrape of glass was followed by a stealthy click and soft, unobtrusive thuds. My mind fumbled for explanations, remembering I was alone in a strange hotel room. Was that rain, gusts of wind, the heating system? I listened, chasing off fragments of dreams. It took a few seconds to locate the rhythmic sound that filled the night.

It was two seventeen. My mobile was at the bedside, next to a bottle of mineral water. Answering it, I searched for a wall switch nearby and the room was swamped with cold light.

'Zoe.'

A rasping whisper forced out my name, dispersing sleepiness. I struggled to sit up.

'Charlie.' It didn't sound like my husband, but who else would decide to call at two in the morning? 'D'you know what time it is?'

There was no answer, nothing. 'Charlie ... Are you still working?' I felt a stab of alarm. 'Are you all right?'

'Listen . . . I haven't got long. To talk.' His voice sounded fuzzy, disconnected. Still I didn't realise what was happening. I imagined Charlie at his computer, intent and unaware of the time or the world outside his head, oblivious to his own needs or his family's.

I tried to suppress the old resentments. 'What is it? Are you coming down to Mayhall after all? Caro'd be so pleased if you did. You'd be making her week.'

'Listen. Love you. Both . . . '

Maybe it was then that I knew he must be in deep trouble. Charlie could spin words for hours if the subject was electronics, but he could never find these kinds of sentiments. Except now. I sat up quickly. 'And I love you, Charlie. Something's wrong, isn't it? Tell me.'

'Can't talk . . . '

His words faded. A burst of music came through instead. It was some rock standard I couldn't quite recognise, a phrase of a song just beyond grasp. It was gone, cut off abruptly. I slid out of the hotel bed and sat on its edge, trying to bring back his voice. 'Charlie, what's wrong? Are you ill? Where are you?'

He began to speak again, but it was all barely decipherable. I heard the word *enemy*, and something about *protection*. Not like Charlie, any of that. He was slurring out phrases, rambling as if he was dead drunk. He had never got drunk, never in nineteen years. I thought then he might have got injured somehow. And that he seemed afraid; that something terrible might be happening.

'I'll come back, right now. Tell me where you are.' I was almost shouting, in case he couldn't hear. 'I'll call someone, the police. Shall I? Or what — '

'*No.*' Charlie was lucid, suddenly and obviously making a huge effort. 'No, don't tell . . . Don't trust. Not anyone. Promise. *Promise.*'

'Darling, I promise. Tell me where you are, then I — '

'Be *careful*. Watch out . . . '

'What is it? Charlie . . . I'm driving straight back.' There was no answer. Then a clattering sound, it was metal or glass. The line had gone dead. 'Charlie? No, don't go! Where are you . . . ?'

A fox barked somewhere and rain fell in gusts on the windowpane. I sat there in the chill night, listening to his absence, then to my own fear beginning. Charlie needed help but I didn't know what was wrong, nor where he was. I called up the number he'd rung from. It had an outer London 0181 code that I didn't recognise. The number rang and rang endlessly. Charlie had moved on, or fallen unconscious. I scribbled down those digits, then tried his mobile but couldn't get through. In some forlorn hope I rang our house, then our office at MakerSeceuro HQ. Of course, there was nobody at either place.

Charlie was in trouble, ill or under some kind of constraint, trying to alert me but incoherent. I remembered the way he had come up with last-minute vague excuses why he couldn't be with us this weekend. There had been something important that he wasn't telling me then but I was too disappointed, for our daughter's sake, to find out what it was. Caro had changed schools for her sixth-form studies, Mayhall was still new to her. How could her father be too busy to attend the first parents' weekend? I had hit the roof. 'What could be more important, Charlie? You promised. She's expecting us both. Everyone else's father will — '

'There's something I have to do,' Charlie had cut in. He had said it in a final, decided way. 'I can't get out of it. I have to see someone — '

'A meeting? A *business* meeting? What the hell is going on? This particular weekend — it's not just any old time, it's special for Caro. She'll be hurt. You must at least explain.'

We had argued for a while but he wouldn't give way and wouldn't explain. I felt puzzled. He was a kind father, well meaning although too often unreachable, distracted. Clearly Caro felt let down. Yesterday, Saturday, she had put on a front, showing me around the places where she hung out, casually and carefully introducing her new friends. It was brave but she was insecure. She was used to being at day school, with us at home.

Charlie had some emergency, and I must go and help sort it out. Two miles away, Caro would be asleep in her bright, yellow-painted room. She had decorated it with her posters and plants, rugs and cushions, producing a cheerfully cramped chaos. Was she going to wake up there to find that I had gone too? I must either return to the school by eight thirty, or call her as soon as they were all at breakfast.

By now I had decided to get back to London quickly, and was pulling on clothes, folding others and repacking my weekend bag. I couldn't have stayed a moment longer, after Charlie's strange call. There would be time on the journey to decide how to go about finding him. Scooping up wash things into their bag, I did a quick calculation. It was two twenty-three and the roads would be clear. Despite the heavy rain, I might make it back to the city in about forty minutes.

★ ★ ★

There was no sound but rain and the wind, gusting through darkness. I stepped out of a warm foyer and ran for my car, a white Mazda MX-3 parked near the entrance, and set off fast. One question kept nagging: was Charlie really lying ill and alone somewhere on such a cold, stormy night?

From the hotel driveway I turned right, through narrow lanes. The headlights' powerful beam lit dense hedges and thin treetops. The lanes led to a sliproad on to the A3 and soon I was speeding north. There was no one about, almost no traffic at this hour. I crossed red lights in Hindhead, threading through the town, around hairpin bends that lined the crest of the Devil's Punchbowl. A sheer drop fell away to my left, almost blotted out by the rain and dark. When I hit the dual carriageway at last, I put my foot on the floor and tried Charlie's mobile again. It was still switched off.

Who might I call? Who might be able to

help? Alison, of course.

No, don't tell . . . Don't trust. Not anyone. Promise. Promise.

He had seemed terribly afraid of something or someone. Could that have been the muddled paranoia of a fever, maybe a sudden bout of flu? Or . . . Charlie might have been involved in a road accident.

'Sorry, Charlie,' I murmured, punching the memory dial. 'But you want to be found? So Alison's our woman.'

Alison was an old friend and was to be trusted. Twelve years ago she had left the CID, around the time she and Charlie first met. Later she started her own private investigation agency. Our paths sometimes crossed professionally with hers through our company, MakerSeceuro. Alison's specialities were commercial and personal security, and industrial espionage — or counterespionage, as she would say. She had some big clients. Finding somebody scarcely came into her category of work, but she had the right connections and experience, with motive enough as a friend of Charlie's.

The phone was purring now in her Hampstead house. I prayed she would be there and not out on a job or some heavy date, not away for the weekend. When she answered, Alison sounded like a hungover mole being dragged into daylight. 'Yes. What?'

'It's Zoe. This is important.'

'Goddamnit — Zoe? I don't believe it. Do you know what the time is?'

'Two thirty-seven on Sunday morning, I know. Alison, it's about Charlie. He rang twenty minutes ago. He's ill or something — and I don't know where.'

There was the shortest of silences, before Alison's voice snapped back: 'What did he say? Where did he call from?'

'He sounded incoherent and — sleepy, as if he was only half conscious. He said to be very careful, to watch out. That I shouldn't trust or tell anyone. About the call? I'm not sure if — '

'Why did he call *you*?' Alison cut in suddenly. There had to be a smart answer to that, but she added quickly, 'You're out of town this weekend, aren't you? I'm assuming Charlie called from London? Wasn't he at home?'

'That's what is really odd. He rang from some number with an exchange I don't know.'

'Let's have it.'

I gave her the number. 'Can you find him?'

'It should be easy to locate the phone,'

she said, noncommittal about what really mattered. 'Where are you now, Zoe?'

'On the A3, twelve miles north of Guildford. I was in Sussex for Caro's parents' weekend. Charlie couldn't make it, said he had to see someone at the last minute.'

'What kind of someone? A client, or . . . Did he say who it was?'

'No. I've no idea. It was important. I think he must've gone out — visiting, entertaining maybe — then left but got taken ill. Or he could've been in an accident. Alison, he doesn't want the police involved.'

'I see. And you want me to go and find him — now, personally?'

'Please. And the weather's a monsoon. Poor Charlie, if he's out in this. Can't have been in his car, he would've rung on the mobile from there. You will find him, won't you?'

'Have you told anyone else?'

'No. But maybe I'll call our MD. Bill might know something if it was business-related, maybe a customer? Or Charlie's assistant — '

'He didn't want you to tell anyone.'

I hesitated. 'Listen, I'll head towards home, check for any clue as to where he went tonight.'

'I'll trace the number, start a search for his car. I'll get people looking for him.'

'Thanks. Call me back as soon as you know anything. Anything at all.'

After that I was alone with my thoughts. The dark outlines of hills and trees were overtaken by clusters of suburbia. The curving ribbon of cat's-eyes got swallowed by serious lights. Concrete escarpments, heavy crash barriers appeared, encasing the road as I carved through a scattering of city-bound traffic. I kept calling Charlie's mobile, getting no response. It was lonely, that. I veered between hope — that we would find him quickly, there would be some simple explanation, he would be all right — and anxiety with a sense of foreboding.

If someone else from MakerSeceuro was alerted, they could be checking the office while I headed for the house. I had Bill Thwaites's number and he was closest to Charlie, but I balked. There was no bond between him and me. Perhaps he was too much of the old school and we were on opposite sides of some glass fence. Once he knew the chairman had gone missing, Bill might go straight into authoritarian overdrive, not do as I asked, even call the police.

But suppose there was some clue at the office as to Charlie's whereabouts right now?

'Madison,' I murmured aloud into the speeding, flashing night. Seconds later I was explaining — not too much, only what he needed to know. Madison 'Magic' Black was our sales and marketing director, ambitious and visionary. He had a rocklike reliability. I would have trusted him in almost any context. 'I'm very concerned about Charlie, whether he's OK. I need your help.'

'Tell me.'

'Do you know about any meeting that Charlie might've arranged for yesterday? For last night, perhaps?'

'A Saturday evening? No, nothing he mentioned to me. Have you tried Bill? Or Jenny — '

'The thing is, your home is close to the office.'

'I'm on my way. What d'you want me to look for?'

I could hear his wife, Ruth, saying something to him nearby. 'I don't want this to go any further. If Charlie's been taken ill . . . '

'Fine, Zoe. I understand that.'

'Check in his diary. Anything that might tell us where he was going. It was a meeting, it should be in there. Who. Where. And Madison — there's one other thing. I don't know why, but Charlie doesn't want the police informed. So we'll leave them out of it.'

He agreed, sounding slightly surprised. 'OK. Let's not get too worried. There's only so many places he might've gone. There's a limit to what could've happened. We'll find him.'

'Let's hope you're right.' I checked that Madison had my number and we arranged to keep in contact. I wondered briefly how much he would tell Ruth. An office emergency could be explained away, but he had said some specific things, and I didn't know his wife well.

The city was flashing past, asleep. There could be no simple darkness inside a web of millions of neighbours with motives unknown. So, security. The long arms of the industry — the giant Banhams and Chubb, Livesey and A-Zander, with young MakerSeceuro and its hundred brothers — had wound around the streets and buildings, gripping tightly.

I overtook a truck, then braked, cornering for a short cut through King's Cross. Rows of shops were closed behind steel shutters and padlocked grilles. An alarm was whooping a solitary warning, its light flashing, unattended.

Everyone has something to hide and

something to protect. We all have things to fear. At MakerSeceuro we prevented crime, while we traded on the communal bad dream.

The rain was pummelling down relentlessly, blanking out visibility. Avoiding the North Circular because of roadworks, I got on to Camden Road for Holloway and Archway. Using the A1, I would reach home around three fifteen.

There's a limit to what could've happened. We'll find him.

My spirits lightened, remembering Madison's closing words. On familiar roads and drawing nearer to our house in Finchley, I imagined Charlie already back and perfectly safe, having forgotten to let me know. He would be sitting in the kitchen, nursing an unaccustomed hangover and wondering what he should take for it. I would have a lot of explaining to do, apologising for sending Alison into action, for alarming Madison and disturbing his and Ruth's night.

I stopped at red lights, waiting to turn north towards Archway. A couple of other cars were around. I called Charlie's mobile again. All the way up from Sussex, every few minutes I had kept on redialling, hoping Charlie might have switched on.

Now, suddenly, he had.

13

Somewhere in the night, his mobile was ringing. Then it stopped. There was silence.

'Charlie? It's Zoe. Please answer, love. Say something.'

I strained to hear. He had answered, the line was open, but he wasn't speaking. Then I heard the sound of some distant traffic, an engine passing: it was passing by him, not me. And I swear that I heard him breathing.

'Charlie! Please answer. I need to know where you are, damnit! Speak. Tell me. *Say* something, anything . . . '

There was nothing at all now. I must have imagined his breathing after all. But he was there on the line. I quelled a surge of anger. It was rage at my own powerlessness to find, to help him.

'Listen, darling — just make some sound. Can you? . . . OK, I don't know what's wrong. If you could just let me know where you are. Let us know . . . Charlie, I called Alison. She's searching for you . . . Listen, I'm getting on to the A1, heading up towards home, right now. Can you hear me? Oh God, Charlie. I'm coming up to Archway roundabout . . . '

I had to pause then, for long enough to concentrate on the road. Something was right on my tail, dazzling into the rearview mirror.

It was making it harder to see through that curtain of rain, among the blurred streaks of light and wells of shadow. I turned off at the big roundabout, heading up the Archway red route, north towards a wide-spanning bridge. I was accelerating when the driver behind pulled out to the right and sped through the darkness beside me, almost grazing the Mazda's wing. It was a white sports car, hovering alongside now.

I hit the horn and swerved in closer to the solid concrete wall which towered on my left as we swung through the cutting. Ahead, something big was lumbering powerfully, and I strained to see through the clouding rain. It had a *Long Vehicle* sign on the tail and a lot of small lights: a wide monster that overhung its lane. The white car had passed me and was streaking along the rails of the barrier, nearing the vehicle in front. Speeding up to level with its tail, dwarfed by those enormous wheels.

The lanes were beginning to narrow and merge. And the white sports car was starting to overtake. To overtake the thing ahead — which was an articulated lorry, I saw in sudden, chill disbelief. It caterpillared out to follow the carriageway, the cab seeming scarcely connected to that massive, trailing body. Its brake lights came on, just as I

15

was starting to brake and steering into an instant skid on the treacled surface. The white car bounced fast through the gap, spinning between the lorry's safety bar and the central crash barrier, squeezing through and vanishing ahead. My car was still skating forward unwillingly, too close to the huge wheels of the braking lorry, when I heard the crash somewhere ahead, a sickening rending of furious steel. The lorry jack-knifed away from solid concrete, across the central kerb, trailing broken railings down into the oncoming red route lanes. Still gluing my brakes to the floor, I steered hard, swerving towards the small space that remained then exploding with a bang into the giant's side.

★ ★ ★

There was almost stillness, nearly silent, terrible. Tiny shifts and moans of crumpled steel, a fall of broken glass. Somewhere a car's alarm was sounding intermittently.

I took a breath, then another. I began to move experimentally and seemed to have the use of my body, arms and legs. The Mazda's nose was concertinaed into the lorry's safety bar. My windscreen was in fragments, the space in front reduced to half by overhanging dash, buckled panels.

The driver's door seemed welded into the bodyframe. I battled out of the passenger side, into the road.

My legs were collapsing under me, pain stabbing through an ankle, lungs refusing to work. Under the ghastly yellow streetlamps, I limped round the giant's tail. Someone was staggering about, directionless. It was the lorry driver. He seemed all in one piece but shocked.

'Crazy car. Crazy wanker. Didn't stand a chance. They came across in front. I didn't stand a chance.'

'You hit the car?' I looked all around but couldn't see anything at first. Then I made out what must have been the sports car. It was as flat as a white sandwich, pasted on its side to the escarpment. 'Call an ambulance! Then bring your first aid.'

I started to run, on rubbery joints. I got to the wrecked car but could see nobody inside. What remained of the engine was smoking and the sparkling rain hit on it, sizzled. Then I saw part of somebody — an arm and their head — sticking out of the caved-in side where a window should have been. There was nowhere for the rest of that person to be. The face was of a boy, who looked about twelve. He was clearly dead.

I heard a small sound, between a moan

and a sob in the throat. Then I made out the body of another kid, huddled down in the front. A white face, closed eyes. A lot of blood. The moan had come from him. 'Can you hear me?' I shouted.

He said dreamily, eyes half opening, 'Fell out of the sky . . . '

I had no idea what he meant. 'You're OK. You're going to be OK.'

There was no way of getting to him. He was trapped under the seat by buckled steel. I could see blood coming out of a wound in his head. 'You're going to be all right. Can you still hear?' The boy made no sound. His eyes had fluttered closed again. I saw that the driver had reappeared and was holding a first-aid box. 'There's a kid down here. He was conscious, he spoke. Can't get to him.'

'Ambulance is on its way,' the man said. 'There's something underneath Suicide Bridge. Someone's lying back there, under the bridge.'

'Stay here, talk to him. I'll go and look.'

I grabbed the first aid, stumbled back through the driving rain in the direction the man had pointed. Someone had been flung into the road and lay, limbs sprawled like sticks, pounded by the downpour. I ran towards them, half aware of voices shouting not far away, of people appearing and sirens sounding in the distance.

I reached that still figure. Then I knelt down in the road. Charlie lay twisted, his bloodied face washed by rain and his beard stained dark. There was a howling, keening sound, cut short. It was me. Desperately I felt for any sign that he might be alive. When I found it, his pulse was very faint, unbelievably slow. There was so much blackness, it was so wet, I couldn't tell where he was bleeding from. Blue lights were revolving somewhere nearby. Why weren't the paramedics saving Charlie?

Lurching to my feet I yelled, 'Over here! Help him!' Two figures looked up from the group around the wrecked car.

Someone else appeared through the dark. It was a man in a black leather coat, face contorted, roaring with anger. 'Fucking coward, to jump — they never stood a chance!'

I held Charlie's head between my hands, and told him to hang on. I touched my lips to his forehead, above his ear. His hair was matted, his skin cold and wet with the rusted smells of blood and diesel oil. 'Don't go.' I started breathing into his mouth, trying to bring back his breath, his warmth.

The paramedics reached us then, and began to help him.

2

'Zoe Maker? I don't think we've met before. I'm Detective Chief Inspector Paul Prentiss. Detective Constable Sarah Quirke.'

We shook hands. The DCI was tall, with slicked-back dark hair and beadily observant eyes. His DC was a redhead with freckles, a friendly face. They looked ludicrous somehow, coming into this elegant Hampstead living room. Having shown them in, Alison was hovering, wanting to go but unsure. 'Perhaps you'd like coffee?'

'That would be welcome.' Prentiss and Quirke settled themselves into one of Alison's sofas.

I was trying to register a new level of acceptance, to overcome some lingering refusal to believe what was true. This interview was really about to happen. My head pounded and I felt sick. 'Chief Inspector, I think you may have known my husband?'

'I met Charlie a number of times over the years. We all knew him . . . Very sorry about what's happened. Very sorry.'

I nodded, unable to speak. Charlie had

died at four forty-three on Sunday morning — yesterday — at the Whittington's Accident and Emergency unit. I had been with him constantly since finding him. He had never regained consciousness.

Prentiss went on, 'You're staying here, with Alison Seely?'

'For a few days. My daughter Caro is here too.'

'Caro. She wasn't with you when you found Charlie?'

'She was at school in Sussex. I hope you won't need to interview her. She's . . . '

'Of course. Not in the immediate future, anyway.'

He was courteous and humane, probably wondering how far he might go with questions, so soon after the nightmare of the previous day. The horror of it all was fresh. My ears still rang with sounds of disaster. Charlie's dying face was floating before me, vivid. Underneath all of it, I recognised one new factor: this had been passed to the CID, and that meant Charlie's death was suspicious. Not necessarily an accident. Maybe not self-inflicted.

'I talked to your colleagues yesterday,' I began. 'The road accident people.'

Prentiss nodded. 'I've seen your statement. Some fresh facts have come to light which don't quite add up — to what we first thought. To suicide.'

'Charlie would never have killed himself. You say that you knew him? Everyone did. Charlie had no thoughts of self-destruction, and . . . he had everything to live for.' Everything: in a life that would never be lived now. I stared at Prentiss's face. A slight reserve had appeared there, making me determined to be believed. 'I would have known if he was depressed, worried about business, money — anything like that. I'd like to see the note you found. He was perfectly OK. Except . . . '

'Except?'

'When Charlie suddenly said he had to stay in London last weekend. There was something wrong, and he wasn't telling me.'

'Was it unusual? For him not to tell you his worries?'

It was clear what the DCI was thinking, that here was a wife unwilling to admit — even to herself — that her husband might have been desperate enough for suicide without her knowledge. That made me angry. 'I knew Charlie for nineteen, twenty years. I *knew* him. He was never suicidal. Where's the note?' I swallowed, suffocating tears, trying not to think what my next question meant. 'Has there been a post-mortem?'

He paused for a minute, shuffling some papers. With immaculate timing, Alison appeared and began to distribute coffee in a welcome distraction. She was being practical, almost cheerful, as she had been through the past thirty-six hours. Only if you looked at her was the strain clearly discernible. She hovered, uncharacteristically uncertain.

'You can leave us to talk,' I told her. At the same moment, the phone rang.

'OK. I'll be next door if you need me, Paul. I'm working from home today.' She went out, closing the door.

'Yes, to your question.' Paul Prentiss was ladling four spoons of sugar into his cup, stirring mud. I felt a sudden hatred for those blameless, nicotine-stained fingers. 'The autopsy's produced some unexpected results.' He put down his cup on the low, tile-topped table between us. 'You haven't seen the note then. It was found in your husband's pocket. Can you tell us if this was his handwriting?'

He produced a small, rectangular sheet of anonymous white paper, still inside a transparent evidence bag. He held it out like an accusation. I took a deep breath, trying to focus, to concentrate through a sudden surge of emotion. Charlie's writing — searing, now that he was gone. The uncomfortable, angular scrawl of someone long habituated to computers. His words sprang out, clichéd and unbelievably painful . . . *Can't go on, better if . . . so sorry . . . forgive me, darling.*

The DC reached across in a practised gesture, offering paper tissues. 'Is it his writing?'

'It looks like his. But someone could've forged it.' I looked straight at Prentiss. 'I don't believe Charlie jumped. Even if — for some reason — he suddenly wanted to, he would never endanger people like that.'

'Half a dozen leapers do it every year from Suicide Bridge. Appears to attract them. It seems very high, because of that view of the city way below. They probably never think of the people driving immediately underneath.'

'I don't believe he jumped,' I repeated. 'Surely someone must've seen what happened? There were cars about!'

'No one's come forward yet. Unfortunately, the hour and the rain make it less likely we'll find witnesses. There was one other fatality, so far.'

That *so far* was chilling. 'The second boy . . . ?'

'Still critical. Head injuries. Badly crushed legs.'

'What the hell were they doing? Was the car stolen?'

Prentiss nodded. 'Fifteen — the one that got killed. He was known to us, been in plenty of trouble. Quite a prize they picked up there, that little Toyota. Wanted to see what it could do, I suppose.'

'They were joyriders who just happened along? In a car looking a bit like mine. Same colour. Similar build.'

There was a brief, uncomfortable silence. Sarah Quirke asked, 'D'you think that had something to do with it? Him leaping, just then?'

I laughed, then suppressed the welling hysteria. She peered into my face, earnest and questioning. 'You think it may've been more than a coincidence. Yes?'

I didn't know what I thought. It was too new, this awful reality. I tried to concentrate again. Charlie was dead. He was being blamed, implicitly, for causing the death of a teenager. Now, suddenly, it looked as if he might've aimed to have me kill him. To keep things in the family . . . When I spoke again, I could hear my voice come out very crisp at the edges. 'I want to know the results of the post-mortem, Chief Inspector.'

'Perhaps you can throw some light on this. Did Charlie ever take a prescription drug called temazepam? Or was it ever prescribed for you, or your daughter?'

'That's some kind of tranquilliser, isn't it — for sleeping? No. Nothing like that. Why?'

'You're sure? We're checking with his doctor.'

'Charlie never took pills. He didn't need to, slept like a log.' I remembered the slow, slurred incoherence of his speech in that last call. 'You're saying that Charlie was drugged, when he . . . ?'

'Large quantities of temazepam were found in him. It appears to have been injected from capsules. Those capsules were banned a few years back in this country.'

Charlie, injecting a drug? Nothing was less likely. 'I don't understand. Someone did that to him — it's the only explanation.'

'He travelled a bit, didn't he?'

'In Europe. The Channel Islands. And to South Africa, a few months ago.'

'He could've obtained the drug in capsule form abroad. I'm very sorry about this. The pile-up, the three vehicles involved — it seems that none of them actually hit him. He had injuries from the fall, which could've proved fatal on their own. I'm sorry to have to go into this. You were never aware of him taking any medication like temazepam?'

I shook my head. 'I would've known if he was . . . In the ambulance, I saw — Charlie had a finger missing. Did that happen during his fall?'

Sarah Quirke intervened. 'We're looking into that. But your husband did not suffer, he remained unconscious.'

I turned to her. 'The bridge has a tall wire fence on each side. How could he have climbed it on his own, in that state?'

Prentiss answered, 'The council's made a lot of effort, with anti-leap measures. People do still manage to jump. But it seems doubtful Charlie could've got over the fence with that quantity of drugs inside him.'

Unable to stay still, I jumped up. Alison's living room swam around, vertiginous. 'Someone got him up there, pushed him off the railings. It must've taken time. There have to be witnesses who saw something. He was murdered.' I paced across the room. A rage was beginning to burn inside me. Charlie had never hurt anyone. He had everything to live for.

I looked at the detectives. They sat there, impassive. Prentiss was waiting, Quirke was writing in her notebook. I went on, 'That's why he tried to warn me, by phoning. Charlie was terrified. That wasn't despair — he was in deep trouble . . . ' And I had failed him. Worse than failed, since I'd somehow become a part of his death: his fall had happened the moment I appeared. I had rehearsed my route to whoever was listening on Charlie's mobile, even told them when I was about to approach the bridge. When a white car similar to mine appeared below, Charlie was pushed.

If this was murder, it was murder of a bizarrely cruel and personal kind. Who could possibly hate Charlie so much? Charlie, and me?

Prentiss asked me to go over everything that had happened. I sat back down, recited the facts one more time. Did he still believe I was unable to see a simple truth? 'Charlie must have made enemies, Chief Inspector. We had done so well in a few short years. You know how it is, security's highly competitive. We were about to take a far larger slice of the market.' I tailed off, because even as I said them the words sounded thin.

'Competition does not add up to homicide,' the DC said, with a calm glance at Prentiss. 'And if it wasn't suicide, or an accident . . . This was not a professional killing either.'

Yes, I agreed silently, aware of a tension between the two detectives. It was obvious that Charlie's death had been too weird, too full of the risk of discovery, to carry the marks of a logically thought-out execution.

Prentiss took over. 'Let me ask this in strict confidence, Mrs Maker. Did Charlie — or MakerSeceuro — have money problems? Debts, anything of that kind?'

'Is that what they're saying? Damnit, we've known exactly what we're doing. Growing fast, using the impetus of a market that's expanding fast. You can't do that without taking a degree of risk.'

'I see. And how was he about to 'take a far larger slice of the market', as you put it?'

For a moment I hesitated, because I had been sworn to secrecy. But could this be what lay behind Charlie's death? 'There was something new that Charlie had developed recently. A very clever, inexpensive way of preventing false alarms — '

'What, altogether?' Prentiss interrupted, looking startled.

I almost smiled. 'Perhaps not. But the existing rate will be cut once the new Goldstar technology is patented and marketed. It's a new concept. It'll push MakerSeceuro into the world market.'

'I see. Who else knows about this? Is it general knowledge?'

'Scarcely, at this stage. Charlie told only our technical and marketing directors. The rest of the board know of its existence, but not any details. It's absolutely confidential. We're about to challenge the older, bigger companies . . . ' How hollow that sounded now. One horrific fact had changed everything. I pushed away the wall of pain, went on talking fast. 'Someone could've been after it. In Charlie's eyes, MakerSeceuro was set up for selling his inventions. He lived for them, and this was his cleverest brainchild.'

Nobody spoke for a few seconds. Then Sarah Quirke asked, 'If he really lived for his inventions . . . Are you thinking that your husband might have permitted his own death, rather than destroy his secret? The way things are, it seems that this technology, the Goldstar, has been bequeathed to the firm. To yourself and your daughter, as I understand it. What kind of value would you place on that?'

'It's impossible to value. I can't think of another reason why anyone would want Charlie dead. People like . . . They liked him.'

'Charlie Maker was a well-respected man,' Prentiss said. 'And I'm sure that went well beyond the local community.'

'But why did he call and say those things? If he wasn't very afraid — mortally afraid of somebody?' I paused, let it sink in.

'What about the phone he used, Chief Inspector? Alison tells me it's not far from the Technopark.'

Prentiss looked annoyed. Quirke asked, 'Can you think of any reason for Charlie being in that area at two in the morning? Did he know people, have friends there?'

'I don't think so. But several security companies of different kinds have premises nearby.'

'Does MakerSeceuro do business with those companies?'

'Not directly, not that I know of . . . This is a radically sexist business, and I was not told everything.'

'You've inherited the company now, I'm told. Is that so, Mrs Maker?' Prentiss asked.

During the trauma of the last two days, there had been little chance to think about the wider implications. I frowned. 'I inherit a major controlling share, automatically. There's a lot to sort out.'

There was a silence. 'I think that covers everything, for now.' Prentiss stood. 'We'll be in touch. If anything relevant comes to mind, please get in touch with myself or DC Quirke.'

'I want justice for Charlie. He didn't want to die, he didn't cause that boy's death.' My voice was shaking and I ploughed on.

'You will be sending the note to forensics? I'll get you a sample of Charlie's writing. If you have to interview people at the firm, please — let's keep this as low-profile as possible.'

He gave a murmured agreement, with a sideways look. I understood then that the rumours must be flying already. How much damage could they wreak for MakerSeceuro? Outside it was growing dark, Black Monday had almost drawn to a close.

As he was leaving, Prentiss spoke. 'We need to know where Charlie was, and with whom, after ten o'clock. Those missing hours after he left Alison Seely.' A tiny but perfectly formed bombshell. He must have seen my expression, quickly covered. 'Miss Seely was the last person to see him alive that we know of. They parted outside Bengal Bertie's at ten. He saw her into a cab, said he had to go and meet someone.'

With a false calm I asked, 'He gave no indication of who he was going to meet?'

Prentiss shook his head. 'Didn't Alison mention to you that she'd been with him? That seems rather odd, doesn't it?'

'I expect it slipped her mind. Goodbye, Chief Inspector. Constable.'

The unmarked car slid away down Fitzroy

Lane, its headlights torching the edge of the Heath. Darkness descended, pooled by the bright security lights of millionaires' row. I went back and into Alison's office, without knocking.

3

Alison looked up, raising her eyebrows quizzically. 'I'll call you back,' she said to the phone. 'No, better if I come in . . . Fine, hang in there.' She swivelled her chair. 'Has Paul finished? I thought I heard them leaving.'

I leaned against the door jamb. 'Alison, why didn't you tell me? You were the last person to see Charlie alive.'

She looked taken aback. 'Didn't I mention we had a meal together? He left four hours or more before he called you . . . I'm sorry. So much has happened — '

'How could you have forgotten? When I called and alerted you, even . . . ?'

'For heaven's sake — you'd just woken me up! And didn't give me a chance, remember?' She stood up, annoyed. 'I called three operatives, then went out in a rainstorm for you. Later . . . I thought I had mentioned it.'

'You were the last person to see him.' I stared at her hungrily, as if she held some answer to it all.

'Hardly the last. Others will turn up — Paul

Prentiss is a good cop. I think you're overreacting. I've scarcely been able to remember my own name today. Listen, darling, I'm sorry that went out of my mind.'

'What was he like? Over dinner at Bengal Bertie's? How did Charlie seem? What did he talk about?'

'Oh, you know, he was preoccupied as usual. Nothing . . . If it was important, I would've remembered.'

I went on staring at her. It seemed a little late to be feeling this inner turmoil. It was just that I'd been taken by surprise that she hadn't told me. His friendship with Alison had predated mine with her, of course. Charlie had introduced us, she and I had grown close in the last few years. She had been wonderfully supportive, yesterday and today. I tried to smile.

'You're still in delayed shock, sweetie,' she said. 'It's hardly surprising.'

'Yes. You're right. Alison — '

'How's the neck, and the ankle? Apart from . . . everything else, that was a bad car smash.'

'They're OK, thanks. Is Caro still asleep? Have there been calls for me?'

'She is, I checked. Why not leave those messages until tomorrow? Listen, Redcliff's

35

got a problem with a client, I've got to nip over to the office for half an hour. Will you be OK?'

Alison's face was lined with strain. She must have been shattered by Charlie's death, yet she had remained a tower of strength. Yesterday morning — her only free day — she had even driven to Sussex and back, so I could break the news to Caro. News there was no way of softening: suddenly, overnight, her father was dead.

I wrenched my mind away from the image of Caro's stricken face, those outraged howls of pain. 'We'll be fine. Thanks for — everything you're doing.'

'Rallying around is the least I can do. Listen, leave all that. Get some rest.'

Gathering messages from a corner of her desk, I clung to them like someone drowning and finding driftwood. They were solid, a link with reality, a chance for survival. 'I can't. Need to be doing things. Need to be busy. I should go in tomorrow anyway. Must clear the ground for that.' Most of the messages could wait. They were expressions of scarcely veiled disbelief, shocked sympathy. *If there's anything we can do* . . . It had got out at once that Charlie had fallen from Suicide Bridge — so he was a suicide. What effect was that going to have? On a tender sixteen-year-old who had loved her dad? On the firm he had founded and nurtured over fifteen years?

Alison was hovering by the door. 'Go on.' I smiled at her. 'Go and sort out that new partner of yours.'

'Ah, Redcliff,' she sighed. 'He's a boon and a blessing, and the opposite of those two things.'

When she had gone, I called Bill Thwaites on his direct line. It rang once. 'Yep,' he said.

'It's Zoe. What's been happening, Bill?'

There was a pause, then a surprised echo. 'What's been happening . . . Nothing you should be concerned with. Or worrying about. How are you now? And young Caro?'

'We're doing all right. Have the police been in touch with you?'

'The police? No. Are they likely to be?'

'You bet. A DCI Prentiss is looking into things. I've talked to him, but he'll be asking for finance details. Whether the firm might be having difficulties. It's a formality. But best to warn Stuart in Finance.'

'That figures. Looking for . . . a reason. But why the CID?'

'Because Charlie didn't jump. Bill, there was somebody else involved.' I listened to his stunned silence. 'We don't know who, or why. Not yet. I've asked Paul Prentiss to keep a low profile, but the police will be interviewing some staff. They'll almost certainly ask to examine Charlie's files.'

The MD's voice re-emerged, hot with outrage. 'It's disgusting, bothering you so soon. At a time like this! They should've come through me, the proper channels.'

'I'll be attending tomorrow's board meeting as usual. Then I'll talk to the staff at HQ.' Here was something I could do, I thought. Something I could do for Charlie.

Bill went silent, but not for long. 'There's no need. I can take care of business. Charlie would want me to look after you and Caro. See you're properly taken care of.'

'Thank you, Bill. But I want to talk to everyone, because people deserve that.' I paused. 'Is there anything else I should know about?'

He said there was nothing. I arranged to see him at two thirty.

By now I recognised the signs: in his misguided attempt to be protective, there were things he wasn't telling me. Needing to know what had really been going on, I punched out another direct line.

'Madison, it's Zoe.' Into the silence, 'So, how's it going?'

'OK . . . How are you?'

'OK. What about MakerSeceuro, Madison?'

He hesitated for just a moment. 'There was a piece in the press, this morning. You didn't see? Four column inches of lies. Damaging lies.'

'Read it to me.'

'I'm too bloody furious to. I'll fax it, if I may.'

When the page came through, I saw exactly what he meant. It was a hatchet job, a diary item under the byline of Pat McBain. A veiled attack on MakerSeceuro, the piece subtly implied that the booming company was crippled with problems, caused by a too rapid expansion programme. The alleged suicide of its founder and chairman, involving the death of one teenager and critical injury of another, was a symptom of the malaise. Did Charlie Maker jump because of the Gill Tarpont case? The writer went on to describe how Tarpont, a prominent retail client, had been murdered in her home. The implication was clear: MakerSeceuro, its products or services, must be in some way unreliable. The words *I'm sorry, terribly sorry* had been quoted, lifted from Charlie's note. The journalist ended, like some cheap prophet of doom, 'Is this the unmaking of MakerSeceuro?'

If I was seeking distraction from grief, I had found it.

Gill's murder had happened only three

weeks ago. Her home alarm system had not been relevant, Charlie had told me. The alarm never went off but for the best of reasons: nobody had broken in. How could Charlie, or the firm's products, be blamed for her getting killed? I called Madison back. 'Have the lawyers seen this?'

'Yes. It's carefully worded. First reaction is, they don't think we have a case for libel.'

'I'll speak to the lawyer. No one should be able to get away with all this false innuendo. Who is 'Pat McBain'? How did Charlie's note get leaked? Was it via the emergency services?'

'It's all we needed right now.'

'Yes, too convenient. Far too timely. Who's behind it, do you think?'

He answered uncomfortably: 'People are very demoralised. Not knowing what will happen to them in the future.'

'And getting a broadside like this one adds to the disarray. At least I can give some assurances about the future, right now.'

I arranged to speak to Madison tomorrow afternoon before the board meeting. Then I went through into Alison's empty living room, took a phial of pills from my bag and raided the drinks cabinet. Jack Daniels, unopened. It was probably the bottle Charlie and I had bought her at Christmas, only three weeks ago. I sat down heavily, poured a tumblerful and read the prescription label.

Temazepam. Hysterically, I laughed. The doctor had prescribed them this morning for sleeping. Temazepam! These were tiny white tablets, not the capsules that someone had used to inject Charlie with an overdose. 'Oh, Charlie. Love, I'm so sorry . . . We'll find out what happened. Who did that to you.'

Alone, I could let down the mask I was creating to shut out the world, to survive behind. Later, when the couple of pills and the whisky had begun to take effect, I commandeered the bottle and went upstairs to the guest bedroom. Caro was curled up asleep, her fair hair spread over the pillow. Softly, I kissed her cheek. She stirred. 'Mum? Was there someone at the door?'

'That was only some people who wanted to talk. They've gone, and I've come up to bed. Sleep well, darling. I love you.'

Her arms came out for a hug, fiercely, like a young child. Within a couple of minutes we were both in a deep, exhausted sleep.

★ ★ ★

When I woke, Charlie flooded my mind. I was grappling with the fact that he would

41

never be around again. Over the years he had become part of me, familiar as an arm or a leg. I wasn't able to take it in all the time, that he'd gone for ever. It was as if he might come back, he had only gone on some trip. Except that my body — with its gut-dragging, stonelike weight of depression — was telling the truth.

His life had been thrown away as if it was nothing. Whoever had done it was going to be found, brought to justice. When I thought about this, depression gave way to a boiling anger. Then I could act.

Caro's bed was empty and it was broad daylight. Ten past eleven, I saw with a shock. My head was muzzy from whisky and pills. I took a fast hot-and-cold shower before getting dressed.

Sunlight filled Alison's stripped-oak hall and the kitchen. Her house had been acquired and done up in the eighties, during her marriage to a well-known architect. The spoils of war, she called it. I filled the cafetière and looked out into the garden. Caro was playing with a neighbour's cat, laughing as it chased the belt of her dressing gown. She looked round, shielding her eyes from the sun, and I waved. The cat pounced again and she leaped back, shrieking.

'Sleep well?' Alison asked. She was pouring

coffee into two cups.

'You should've woken me. My God, that was a fourteen-hour night. Caro looks better.'

'She does, poor lamb. I've got plans for you both.' Alison sipped coffee, then slid a sheet of paper towards me. It was Madison's fax. 'I found this. Damn them, whoever they are. Blaming Charlie for what happened to Gill Tarpont.'

'It's complete nonsense, anyone can see that! But mud sticks. I shall write a strong response — after I've spoken to our lawyer.'

She said, after a pause, 'Of course Charlie *was* affected by it. He'd known Gill at least fourteen years, since she bought the very first of her gift shops.'

'She was more than a customer,' I agreed. 'It was devastating that she was killed . . . ' On some instinct I turned to Alison, searching her face. I remembered hearing about Gill's stabbing. There had been surprisingly little press coverage and no details had been released. The killer had not been caught. I remembered vividly how deeply disturbed Charlie had been. Too disturbed to talk much about it. To me, at least. And now Charlie, too, was dead. 'Did he say anything to you about her murder? He did, didn't he? On Saturday night, when you met, did he talk about it then?'

Alison broke into a broad grin. 'Sweetie, you met Thisbe again.'

Caro had come in through the back door. Her face was flushed with laughter, eyes sparkling as we kissed a greeting. Seeing her happy was such a relief, but it brought home to me just how desperate her grief was. To survive her loss as unscathed as possible, she would need time and distraction, not only affection and safe familiarity. 'I thought she'd grown up too much to play. But she's still like a kitten. It's cold out there,' she went on. 'Mum, I need my big Peruvian jumper.'

'Well, I'm going home this morning. To collect things,' I added, seeing her face fall. She was afraid to return to our house yet, unready to face the fact of her father's absence and the reminders which would be everywhere. 'You could make me a list of what you want.'

'OK. Alison's taking me to lunch at Now And Zen. She says we ought to go away on holiday, Mum.'

'Oops,' said Alison. 'I was going to suggest it, Zoe. Good idea?'

I looked at Caro. Her face was clouding again already with the grief that had knocked her sideways, with inner conflicts I could only guess at. She needed me. The firm did too, but once today's meetings had been got through, it could wait for a week or so. There must be consultations, including with the lawyer and the accountant, before making any cast-iron plans for the future. A break would give us time together, away from pressure and rumour, to start coming to terms with what had happened.

'We can, can't we, Mum? You and me. And Alison?'

Alison and I glanced at each other. A wary acknowledgement passed between us in that moment, of a rivalry that had always existed, always unspoken. I nodded slightly to her but she turned to Caro, regretful. 'It would be awfully difficult for me to get away.'

'We could go skiing, darling. How about that? A week or two in the Alps.' I thought about the pure mountain air, bright sun and uncomplicated social life, pictured Caro honing her expertise on the slopes.

'You must be joking.' She scowled. 'All those people. I don't want to be surrounded by people.'

Charlie had always come with us to ski. Those holidays had been special family occasions. Alison broke the silence. 'How about Jersey? That would be quiet. If you went for a fortnight, I could pop over for the weekend.'

Caro perked up, then frowned. 'I don't

45

want to stay in a hotel.'

'I'm sure you could borrow Colin and Liz's house. It's just sitting there while they're in Barbados. That would be more private. Let me fix it with them — this girl needs a holiday, and I could get flights for tomorrow . . . Ah. For a moment I forgot. Your phobia about flying.'

I hesitated. A fortnight, almost alone together and with little to do: was that a good or bad idea? There would be acquaintances we could visit, but even so . . . 'Let's not rush, let's decide this evening.' Of course I couldn't fly. 'There'd be no need for you to book, Alison. Jenny could do it, and get us on to a ferry.'

* * *

An hour later I was in the back of a taxi, heading for home and wondering about Alison. She seemed anxious, so active on our behalf that she was almost interfering. There was something that she — and maybe Charlie, too — had been concealing from me; something to do with Gill Tarpont's murder. Alison had been too intent on rallying around Caro and myself, as if she was trying to make up for things. Almost as if she felt guilty.

I filed the thought away in my mind. I

would get the truth out of Alison.

The cab reached Finchley and turned up Eldon Avenue. Our home, Cedar Court, looked mellow in the deceptive cold sunlight. Built of honey-coloured brick and green tile, it had always been too big for us. Charlie and I had wanted more children, but our marriage had difficulties while Caro was still an infant. It had been patched up — I was deeply fond of Charlie, if not in love — but the separation seemed to have changed our future. More children never happened and we had made the best of things.

I let myself in to an eerie, resounding silence. A pile of condolences waited on the table and flowers were in vases everywhere. Mary had come in, sorting things as usual. Without giving myself time to think or feel, I went upstairs and packed clothes for Caro and myself. In the kitchen, I poured a glass of mineral water then went to the room overlooking the side lawn which Charlie had used as an office. It was both cluttered and desperately bereft. His things filled the place. I touched them. Noticing our shared diary, I glanced through it, then stowed it with my documents.

A memory, an impression came to me of the last time I had seen him here. Our final encounter, before I had left for Caro's school.

He had looked round from whatever he was doing, the lamp lining his rather anxious face with light. I had pecked him on the cheek, said coolly that I would see him on Sunday night. Then I had gone.

'Goddamnit, Charlie . . . '

I struggled.

I sat down at his desk and looked at the photo he kept there. It was of the three of us beside a fishing boat, on Aldeburgh beach.

'There's nothing I can do for you,' I said softly. 'This is the only thing. I'll need a hand here, Charlie.'

At first it was hard to concentrate. I made notes for my meetings and priority calls, drafted a public rebuttal to 'Pat McBain' and a personal letter for circulation to all MakerSeceuro staff. The shock and even the grief began to fall away. Concentration, action was a balm.

I changed into a suit and called a minicab.

The driver set off for MakerSeceuro. It was time to become visible, to vanquish fears and raise morale, to be the boss. I wondered if I could do it. For Charlie, I would try.

4

In MakerSeceuro's headquarters, Charlie's last words came back to me. *Don't trust. Not anyone . . . Be careful . . .*

He had built the company from nothing, over fifteen years. From the MD down, these people owed Charlie their jobs and their loyalty. I was a lot less essential. Although on the board I was seen as almost peripheral, working on the promotional side.

Now word had gone round that I was the new owner. As Charlie's widow, I now controlled this company.

As I walked through the building, greeting personnel I had known for years, suddenly I was an object of intense curiosity and speculation. These people's futures were on the line. What was going to happen to them?

They expected me to sell out, that was in their faces. It came home to me that if I kept the business and took an active role, I would be judged against Charlie's achievement.

Only two days had passed. Everyone here was still reeling from the news of their boss's death, from those stories about suicide. Why

49

would he have done it, unless there was something terribly wrong with MakerSeceuro and its future? The rumours were so thick they could suffocate us.

There were six of us at the board meeting. It was testosterone city — Bill and Madison, flanked by directors Stuart McDale, Keith Naylor and Den Morton — and myself taking Charlie's place. Bill Thwaites was looking troubled already. He and I had just spent twenty minutes together, at cross-purposes.

Charlie would have been startled by the eulogies. I could not afford to feel moved by them, and yet I was. I thanked everyone for their messages. 'We're all suffering from shock. We'll miss Charlie — he was a one-off, nobody could ever replace him. But he's here with us in spirit. He dedicated himself to the firm. MakerSeceuro was the most important thing in Charlie's life.' My voice wavered. I took a deep breath. 'With all your talents and hard work, this is a great team — he built a company that we're proud of. Charlie would want us to keep moving. His death's a terrible blow, but we must recover fast — for his sake.' I looked around. Most of them were avoiding my eye, until I added, 'The CID have begun a murder inquiry. Someone killed Charlie. Nothing can alter that. But they are not going to murder this company.'

There it was, spoken aloud. A flurry of questions followed and I told them what I knew. 'We need to destroy the rumours immediately. Someone's trying to bring us down. We know that we're totally reliable. We know that we're healthy and achieving steady profit growth.'

'We're well on target for this year,' Stuart confirmed. 'But any adverse publicity, especially right now, could leave us vulnerable.'

'We should look at using an outside PR consultant, now I need to concentrate on running the business,' I suggested.

I could feel Bill bristle. He said with obvious distaste, 'We've never needed public relations as such.'

'But we need to protect ourselves now,' Madison took him up. 'An outside consultant would make very good sense at this stage. With Charlie gone.'

There was assent from Keith and from Stuart. I took three sheets of paper from the stack I had brought to the meeting, then caught Bill's look of dismayed surprise. He had recognised the hatchet job which lay on top, and his face was flushed. I could see him thinking: who showed her that?

'You've all seen this from yesterday's rag,'

I said. 'We're a target already — somebody wants to kill off MakerSeceuro.'

Bill muttered something fierce about lawyers. Den was asking, 'Who's Pat McBain?'

'I doubt if he exists. We have to realise that this could be only the beginning. Don't let's underestimate the threat we represent to future market share.' I showed them my written rebuttal, which was with our lawyers for approval.

Right now we were about survival, but Den Morton brought up one looming future dilemma. 'This is not the time for it,' he acknowledged, 'but to keep our research and development, we'll have to headhunt major talent.' I had my own ideas about this: without Charlie, we should rethink. Technical innovation had been our great strength because of him, but over the years we had become an anachronism. Other installation firms no longer made their own equipment. We must explore that alternative before replanning.

We had the existing ace of the Goldstar and it must be pushed through, the impact of our competitive advantage maximised. The marketing department would continue to work like Trojans. After dealing with other business, we agreed on a brass tacks meeting in a fortnight.

Since MakerSeceuro's beginnings, I had been completely involved. Charlie had consulted me but he always preferred to be seen as the decision-maker. Although my long-term grasp of the business was probably as good as anyone's, I wasn't sure if I could lead the company. The shock of Charlie's death was confusing, masking response, but I sensed scepticism, especially from Den Morton. Bill's air of bafflement was tinged with hostility. He hadn't guessed that I might rebound into the firm and start taking control. He seemed upset and, worryingly, he was sometimes inflexible.

Now I had to look at who I supported, and who I did not.

The meeting with HQ staff was a simpler, emotional affair. Charlie had attracted a loyal workforce. We had looked after these people and some had been with us from the start. Wanting a new kind of rumour to circulate, I told them that the chairman's accident was under investigation by the murder squad. That it was my intention to keep the firm, to hold it together as before. We were all mourning, devastated. But the best tribute to our founder, the only tribute really worth making, was our continued commitment to the firm and its success.

It was twenty past five when I got back to

Charlie's office. Jenny Styles had worked as his PA for five years. A super-efficient and likeable woman, she had coped with Charlie's sudden death with her usual, miraculous reliability. She knew her own value and I was desperate to keep her. We started conferring together. It must have been obvious to her that by now I was right on the edge of collapsing. Promising to look after things, Jenny suggested tactfully that I might want to go home.

With a heavy armful of holiday reading, the latest reports and accounts for getting right up to date, I walked out through the quiet corridors.

★ ★ ★

The evening was cold and dark, with a fine drizzle falling as I left the building. Ahead lay the company car park, a floodlit expanse of shining tarmac and almost empty by now. I started towards the dark-red Volvo, our people-mover, unused since last week. I was beginning to shake from all the effort. Unable to go on, I leaned heavily against the rough surface of the brick wall.

For all those fighting words about the business and about Charlie, I had never felt more alone. He had been many things

54

to many people but, in the end, Charlie was simply a man I had loved, a person very much missed, and I felt desolate from loss. An intense longing swept through me for his presence, his familiar voice, for words I needed to hear from him. There was no way, then, of holding back my feelings.

After a while — I don't know how long it was — finding some tissues I took a deep breath and started blindly across the tarmac towards the car. I felt a prickling of awareness and looked round. A shadow had detached from the wall's recess, at the entrance to an alley ten yards off. I had been absolutely certain I was alone.

Someone was approaching, and I hurried to the car.

He paused under the lights — a tall, solidly built man in a heavy coat and dark trousers. From inside the Volvo I watched him come up, then look in. He was twenty-something, not an employee, but I had seen him before. He had pale-coloured hair and wore dark-rimmed glasses. He was saying something inaudible. Reluctantly I pressed down the window.

'I was just passing.' He smiled slightly, nervously. 'And I thought you might be ill. Is everything all right?'

After a moment I answered crisply:

'Everything's fine.'

He looked taken aback. 'I thought . . . Oh.' Then shock filled his expression. 'Mrs Maker? I didn't realise it was you.' He hesitated. 'You don't know me, but I heard about what happened. To your husband. I was — very sorry. It's terrible.'

His words tumbled to a halt. His unease was palpable. It was the awkwardness of anyone trying to speak condolences, magnified by his lack of years. He had a gentle charm.

'Yes. Thank you.' Suddenly I remembered who he was. We had bought the freehold of our office block and then, a few years later, that of the neighbouring shop. Two flats above were let out to rent, furnished. This was one of our tenants.

He must have seen the recognition, and recovered his poise. 'Sorry I disturbed — startled you. Just wanted to help if something was wrong. Forgive me. Please take care.'

Murmuring some denial, I turned away to end the conversation. He had intruded massively. In the mirror I saw him retreat across the car park, turn into an anonymous shadow again. He climbed the narrow black fire escape which led to the flats, and was soon out of sight.

From tomorrow, there could be a degree of anonymity. If we went to Jersey, not many people there would know who we were. The house was private and well screened, and we could see friends or not as we wanted.

I drove carefully, shaken still by the depth of my feelings and full of buried anger because of their interruption by a stranger. I was too churned up to be driving.

No one answered when I called Alison's house, so I tried her office. Caro was there. 'I'll pick you up, darling. How are you, how was today?'

'Dullsville. You know.' Her voice was brittle.

'Was it boring? I'm sorry. What about your lunch at Now And Zen?'

'That was all right. And then we went shopping. I've got some new boots, they're great.'

'Have you, indeed?'

'Oh, Mum. Anyway, you said we're going to do lots of trudging around. We are going to Jersey? Fresh sea air and ghastly things like that? So I need the boots, don't I? Anyway, I've been working here.'

'OK, OK. Yes, we'll go to Jersey if that's still first choice. Listen, I'll be by in about twenty minutes. Can you come down?'

'Not really. I'm working with Redcliff

now,' she explained, 'in the archives room. Oh, and Alison wants a ride home with us.'

I had turned off the North Circular and was heading south among the traffic on Finchley Road. 'Fine. See you soon, sweetheart.'

Alison's office was at the edge of Regent's Park. There was no meter free so I left the car on a double yellow line. Her building was a converted house in a gracious, curved Regency row, a carefully preserved time warp. Inside was uniformed security with CCTV and a visitors' book, a reception area and the lift beyond. Quest Associates had the third floor, above an insurance company, an investment broker and solicitors. It was all pretty empty at this time of the evening. I started for the stairs, then changed my mind. As I pressed the button, a man squeezed in through the closing lift door. He was tall and weasel-faced, with a sandy moustache, his grey mac darkened from the rain. By now, bad vibes were combining with a sense of nausea. I got out at three, and so did my fellow traveller.

I was heading for Quest's reception when someone appeared from nowhere, pushing past me. He was about thirty, broad-shouldered and muscular in black sweatshirt and jeans, his hair close-cropped and face set grimly. That bulldog stance, everything about him spoke of intimidation. I felt a rush of anger. He went striding on to confront the man who had shared the lift. 'Hello, Eddie.'

For several tense seconds they stood inches apart, eyeball to eyeball. The weasel-faced man held his ground. 'I've a message. And that's all.'

'Sure it is.' That voice was cutting steel, honed by threat. 'Forget it. Get back in the cage! Beam on down to where you belong.'

That was when I glimpsed Caro, caught in the corridor just beyond them. She was hovering there, white-faced. I called out to her.

The weasel-faced man shot out a hand. A split second later he was felled by a heavy punch. Gasping for air, he was being gathered up into a bundle, arms bent back like chicken's wings.

Something had tumbled to the floor. An open double-sided knife was lying there. The bulldog man aimed a kick. The knife flew across the floor like so much trash.

Then he snarled round to me, in our mutual recognition, 'Thanks for nothing, lady!'

Hatred welled in me as his earlier words came flooding back. Only two long days ago, under the bridge in the rain and dark, across my husband's pitiful, dying form. This man's face, contorted with rage or adrenaline then as now. *Fucking coward, to jump — they never stood a chance!*

I leaned in close now. 'Well, look who's talking,' I hissed to him, quietly. 'I'll show you who's a fucking coward! If only it had been you that died.'

Those narrow green eyes turned to slits. 'I take back that 'lady',' he said. The next moment, he was hauling his victim to his feet. The visitor, still gasping for breath, was frogmarched unceremoniously to the back stairs.

Caro was with Alison at the reception desk. Her eyes were wide from reactivated shock. Shaking from my own reactions, I went to her.

'What was he doing with a knife?' she asked.

By now I had realised, of course, that weasel-face had meant trouble for Quest. Things just hadn't looked that way at first. I was still furious because of the way Caro was being affected, and couldn't find any words. Alison told her, 'It's all right now. There's no harm done.'

'But who was he?' Caro asked. 'What did he want?'

'That was just somebody's hireling. Come to deliver a message.' She shrugged, lightly and unconvincingly. 'Redcliff was watching out for him on the monitors. He doesn't like him too well.'

I was incredulous. 'Redcliff? You mean *that* was your new partner? That great thug?'

'He's sharp. He's good,' she retorted, annoyed.

'He's got a real attitude problem. He must go down a bomb with your corporate clients!'

'For heaven's sake.' Alison sat on the receptionist's chair, crossed one elegant leg over the other, lit a cigarette and lapsed into silence. She was watching one of the CCTV monitors. Moving round, I watched with her. Her thug partner was taking a long time saying final goodbyes to weasel-face.

'The car's on a double yellow,' I told her.

'Can you hang on just for a minute? I need to have a word before I go.'

When Redcliff made it back to the office, Alison went to confer with him. 'Was that what we thought it was?' I heard her ask.

'It's sorted. We'd upset a client of his . . .' And he added a name, too softly to hear. Then he put a hand on Caro's shoulder, and saw she was still looking troubled. 'OK?' he asked her. 'I had to get him out of here, and quickly.'

She said, 'It was OK, it was exciting.'

'This is Jay Redcliff,' Alison introduced us. 'Zoe Maker.'

I watched comprehension dawning on Redcliff's face. He was beginning to look stricken, but I was still too furious to be gracious. 'We've met, two nights ago. Come on, Caro . . . We'll be in the Volvo.'

We went out and waited in the car. It was several minutes before Alison appeared. 'Sorry about the delay. Also the drama. Life at the office is usually so dull.'

'I'm going to be a private eye,' said Caro nonchalantly. She was quite recovered by now, with a new gleam of interest to her.

'Oh no you're not,' Alison countered. 'You wouldn't have enough patience. Endless watching, endless checking of records — '

'You wouldn't do it if it was boring,' Caro pointed out. 'You do it because it's exciting.'

I caught Alison's eye, then looked away. Caro had always alternated between hero worship of her, and ambivalence which seemed to contain distrust. I had never understood why. And Alison seemed to envy me, although she would stay childless from choice. She was committed to her independent relish of life and her succession of sexual conquests. Might that explain the new tension between us? I was suddenly single, like her.

'A girls' evening in,' she announced half an hour later, opening her freezer and glancing over its contents. 'How nice. We could phone out for dinner.'

'All we really need is a bottle or two.'

I had a lot of questions to ask Alison, but waited until Caro had gone up to bed. Listening at the living room door, I left it almost closed to muffle the sound of our conversation. 'Your new partner,' I began. 'How come he was right there at the bridge — just when Charlie was?'

'Because I'd called him out. I used two operatives, and Redcliff himself. We were in the Lea Valley area, and had a search on for Charlie's BMW — which turned up, abandoned outside a park there. Redcliff went to where I'd last seen Charlie.'

'Then how did he miss seeing him on Suicide Bridge? Or *did* he see him? Have the police interviewed him?'

'Yes, of course — Redcliff made a statement. He was searching the streets under the bridge, trying to find anyone there who'd seen Charlie or his car. It was a long shot, and he had no luck. When he heard sirens arriving, he went straight to the scene. I didn't realise you'd met there.'

'It wasn't a tea party . . . Your thug partner decided then and there that Charlie had jumped so was to blame for — the mayhem.'

Alison reached for her cigarettes. 'I think everyone assumed that at first. Be fair, darling.'

'With friends like that, you don't need enemies.' I still felt angry. 'Where did you find him? He's not another ex-cop — that's for sure.'

She lit up, and blew out smoke. 'You've only seen one side of Redcliff. Believe me, there are many others. I'm sorry he upset you. Zoe, you really need this break — it's like treading on eggshells, dealing with you.'

I nodded, because she was right: everything was making me angry. I stared at her, still sure that she was keeping something vital from me. Alison had made detective sergeant quickly despite the strong gender bias which existed then. She kept good close contacts among the police. I asked coolly, 'So what is the connection — between Charlie and the Gill Tarpont case?'

'Darling, I don't know.' She ran a hand over her auburn bob, burnishing its gloss. I felt sure she was lying. 'Yes, he did talk about Gill's murder that evening. He was terribly affected by it, you know he was.'

'Was he trying to find out who had killed her?'

'How on earth should I know?'

'Why weren't there any proper details about Gill's death in the papers, on the news? There's been some kind of censorship, hasn't there? Have you asked Prentiss — '

'I don't meddle,' she snapped. 'I do my job, which is quite enough. Police contacts wouldn't wear it for a moment if I meddled.'

We stared at each other. 'Would you do a job for me? For Charlie?'

She pulled a face, probably at the emotional blackmail. 'What then?'

'Trace Pat McBain.' I saw an expression of relief flit across her face. Then it was gone. She had expected, or feared, something else. 'Charlie was killed — most likely somebody paid to have him killed. I want to know who his enemies were. Whoever was responsible may've hired the hack who cobbled together that 'Unmaking of MakerSeceuro' piece.'

'Pat McBain,' she echoed, thoughtfully. 'I suppose it's possible there could be a link.'

'Find out who he is, who got him to write that piece.'

'It could have been — just opportunistic . . . '

'It was far too quick. And just too neat. Will you?'

'I can probably trace the journo for you.'

'Right. Get to him, and we might get some answers to the big questions.'

She shifted towards me, restlessly. 'Why not leave it to the cops? Haven't you got enough to deal with right now?'

'I want justice for Charlie. However much that costs. There's one other thing.'

'What?'

'Don't let that crazed partner of yours anywhere near this. OK?'

'You need a holiday,' she repeated. 'Don't worry, we'll find your Mr McBain.'

That night I lay awake for a long time. I was going to get justice for Charlie, whatever it cost and however many people I had to alienate. I slept patchily until the alarm woke me. Caro and I packed for the trip to Jersey and by ten I was on the phone to Prentiss. He probably thought I'd remembered something new. He was disappointed.

'I've been thinking things over. Charlie had been very shocked by Gill Tarpont's murder,' I told him. 'We'd known her for a long time. She was practically a friend, as well as a customer. I think there's a connection.'

Prentiss was silent. He asked cautiously, 'What kind of connection are you thinking of?

66

The two cases appear to be very different.'

'She was stabbed, wasn't she? In her home. Charlie was devastated when he heard. Suppose he was trying to find out who killed her?' I listened to another silence. 'There's been nothing in the news about any possible motive. Was it robbery, a burglary?'

'I'm afraid I can't comment, Mrs Maker, on that case. Not at all. If you have anything new for us, you'll get in touch then?'

Inwardly fuming at his refusal to give an answer, I assured him that I would. I cut the line, thought for a moment, then pressed redial and asked for DC Sarah Quirke. She answered in two seconds flat. 'I've something for you. DCI Prentiss wanted a sample of Charlie's handwriting. I've got that — and also Charlie's and my diary, from home.'

'I'll come over and pick it up,' she said at once.

'Caro and I are leaving right now, for a fortnight's holiday. Could you meet us on the way?'

★ ★ ★

DC Quirke walked into the busy café, looking for us. I raised an arm to catch her attention, assessing her as she approached. She was tall, lean and fit, around twenty-three or twenty-four. There was something a bit unorthodox or even wild about Sarah Quirke. The red curls were dishevelled and her wide grin suggested a sense of easy triumph. She was not your average young detective. In her old leather jacket and jeans, she looked like just anybody passing through.

'Caught you, I made it.' She sat down at the table, cheerful. 'On your own?'

'Caro's exploring the shopping possibilities.' I took out the diary and put it down on the formica surface between us with a page of Charlie's handwriting.

'Right.' Sarah Quirke's eyes were keen. 'This is nice for me, taking in something new which might prove useful. We didn't know you and your husband kept a home diary. Why didn't you tell us before?'

'I didn't have it before. And there is something I need from you, Sarah.'

'I see.' Her expression darkened with caution, at my words and at the familiar use of her name, perhaps. 'And that is?'

'I need a bit of quite ordinary information, about the Gill Tarpont case. Gill was a friend of ours. I want to know how — and why — she was murdered. What was the motive?' Sarah said nothing, and I went on: 'I asked your boss this morning. Got a brush-off.'

'Then I may not be able to tell you anything, Mrs Maker.'

Urgently, I leaned towards her. 'It's Zoe. If you can, then will you? Please. Because . . . Gill was a friend. It would help me to know. There was so much secrecy around her death, and now . . . I just need to know — why *that* happened. To start making sense of — something, at least.'

Watching my expression carefully, she considered, then seemed to relent. 'I'll find out what I can.'

'Thank you. This is our number for the next twelve days. Thanks, Sarah.'

Sarah Quirke picked up the diary and clasped it to her, looking serious. 'You won't keep anything else from us, will you?'

'Of course not. Listen, I want this solved — more than anybody does.'

5

We took the ferry to Jersey. We were free to begin the worst time of our lives. It was the beginning of Prozac time, days which are best not remembered too well, especially that first week. In our different ways, Caro and I both fell apart.

She had quickly retreated, withdrawing into long silences, when any interruption to her thoughts drew a spiky response. The bright, joky sixteen-year-old was gone. I sensed bitter, searing recriminations: why had her father been allowed to stay behind, alone in London for that last weekend? Why had it been him who died? In so much pain, she was turning against me. How could I help her? The teenage angst which had begun to ease in the past year was back with a vengeance. Poor Caro. My heart ached for her even as my own anger, so near to the surface, was being set off by her.

The island was quiet under a pale sun. We were staying in a grey stone house, a hundred yards from granite cliffs and an empty beach. Hedges surrounded the garden, keeping the world out, enclosing us in the absent lives of Liz and Colin. They were on holiday in Barbados with their four children. Their house spoke of family togetherness and loss.

Had it been a mistake to come? Caro tried hard to sink into couch potato mode. She put on the same clothes each day and watched endless TV. The first night I had gone into her bedroom, borrowed from a ten-year-old, and held her. We cried together. After that, we both slept in the master bedroom. She grew calmer, then more deeply withdrawn. She wanted me near, but to be alone. Attempts to get her to talk were all failing. Caro needed time.

I dragged her out on those promised long walks, and she raged at me for that. We targeted cafés, bars and restaurants, stopping there a while before walking home again, worn out and windblown, full of sea air. We hired horses and went riding — something we both loved — and this cheered Caro.

There was time to think, and sometimes guilt overwhelmed me. I had failed with Charlie — in getting him to Sussex that weekend, then in reaching him and responding to his call for help, until it was too late. I could have tried harder with our marriage. During the early years, I had left him. Was that a very bad time for him? I had never really said sorry. Might that be why things had never worked too well between us afterwards?

I forced myself into holiday reading of accounts and reports, plans and projections. I had to step into Charlie's shoes, decide on the right options and guide the firm onwards. There could be no standing still, no fudged decisions or delays. Yet it seemed all wrong, this necessary haste. It seemed inhuman. If Charlie had been here with Caro and myself, there would have been the usual sightseeing trips and visits to friends. Not doing these things — not having the heart to — brought home our loss. A million videos of Charlie and our life together were tumbling through my head each endless night and day.

★ ★ ★

We had been on the island for nine days. Alison's promised visit had been put back to the second weekend.

That Friday morning dawned grey and windy. Caro was watching cartoons, so I set off down the lane alone. The blustery, fast-moving clouds swept low overhead in changing patterns of oppression. Several sleepless nights, with pills no longer working their easy magic, had left me ragged as the day. Without noticing, I had climbed gradually and was standing high up on the cliffs. Suddenly I was gazing down at black waves breaking over and over, far below. My breath jagged into panic, abrupt. Those rocks were beckoning irresistibly. I had woken up to death, to its inevitability and permanence — and that had happened before. No wonder we live like sleepwalkers, doing all that we can to avoid its stare. Catch death's eye and you are marked.

Caro was so young for this. She needed to talk.

Back at the house I found her in the conservatory, curled up foetally in a round basket chair. Music was playing from the living room. A singer, a haunting sound that stirred in my memory. It was something important, and recent, which I couldn't quite place.

'Darling, how are you?' I stroked the overgrown fringe back from her eyes.

'Don't ask, Mum.'

'It would be better to talk, sweetheart. Don't keep things shut in.'

She didn't speak, just closed her eyes. It said clearly enough: go away, leave me alone.

'We need to shop for the weekend. We could go in to St Helier. To the market.' I recognised the singer, now, as Sting. But that song . . . what was it? The back of my neck was prickling at those soft repeated chords.

'What's up, Mum?' Caro was staring at me, sitting up crosslegged now in her chair.

'That song. I've heard it somewhere recently . . . What is it?'

'It's 'Fields of Gold'. OK,' she volunteered, unexpectedly. 'Let's go to St Helier.'

'Great. And we could have lunch there. Yes?' I went into the kitchen to make a list, then stopped in surprise. Deposited casually on the draining board was a bouquet of flowers, tightly encased in cellophane and tied with ribbon. 'What are those doing here?'

Caro stood on one leg in the doorway, eyeing my reaction. 'They're lying on the draining board, Mum.' I gave her a look. 'The florist delivered them just after you went out.'

'They must be for Liz and Colin. I'd better call — '

'They were for Maker, the woman said. Some secret admirer?' she asked, beadily.

'But nobody knows we're here.'

'Somebody does.'

I searched for a card but there didn't seem to be one attached. The flowers were a great mass of long-stemmed red roses with giant waxen lilies. As I unwrapped them, the card fell out from amongst the blooms. We both pounced.

'Who're they from? What does it say?'

' 'I will call you, if I may.' Signed . . . '

'Let me see . . . Ian?'

'Mm. It might be. Do you know any Ian?' She shook her head. 'Neither do I.'

'A *very* secret admirer, then. How fascinating, Mum.'

I puzzled over the flowers and their card. Red roses for passion? White lilies for death . . .

'There'll be a simple explanation, something prosaic. Can you pop them in this vase, darling? I'll do a list of what we need to buy.'

Caro wouldn't leave it alone, and the mystery seemed to have cheered her. She was making up Ians throughout our tour of St Helier. Was he the naval type at the fish counter, or the young farmer in a Land Rover who almost drove into our hire car? At lunch, she asked the moustachioed waiter if his name was, by any chance, Ian. 'My name's Paul,' he told her with a smile. He agreed to become Ian for her, for the duration of our lunch.

As we drove back from the town, Caro's mood shifted abruptly again, from the manic all the way down to her silent withdrawal, in one all-too-easy sliding change of emotional gear.

I stopped the car, looked across at her. 'Come on. Speak it.'

'*Why* did he go? I feel so *angry* with Dad! For — jumping *or* being pushed! So stupid . . . I feel so ashamed, Mum, at being angry . . . *Poor* Dad . . . Why?'

Her heart had been broken. She had been channelling her grief into anger, just as I had. The tears subsided and as we searched in vain for enough tissues, she giggled a bit. I said, 'Of course you're angry with him. That's natural, it's nothing to be ashamed of. One way or the other, he's left you without him. It's absolutely all right to feel really pissed off about that.'

When we drove on, I headed towards the end of the lane and parked there. The sun had come out and we walked for half an hour beside the sea, hurling rocks at breakers and getting knocked sideways by the wind. I knew that part of Caro's rage was caused by Charlie's many absences from her life — and his emotional unavailability when he was around. I knew that because I felt her resentment too. He never had been present enough, and now he was gone for ever.

We were standing on that beach together

when something passed over, flitting between us and the sun, for a moment blocking out its light. I looked up. It was a small aircraft, a white Cessna two-seater, with its shadow trailing now across the sea. The panic surged back — my skin had grown icy, my legs were collapsing. My terror of flying was extreme, even standing safely on the ground. Caro was looking after the plane, that harbinger from our distant past, until it disappeared. Now almost all her family was gone, and we must have been having the same thoughts, not speaking them.

We ought to talk about the distant past, but I could not: not yet.

'Good walk,' I said. 'That's brought some colour back into your cheeks.'

'That's because I'm freezing, Mum!'

'Think log fire. Think toasted muffins for tea.'

We found a message on the answer machine. 'It'll be from Ian,' I joked. 'Ian said he'd call.'

It was Alison's voice, quick and busy from another planet. 'Hi, you folks! How's it going there? Look, so sorry, can't make it after all. We've got something really urgent here, so bang goes my weekend. Don't be cross — I'm sending someone else to look after you instead. Expect a visit from a tall, dark, handsome friend . . . Enjoy! Byeee . . . '

'Trust her.' Caro was scathing, from her disappointment. 'Alison's always letting people down.'

'It goes with the job, I suppose. So we're to expect a visit . . . D'you think she means — from *Ian*?'

★ ★ ★

Saturday began with the phone call. Struggling awake, I heard Caro's voice on the landing. ' . . . terribly nice. We would be delighted,' she was saying, overpolitely and not at all like Caro. 'Yes, absolutely.'

Stumbling out of bed, I saw her putting down the receiver. She turned, with a pleased grin. 'That was Ian.'

'Oh, Caro. Who was it?'

'Seriously. His name was Ian Something-I-couldn't-catch. Said he was a friend of yours? Visiting Jersey. I thanked him for the flowers, Mum. And he's coming here at seven to take us out to dinner. I accepted.'

'But — we don't even know who he is. You shouldn't . . . Well. What did he sound like?'

'Oh, you know. *Oily.*'

'How peculiar. We haven't any friends called Ian.'

The mystery diverted us throughout the day, while Caro enjoyed the Ian game again. We cleaned the house, baked cookies and walked in the lanes. Then she showered, emerging transformed. She had pinned up her hair into a knot, which was already beginning to tumble artfully, and had teamed a black scoop-necked top with her white chinos.

'You look good. Where did you get that top?'

'From a wardrobe. Don't worry, I'll wash it after. Mum, you must change to go out.'

'We don't know that we are going out,' I reminded her firmly. 'Since we don't know who he is, Ian-Something-you-couldn't-catch.'

'At least change out of those jeans, put on a skirt.'

I laughed, at the role reversal and because Caro seemed almost happy.

By ten to seven, she had stationed herself in the living room window to watch. Sitting there with the light illuminating the curve of her brow and nose, suddenly she looked unbelievably like Charlie. Then it was as if he hadn't died but still lived on. I felt a glad rush of relief.

A few minutes later, she let out a cry and I went to look. A scarlet Spitfire was approaching through the dark up the drive. It pulled in before the house and someone got out. He was tall and slim with neatly styled dark hair, and was dressed immaculately in casual pale jacket and trousers.

Caro stared at our visitor. 'Who is it, Mum?'

★ ★ ★

Everything was falling into place.

Ian Darius had been better known to Charlie, since I had only met him a handful of times at industry functions. He was more of an acquaintance than a friend, and more of a business competitor than anything. His company, the A-Zander group, was a giant revamped for the millennium. They covered almost very kind of surveillance, guarding and physical security, commercial and industrial, static and investigative work. Sometimes it seemed their alarms were attached to every building, their mobile patrols filled every high street.

A-Zander was a hungry beast, with many new tentacles. I didn't need to guess very hard as to why Ian Darius was here. There had been an attempt by him, a few years ago, to buy out MakerSeceuro. Charlie had resisted tooth and nail. In the end, the whole affair had strengthened us, while Charlie had increased his own control. That was then. This was now, and a lifetime later, or so it felt.

Caro and I had come to Jersey for a respite from pressure. Charlie had been dead for less than two weeks. I felt unprepared to deal with this visitor, and with what he wanted.

'Who is he, Mum? Is he a friend, like he said?' She was sensing my reluctance.

'His name's Ian Darius,' I said slowly, making an effort to sound nonchalant. 'And I suppose you could say that he is.'

When the doorbell rang, she hung back as if she had become uncertain. That decided me. The evening should happen and be fun for Caro, to give her a happy memory amidst the wreckage of a desperately bleak time. If this rival wanted to pay court, then he would be allowed to do that.

So I welcomed Darius. 'What a pleasant surprise, Ian. Thank you so much for the flowers.'

'Zoe. What can I say?' He took my hand. 'It's such a terrible thing. Are you both all right? You look lovely, despite everything.'

'We've been having quite a relaxing break, in its way. This is Caro. Ian.'

Suddenly the Ian game was reborn. A fit of the giggles erupted, flitting through

Caro, barely suppressed. Then she blushed, aware of the admiration coming her way from this tall, dark and handsome stranger. Darius was, as she might have remarked, a hunk. He had the chiselled good looks of some virtual-reality hero, with a lean and well-proportioned body, his thick black hair beginning to grey a little at the temples. Only his mouth spoiled the effect, because his lips were narrow.

As we sipped drinks by the fireplace, I couldn't resist asking innocently, 'Are you here on business? Or did you happen to be passing?'

He smiled, answering indirectly. 'I'm visiting a colleague who lives here with his family. Just for the weekend.'

'We happened to coincide, then. I wasn't aware that you knew Alison Seely?'

'That sounds like a question. I know Alison a little, not terribly well. You were staying with her, I believe?'

'She's been very kind.' Secretly, I was grinding my teeth. Alison must have directed him here, knowing or guessing what he almost certainly wanted.

'Should we go, perhaps? I've booked a table for seven thirty.'

We ate at the Grand Hotel. Darius switched his main attention to Caro and she threw herself into the spirit of a lavish dinner out, with hunky escort. Soon, encouraged by him, she seemed to be ordering most of the menu as he persuaded her to try new things — grenouilles, an escargot or two — that would normally have elicited a resounding 'Yuck! *I* don't *think* so!' And of course, the Ian game proved irresistible. By now his name was a code producing gales of helpless laughter, in a release of pent-up tension from the past ten days.

Darius began to look slightly at sea. He was clearly a person habitually in command, used to getting what he wanted. He wasn't sure what was going on, how to respond to a slightly tipsy sixteen-year-old, except with more gallantry and indulgence. He kept trying to bring us back to sobriety, things he understood. What had we been doing these past few days on the island? Watching cartoons and riding horses, throwing rocks at the sea. What did we have planned for the days left? Probably the same . . . He gave up, still with a smile.

I was indulging Caro too, but only up to a point. By dessert time, she was beginning to change colour and Darius was pouring the third variety of wine. I stopped him, firmly, from filling her glass. 'That's enough, Caro.

Truly, darling — you've had more than enough.'

'Oh, *Zoe*,' she complained. 'Stop being my *watchdog*!'

Halfway through the profiteroles, like some valiant but overladen vessel, Caro slowed, ploughed on a little further, then gradually stopped. She agreed it would be all right to leave and we were back at the house in ten minutes. She was reeling slightly, happy but not entirely conscious. In the hall, she turned to Darius. 'Thanks for a super evening. You're the best Ian.' And she giggled.

'It was a great pleasure. Perhaps we could do it again some time? Goodnight, Caro.' He added to me, 'You have a charming and beautiful daughter.' It was loud enough for Caro to hear from the stairs.

'Yes, she is. I'm lucky to have Caro.'

Darius began to stoke the log fire in the living room. When I took in a coffee tray, he was rekindling the flame with a pair of old bellows from the hearth. He looked strange in his smart clothes, kneeling with the bellows. He was too urbane, far too much a part of the techno revolution.

'That was very pleasant. How kind of you to think of us.'

He sat down in one of Liz and Colin's

armchairs, leaned back and sipped his brandy. 'I was concerned as to what will happen to you. Charlie was well respected by us all. Zoe, what will you do now?'

Drink a couple of Scotches, swallow pills and go up to sleep, I almost answered. I wasn't going to make things too easy. I stirred the fire with a poker. 'In what respect?'

'Given the nature of our security world, I wonder if you've considered things at all yet? How a female owner, or boss, would fit in?' I waited, with an enquiring expression. He saw that I wasn't going to take this up. 'She would be likely to have a difficult time. It's a most unusual situation.'

'Ian, there are lots of service businesses led by women.'

'Not in security, you know that. A woman like you could be having a marvellous life. Would she really want to be tied down, plagued by business worries in the future? When she could have anything she wanted?'

He had made up his mind what I ought to want. Biting back a retort or two, I left a silence between us. Why shouldn't he think his words were having the desired effect? It was interesting, this definite confirmation. MakerSeceuro was tasty, we were a target. Our main competitors, the giants of the trade, would like to gobble us up to protect their future market share. Ian Darius had come all this way to catch me alone and begin to woo me into selling. How much might the company be worth right now?

I realised just how much I had been missing the frenetic activity, the enforced distractions of London and the business.

'It would be a pity,' he went on quietly, 'to allow MakerSeceuro to run downhill, after all Charlie's years of building.'

Darius's presumptions were so startling, I found myself studying him carefully. I thoroughly disliked his attitude, but something else existed too. It was a kind of attraction, as unexpected as it was misplaced. Perhaps attraction had always been there, buried between us. Or was this some odd side effect of bereavement? A sexual need, almost impersonal, as if only sex could provide the proof of my own survival.

Leaning back into the sofa, I relaxed. Stretched my legs out towards the fire, crossing one knee over the other. 'Ian, whatever would I do for interest, for an exciting life, if I sold the firm to you?'

'You could do anything. I expect you'll remarry,' he said after a moment.

I went on studying him, his quick glances towards me and away. He must have been approaching forty, a year or two older than me. 'You and I are contemporaries.'

He was quick to flatter. 'Oh no. You're younger, by some years.'

'Yet you think I ought to be put out to grass. While you forge ahead?'

'Heavens, no — I didn't mean it to sound like that! You could go into business for yourself,' he suggested. 'In a more suitable area. I really would hate to see you having all those future problems which I can foresee. You deserve better, Zoe.'

'And you'd like to help me out?'

Darius made an expansive gesture, both arms wide.

I got up and poured fresh drinks for us both, then stood, swirling the liquid amber slowly around the bottom of a glass.

'Charlie has been gone for less than two weeks. And I came here just to grieve for him.' I shrugged. 'I don't know. Perhaps I'll talk with our firm's accountants, when I get back. Maybe I could obtain some ballpark figure, and then see . . . '

Ian Darius's smile was a thousand-watt affair. It would have lit the grave. Abruptly, I felt a real dislike for him.

★ ★ ★

'I don't mind, Mum. If you want to sell the business.'

I shot a surprised, questioning glance at Caro, beside me in the back of the taxi. The remark had come from out of the blue, at the end of an almost silent drive from the ferry terminal to home. 'What makes you say that?'

'I overheard you on my way to the bathroom . . . Oh, OK, Mum, I eavesdropped. Anyway, it's up to you what you decide to do.'

'You really wouldn't mind then?'

'Not if you didn't. Burglar alarms . . . dead boring. Not going to bring Dad back, is it, if you carry on.' A slight quaver in her voice. We were heading up Eldon Avenue, with a glimpse of the house around the curve ahead.

'No. It isn't going to bring him back. But I don't feel that I'll want to sell. We need — I think we both need — some continuity.' We had reached the gate. I operated its code and the cab crunched up the short gravel drive.

'Have you quarrelled with Alison?' she asked, as the driver carried in our bags.

'I'm annoyed with her for telling Darius where we were.' I paid the cabbie and followed Caro through into the kitchen. A note from Mary announced that she had done the shopping and would be in tomorrow as usual. Caro was taking a Coke from the fridge, popping the top off. 'Is it nice to be home?'

She nodded. 'It's OK.'

'You don't need to go back to school yet. Give it a few days.'

'Yeah . . . I might phone Penny later. See what she's doing.'

'That's a good idea.' Penny Harker was a close friend from Caro's old school and lived not far away. 'You could ask her over.'

It was odd being back. The house was the same, yet somehow totally different now with Charlie not around. Walking from room to room, I felt that difference. Our home seemed to be in suspension, waiting for something to happen. It was as if his spirit still hovered here, possessing old haunts and urging me on with an edgy presence.

That was complete nonsense, of course. Charlie was in the morgue, the subject of a police investigation.

I went to the living room phone, switched on the answering machine and began to filter messages.

Bill, I scribbled on the pad, as the MD's voice plaintively asked for an urgent conference before Wednesday's board meeting. *Car insurers . . . Doctor's receptionist . . . The* message I wanted was right at the end. 'Mrs Maker — Zoe? It's DC Sarah Quirke, Tuesday lunchtime. Can you get in touch with me or DCI Prentiss, soon as possible? There's been a new development.'

I called at once. Neither Prentiss nor Quirke was available and I had to leave a message. Forty minutes later Sarah called back, sounding rushed and cheerful. 'Good holiday, I hope?'

'It was fine. Sarah, what's happened?'

'We've had a breakthrough, just last night. Actually, this morning. We seem to have got hold of a witness — someone who saw Charlie on the bridge.'

Everything was about to open up. 'What was he doing? When was this?'

'Three o'clock, on the morning of the sixteenth — very shortly before the incident. Listen, I can't tell you any more right now, but the DCI wants to see you. He'd like to come to your place. Would five thirty be OK?'

6

Let me tell you a little Home Truth, in case you remain unaware of this. You are being watched.

Everyone is being watched.

What would we like to know about you? Your day-to-day life is being recorded secretly by covert cameras, transmitters. We don't need light to record the visuals and we can do unattended operations. No need for closeness to the target — no need to be close geographically, I mean. All that's to be seen is a pinhead lens in the ceiling or in a briefcase, fitted in a doorway or on a roof, concealed in places you wouldn't dream of.

Tiny bugs are transmitting what you say — from inside your phone, from this electric plug, that light fitting; from inside a simple cigarette lighter or calculator. Are things really what they seem? You're being watched, overheard in what you do. My job can be done under any conditions, your voice relayed to anywhere across the globe.

You name it. It's being done.

Personally I like to be up close. From the beginning, I've wanted to be right there. I wanted everything except the eye contact. That way it means more.

It used to be my hobby but now it's business. Big business. You learn so much about people, you wouldn't believe it. When they've no idea they might be under surveillance, you finish up learning everything in the world about your target.

THE WIDOW MAKER (My present target.)

Arrives at Cedar Court 15.47 hours with Maker's daughter. Home from those happy hols in the Channel Isles. The daughter, age sixteen, goes off to friend's house after calling: make a note of those details. Widow has meanwhile gone through her phone tape, found the police message and swapped a call. Detective Chief Inspector Prentiss wants to come to Cedar Court to unveil his news about The Witness! Not to be missed . . . Someone saw me? Witnessed Maker and Myself — pas de deux — on the bridge? Stay tuned!

The widow Maker takes a shower. She takes a long time over this. Dries her hair, gets dressed in jeans. Then she unpacks. Does what she tends to do, walking around talking to her husband. 'Charlie, I miss you . . . '

Weird or what? I've news for you,

sweetheart, comprenez — he's dead.

She's waiting for DCI Prentiss. So am I, so am I.

Two weeks gave me plenty of time.

Partly while the widow was out of town, I've been reviewing material from that board meeting. MakerSeceuro's paymasters, calling their little tune. Not a major player, merely minnows. What a popular sound, X billion pounds, a jingle sung for fervent masses. Where would any of us be without all the frightened people? Where do they all belong? And then I did the edit. No surprises, beyond herself fancying a taste of power, of course. That could well surprise us all — it does me — and must be taken into account.

Also I set up traps on the sergeant, Alison Seely: clever stuff, although I say it myself, exquisite stuff to ensnare a well guilty Lady. That's private, for yours truly. That's in hand.

I KNOW EVERYTHING THAT YOU DO: I'M WATCHING YOU!

When you think I'm not there, I see and hear, I know everything. Everything! So watch it. He would say that to me often, just before He went out. A big man with plenty of meat. His big hands chopping through the air. Blood, bones, offal. The eye. No one else was such a giant — on giant shoulders I was carried — not like that. None of them counted for everything the way He did. When I went off to school, slipping out on the street to play, or going up to bed at night. Just you remember what I said, He'd say. Remember? I wanted to please Him, wanted Him to be proud of me. My God. No. I've come so far, but I won't forget.

Detective Chief Inspector Prentiss not showing yet. Nip down from the loft for a can of NRG, nice and cool. Quick look in the freezer: fond memories, all freezer-wrapped in polythene. My unofficial sample matter. Phials filled and filed: the precious Blood. Just a quick look at my newest little memento — here among my other mementoes — at the back of the lowest drawer. Its pink skin has been paled by ice to a sugary tone. It's a delicate pearly almost-white, a faded fashion-aware Rose White. Inside its see-through wrapper, rock hard, my little stick of holiday candy. Wrap it tight, pop it back nestling among the others. Nice and snug.

THE LAST TIME THAT WE MET UP.

'Hello, how are you?' Maker said. Recognition as always, with just a small smile for me. Trusting me — as the widow does — and so he should have done, of course! (And she'll soon believe in me even

94

more.) Our Charlie, popular fellow that he was, definitely gave me a friendly grin of sorts. Not having an inkling that I had his execution taped, all planned out. Justice. The end of the line. He didn't plan on losing his digit or his life.

Deciding to take Survival Rations up to the loft, I hunt around. Want to catch it live, this meeting with Prentiss. It could go on a bit. As meetings will, all too frequently. Decide to make a brew and find Sports chocolate, rice biscuit. Up to my hide, dig in and settle down. Still nothing. I'm alone in the world. Monitors empty, except she crosses walking through, across and back again like a rat in a maze of tunnels, trapped in there. The widow is not what she appears to be.

WE ARE NONE OF US WHAT WE SEEM.

I'm just the same — I look the same as anyone — you could see that if I let you look at me. People depend on me, I do the job: I'm liked, I'm highly valued. You need me and if you're smart you know that. Fitting in is just an art, everyone learns how to do it sooner or later. You study it, because that's survival. I have what everyone has — work, home, relationships — because if you don't, they crucify you.

A model man, I have my own life plan. I am here to kill.

Detective Chief Inspector Prentiss now arriving, front entrance Cedar Court, 18.09 hours . . .

7

Prentiss was late. Caro and I had come back to one of those English winter days when the cloud lies so low, it presses out light and flattens time. A pale kind of dusk, all through the long day, had merged almost unnoticeably into evening. When Prentiss rang the doorbell I jumped, as if his visit had been the last thing on my mind.

As I took him through to the living room, for the first time I noticed how he resembled a bird of prey. His eyes were too close, under straight brows that nearly met, and his face seemed narrowed by the length of an aquiline nose. The almost black hair, slicked back, clung gleaming to his bony skull and feathered down over his collar.

I brought him a cup of tea and found him at the corner desk, not touching but staring at the array of papers and pigeon-holes. 'That's mine,' I told him. 'Charlie kept a small study in the room next door. I'm told that you've been through his things at headquarters. You took away some disks and papers.'

Adding his four lumps of sugar, stirring

the tea, he was checking me over. 'We've also read through the home diary, and would like explanations of some entries. We must go through all documents kept here, it's a process of elimination.'

'Yes.' I was unable to keep quiet any longer. 'You've found a witness, then? Somebody who saw Charlie.'

'Mrs Maker, I hope you and your daughter had a good break? As restorative as possible, in the circumstances.'

I nodded, thrown by the question. Waiting impatiently. It didn't occur to me until later that he was being kind, and responsible, because of what he was about to tell me. Prentiss drank his tea, put down his cup. He tilted his head to one side, regarding me. It was so birdlike that, filled with unbearable tension, I almost laughed.

'Do you know anyone,' he asked suddenly, 'who owns a van — dark navy, black or even green — with an elevated roof? Might be a Mercedes. That ring any bells?'

'I don't think so. Why?'

'It was possibly an M registration.' I shook my head. He looked disappointed. 'We picked up a lad early this morning for burglary. We've got a lot on him, because he's been using the same chisel to force a number of windows. Including a job on

Hornsey Lane the night your husband died.'

'Did he see this van? And Charlie . . . '

'Our burglar wanted to get back across the bridge. He was carrying a VCR and other goodies, under black plastic. Must've felt a trifle conspicuous at three on a Sunday morning. It was raining hard, but the bridge is well lit. And there was this van. Parked right up on the pavement against the railings, the witness says. Showing no headlights or sidelights — but then a light went on inside, in the front.'

'Did he see Charlie?'

'He thinks there were two people in the front. One had sandy-coloured hair and was leaning against the passenger window. He can't describe the other person. The lad watched the van, hoping it would clear off. It didn't. After a few minutes, he ducked down and ran past.'

'Charlie was still inside . . . Can you trace the vehicle?'

'There are a lot of that type on the roads. We're doing our best.'

It all made some kind of sense. A dark-coloured van with a high roof. Maybe with a hatch that opened, or a sun top? Parked right on the railings of Suicide Bridge . . . Waiting for a white sports car — my car, as someone thought — to appear on the road below.

But why? And how did they know so much about us?

'Might he remember any more? You've got him in custody?'

'While the burglary inquiry continues, we've got him. It gives us a few things to go on. There's more, but it gets contradictory in a way. The letter your husband wrote?' He paused, with an air of carefulness. 'The note turns out to be genuine. It was a suicide note, and it was written by Charlie . . . Something else, though. Not sure if you'd want to know this or not. But it's important — we need to ask, check a few things.'

'Go on, Chief Inspector. What?'

'The small finger from the left hand . . . How it was severed?'

'Go on.'

'Mrs Maker, that finger was taken off — it seems — deliberately. It was done rather neatly, with a bullet fired at close range from a small-calibre handgun.'

* * *

No, I answered Prentiss automatically, then, Charlie did not keep any gun. I didn't know anyone who kept firearms, not among our personnel, nor anyone else. Yes, we lived defensively. We feared the rising tide of violent crime, but Britain had no real gun culture after all. Yes, Charlie himself had been an expert shot as a hobbyist. He had owned several handguns before they were banned. And the police knew that . . . *And so what*? I felt like screaming at him.

Someone had shot Charlie in the left hand, to force him into writing a suicide note. That seemed obvious.

My voice was saying things, angrily and remotely, as if from a long distance. Some time later, DCI Prentiss left.

The minute he had gone, I pushed out blindly through the back door. Cold light illuminated a sparse, wet lawn and barren earth. I went down the crazy-paving path, out of the light's range, to the cedar bench we had bought last year. It was in a small rockery, a private place that Charlie had made. From here the noise of the city was muffled, light shaded by a winter-blooming jasmine.

He had been threatened and injured before he was murdered. I felt sick. Had the driver done it? Perhaps there were other men hidden in the back of the van. Had they tried to get information about the Goldstar project? They might have tried to persuade him to sign something else, before the suicide note. To sign away rights — to the Goldstar, or to MakerSeceuro? Was someone trying to force a deal Charlie didn't want?

In my heart, I knew no one could have been that desperate, taken such a huge risk. But he had been kidnapped, then coerced. Somehow he had managed to call me, to raise the alarm. He hadn't been able to say where he was. Already drugged and confused, he had probably been discovered and interrupted mid-call. He must have known who his captors were. Nothing remained to them but to kill him, using his suicide note to cover their tracks.

I sat huddled on that bench for a long time, obsessed with one idea. Charlie hadn't called the police but he had called me. He had wanted me to help. There were things I could do now, people I could question, and records, papers kept at the house which might be revealing. I wanted to search through his personal things myself. The police still had his BMW, which Charlie had been driving on the night he died. It had been left outside a park, within reach of the canal and the payphone he had used. His mobile — that I had spoken to, just minutes before the murder — still had not been found.

By now I knew what to do. I needed to be in denial, channelling grief into action of one kind or another. The next few days were full of essential business.

Wednesday began with the MD's resignation, which was accepted. Bill Thwaites wanted to leave now that one rule was over and another, already promising to be very different, about to begin. I had more or less expected it, but not with such abruptness, so close on the heels of the chairman's death. That was puzzling. Was our personality clash affecting my judgement? It seemed unlikely that Bill was connected in any way with what had happened. And yet . . . Now that Charlie's death was no longer being passed off as suicide, whoever was responsible could well be panicking.

Bill insisted that he had no definite future plans. He wanted time with his family. He was too cautious an operator for this to be strictly true. Which of our rivals was he going to join?

'Watch this space,' Madison agreed. 'He's got plans, all right.'

We would keep Bill Thwaites under observation. There was a non-competition clause in his contract, but that could be difficult to enforce. We had imposed strict conditions, tying him in with a loyalty and secrets agreement. It was all amicable enough, on the surface.

That afternoon I met with Joshua Keanes, a senior partner at Whyte Majors, the firm's accountants for the past nine years. We were looking good, Keanes confirmed. Selling MakerSeceuro could make me a wealthy woman, and there were ways of making the future very comfortable indeed. He advised that selling was the best option.

I was only confirming what I wanted. It was partly — not wholly — for Charlie's memory. Caro would soon return to her studies and her friends, while my life looked unbearably empty. I would keep MakerSeceuro for the challenge, and to prove myself. I wanted control without the everyday restraints of running the company.

Madison Black was burning for that chief executive role, and he was an easy choice for us. It was agreed that he would remain in charge of marketing decisions until we had found someone else, and the Goldstar would still be his to market.

MakerSeceuro's present structure had only made sense while Charlie was in charge. We had to look at the alternatives, to evolve a vision for the future, decide on strategy and implement some immediate changes. These included a set of detailed new financial forecasts and the recruiting of fresh talent with a new head of sales and marketing. Phase two was planned to bring a rationalisation and streamlining of our entire future operation.

There was satisfaction in the relentless pace of those few days. They were fraught and exciting, allowing no thoughts about other, torturous events. Messages were arriving from both Darius and Alison, but, hard pressed for time, I took only essential calls.

By three o'clock on Friday afternoon, temporarily free, I was headed for home and the vacuum created by Charlie's loss.

* * *

I showered, and dressed in an old shirt and jeans, then put through a call to Sarah Quirke. Over a fortnight ago, she had agreed to find out the facts about Gill Tarpont's murder. Now she wasn't in. I left a message, carefully phrased, about needing the information which had been requested.

In Charlie's little study, I switched on the overhead light and desk lamp. I needed to search through his remaining papers and disks now. Soon all his things would need sorting, then giving away or . . . I felt swamped by guilt. It was many years since my parents' deaths, and my mother had died as suddenly as Charlie. Then, as now, I had blamed myself, and with good reason. It was

105

seventeen years ago, but the sense of guilt felt as strong as it had been then.

For a moment, they were all there in the room, mutely with me. So many ghosts. Even my sister couldn't bear to be around . . . I had to suppress those memories, and the feelings.

It seemed wrong and disturbing, rifling through Charlie's desk, but there had to be some clue somewhere to that final appointment on the night of the fifteenth. Maybe documents would be hidden here, kept away from the office deliberately? He had been keeping secrets and they had to do with MakerSeceuro.

Charlie had left his presence and personality in every corner. Memos and jottings, letters and bills, his personal documents and some unexpected keepsakes. Often he had been remote towards us, without any hint of sentiment. But in these private places, among the stuff of everyday existence, I found some of Caro's earliest efforts at drawing, carefully stored along with old birthday cards. Postcards too, that I had sent from the holidays he was too busy to share with us. This was a side to Charlie that I had never known existed, this keeper of loving mementoes.

Then I found the letters.

In the desk's bottom drawer, an old cigar tin was wedged at the back. Charlie had given up smoking years ago, when he hit forty. Absently, I opened the tin. Inside were folded papers. I began to open them and the handwriting leaped out, a heavy hand in dark-blue ink with flowing tails and large, florid capitals. Alison's writing. Not much different from the way she wrote now.

They were love letters. Sitting back on my heels, hands trembling, I read the pages. Three letters, undated, and each signed with that big, swirling capital A . . . *Thursday afternoon, so special! I can still taste you, and smell you on my skin . . . Darling C, can't wait til next week! You will call, won't you . . . I'm sure you'll make it to Basingstoke somehow, sweetheart? . . . Of course I understand, you're her father, after all . . .*

'Damn it, Charlie! What else are you going to . . . ' Refolding those pages, I stuffed them back into the tin and snapped it shut, closing my eyes. That didn't undo what I had seen.

I felt bewilderment, followed by a huge anger. Then it was as if I had lost him all over again. There was no reason now to suppress what had been unleashed. It was a long time before I felt calmer again.

Thoughts began to appear. Was this why I had never asked Charlie or Alison about the beginnings of their long friendship? Thirteen years ago, when they met, our marriage had been on the rocks and we were living apart. On some level had I known they were lovers then? These letters were old, the paper discoloured and the creases frayed. Perhaps from rereading.

I comforted myself with the idea that he had protected me with silence. They both had. But now a lot of things made sense. That old habit of secrecy had led Alison to keep quiet about their dinner together on Charlie's last evening. The residual guilt I had recognised in her, since Charlie's death, was her trying to make up for the affair. That competitive edge between her and myself, I had never fully understood before. Those sharp cracks of insecurity, which I often felt around my freewheeling, uncommitted friend, were because she was the rival that I never knew existed.

It must have been over ages ago. Alison had flitted off to other conquests, other temporary passions. He and I had returned to each other, struggled to build enough to stay together, for Caro. Alison and Charlie were history. Perhaps it was better that I knew now.

After a while, I went on searching. What other personal secrets might come to light? The top drawer of his filing cabinet was locked and no key seemed to fit. I tried forcing it, unsuccessfully. The other place to look for papers was in the loft. Although we had an unused bedroom, Charlie had stored boxes and a trunk in that less accessible roof space, and by now I was wondering why.

It was a couple of years since I had been up there. The light was inadequate, with only two sockets to cover the entire area of the house. I pulled down the ladder, then found a torch and scrambled up through the hatch. Layers of felted dust lay undisturbed. Whatever had been hidden here could have no recent relevance. I decided to look round anyway, and stepped on to the boards placed across the beams.

Charlie had stored furniture here, left to him by his parents. They were awkward, old-fashioned pieces which could have been sold or given to his cousin in Edinburgh. It took a while to locate the trunk and two boxes, which I knew he had put up here last year. Gingerly, I opened the trunk's lid. Inside were more boxes, papers and old photographs. I was shining the torch in, beginning to sift through, when the doorbell rang. I ignored it.

Six seconds later it rang again, longer, imperious. I scrambled down the ladder and down the stairs, because it might be Sarah Quirke.

Alison's partner, Redcliff, stood looking up into the camera. He wore the expression of someone who knows they're unwelcome. 'Jay Redcliff. Mrs Maker — Zoe? Could we talk for a minute?'

I wiped my grimy hands on my shirt. It left me looking like a Victorian chimney sweep, even more than before. Then I pressed the buzzer.

Jay Redcliff was almost unrecognisable in a pristine suit, collar and tie, which fought a style battle with his pugnacious young features and bullet-like, almost shaven head. I had never felt grubbier or at more of a disadvantage. He showed a flicker of surprise, and a faint smile passed between us at this reversal.

'I called your office, was told you'd gone home. Is this all right? There's something — a couple of things — I need to say.'

'Come through to the kitchen,' I suggested, reluctant.

'I'm the peace-keeping dove. Bearer of olive branches.'

'Did Alison send you?' My voice sounded sharp.

He frowned. 'Why would she?' I said nothing, so he answered himself. 'You didn't take Alison's calls. She began to imagine you lying totalled somewhere.'

'As you can see, I'm all in one piece. What's the message?'

'OK. First thing — she's traced the person that you wanted information on. She's going to be home after seven. You're invited. She'll be cooking Japanese. That some kind of a code?'

I laughed. Alison's home-cooked tempura was the best, and she knew it. Beginning to like her messenger, I felt ashamed of my earlier bitchiness.

'Second, Alison filled me in. On everything that's happened in your life recently. And — those things I said? I'm sorry.'

'That's all right — '

'I didn't know what had really happened. I got to the scene, and there was a dead boy, just a child, killed! It looked like . . . Your husband — it looked like he caused a head-on. That was ignorance. I didn't know who you were, but that's no excuse. Both times — I was well out of order.'

His speech had a disarming effect. Hurriedly I said, 'It's OK. I overreacted too. At Quest, that fight — I'm sorry. Everything came rushing back. I keep feeling so much rage since Charlie died. There's just darkness and rage. That's all. Does that sound crazy? Maybe I am.' Suddenly aware of confiding in someone I didn't know, I stopped abruptly.

'That happens. Death leaves a crater of change. You can never be like you were before.'

I nodded, grateful that he understood. Looked down at my hands, and saw their layer of blackness. I went across to the sink, began to scrub at the dirt.

'Been doing some clearing out?'

'Yes.'

'Are you being kept informed? How things are going?'

'The police don't tell me much. There's some new evidence . . . ' I shut down again, not wanting to discuss the case with him.

After a minute he asked, 'Anything at all I can do to help you?'

'In what way?' I shot him a glance, and he shrugged: anything. 'There might be. Are you any good at picking locks?'

★ ★ ★

In Charlie's study, Redcliff examined the lock on the filing cabinet. He found a paperclip and bent it open, then slid the wire in delicately, his head on one side as

112

if he was listening. Gently tweaking the lock a couple of times, he slid the drawer open.

'Great. Thanks.'

'Easy,' he answered in a self-satisfied way, then looked into the file drawer as I did. 'Disks, hard copy in there. Looking for anything special, are you?' I didn't answer. 'This house, the size. You must rattle around, it must seem empty now.'

'It was always too big.'

'Who's around? Caro — how is she?'

'She's rediscovering her London friends, and that's a good thing. But she'll have to get back to her school in Sussex.'

'She's a great kid, Caro. Must be really hard on a girl — losing her dad at sixteen. I've got two kids of my own. If anything happened to hurt them . . . How d'you go on?' He frowned. It made him look grim again. 'You going to Alison's tonight?'

'Yes, I'll go.' I would take those letters of hers. They would be returned to sender.

'Right. You didn't get that pig-dirty failing to open a file cabinet. So what else can I do?'

I eyed his neatly pressed suit. Was this some kind of an act of contrition, or what?

A minute later, having taken off his jacket and tie, Redcliff was shinning up the loft ladder. His physicality was impressive. Once he was set into action, that pent-up aggression made a different kind of sense: it was more about achieving, less to do with intimidation. I was trying not to look impressed, as the storage boxes and trunk were rapidly carried down. He put them in the spare bedroom, which had a much better light. When he had gone I would have a look through.

Redcliff pushed the ladder up into storage again, closing the hatch.

'Well, thanks. That's a real help.'

'No problem.' He wiped his hands against the already dusty knees of his trousers, then went off to wash.

When he came back downstairs to where I waited in the hall, I offered him a drink. Redcliff glanced at his watch. 'I've got to drive to Hereford, but thanks. Got time for a brew.'

'A brew. That means tea?'

He nodded, boyish then as he grinned. He followed me through to the kitchen again, where I made a pot of Darjeeling. By now he was settled, sprawling in the chair that had been Charlie's. I tried not to mind. 'Are you staying the weekend in the country?'

It turned out that his family was there. He had an eight-year-old, Lisa, and a boy of two called Danny. He didn't mention his wife but I gathered the children lived with her there.

Redcliff was cute about them, especially his daughter. When he spoke of Lisa, everything about him softened and I got the impression of a devoted dad, reduced to putty in those young hands. 'Why Hereford?' I asked. 'It's quite a way off.'

Suddenly I wondered if he might have been in the special forces, based there. Yes, he had something about him, ill-fitting to civvy street. Alison's rough diamond. But no one ever really leaves the SAS, or so I'd heard, unless they were asked to leave for some reason.

'Lisa's at school, her friends are there.' He added with a shrug. 'And the grandparents. So that's home. I've a flat for weekdays in north London.' Glancing at the time again, he stood. 'I must go. Thanks for the tea.'

'Thanks for helping out.'

He paused in the hall. That heavy frown came back, making his whole appearance daunting. 'I'll drive you over to Hampstead, Zoe. Come on.'

'No thanks. That's all right.'

'But I want to. It isn't — '

'I'll drive myself,' I said firmly. 'Later, after I've made some calls.'

Redcliff shook his head, then turned to pick up his jacket from the banisters. His voice sounded curt. 'It's not right.'

I was beginning to feel annoyed, because a helpful gesture was one thing but interfering arrogance was another. 'What isn't right?'

'Being on your own.' He was turning straight back into the pig-headed oik that I'd first encountered. 'You need protection. Shouldn't be on your own, with all that's — '

'Thanks very much,' I told him, 'but the condition is not crippling. I happen to be perfectly capable and don't need any — '

'You've demonstrated *that*,' he flashed back.

I was fuming. I felt like offering a tip for those jobs — anything to insult him. My voice clipped out: 'It was terribly kind of you to offer assistance.'

Redcliff glowered. 'I suppose one could put it like that. If one was to put things in a tight-arsed, middle-class way — one might say that.'

As if he meant to be as objectionable as possible, he put on his jacket in slow motion before drawing out a mobile phone from its inner pocket. Unhurriedly, he pressed out a number. 'Redcliff. I'm at your friend's, and I'm leaving. You're on for tonight.'

8

'They've found a witness,' I told Alison.

Busy with her cafetière, she looked round to where I stood watching by her back door. For some reason, she looked almost alarmed. 'Tell, then.'

I shook my head. 'You tell first. Who wrote the 'Unmaking of MakerSeceuro' piece? And — who did they concoct it *for*?'

She turned back to what she was doing, without answering. Angry with both Alison and her Quest partner, I had turned up too late for what, she assured me, had been her best-ever tempura and sushi. Her letters to Charlie were burning a hole in my jacket pocket. Return to sender: but first things first.

'Let's sit down,' she said, throwing another glance in my direction. She pulled out a chair and sat at the table. 'Pat McBain doesn't exist, it was a pseudonym. That piece was written by someone called Patricia Abel. She's a crime journalist, generally reckoned to be top of the league, and was only guesting on the diary while the regular chap was on holiday. Abel herself brought that item to the editor at short notice. Her sources are not known.'

'Her source must've been someone who read Charlie's suicide note, then leaked it to her. Or, worse — it was somebody who knew what the note contained, because they had dictated it to Charlie. Have you talked with Abel yet?'

She shook her head. 'But Charlie didn't write the note himself, did he?'

I sat down opposite her. 'Yes. He wrote it. With physical persuasion.' She said nothing and her face was grim. 'You know when he was found Charlie had a finger missing? It had been shot away at close range by a small-calibre handgun . . . They tortured him.'

Alison was looking stricken. 'Oh no.' Then, softly, 'Charlie.'

She had loved him, I realised then. Perhaps she had gone on caring for him. All the promiscuity since looked like some search for the impossible. Could he have been the one who ended things, for Caro's sake, and mine?

I sat down opposite her and started to describe the tall, dark-coloured van which had been seen parked at the bridge railings with Charlie inside. 'He must have been pushed to his death from out of that van, as I approached — someone was listening

118

to me talking on Charlie's mobile.'

'It was really *that* personal?' She was frowning, puzzled.

'It was dead personal. Someone knew what car I'd be driving, and the route I'd take. They even knew I was going to avoid using the North Circular because of roadworks. They were very familiar with Charlie and me . . . It was someone close.'

'Or else they'd had you under surveillance. That van sounds almost like a mobile patrol — a security vehicle — doesn't it? Maybe from another security firm.'

'If we're looking at all the possibilities, it could've been someone in the police.' There was a brief silence between us. I added, 'There's more to Gill's death than we've been told. I'm getting information about it.'

'Who from?' she asked, with a sort of wariness. 'What kind of information?'

'There's been nothing in the papers, or on the news, about motive. Break-ins are usually the work of burglars. What was stolen, and why hasn't that been mentioned? It usually is. If Gill surprised a thief, how did she get stabbed to death? Burglars don't often commit murder, especially in that way.' I looked at Alison's disturbed expression, and wondered about it. 'You must agree we ought to know more? Perhaps you could find out about her from one of your contacts?'

In the split second before she started to answer, I saw that she knew already. Alison knew all about Gill's death, so why wasn't she telling?

She said quickly, 'I agree the reporting on that case must've been restricted. But that may not be significant. I keep wondering . . . How premeditated could Charlie's murder have been? Because — I know it was three in the morning, but anyone could've seen it happen there.'

'And they almost did. That's why I don't see it as premeditated — or not in that way. The killer had him shut in that vehicle, pumped full of drugs . . . But the time and place? Perhaps it was opportunism.'

Alison said, 'But what was the point of killing him like *that*? It was so elaborate, and risky.'

'Yes. It's crazy . . . It could only have been done like that as some kind of deliberate statement: a message. But I'm sure now of how it began. Charlie met someone — that mystery appointment — and he was kidnapped. He must've been held prisoner somewhere — '

'And then coerced.' Alison looked as sick as I felt. 'But what did they want?'

'Secrets, to do with MakerSeceuro. If we

knew where he was taken, it might help. That payphone he called from — by the canal? Have you looked around there?'

'I've been up to my eyes in work. You want us to check out the area?'

I nodded. 'I don't care how much this costs. Someone may've seen Charlie near the canal. He was already drugged, and would've been conspicuous. OK, I know the CID are working hard — but Paul Prentiss never tells me what they're doing. Not even what they're finding out, half the time.'

'I'm not surprised,' she countered mildly. 'Since you're over-involved already. He's trying to keep you at a healthy distance.'

'How can I possibly be *uninvolved*, until Charlie's killer is brought to justice? Unless I know for sure that everything possible that can be done is being done?' Alison looked away. On the wall behind her, the electric clock said eleven thirty-two. I watched its second hand inching forward — unstoppable time — and remembered vividly that frantic drive through the night after Charlie's call. I had failed to help him, so I felt to blame for his death. Now Alison had placed herself, like an obstacle, between me and his memory.

'What?' she asked quietly, after a minute.

Perhaps she sensed my anger. I wanted to take those pages from my pocket, to call her a traitor. To be given some comfort, maybe. But I couldn't do it: not now, like this, howling inside with conflict and need. That last abandonment by the dead is unanswerable.

Alison must have been going through something like this too.

'Another thing,' I went on. 'You should talk with Patricia Abel. One way or another, we have to find out her source.'

'Abel's abroad on assignment, so that'll have to wait.' She sounded pressured. 'We've another big investigation going on — that's riddled with annoying problems.'

'If it's a really nasty job, why don't you give it to Jay Redcliff?'

She laughed. 'The two of you will never rub along.'

'At least the feeling is mutual.' I shrugged. 'It's late, I should be going.'

She began to potter around her gleaming kitchen, clearing a few things from her cooking session. The set of razor-sharp French knives. The giant wok. Alison's kitchen matched her. It was stylish and pleasing. From poor beginnings, she had trudged through her stint with the police, then danced into a surprising marriage to a respected architect. She had worked hard at putting herself together and at mending the cracks. Her life now provided comfort and gave her authority, plus the excitement she always craved.

With a wickedly innocent gleam in her eye, Alison swung round. 'You still haven't mentioned last weekend, with Ian Darius. How did it go?'

'I suppose you knew he's got his eye on MakerSeceuro?'

'Has he, indeed? Well that could make sense, couldn't it. So what? It gives you a choice. I hope he showed you a decent time.' She was studying my expression, which must have been as closed as I felt. 'How did you find him? He is rather good-looking, don't you think?'

★ ★ ★

It was Saturday, early afternoon, when he rang. The last thing I wanted was a business chat with Ian Darius. 'Tell him I'm out, or busy — anything.'

'I already said you were right here, Mum.' Caro handed over the phone, uncovering the mouthpiece.

Why couldn't he have gone through the proper business channels from the beginning? Our home number was ex-directory. It was annoying that he had somehow got hold of it. 'Ian,' I said, cool. 'How unexpected.'

'Zoe, I've been trying all week to catch you, as you probably know.'

'It was a rather full week for us. There's been a great deal to sort out, as you can imagine.'

'I imagine that you and I have one or two very interesting things to sort out. And to talk about. Don't we?'

So our thinking had gone in opposite directions. I cursed my previous wish, only one short week ago, to leave all options open. 'To be frank, I don't think that we have — '

'But of course we have to talk!' he broke in, forcefully, with an odd kind of jollity. 'You can't decide anything without a full discussion with me. When can we meet? Tomorrow?'

'That won't be possible.'

'Not at all? All day?'

'Caro and I are driving down to Sussex.'

'Tonight, then. Dinner. Yes?'

'I'm sorry, that's not possible.' I was having dinner with a couple of old friends.

'Then let's meet earlier. Just for a drink, a brief chat, Zoe. Tell me where.'

Darius seemed in a great hurry to know where he stood. So why didn't I tell him, and get it over with as soon as possible? I gave him the name and address of a wine bar and we arranged to meet there at seven, until half past.

'Excellent — we've a lot to talk about. See you there.'

He rang off. Slowly I put down the phone. 'Damn. That's the last thing I want to do.'

With an anger that startled me, Caro said, 'You're seeing him? Tonight? Why's he all over us both? Dad's not even . . . That Ian Darius — *greaseball* or what. D'you think he's revolting, really?'

'It's just business, I think. You were going to Penny's place, weren't you?'

'Yeah. I'll be stopping over,' she added.

That would be the third night this week she'd slept over at her friend's. 'Hey, what's the big attraction suddenly?'

Caro shrugged. 'You're going out anyway.'

'Only for a drink, then supper. Well . . . I'll drive over and pick you up at ten tomorrow. That'll save you — '

'I'll be back here by ten, Mum.'

I looked carefully at Caro. She had been confiding less than usual and I had been too busy to seek out confidences. The evasiveness was new and, given what she had been going through, it was worrying. 'Is everything OK, darling?'

'Course it is.' She added, scathingly, 'I'm

125

only going to Penny's.'

'You will be all right, returning to school now? It just isn't a good idea to get too far behind in the curriculum, with A levels — '

'Don't fuss, Mum. I'll be fine, honest.'

'Well, remember I can drive down — if you don't want to get the train back — any weekend.'

'Yeah, Zoe. I'll remember that.' She pulled a long-suffering face and I stopped nagging. At least much of tomorrow would be spent together, in the car and in Caro's favourite lunch place.

At a quarter to six, she went off for the night. I showered and changed, then left for the wine bar in Hampstead.

Ian Darius was late. Seven o'clock passed, then seven fifteen. At twenty past, a message arrived: he had been held up after being involved in an accident. He would be here in a few minutes.

When Darius walked in, he seemed unbelievably cool and calm for someone arriving half an hour late, straight from the scene of a road accident. 'Zoe. That dress! New hair? You look absolutely stunning.' He leaned close and kissed my cheek. 'So sorry I was delayed. Who's the lucky man?'

He certainly had a knack of making things appear personal when they were not. I took a breath, my heart thudding unexpectedly. It would be better to disillusion this rival, on both fronts. 'I'm sorry too.' I smiled sweetly. 'I can only stay for another ten minutes. I hope the accident wasn't a bad one?'

'Just an annoyance. Some idiot cyclist, shooting out of a side turning with the ridiculous arrogance they have.' He paused to order himself a drink, while I shook my head to refuse another. Then he went on, smoothly confident, 'We don't have much time for discussion, but I've been doing a little research and — '

'I'm sorry, Ian. It seemed better to say this in person — '

'All we are doing here is merely discussing a principle. You are going to need me. And here I am.'

'I have no interest in selling MakerSeceuro.'

His dark eyes changed, glinting. 'Oh, come on, Zoe — these are games! You've been talking with your accountant at Whyte Majors. Someone I know saw him coming out.'

'But I won't be looking for any buyer.'

'That's a bad mistake, if I may say so. Right now, MakerSeceuro could command a very healthy price. You could name your figure. But frankly, within a very short time — '

'Thanks for your vote of confidence! Yes, I've been meeting with accountants, with everybody — of course we've all had a lot to discuss. And we've made our plans for the company's future.'

For several moments he was silent. His face wore an expression of rampant egocentricity, thwarted. There was cruelty in that thin, wirelike mouth. Ian Darius could be an unpleasant enemy.

I made an effort to smile. Touched his sleeve lightly, briefly. 'We shall be colleagues in the field.' And I gathered my coat to go. 'I thought you had a right to know quickly.'

He smiled back, recovering charm. 'Zoe,' he said, with that glint in his eyes. 'You would regret it so much. I can't take no for an answer, not from your delightful self.'

* * *

The next morning, Caro and I drove out of town and into Sussex. 'How was your drink with Mr Greaseball?' She was giving me sly glances. 'Then chewing the fat with old pals? Mother's got a hangover, I do declare.'

Yes, I had a kingsize hangover. Charlie's and my old friends had been very kind, and supper with them had been low-key. Nothing could have softened the fact of

128

Charlie's absence from the evening.

'Ian Darius turned up for ten minutes. And I'm not selling . . . The rest of my evening was nice enough. How about yours?'

Caro seemed in good spirits, describing in detail the new film she and Penny had seen last night. 'Exciting! But not a patch on your drunken night.' About to answer, I sneezed instead. 'Bless you, Mommy dearest.'

'Thank you.'

'Oh *no*! If somebody blesses you, never say thank you. 'Cos if you do, a fairy dies.' I gave her a look. She went on cheerfully, 'D'you know why we shut our eyes every time we sneeze?'

'Can't say I've thought a lot about it. Why?'

'Because if you didn't, your eyeballs would burst out — fall out of their sockets. Splat. Grisly but true.'

'Caro, that's horrible! Who's been telling you things like that? I suppose it might even be true.'

She laughed, gargoyle-like, at my disgust. It seemed things were just as Caro had said. She was going to be fine. Still, I met with her school houseparents, Bob and Sheila, asking them to be watchful. They must let me know about any changes in Caro or her studies. If she needed me, they must get in touch.

The headmistress, Rosemary Lomax, seemed to think Caro should be offered counselling. 'It's not only that her father's died, but also the suddenness, the violent nature of it. With his death under investigation, that will make it harder coming to terms with what's happened.'

I was surprised, pointing out that Caro seemed in good spirits now. 'Although she has been having bad dreams, then not getting back to sleep . . . How does one find that sort of help?'

Rosemary smiled. 'We happen to have Dr Simon Tyrone living nearby, outside Haslemere.' She paused, clearly expecting me to recognise the name.

'Doesn't he write books?' I remembered. 'And do profiles — radio interviews?'

She nodded. 'He's an eminent neighbour, but also a friend with personal connections to the school. He stepped in once before, although he's retired from clinical work. He's very good. Shall I speak to him, ask if he would meet her?'

I still felt doubtful. 'We don't want to risk stirring up anything more . . . '

'But in the longer term? It would provide someone to talk to, a professional — to make sure she does recover.'

When I asked Caro that night, she had no

doubts. Scorn and ridicule set the phone on fire. 'A headshrinker? Some mad old fogey giving out sermons?'

I laughed. 'It mightn't be like that. A chance to talk? About your bad nights — '

'I *don't* think so!'

'OK. We'll drop the idea.'

That week were were busy at HQ but MakerSeceuro was not my only concern. Gradually I was gathering information about Charlie's last few days, making a list of the people he had talked with. A clearer picture was emerging.

Jenny produced copies of Charlie's phone statements. 'These are the last calls he made. This is for his mobile . . . We've gone through, putting names beside numbers where known. I expect some were personal — I've no record of who they were.'

'Thanks, Jenny. I'll have a look.'

Sarah Quirke had called back, arranging to come in at three that Wednesday. After her long silence, I sensed from her tone that something new had happened. By the time she arrived, I had studied all the call statements. Some names jumped out from the pages. Christopher Houghton, chairman of the Livesey Security Group. Quest Associates, plus Alison's home number, four calls. The Metropolitan Police, local branch CID. Ian

Darius, and a second, unknown private line at A-Zander Security. Gill Tarpont's retail chain headquarters, five calls.

All Sarah's directness seemed to have deserted her and she met my eye unwillingly. I waited until we were alone, then closed my office door.

'Have there been any developments?' I prompted. 'Has the witness remembered anything else?' She ran a hand through her hair, in that gesture which meant she was troubled. I attempted a bad taste joke. 'What's wrong? Did he die in custody?'

'Not quite, but it's still bad. The lad retracted all his evidence — everything. Never saw any van. Never saw Charlie or anyone else on the bridge that night. He'd made everything up, he said.'

I couldn't believe it. 'But why on earth would he have made it up?'

'To get leniency, when his string of burglary offences were considered in court. I'm sorry.'

'Then why retract? And everything he saw — that he said he saw — made perfect sense. How *could* he have invented it all?'

'Charlie's death, the manner of it, was reported fairly extensively. We issued posters with his picture on, with appeals for information. Perhaps Mark Jones was an enterprising lad, put things together. Just hoping to get his sentence reduced for volunteering information and cooperating.'

For a fleeting second, I wondered why she had revealed the witness's name. I was filing it away in my mind at once — together with the past tense that she had just used.

'Even so, to come up with the description of that van, the details, the other man with Charlie . . . Perhaps,' I went on, levelly, 'Mark is a lad who has been frightened now.' I watched her expression. 'If someone got to him, scared him . . . '

Sarah shook her head. 'Nobody got to him.'

'But it's a possibility, isn't it? That he did tell you the truth — and then thought better of it? Thought of his health when he got out?' She was giving nothing away. Did she agree with me? 'Sarah, let me talk with him, make an appeal to him. As the victim's widow? While he's still in custody. It just might work.'

'That would never be allowed. You know that.'

'But you think he was telling the truth too?'

'It's too late anyway.' She looked thoroughly unhappy. 'He was released on bail. Day before yesterday.'

I sat back. 'I don't believe it. Who put up the money for bail?'

'I can't tell you.'

'Wasn't there any way of keeping him in? Couldn't you have got bail refused? He was a young lad, surely in need of care? Apart from being the only witness in a murder case!'

'Once he'd retracted everything, Mark was no longer a witness.'

'But — Paul Prentiss could've found out if someone was frightening him, surely? Or somehow blocked his getting released?'

She spread her hands. 'I can't tell you any more. Off the record, this could turn out to be the kind of cock-up that bad dreams are made of . . . Because it gets worse, you see — he's skipped bail and disappeared. Did that the first chance he got.'

I sat there behind my desk and stared at her, unable to speak. Thoughts and feelings raced through me. 'He disappeared,' I prompted at last. 'You know that for sure? Already?'

The hand went through her hair again. 'Of course, we'll keep looking.'

I wasn't going to disguise just how let down I felt. Mark had been our only witness, so far as I knew. The only lead that I had heard of. And he had been lost, thrown away. 'You'll keep looking,' I repeated. 'In case he changes his mind back again.'

'We're really pissed off as well. Once Mark had insisted that his statement was complete fiction, there was nothing we could do.'

'You don't believe that it was made up, and neither do I.'

She was silent for a minute. 'Well, if there's anything else — '

'There is. Something else.' I looked across at her. 'You were going to tell me how Gill Tarpont died.'

Sarah didn't answer for a full minute. Then she sighed. 'OK. I can tell you how Gill was murdered. If you're really sure you want to know.'

'I'm sure.'

She began, quietly, 'It wasn't a robbery. Whoever murdered Gill Tarpont was a real sicko — a psychopath.'

★ ★ ★

Mark Jones, Flat 68, Level Four, As You Like It, Penton Meadow, N17.

I eased the car to a halt at the end of the narrow street. Ahead lay Penton Meadow: a dozen concrete cubes and towers jostling for space, each block stabbed with small windows. The estate was an Alcatraz of connecting walkways with heavy iron bars,

135

across yards of flat, empty concrete. A ramp leading down to parking beneath sported a painted landscape of bright-green meadows with flowers and trees. The council had commissioned the mural after a policeman's murder in the riots here a few years ago. Even from this distance, CCTV was visible everywhere.

Glancing at Mark's address again, I folded the sheet of notepaper and thrust it into my pocket. For the hundredth time in twenty-four hours, I wondered why Sarah Quirke had left the page behind. I had been so shocked, nauseated by what she had told me about Gill, it must have been half an hour before I saw the page lying under her chair, as if dropped there by accident.

I wondered if Sarah Quirke would make it to detective sergeant.

Leaving the car in a street of Victorian two-by-twos, I approached the estate on foot. A board plan at the entrance showed blocks of flats named after Shakespearian dramas, favouring the comedies and histories. As You Like It was the third tower block on the left, after Comedy of Errors and before Twelfth Night.

I began to pass the concrete dungeons. A flicker of movement caught my attention. Three lads, melting away from whatever they had been doing, emerged into the semi-daylight. Lounged there, following my progress with their eyes. They began to saunter alongside, still in the shadow of the garage lot. Making clucking, sucking, lipsmacking then retching sounds. I had put on a faded old coat, jeans and worn-out trainers, good for running. Now I walked faster, my hand on the shriek alarm in my pocket. If I did have to use it, no one was likely to come to my aid in this desert of frightened people.

Then I heard shouting from back at the entrance to the estate. The lads dropped away. Walking so fast I was almost running, I made it to Mark Jones's block, up flights of concrete stairs to Level Four, and found my way round the Alcatraz walkways. Everywhere seemed completely deserted. Flat 68 had nets over the windows and a uniform faded-blue door. Sounds of a game show could be heard from inside. I rang the bell, then knocked loudly.

After I had knocked a second time, the television was turned down a bit. I yelled through the letterbox, 'It's Sue, from the Social.'

Another minute, then the curtain moved at the window. I whipped a card from my pocket, flashed it and smiled. It was a video shop membership card, but at this distance they weren't going to see that.

The door opened a crack. A woman's white face behind it. 'He says, what d'you want then?'

'Hi, I'm a friend — of Mark's. Is he there?'

The door opened slightly further, then stuck. A wiry, birdlike woman was inspecting me. She turned away, yelled, 'She wants our Mark! It's his legs,' she explained, turning back to me. She wrestled the door, got it open. Folded her arms. 'We don't want trouble no more. He's gone.'

'There won't be any trouble. I'm Mark's friend, I just want to know where he went. And if he's all right, your son.'

Someone else laughed wheezily, then started to cough. A man appeared, shuffling up behind the woman. He was older looking, and wore a dressing gown. His legs were misshapen, ending in flattened bedroom slippers. He looked at me suspiciously. 'She's his aunt, that's all. We're not getting him back here again — you hear that? Nothing but trouble since the day he arrived.'

'OK. Where did Mark go? Where is he now?'

'They come and took him, all over again. I said that's the last time, didn't I?'

'Who took him?'

'Police, weren't it? The usual.'

At the aunt's weary tone, I said sympathetically, 'You must've had an awful lot to put up with. When was it that Mark got taken in, this last time?'

They argued about when it had been, finally agreed *Coronation Street* had just been ending. Eight o'clock on Monday evening.

Just hours after Mark was released on bail, he had been picked up and taken away again. By men posing as police officers?

'Were they in uniform?' I asked. 'Did they have ID cards, or warrants?'

The woman looked pained. 'Police, weren't it? You could tell. He went with them. The usual.'

'Were there two men? What did they look like?'

'What d'you want to know for?' the man demanded, hostile.

Quickly I began to explain: 'I'm in a bit of trouble myself. I was supposed to talk to Mark and do a report. But I never did. I know all the police down at the local station,' I improvised. 'So if you can tell me who collected him, then I'll know who to go to.'

They both stared now, eyes beady. The man said, 'If you're from the Social, I'm the Spice Girls.'

I smiled. 'But I am a friend — a friend of Mark's.' I took out a crumpled note and smoothed it.

They both looked at the twenty pounds. The man took the money, pocketing it.

Then he began to describe the two men who had abducted Mark Jones on Monday night.

★ ★ ★

I arrived back where I had left the car, unlocked it and got in. From that safe vantage point, I looked again at the towers and cubes of Penton Meadow. Dealing drugs or thieving was the usual employment for kids raised here. Mark had gone for the softer option. Then, I suspected, he had stumbled into something far more sinister, become entangled with someone deadly.

Where was Mark Jones now?

Setting off north-west, I got on to the North Circular and headed back towards HQ. Then changed my mind on impulse and drove on past the turning which led to the office. A little further west, I struck off down the A1 southbound and headed slowly through that busy traffic, towards where it had happened.

Ten minutes later, there it was in the

distance, growing nearer.

The bridge, of glossily painted Victorian iron, stood spanning the cutting in a great wide arc. One hundred years old and sixty feet high, long like a pair of kestrel's wings. Hovering there, it seemed to spin and blur a little, watching over the dreaming city of London. A dozen suicides every year, drawn by the beauty of the metropolis. The mirage of plenty, of happiness.

I stared up from the red route below, approaching in clogged traffic that lurched forward in fits and starts. That lacy black fretwork took off, soared into the sky. Perhaps Charlie's death had made it a baker's dozen. Unlucky thirteen. Someone pushing him off those railings. To be crushed, right here.

Somebody, maybe local people, had placed flowers at the side of the road. For Charlie. For the boy in the white car, carelessly killed.

My vision grew blurred. I wiped away the tears.

Like an automaton, I kept on driving, down through Camden and in the direction of Regent's Park.

9

I left the car on a meter in a side road, then walked round the block to Quest Associates. The lift produced its usual surge of vertigo, but there was no other occupant on this visit. The third-floor reception boasted a new, smartly uniformed security guard. My own disreputable clothes had him looking alert.

'I need to see Alison. Zoe Maker.'

'You have an appointment?'

'No. Just tell her it's urgent.'

When I went through to her office, Alison was droning into a microphone, dictating a report. She paused in mid-sentence, staring as if she couldn't quite recognise me, then clicked off the machine. 'What *are* you wearing? What on earth have you done — the hair?'

I smiled briefly at her dismay. My blonde bob had been cropped very short a couple of days back. It fitted my mood.

'So what's wrong?'

'I've been asking some questions.'

'Damnit, Zoe, why can't you leave things to us? It won't bring him back if you get yourself killed.'

I sat down opposite her power desk. 'Charlie's death was to do with Gill Tarpont's murder, I'm quite certain now. He got killed because of the people he was putting under pressure. He had information, knew things that were too dangerous. Someone had to get rid of him.'

When I paused, Alison just sat back with a sigh. So I went on. 'What I didn't know before . . . Gill was murdered by someone who is clearly psychopathic. Deranged. Who's killed before sometime. And he'll kill again.'

'You don't know that.' Her voice was angry.

'Nothing was stolen from Gill's house, although she was wealthy. She got targeted for whatever sick reason, by a man who went to a lot of trouble, was absolutely intent — not on killing just any woman, it had to be Gill.' I scrubbed the tears from my cheeks furiously. 'Her wrists were tied with strong-gauge wire. She was dragged across the bedroom to her dressing room. She was suspended from a clothes rail. Her clothes were cut open. Then her breasts. He was using a knife from her own kitchen, downstairs. He used the knife in her vagina. Cut her open, eviscerated her like a side of beef . . . '

143

Horror and pity were between us, sharp and edgy as metal. Alison had got to her feet a bit unsteadily. She was standing with her back to me, at the window looking out on to Regent's Park.

Some time passed. I went on: 'Why did they hush it up, silence the press? Surely people need to know that some crazy — '

'Not necessarily.' She snapped round. 'He won't go for just anyone. Zoe, *trust* them!'

'Not with all this silence, the secrecy. And with nothing happening. There are killings which go unsolved, whoever did them walks free. I won't allow it. That Charlie, and Gill, should be among those victims.'

'You're talking about two completely different murders,' she tried, coming back to the desk.

'That's bollocks,' I told her, angrily. 'You can't fool me — not any more. You already knew exactly how Gill had been killed. Because you and Charlie had talked about it just a few hours before he was murdered.' I was guessing: Alison said nothing, and I knew it was true. 'So — why was Charlie so involved with it? Both of you — why? You knew everything about Gill's murder, but pretended not to. Why didn't you tell me?'

'Because it was too frightening — '

'Bollocks again. Charlie was hunting a

psycho — who killed him. This whole thing is a weird mixture of the personal and the purely crazy — with something very big. Big, and professional.'

Alison was frowning, about to argue. I went on, 'First hear this. The witness who saw Charlie on the bridge was a lad called Mark Jones. He got scared and retracted everything. Then he got bailed. I've just been to Penton Meadow . . . He was abducted from his home there by two men posing as police officers. Unless, of course, they were for real.'

'When was this?'

'Monday evening, at eight. Five hours after the magistrate granted his bail. It would be worth finding out who put up the money.'

'What a pig's ear.' Her voice was quiet and thoughtful now.

'I want you to find Mark Jones, and find out who took him. Whether he's safe. His aunt sold me his picture for a tenner.' I handed Alison a polaroid photo, then told her every scrap of information I had gleaned, about Mark's interests and where his mates hung out, descriptions of the two abductors and their car.

She studied the photo, put it down. Mark's face, looking younger than his seventeen years, grinned up cheekily from her desk.

'Interfering with witnesses — you could damage the prosecution case when all this gets to court.'

'It'll never go to court unless we find Mark and learn who's behind it. So far as I know, Prentiss's team haven't got *this* far. You know the residents of Penton Meadow would never give zilch to the police — unless they were forced to.'

She nodded. 'But we can't — and must not — withhold this information.'

'I'll tell Sarah Quirke,' I promised.

'This is not our usual line of work.' Her voice was wry.

'If you won't look into it, then I will.' Our eyes met. 'But you'd do it much better.'

'Of course we would . . . You know I don't mix the professional with the personal. Although I suppose it would stop you from — '

'Do it for Charlie. You know you want to. There are things you only learn about people when they've died. When you have to go through all their things. Decide what to do . . . with old love letters.' I saw the dawning worry in her eyes. 'Would you like to have yours back?'

She was too shocked to speak for a minute. When she did, I had taken her breath away. 'I'm so sorry. What rotten timing. What on earth did he keep? Maybe you think — ' She broke off, then started again. 'It was history. While you were living apart, we met. He was on his own. He wanted you never to know. He didn't want to hurt you.'

'I know.' After a moment, I leaned towards her. 'Do this for Charlie. Because you were close. Because you loved him too. Help Charlie now. There are things the police can't do that you could — on the quiet.'

'I can't break the law. That would mean losing everything, my credibility, and reputation. My livelihood.'

'Only if you were caught.'

'Or if I had to give evidence as to how — '

'There are ways and means,' I interrupted impatiently, focused on her. Alison was refusing to look at me. 'That are less strictly legal. The CID have to always go by the rules, they're always under scrutiny. While you're not. I want a full private investigation into Charlie's killing. Because maybe you owe it.'

'I'm too involved,' she began, sounding cross. 'I can only take on . . . What else can you tell me?'

I showed her Charlie's phone statements. Pointed out the number of calls he had made to Gill's gift chain, and to MakerSeceuro's biggest competitors. The Livesey Group chairman. The direct line to Ian Darius — and to someone else, unknown, at A-Zander. I had tried that number, found out it no longer existed.

Alison was making notes. Why was I trusting her? I had a strong sense that she was still holding things back. Even the moral blackmail which I had just resorted to had failed in persuading her to reveal all that she knew.

For some reason, Alison wasn't confiding in me yet. She took on the job, though.

★ ★ ★

It should have been enough then, knowing Alison's team was taking care of things. For a few days, while I tried to concentrate on business, it seemed enough.

Still, Charlie was never out of my mind for more than a few brief moments. There was something about Gill's murder and its horrific, pathetic mode, which was reminding me of something else in the past. I couldn't quite recall whatever it was, but the submerged memory was deeply troubling. It was filling me with a sense of dread.

Perhaps this was the reason I couldn't leave things to Quest, couldn't quite stop.

By the following week, I was poring over a London A to Z and marking places where things had happened. Archway Road's Suicide Bridge, the park where Charlie's BMW was left, the pub with the phone that he had somehow rung from and the canal itself: all were contained within a five-mile radius. Even the Penton Meadow estate came within the same small area.

I sat at my desk, doodling, staring at the geography and trying to make sense of where Charlie had been on that last night. I went through the list of people he could have been meeting before he was kidnapped, then killed. Had he been held by his captors at the canal? The place could offer some important clue. I knew Alison's operative had not yet been there. She was concentrating on finding Mark, while that trail was still warm.

For the second time that day, I called Alison. She was unavailable. Waiting for her call back, I felt thwarted by the lack of progress, frustrated in my need to know Wanting action . . . It was mid afternoon, there was nothing urgent to keep me at the office. I couldn't concentrate anyway. Why not take a look around and try to put it all together? It would be better than just sitting here.

I dialled Alison's direct line at work.

She had her answer machine switched on. 'Alison, it's Zoe. If you're there, can you pick up? . . . OK. Listen, I'm going to take a walk along the canal. Just to look at where Charlie's car was found. And the pub, that phone. I'll catch you this evening.'

Half an hour later, changed into old jeans and coat, I was setting off again, this time from home. In my pocket was a personal alarm, a Mace spray — illegal but comforting — and a holiday snap in my wallet. Maybe someone would recognise Charlie from that night. Driving east through Tottenham, I approached the Lea Valley and found the street where Charlie's car had been recovered.

I parked where I thought he had parked. It was a narrow cul-de-sac lined with ancient cars and a terrace of houses, heavily curtained from prying eyes. At the end, a gap in the railings led on to a grassed recreation ground. Weeds were growing over the gate which was clearly never locked. I went through into that square expanse of grass, bordered by tall plane trees with a few benches. Charlie had come here to meet someone, it seemed, but what had happened then? He must have had a mightily urgent reason for coming to this lonely, open space late on a stormy winter night.

Crossing the empty recreation ground, I came to a bare expanse of mud pierced by thorny stumps. An out-of-season rose garden. Beyond lay a playground, full of bright steel bars but empty of children. I walked towards the canal through long concrete drainage pits. They were cracked and open to the sky, littered with weeds and pages from *Hello!*. Beside them was a building with fenced-in play space, half constructed then abandoned. Sandpit and pool were stuffed with sludge and cans. I ducked through a low tunnel and came to the canal.

Under heavy skies the water lay solid, seeming breathless. Willows fell from behind a spiked fence on to stagnant debris. I began to walk up the towpath. A couple of cyclists, commuting home, spun past silently. Soon blocks of flats, built of new brick with aluminium, replaced the willow trees. Further on, moored to the opposite bank, were narrowboats interspersed with old cabin cruisers and rusting, tarpaulined oddities. A heavy steel hull, industrial grey, seemed to be nameless. A holed wooden barge had its rotting cabin brightly painted in fuchsia, purple, orange and rust. Signs of occupation lurked, in a black mongrel dog and plants that struggled from pots, smoke wavering from a thin chimney. Behind the boats, miles of reservoir gave way to miles of empty marsh.

The flats petered out, into the lingering remains of old industrial wharves, past commerce. Warehouses and factories had their windows boarded, yards fenced off from view. Rusting cranes hung gibbet-like, suspended over the water. Brambles and nettles were growing camouflage.

Suddenly I felt I was being followed, and turned, scanned the meandering mud path.

Empty.

By now I had walked for two or three miles but there was still no sign of the pub ahead. Surely I couldn't have missed the place? It seemed odd that Charlie had come all this way, in the dark and pouring rain. Perhaps he had gone around by road to the pub somewhere ahead. Maybe in the car of whoever he had been meeting?

There were so many things I could only guess at. Perhaps there was nothing to find here. Discouraged, I stopped and glanced about.

That was when I saw it.

Dotted around among abandoned factories and warehouses, there had been odd survivors: a builder's yard and scrap merchant, a sawmill and timber wholesaler. Now I saw that the wall bordering this stretch of canal had been quite newly built. The windows, small and heavily barred, were lighted inside. Anti-climb paint had been used on the wall, which had an electronic alarm system. Livesey's. The narrow eye of a camera was tilted down, spying on me.

I was not quite alone.

A small plaque had been screwed into the bricks, high up, its information almost too small to read. *Wesey (UK) Ltd.* The company address below was that of the Livesey Group. I remembered now: Wesey was a subsidiary of Livesey, and makers of the most advanced surveillance equipment in the world. Their inventions, designed for espionage purposes, were generally manufactured for export. I hadn't known they had a site here. It was probably just a coincidence.

Or could this be where Charlie had been heading? But if he had been, then whatever for?

There was no way in. To get to the entrance, I would have to find a way around by the road. Caution held me back. In the security world, my identity was too well known. I could never ask questions with any degree of anonymity.

I walked on slowly to the end of the Livesey premises, then paused. Fifty yards ahead was a low brick building, which looked like a pub but had no name. Before that, another derelict factory and yard. This one had been fenced off with tall sheets of corrugated iron, bolted together and cut into spikes at the top. Around the outside ran a strong wire-mesh fence. It caught my attention because, at the far corner, the iron sheets had been unbolted and could be slid apart to make an opening. From closer to, I could see the wire mesh had been neatly cut just enough to allow someone through. The cuts were new, unrusted.

Glancing back, I reckoned that the Livesey camera almost certainly couldn't see this far. I would be right at the perimeter of its range. Even so, I hesitated to go inside. It was a hesitation full of a growing suspicion. If Charlie had been held in here, then managed to escape and find his way out, to the pub next door . . .

I would check out the pub and its phone, then maybe explore some way along on the other side of it. On the way back, I would look around inside this abandoned factory.

Any doubts as to whether this was the right place quickly gave way to certainty. The pub's sign, The Navigator, had fallen down and lay propped by the path. It was a cluster of small, one-storey buildings, unprepossessing, not interested in passing trade. As I approached, a frantic barking began. A pit bull terrier, its piggy eyes turned to slits in ferocious effort, was hurling itself at the yard fence between us. It was guarding the bungalow attached to the pub.

Around the side, in a small entrance lobby, was a payphone. It was coin operated and bore the number that Charlie had called from. The lobby door had a bolt and keyhole. It would certainly be locked at night. Had it really been left open at two on that Sunday morning, or had Charlie got the landlord to open up? What about the burst of music I had heard in the background?

The lobby's inner door, of frosted glass panels in a wooden frame, led directly into the pub. Inside was starkly lit, with just three people, two of them behind the bar. Conversation between them ended as I went in. All three turned to stare.

Asking for a small Scotch with ice, I brought out the photo of Charlie and laid it on the bar. The landlord was an East End bruiser gone to seed, with a paunch like a nine-month pregnancy: no, he had never seen Charlie before, not in here, not anywhere. The landlady came to have a look, saying nothing. 'I'm his widow,' I told her, pressing them. 'Nothing to do with the police, or anything like that. A few weeks ago Charlie had a fatal accident. It was a Saturday night, Sunday morning on the sixteenth. He called from your payphone at two in the morning. I need to know just one thing — was somebody else with him?'

They both swore they had never seen Charlie, the pub would've been shut, the lobby locked and bolted. Their only customer — a man who looked as if he lived in that chair by the radiator — just shook his head, saying nothing and drinking up. I was getting nowhere fast and it was pretty obvious why.

At the far end of the bar stood an old-fashioned jukebox. I put in a coin and selected a track: Sting, singing 'Fields of Gold'. It was the snatch of music I had heard when Charlie was on the line and which I'd recognised, when Caro played it. A private party must have been going on here a couple of hours after closing time. Charlie had been on the phone when someone had opened the inner door, briefly letting the music through while he was talking to me.

By now, the landlord's cold shoulder was turning frosty. I finished my whisky and left with the music still playing. But I felt tantalisingly close to finding a witness, someone who would describe how they had seen Charlie.

Hovering there on the towpath, I looked back at the sound of the pit bull. It was barking at the solitary customer, who was making his way to the Gents' across the yard. Instinct made me wait, leaning against the fence. A few minutes later he came out, saw me. He stopped and I went over to him.

'You did see Charlie that night, didn't you?'

He took out a cigarette. 'I might of,' he answered, eventually. 'Seeing as you're the wife . . . He come in through the side — the door was open. He'd had a skinful, but not in here. Been in a fight — blood down the side of his clothes. Wanted a phone. So they let him use it.' He lit the cigarette. 'I've never told you nothing.'

'Thank you. Just one thing — did somebody else come, and leave with him?'

'Another bloke, his mate, helped him away. 'Cos he was pickled. Had a skinful, somewhere else.'

'What did he look like? The other man?'

'Couldn't tell you. It was dark out, anyways. It was your husband then?' He clicked his tongue, then shambled away down the towpath, in the direction I had come.

Perhaps I hadn't learned very much but the confirmation was enough to send me on. Lost in thoughts about Charlie and that night, I set off again, steadily forwards along the canal path.

The silence was deeper here, although the canal was thrusting through the heart of the city. A moorhen called, loud enough to startle. Something surfaced in the murk, vanished again in a trail of bubbles, leaving ripples. On the other bank, houseboats huddled by acres of marsh. Before me lay a flat, empty park. There were no shadows . . . Because everything was in pale shadow now, light fading early into an eerie afternoon dusk. There was nothing else to see on this side of the pub. Charlie, and his captors, had not reached this far.

I decided to turn back. That was when the world exploded.

A heavy weight had struck me squarely between the shoulders. I was lying on my face in the mud, winded, too shocked to move until moments later the adrenaline rush sent me writhing, struggling. I was grappling with someone heavily built, in a black sweatsuit, hooded. Their breathing came in growls, intent and maddened. Coiling away, snaking out an arm, I grabbed the hood, ripped it back. Looked into — not a face, but a black-knit skin of balaclava with eyes and mouth cut out, an executioner's mask. Eyes black pins, mouth snarling teeth. I punched the mouth, with not enough weight behind the punch, but got to my knees as his head snapped loosely back. Grabbing the Mace in my pocket, I dragged it out — then saw steel in his hand. A knife. Raised the spray as he pulled me over — then suddenly, inexplicably, he was twisting, catapulting away to the side.

He was scrambling to his feet when I heard it too. Shouting, from somewhere nearby. The man was racing away, fleeing across the park towards houses and streets. I crouched there, catching my breath. Straightened up in time to see that someone else had joined in the path of his flight.

His accomplice, or a public-spirited pursuer?

Then they were both out of sight. I still held the Mace spray, but knew that wasn't what had scared him off. This place was a mugger's paradise, so quiet and well concealed. Every now and then a lone cyclist or jogger would come past. Had a passer-by disturbed him?

I would have disabled the mugger if he hadn't run off: I told myself that. I stood for a while on the path, recovering. My body was awash with sensation, a mixture of aggression and fear. I was ready for anything — fight or flight — anything except a quiet walk back to the car, the tame drive home. Perhaps that explains what I did next.

Retracing my steps, alert to every small sound or movement, I passed the pub and came to the derelict factory. I could walk straight by, or look around inside as I had planned. Somebody had gone in there recently. It could've been Charlie and his captors. If I didn't go in now, I would always wonder what might have been there and whether the puzzle might have been solved.

Fear, and exhilaration at escape, were pounding through my veins. I remembered Alison's words: *It won't bring him back if you get yourself killed* . . . Perhaps, since Charlie had died, part of me did want my own death too. Perhaps I had become crazy. Even while I was thinking this, I was glancing up and down the towpath, then squeezing in flat against the perimeter fence, away from the all-seeing Wesey eye. I pulled open that recently cut stretch of wire, slid apart the corrugated-iron sheets and squeezed through into the factory yard.

The asphalt was almost concealed by tall

nettles, bramble bushes and dead yarrow. I traced a trail of snapped stems, leading from the gap in the fence: of course it could have been just kids, or someone seeking night shelter here.

The door to the brick-built factory was easy to push open, because the lock had been snapped. Whoever had done that could still be in there. I stepped through silently, heart skipping.

Darkness, with the smell of mould and rotting things. A frantic scrabbling: some small creature escaping in fright. The windows were boarded up but slits of light came from holes in the roof. Very gradually, my eyes adjusted to the dark and began to pick out solid shapes. Heavy antiquated machinery, abandoned a long time ago, stood cloaked in brownish dust beneath patches of oily resin and cobwebs. The floor squelched slightly under my feet. It was too damp, too lacking in light for any homeless person to seek shelter here. And kids would be too spooked, surely.

I stepped slowly, as silently as possible, around the factory floor. Holding my breath, searching the place for any hint of occupation, any sign at all that Charlie had been in here. A couple of poky offices had been partitioned off from the factory floor. Scouring these hopefully, I cursed myself for not bringing a torch. Filing cabinets stood like guards. A stack of mail or documents had been left on a desk, and had grown brown and curled, gnawed away at their edges. On the floor behind the desk, old coats or blankets lay in a flattened heap. Perhaps someone had been sleeping in here after all.

There was no sign that Charlie might ever have been in this place. I wondered what I had hoped to find, what could have been left if he had been kept a captive here. His captors' calling card, perhaps? When I laughed softly into the gloom, the sound spread out and echoed, unfamiliar, almost mad.

Giving up on the offices, I made my way carefully across the factory floor to a flight of steps in the centre. They led up to some kind of inspection walkway or gallery. There was slightly more light here because a part of the roof had fallen in. I had taken three steps up when, without warning the handrail above swung loose, lancing out in a wide arc through the air. Instinctively, I ducked: the metal rail grazed past my head with a whoosh. It landed inches away, crashing steel on steel. A cloud of dust flew up. In the silence that followed, I knew I was not alone.

I was visible, lit from the roof.

As the dust thinned, dancing down, my eyes dragged unwillingly to that other source of fading light, the long, thin rectangle of open doorway. A man was standing in its light, solid among the filtering debris.

In a rush of dread, I took in that heavy build, the black clothes. The still, poised stance of the fighter.

10

I froze. His silhouette flitted sideways and vanished against a black wall. Nothing. Silence. He had disappeared.

This was my attacker; he was somewhere in here. Had he really been staring straight at me, or just trying to see in the dark? He had come back, and I had walked into the perfect trap. In this lonely place there was nobody to hear me scream, and in those seconds of terror I thought of Charlie: was he a prisoner here before they finally killed him? Was I about to take his place, find out exactly who had killed him?

Whoever it was, he knew I was here. He was waiting for something, or creeping up on me soundlessly, and soon his eyes would adjust to the dark. Very slowly I slid down lower, began to ease towards the doorway. Something gave softly, fleshily beneath my right foot. From nearby, a steady drip of water sounded like the cracking of small bones.

Light flashed out. A powerful beam. It held me trapped there, caged in the shadows.

'*Zoe.*'

A harsh whisper, familiar and haunting. Charlie's voice. His whisper that night. Cold bands of shock were squeezing my spine. My lips were trying to form his name but I couldn't say it. I had seen his dead body. It couldn't be him.

The voice cracked out an order. 'Come out, damn you. Step into the light, where I can see who you are.'

Slowly I pulled myself up, using the steps. The torch beam was blinding as a spotlight.

'Crazy lady.'

The words were drawled, between disbelief and some other, lighter emotion. A sense of reason began to return. The voice was no longer Charlie's. There was a trace of a Midlands accent, familiar but nothing like my husband's lingering north London heritage. The light was moving now, edging closer. It shifted away from my eyes and illuminated the ground. The voice went on, changing to a quiet tone. 'It's OK . . . You're OK now.'

I looked up into his face. It was Redcliff, somehow here. I leaned against the steps. Relief washed through me.

'Zoe Maker.' He made an exasperated sound. 'I chase off one bit of trouble, and you go straight on looking for more. Did

I scare you?' He laughed shortly. 'I knew you'd go back down the towpath — and that somebody had come in here. What the bollocks are you up to?'

I too was experiencing the anger which often happens after fear, in the wake of relief. 'You were following me?' The words sounded sharp as an accusation. I did not want Alison's partner around. My instructions to her had been clear. Yet I was desperately glad at the sight of him. 'Redcliff, how did you know I was coming here?'

'You rang Quest and left a message. I fielded that. Right?' He peered down at me, his features weirdly lit from underneath. 'You must've already been here by that time. I tracked you and caught up, saw it happen. I just wasn't in time to stop the guy. You're not hurt?'

I shook my head. 'He must've been after my wallet. D'you think?'

'Come off it, Zoe! That knife? The way he went for you? Somebody meant business — somebody didn't want you around. He would've killed you.'

His words echoed through the desolate warehouse. 'You frightened him off, shouting.' I was trying to remember the sequence of events because everything had happened too fast.

Redcliff grinned. 'I'd have put even money on you winning. But the guy was armed. Had the advantage of surprise, and weight.' His expression had darkened. 'Did you see his face, get a description?'

'He had a mask on, a balaclava under the hood. He was tall, maybe six three. Heavy build, he was built like you.'

'I'd have nailed him. Dropped him with his own knife. I was gaining on him. But he had a car waiting, other side of the playing fields. He got away.' Redcliff came back out of some private world of revenge and regret. 'That was no ordinary thief. He was special. We need to report this.'

'To the CID? What good would that do? I'd get warned off again.'

'And we need to talk about that — warning you off,' he said evenly, deliberately. 'Let's go somewhere and talk, Zoe.'

'There's something I want to check first.'

He was sharp. 'What were you doing anyway? What're you looking for?'

'I asked Alison to search here. I instructed her to. Apparently everyone at Quest has been too busy.' I hesitated, wondering how much Redcliff knew about the case, before deciding to tell. 'Charlie was held prisoner for several hours. And he was shot. Probably somewhere remote like this — '

167

Redcliff interrupted, acid with scorn. 'And you think the police haven't turned over every place, scoured every possibility?'

'Not here,' I answered firmly. 'Why would they, when he was killed on Archway Road? They think he was shut up in that van or a business premises. But I've had a feeling about this stretch of canal. And there are people who don't talk to cops. They've talked to me — and Charlie was seen here after he was shot.'

'Who saw him?'

'Lend me your torch. I'm going to search upstairs.'

Redcliff didn't argue but looked at me briefly, then turned to lead the way. It was colder now, the air was raw. We reached a narrow landing and the factory floor spread out below. The rusty hulks of plant seemed to confer across that sea of debris, ghostly delegates from a past industrial age. For decades, no one had made use of the site.

'I hate this place.' The words came back, quietly ringing. The echo must have been caused by the hollowness of the upper floor. As Redcliff circled the torch slowly around us, it became apparent just how much of the roof had gone. The resulting damage was spectacular. Most of the office partition walls had warped and rotted, collapsing to leave the floor like some drunken premonition of open planning. When he aimed the light straight up, we saw the sky and jutting beams.

'This is unsafe. We must get out of here. Zoe, come on.'

'Wait a minute.' Something had caught my eye. It was a different kind of debris — plastic bags, stirred by a breeze and ballooning, scuttling over the boards. I took the torch from Redcliff's reluctant hand, trod carefully across the floor. Here was a solid corner of roof and, beneath it, definite signs of occupation. The blankets were in good condition. Empty tins and bottles lay around.

He was at my side. 'Train it here, right here. And stay back. Mind where you tread, or we'll spoil it. Yeah,' he breathed, talking to himself. 'Recent, all right.'

The torchlight revealed the ashes of a fire, charred wood. A cleared area of floor beside some metal pipes, and something else. Some staining, I thought. Redcliff crouched, intently examining. The fire, the pipes. That dark stain . . .

The beam of light was wavering off course. He took the torch back, but not before I saw the chain which lay around the metal piping. He glanced up at me then.

'They're bloodstains, aren't they?' My voice sounded strange. It was Charlie's blood. We had found what I wanted.

He grasped hold of my arm. 'Let's get out of this place,' he said again. This time I didn't protest.

★ ★ ★

We made our way out to the canal towpath. Redcliff put through a call to Prentiss and I sat down on the concrete bank, waiting for the nausea to pass. A large bird crashed out of the water, flapping away. It left a deeper silence. The vein of black water was stagnant, jammed with stinking weed and trapped white shapes of polystyrene. The night's heavy cloud had begun to leak and we were enclosed by raw drizzle.

Redcliff pocketed his mobile. 'They're sending someone along. I said we'd both wait here for them. Then I'm taking you home.' Glancing up and down the empty path, he squatted beside me. 'OK?'

I turned to him. Although we were so close, I couldn't see his face in the dark. 'Listen, Redcliff. Let's get one thing absolutely straight. I don't need baby-sitting.'

'That seems to be exactly what's needed.'

Maybe it was time he remembered that I

was the client. 'I didn't hire your firm for a minding job. I asked Alison to investigate my husband's death — she took that on.'

'Then why did you come here?' he demanded. 'We would've done this search. Why weren't you willing to give us time to carry it out?'

There was the exasperation again. I ignored it, along with his questions. 'Charlie came here — or to the park where his car was found — to meet someone. And the Livesey Group has premises practically next door to here.' I nodded towards the CCTV. 'Their camera's recording us right now.'

'I saw that.' He was impatient. 'And . . . ? You think they — '

'Probably they want our technical secrets. I'm sure that's connected with — Charlie, what happened . . . ' I paused for a moment. 'When's the next case conference?'

It was his turn to hesitate. 'I'm not sure it's been set up,' he hedged. 'Probably some time next week. Why?'

'I've found this new witness. Charlie was shot before he used the phone, before he tried to get my help . . . to warn me. I've new information and I need to attend that meeting.'

'You shouldn't be involved. No . . . It'll

be Alison's decision,' he amended quickly. 'This is her case.'

'And it's my investigation. I need to know what she's got cooking. And I am already involved.'

'You know the form. These are internal conferences.'

'Of course I know. And I *will* attend.'

Redcliff sat down on the bank, stared intently at the invisible water. It was my field of vision he was searching: he wanted a key to my thinking. 'Listen,' I said again. 'Do you think I can just pick up the pieces — of Caro's life, as well as mine — and carry on, without knowing the answers? The police usually catch murderers very soon after the act — or not at all. You know that as well as I do. And they haven't caught Charlie's killer.'

'OK,' he said slowly, finally. 'And I think you're crazy. It took some courage but — '

'D'you think there's any choice?' I interrupted. 'Redcliff, I want your support. To be let in.'

He was suddenly tense. Jumping to his feet, he glanced quickly behind us, then relaxed. 'Motorbike.'

I heard it in the distance, a soft swarming that grew to a roar as it came closer. A single light appeared, bouncing off patches of the canal, the towpath and bushes. The bike sped up towards us then slowed to a stop. Its rider cut the engine.

Redcliff strode forward. 'Nice one, Sarah,' he called. 'Is it yours?'

Sarah Quirke spoke briefly into her radio, then left her motorbike on the path. She looked at the warehouse, assessing it, unfastening the strap of her helmet. 'Right, let's see what you've found. And whether I need to get the SOCO boys over. Then,' she went on with a touch of malevolence, 'we'd like to know exactly what you were doing here anyway.'

★ ★ ★

Half an hour later, the DC had alerted scene-of-crime and I was heading for home. Redcliff, who was driving up to Hereford, stayed glued to the tail of my car, detouring via Finchley. Maybe he had decided I was accident-prone. Driving in through the gates, I was glad to see the house lights were on. Caro was back for the weekend. It would be good to see her, to chat and cook a meal.

Redcliff's car was still waiting in the road. I raised a hand to let him know everything was fine, and he flashed his lights. When I glanced back from inside the hall, he was moving off.

'Caro? I'm home.'

She wasn't there, I realised a few seconds later. She had come by and left a note on the kitchen table, saying she had gone over to Penny's place.

Caro seemed to be living with Penny Harker these days. The house was very empty. Heart sinking, I saw the time was barely eight thirty. After all that had happened, it seemed much later. I was still feeling shaken, as well as thoroughly cold and wet. From the bedroom mirror, a drenched and mud-plastered figure stared back.

I took a fast shower, then a long hot bath. Caro obviously wasn't coming back for a meal. After two Jack Daniels and a bowl of soup, I pottered around the house, still unable to relax. I cleared the airing cupboard and put things away — more often one of Mary's tasks — belatedly checked the phone then switched on the news. My heart was still in my boots and I couldn't quite think why, at first.

It was the brevity of Caro's note, the fact that she never seemed to be home. Since her father's death, we should have been closer. Why did she never seem to want to talk?

Wishing I had been back before she arrived, I decided to call her.

Penny's mother, Molly, answered, seeming slightly surprised. When I asked if I could have a word with Caro, there was an odd silence. 'She is with Penny?'

'I don't think so. Penny's gone out with her new gang. I suppose they might've met up . . . We did see Caro once — after it happened. But she hasn't been around in quite a while. We've been wondering how she was holding up . . . Why d'you ask, Zoe? Did she — '

I interrupted hurriedly, instinctively covering for Caro: 'I probably misunderstood. Thought it was Penny she was meeting tonight. Must've been someone else.'

'Well, they could've been meeting up. Penny will be back at eleven thirty. I expect Caro will be too, won't she?'

'I expect she will,' I answered. 'Not to worry.'

Caro had been fibbing. By now, my head was spinning. If she hadn't been going to Penny's house recently, who had she been seeing? She had been staying overnight with them, and she didn't want me to know. I read her note again. It was an essay on teenage uncommunicativeness. *Gone round to Penny's. Might stop over. XXX. C.*

It seemed so obvious now, if only I had put the signs together earlier. All these nights of 'stopping over at Penny's' had been spent with a boyfriend. If it was true, if she was with a person I didn't know about, why had she felt that she needed to go to such lengths?

Slowly I went upstairs, to Caro's room. Guiltily, I searched through her things. The condoms were easy to find, beneath her undies in a drawer. They weren't really hidden: Mary or I always replaced her clean clothes in here and I had done so just a couple of hours ago. Feeling like a sneak, I looked inside the packet. Two were gone.

Caro was sixteen, she was both a girl and a woman. She had always brought friends home and told me about new people in her life, or so I had thought. I hadn't expected her to stay a virgin for ever . . . but why hadn't we talked? She was my daughter, and so young. Vulnerable, especially right now after Charlie's death. Was that the reason? She had begun seeing someone in the wake of suddenly losing her father. She must have known I wouldn't approve.

What was he like, this boy who would seduce a recently bereaved sixteen-year-old schoolgirl? Caro wasn't in a state to take care of herself or to exercise good judgement. Did he give a damn about her, or her welfare?

Throwing on a coat, I grabbed my car keys. It was eleven seventeen when I drew up outside the Harkers' house in Maryland Road. I parked by their front gate and waited, hoping to catch Penny. I didn't want to reveal to Penny's parents what Caro had been up to. I didn't want to embarrass her in those relationships, but there was no way things could be left as they were. I wanted Caro safely home tonight, talking about this.

There was time for reflection then. I couldn't really blame her for the secrecy — and just maybe not even for the deception. She had been going through a terrible time, while I'd been distracted by business, then by my stupid obsession with catching Charlie's killer. Suppose she was seeing someone who was just using her? Last year she'd had a close friendship with a boy for six months, but that had been unserious. If this was her first real involvement, it could lead to terrible hurt: and she was so hurt already by Charlie's death. I longed to see her and know she was all right.

Cars passed now and then, in that quiet avenue. By quarter to midnight I was convinced it must be too late and Penny had already got back. The lights of the

Harkers' house were still on but I hesitated to ring their bell. In the past I had trusted Caro, knowing she would choose the right thing for herself. I didn't want her to become distrusted — especially by these people, her friend's parents. How urgent was the situation really? She was doing what teenagers do, experimenting, moving away from me. Was I making too much out of it?

A small voice was warning: but we make mistakes. Sometimes serious mistakes. She's too *young* . . .

I got out of the car and locked it. At the same moment, a red Scirocco drew up at the kerb in front. Penny climbed out. She leaned in to speak to someone and for a glad instant I thought it was Caro, that they had been out together and Caro was here, being driven home by a parent. Then I saw there was only one person, the driver, still inside.

The Scirocco drove off. Penny turned towards the wooden gate set in the low beech hedge. I had been standing very still and she hadn't seen me yet. When she did, her face said everything.

'Oh, hi.' Shock and dismay turned to the anticipation of trouble as she adopted a studied nonchalance. Penny had been in Caro's year and was the same age. Now, despite her black leather jacket and tall boots,

178

she looked about twelve years old.

'Hi, Penny. I'm looking for Caro. She seems to've disappeared.'

She was trying to think what to say. 'Right. She's not home yet, then.'

'It's rather worse than that, Penny.' Angry at being deceived, I felt like wringing her innocent little neck. It took an effort to speak calmly. Caro could be very persuasive in getting her way. Probably Penny hadn't been given much of a choice. 'She's been pretending to come to your house — as a cover. I've spoken to your mother, and that much is clear.' She looked almost comically woeful then and I suppressed an urge to laugh. I was tired. It was late and I wanted Caro home.

'I told her she should tell you,' Penny wailed crossly. 'And now I'll be for it.'

My voice was grim. 'I'm sure you tried. And perhaps I won't blame you — but you'll have to fill me in now. Where is she? She's with a boy, isn't she, and staying overnight? What's his name? And who is he?'

'Peter. That's all I know!'

'You've met him, I'm sure you have.'

'Honestly, Zoe — I'd tell you if I had. She just said that if you asked then she was at my place. I told her it would get out — Dad'll kill me. All I know is, his name's Peter and

179

she won't let anyone around him, or not yet. He's older. He's a graduate, a scientist. And that's all.'

'All right, Penny. But I'm sure you know where to find her, don't you? Listen, if you can get her back home tonight, then I won't tell your parents what's been going on. Will you do that?'

Her face screwed up into a grimace. 'I would, but — '

'Listen to me,' I repeated, voice rising. 'I've been worried sick about her. She shouldn't be doing this. I don't need to tell you what she's been through recently.'

She shouted back, 'It's not my fault! And I would help, really — 'cos I can see how worried you are. But I've just no idea where she is, that's all.'

* * *

It wasn't really a crisis, or even a drama. Caro had started dating somebody. She was sixteen and was able to look after herself. She had a new boyfriend, just hadn't got around to telling me yet. These were the things I repeated to myself, driving home. She would be back in the morning.

I slipped in and out of shallow sleep, anxious dreams, as if I feared the loss of my daughter — that I might never see her again. As if, like Charlie, she too might have died.

At first light, frayed and despondent, I went downstairs to make a pot of strong coffee. She'll be back soon, I thought, turning on the radio. It was news time and I listened to disasters. Just after eight, the phone rang and I fell on it.

It was Alison. 'Isn't it a bit early for you to be up?' I groused, disappointed.

'Who said anything about going to bed last night — at least, for sleeping?' She sounded smug, horribly cheerful, and I left a pointed silence. If she wanted to boast about her latest conquest, she was on her own with it because I wasn't in the mood. 'What's up?' she asked, finally.

'Nothing. Having the odd problem,' I amended, feeling slightly ashamed. 'With Caro, actually.'

'What sort? Just teenage stuff, I expect? Well, take it all with a pinch of salt,' she advised airily, as if she had been mother to a sizeable brood herself. 'It'll blow over. I've just talked to Redcliff, and I ought to be extremely cross with you, Zoe Maker. All this snooping around on your own — and being threatened with a knife? Come on. Isn't MakerSeceuro enough for you?'

'I found valuable new evidence, did Redcliff tell you that?' She said nothing. 'I'll tell you all about it — but only at the next case conference. When is it?'

'We'll have to talk that over. Clients have separate briefings, you know that. Listen, I've got to make tracks. I called because I've got hold of that journalist at last. Patricia Abel. She's back in town.'

'That's great. And?'

'She'll never reveal her source.'

'We'll get it out of her.'

'She says she believes what she wrote was accurate. But she is willing to hear your side of things.'

'And to write that?'

'She's willing to listen. Can you make it to Islington tomorrow night, and I'll come along as ref? Nine o'clock, in that pub by the canal. The Narrow Boat.'

'I'll be there.'

Putting down the phone, I heard the front door open quietly as Caro came in.

11

'Oh, hi.' She came into the kitchen with her old, cheerful grin, dropping her bag on to the floor. 'Any breakfast going? I'm starving.'

The house seemed filled with life again. Caro took a packet of cereal from the cupboard, poured it into a bowl and added milk. I was giddy with relief, watching her. 'Like some coffee?'

'Mm.' She nodded. 'Molly had to go out and — '

'No, don't say anything else.' I had cut her off sharply and she looked up, breakfast forgotten, our eyes meeting briefly in recognition. She didn't seem surprised. She had expected to be found out. 'Oh, Caro. Why couldn't you have told me you were seeing someone?'

She took a while to answer, pushing away the cereal bowl and fiddling with a napkin. 'It's nothing to do with anyone but me, that's the reason. I knew you'd be up in arms about it. I knew you'd want to interfere and stop me.'

If only you were here, Charlie, I thought. Adding your words and keeping the balance.

She needs you, we both need you.

'Caro, you're only *sixteen*.'

'So? Does that make me less of a person?'

'Stop being obtuse. I've been out of my mind with worry! I called Molly yesterday evening, for a chat with you — '

'So, I was staying somewhere else. What's the big deal?'

'The big deal is the lies, all those fibs, Caro. I found the condoms, so I talked to — '

'Checking up on me, like some Victorian granny? You've been searching through my things — really? And quizzing my friends.'

'Because you weren't where you'd said. You could've been — anywhere at all. I shouldn't have had to do that.'

'Then why do it?' She was furious now, and my own latent anger was bubbling up in response. 'Why not just wait? I'm here, aren't I?'

'You could've been in trouble,' I snapped. 'And you've been doing this for weeks, haven't you? Lying.'

'I feel like a prisoner! And I don't even live here — I live at school.'

'You do live here. And what kind of boy would sleep with a schoolgirl, deceiving — '

'Leave him out of it!' She was shouting, in a voice of panic, not just anger.

184

'Don't be silly, we can't.' I breathed deeply, trying to get calm enough to understand, to reason with her. 'We've got to talk this through now. I didn't mean to . . . Didn't mean to attack you, or him. I don't think you realise — how it was, finding out. Waiting, not knowing if you were all right.'

'That's your problem.'

What had happened to us? Our closeness, and the trust? Under that cold-seeming, spiky manner, she must be feeling as bewildered as me. Then I saw, or remembered, the obvious — this was all about losing Charlie. We were floundering in that morass of emotions again. It wasn't about her having a boyfriend. Poor Caro. She was trying to leapfrog straight into adulthood, at a time like this.

'Caro.' I sat down next to her at the table, longing to touch her but knowing right now she would move away. 'Since Dad died, we've got to pull together. We must, or there's no hope for us. D'you see that?' She said nothing and I went on, 'I'd like to know about Peter. Tell me.'

Unexpectedly she said, 'You're hardly ever around.'

'At weekends? But I am! Yesterday — '

'When I call here, during the week.'

I frowned. She hadn't been leaving messages — and why hadn't she tried the mobile? Perhaps she had been checking up on me, then? Or feeling lonely at school and trying to touch base when I wasn't here? 'I didn't know you had. I'm at the office quite a lot. We all have ways of coping, and mine is keeping busy.'

'Yes. Mine is Peter,' she said, and smiled. I smiled back.

'Is he nice? Penny said he's older than you. And a scientist.'

She answered proudly, 'He's twenty-two. He works in genetic research at the university.' Unexpectedly, again, 'You met him — last year, and recently. But Peter thinks you might not remember it. In the car park?'

'What car park? When?'

'*The* car park.' Enjoying herself now. 'I don't know when. It was at HQ, Mum.'

Of course it came back then. Only two or three days after Charlie's death, the emergency board meeting, addressing the staff. Breaking down afterwards, on the way to the car. 'He's tall, with light-coloured hair? Does he wear specs?' She nodded, watching my reaction. 'That's Peter? He's one of our tenants.'

Butter wouldn't melt in Caro's mouth. But had she really spent last night — and several other nights recently — in one of the flats

186

at the MakerSeceuro building? She had been snugly close by all the time.

'I knew you'd be like this!' she burst out then, misunderstanding my silence. 'Nobody could be right, could they? Just because he pays you rent.'

'Perhaps nobody could be good enough,' I agreed. 'But I was actually thinking . . . Never mind.' We had got this far and I wasn't going to risk more alienation between us. I wanted to meet Peter properly. 'So he's a scientist. That sounds . . . impressive.' I was wondering how long she had known him, whether she had jumped into bed with him. Would Caro do that? Suddenly it was as if I didn't know her very well any more. 'Caro, is he nice? Penny said — '

'Just because he isn't in business! Because he's six years older than I am, that doesn't mean I can't love him. You don't understand. He warned me people wouldn't understand.'

'But I think I do. It's just that you're terribly young. It's so recent that your dad died. You've just started your A levels. And I really do not like being deceived.'

She looked a bit hangdog. 'Peter had nothing to do with that.'

'But he must know you're a minor. Just sixteen. Are you sleeping with him?'

'That's what this is all about, isn't it! Just sex. All anybody cares about. You don't have to worry. It's nobody's business but mine what I do.'

'Caro. Please be careful . . . Did he really imagine your parents would be happy with the situation, not giving a damn where you slept, not knowing who you were with?'

'Dad's dead,' she stated bleakly. 'And you — keep busy.'

My heart contracted and I reached out to her. 'I will always have time for you. You know that — you know it. And even after all this subterfuge, I want to believe that Peter is OK.'

'You'd *like* him. You checked him over when he took the flat, and thought he was OK then.'

It was hardly the same thing, and I bit back several retorts. 'Then why the secrecy? You could've brought him home before this.'

'Because you would've interfered, like this. That's why.'

'Is it interfering to care? Come on, Caro. If Peter cares, then I'm sure he'll want to meet your mum. Just as much as I want to meet him.'

That silenced her for a few moments. I got up and began to tidy things away.

Caro opened the dishwasher. 'It sounds like a summons.'

'Let's turn it into an invitation,' I answered lightly, then became serious. 'Given all that's happened, I can't allow you to see him again. Not until I've had a chance to talk to him . . . Until then, you're grounded.'

★ ★ ★

After a few hours of mulling things over, Caro called Peter and they talked for a long time. Eventually she emerged from her bedroom looking pleased. He had agreed to come to Sunday tea.

After that she was fretful, nervous of our meeting and angry at missing a Saturday night out. She seemed to have lost all interest in her other friends. Her feelings for Peter were intense. I was trying to mend bridges between us and so, in her own conflictful way, was Caro. She owed me an apology and I think she knew that. Single parenthood was a whole new ballgame, in terms of authority and of closeness. Caro must have found it disorienting — among other things — suddenly having only one parent. We needed new rules.

On the dot of three thirty the following afternoon, Peter rang the doorbell. There was a low-voiced exchange in the hall, several minutes of near silence before Caro brought him through to meet me. By this time I had realised how infatuated she was. I was worried, because of her age.

He was a gentle giant, taller and broader in the shoulders than I remembered from that little encounter in the dark. His features were plump, the fair hair was a bit overgrown and he was hiding behind those studious, heavy tortoiseshell spectacles. He seemed formal and was wearing a suit. That first impression was confirmed — Peter Doyle had a vague, charming unease about him, a shy clumsiness which disarmed. A blond Clark Kent, I thought as we shook hands. Was he about to dive into a phone box and change into a cloaked avenger, saving the world?

We went through into the conservatory, overlooking the garden. 'This is . . . What a beautiful house, Mrs Maker. Caro's told me — described it to me, but I hadn't realised.'

'Sit down, Peter. Caro will make us some tea. Where are you from — the voice?'

'There's a touch of Scots in it, isn't there? I went to school in Edinburgh. We lived outside the city for some years, when I was a kid.' Sitting down at the table, he knocked over a plant, apologised profusely and tried to right it. He was very nervous.

Caro said, 'Mum, can we save the third degree? Would you like coffee?' she asked him. 'I've made an angel cake and you've got to eat some.'

When she'd gone I told him, 'I don't intend to sound like an interrogator — but I do want to know all about you. I'm sure you understand that?'

Peter flushed red and looked down at his hands. For a moment I imagined he was angry at the prospect of being vetted. Then it became clear he was just embarrassed. 'I'm sorry,' he said, still refusing to meet my eyes, 'about you not knowing . . . I've not been seeing Caro for all that long, but — '

'She's just lost her father, in the most terrible way imaginable,' I told him. 'She's sleeping very badly. And she's started sixth form at a new school. Apart from everything else, she shouldn't be getting exhausted every weekend up here in London. This is all just too distracting.'

He was nodding earnestly. 'I understand all that. And I did want Caro to tell you sooner, Mrs Maker. I want whatever's best for her, you see.'

That foxed me, since it was what every mother would want to hear. I eased off, stopped acting the terrier. Watching them together was slightly reassuring. Peter seemed fond of her in a friendly way, fairly mature emotionally for his twenty-two years and not in the least wild. It was Caro making the running, pushing things ahead in a hurry. She had a restlessness and a worrying neediness about her which had never been there before: it had appeared since Charlie's death.

Beginning to relax a bit, Peter talked without much further prompting. His father was a lecturer in biology, his mother taught in primary school and he had one brother, now at university. He seemed more confident in describing his family, as if they were a close unit and his childhood had been a happy one. The thought crossed my mind that the tenancy papers would contain facts about his job, plus references. Those could easily be dug out at the office tomorrow.

With a good appetite, he was steadily devouring the angel cake which Caro had baked this morning. 'You work in genetics, Caro tells me. In a laboratory, is that right?' With his shy, studious manner and those specs, it was easy to picture him peering down microscopes. 'What kind of research is it, Peter?'

'I work in a team. We're mapping for genes

that influence human behaviour.'

'That's interesting. It sounds — very important research. I thought genes were about inherited physical characteristics. Health, and appearance?'

'Oh, Mum,' said Caro in an embarrassed voice. 'They're much more than that.'

'So there are genes for behaviour? That actually influence what we do?'

'You bet there are.' Peter was getting into his stride, in his territory now. 'We *are* our ancestors — it's a bit like a lottery draw, from our forebears. We really only exist as two sets of chromosomes, a few million genes. That's us, and that's our behaviour. We're programmed, Mrs Maker, and it's far more than phenotypic effect.'

'I hope you're not saying there's no free will? I don't believe that, Peter. Surely even the most fervent geneticist would allow that environment plus upbringing has a big influence on behaviour?'

Peter made an uncharacteristically expansive gesture, totally dismissive. 'So we work with behavioural psychologists, as well as with neuro-scientists. But believe me, very soon indeed people will be looking back on this as a dark age, Mrs Maker. An age of excuses and fudging the issues. People are biology, plus chemistry.'

Peter was a new graduate, Caro had told me, working as a lab assistant and hoping to do a PhD. Clearly fanatical about his field, he was maybe too young to put the work into a broader perspective. Unless, of course, he was right? I began to argue: 'It sounds a bit like religious fatalism — the idea of predetermination, chosen ones? And what about eugenics and — '

'Mum, you just don't get it,' Caro sighed. 'There's a lot of sentimental ignorance around still.'

'I don't know anything about it — that's true. Darling, you need to phone the school. If we get you on to the eighteen twenty from Waterloo, Bob can collect you from Haslemere. And don't forget to take that form about your course visit to Strasbourg. Peter, perhaps you could help with carrying the tray out?'

In the kitchen, all his nervousness returned. He scrambled to retrieve the cutlery he had just sent bouncing across the tiles, then blurted out, 'Are you going to let us go on meeting?'

'That depends — mostly it depends on you.' I looked straight at him, and again he seemed too shy to meet my eye. 'Caro needs time to recover emotionally. If you want to be a part of that process, then it has to be as one of her circle of friends. Nothing more.'

He flushed again. 'I wouldn't — I wouldn't want to . . . '

I waited, but whatever he was trying to say had fizzled out. 'She hasn't introduced you to anyone yet, has she? It wasn't only me . . . I wonder why.'

'Caro's very intense,' he said, and stopped again.

'Then you must both cool it. Mix with her friends, and yours — go out in a group. OK? And you're welcome here any time. But no more sleeping over.'

Peter nodded, seeming to have no problem in accepting this. Caro was less easily persuaded. Her first reaction was fury — and yes, I was certainly interfering — but when Peter reasoned with her, repeating all the things I'd said to him earlier, she quickly calmed down. That was reassuring. I was banking on the hope that, despite the questionable beginning, he could turn out to be a good influence as one of her friends.

On the drive to Waterloo station, I said cautiously, 'Peter seems all right. But you must remember you hardly know him yet — and you're much too young for any heavy stuff, Caro. Please believe me.'

She said, in a too reasonable voice, 'I just wish you wouldn't interfere, Zoe.'

I pulled in near the taxi rank and turned to her. 'I only want to protect you. Because I love you. I'm so sorry you've lost Charlie. But please don't try to replace him with someone else, darling.'

Caro leaned across and gave me a hug. 'I love you too, Mum. But sometimes you're such an idiot. Now quit worrying, huh?'

★ ★ ★

That weekend with Caro had been a shock. Thinking back, I could see there had been some signs of her romance — or her infatuation — with Peter. She had been royally moody and uncommunicative, then buying a lot of new clothes, more preoccupied than usual with the mirror. I had just assumed she was knocked off balance, then compensating for what had happened to her.

By Sunday evening, my instinct was to concentrate on Caro and the business, leaving everything else to the police and to Quest. Wanting to discuss cancelling the meeting with Patricia Abel, I called Alison, but she wasn't at home and her mobile was switched off. I would have to go along to the Narrow Boat. Perhaps talking with the journalist could help MakerSeceuro, even if I learned nothing of any use about our enemies.

There was a raw, fine rain falling that winter night. The pub turned out to be well removed from Islington's renovated terraces and crumbling basements. It clung to a bridge on the Regent's Canal, between blocks of council flats and industrial wharves. Inside was as narrow and boatlike as its name, with board floor and tobacco-yellow walls. The clientele was local, making this a discreet meeting place.

It was just before nine. I bought a whisky and settled at one of the long windows. Below, boats sat moored in watery black shadows between the brick walls of converted warehouses. The choicest moorings were a couple of hundred yards away, among willows and lawns with private jetties. Those boats were shiny and sleek, their bright, ornamental colours turning them into favourite toys for those who loved damp living.

Ten minutes late, Alison made an entrance with flapping fur coat, scarcely used umbrella. She bought a drink and came across, looking wrecked.

'Good weekend?'

Ignoring that, she settled on to the hard wooden chair with clear disdain. She fished for cigarettes. 'I didn't choose the

197

venue — I'm innocent, OK. No sign of the journo, then?'.

'Not unless she's that old salt propping the bar up. What's she like?'

'The horns and the tail, d'you mean?'

'I mean . . . Is it all opportunism with her? Could somebody have paid her — not the newspaper, but some interested party — to do that piece against MakerSeceuro?' Then I realised: already I was in danger of breaking my new resolve to leave things to the investigation agency.

'We've only talked on the phone. But if you want my impression, I think she might actually be interested in learning the truth.'

'We'll see.'

'Good weekend, yourself?' she asked, brightly.

'I've known better ones. Why?'

'You certainly know how to stick your nose in where it's not wanted.' She was making an obvious effort to sound mild. 'Why didn't you wait for me to send someone to the canal?'

I shrugged. 'You don't know what I found out yet. Not everything. Redcliff only heard the telegraph version — '

'And now you want to start attending our case conferences? Clients never come to those. It's a house rule.'

'That's all right. I've changed my mind about it.' She looked puzzled, almost put out, and that was unexpected. We stared at each other. Her expression held an emotion I couldn't name. Relief? Or fear? I stopped her next question, because there was something I needed to know. 'That — stuff we found in the warehouse . . . Were those definitely bloodstains? Have the police said anything to you?'

'There's no proof yet that it's anything to do with Charlie. I've had this ghastly feeling you'd want to be even more involved with our investigation, and Redcliff says — ' I was shaking my head, and she paused abruptly before going on. 'Redcliff told me you want to. I've decided that you can attend. It'll probably be Tuesday, the next in-house meeting . . . ' My expression must have told her she was wasting her breath. 'Why the change of heart?'

'Why *your* change of heart?' I asked, looking her over carefully. Had she just decided that I was too much trouble if left out of things?

Alison stubbed out her lipstick-stained cigarette. 'My partner thinks we should liaise with you more than we have, that you could contribute to solving this case. Or anyway, that you're too pigheaded to keep out. But it seems . . . Was he wrong?'

'I need to concentrate on Caro. So it would be better if I leave things to Quest. To you.'

'We make an exception — and then you turn us down?' Alison gave a short laugh. She was looking at me, wondering.

She and I had been fencing, parrying small attacks across the narrow table between us, ever since she had sat down. Was this to do with Redcliff and his shift in attitude? I suspected it might be a lot more important, to do with the investigation itself. Alison seemed to be pushing for my involvement, after massively resisting it all along the way. I had the feeling that something else might have happened, quite apart from the bits of evidence I had managed to turn up.

Stop this, I told myself.

'How *is* Caro?' she asked suddenly. 'What's the problem — boys? It usually is.'

'There is a boy.' I was longing to share the weight of the past two days. 'He's six years older than her, and six years is a lot when you're in your teens. She seems more than a little bit keen and that hasn't really happened before.'

'She's about the right age for it. Is he OK?'

'I'm not completely sure about that. And

this is just not a good time for her.' I began extracting myself from our corner, to get us another drink. 'If only Charlie was still alive.'

'That, my friend, is my sentiment exactly. If only he was.' She took out a mirror and checked her watch. 'Look at the time, it's gone nine forty. A bit late, isn't she?' Glancing at the black, rain-patterned glass of the window, Alison leaned towards one of the pub lights. She was applying fresh scarlet lipstick. 'I wonder if our Patricia Abel is going to show?'

12

And life is gone. Easily — quieter than anything else in the world — only a little surprised reaction, a small physical readjustment. And Death. Letting go then, letting the kid slide down. The ground's pretty muddy, the rain's grown steady as the night's drawn on. Under the arches, everything bounces off concrete. The rain, streaks of light and echoes. The wheels of a train setting off overhead. A thunder and lightning of cars passing by, so close you feel the whoosh. In the thick of it, you'd think.

Too easy, really. A desert of cars, peopled by pillars. No passers-by. No one to see. Old proverb: it is Better not to Bear Witness, or your life Will be short and unhealthy!

The imprint of my boots, and fibres, perhaps. I can see to those. Under the maze of the viaduct, back to the car.

Will they be bright enough to connect? After all, not my usual modus operandi. Not even a souvenir — I didn't bother taking one. Perhaps they'd like a different clue, a signature — maybe an autographed photo would help? Ha ha. Let them take their tiny brains for walkies. It's always interesting, reading the papers. It's a mad world, my masters. A dumb world.

Driving fast through a dumb, asleep world: watch out, because here I come! Elation — streaking ahead through streets that are almost empty — so few cars around and an hour or so till dawn. All so EASY. I CAN DO ANYTHING, ANYTHING — AND GET AWAY WITH IT! NO PROBLEM . . . Adrenaline's the best drug in town, kicking in with a special speed. I understand these things, I've studied the human brain. Finding out, that's my bag. Learn what you need, then move on.

Slow down, now. And stop for red lights. Dumb, dumb world. Play the game.

Still dark and still raining, as I park near the water. To the boat, for getting shipshape. All's secure.

Aboard, my first step is to light the stove. Get it burning to a furnace, then begin my clean-up operation. Strip off. Bundle up the wig, clothes and muddy boots, for incineration. (I didn't get where I am today, through carelessness or lack of self-discipline.) Take a shower, followed by a shave. Clean clothes for the day's work and my next appointment. By the time I'm ready to move on, all the stuff I wore has been reduced to cinders in the flames. Leave that tamped down and take a quick check round. All shipshape. Time to take care of business.

No one around the boats yet. A grey morning, still and silent as I step ashore, carrying my briefcase to the car. The rain's cleared at last but you'd scarcely notice, the air's wet as well as the ground. Wondering if they've found the kid, tuning in to London news on the way: nothing. It's too soon.

My second rendezvous in this café: some choice. Enough punters are already eating, sharing a table looks almost necessary. I buy a cup of tea — although I'd never dream of drinking it — and check the position of my contact. He is in the promised bower of plastic ivy, behind a plastic trellis — reading The Times. Nice touch?

I sit down opposite and we ignore each other. My briefcase goes on the floor between our feet. His identical briefcase is there already. Information For Cash, it's a fair deal. I'm getting technical hardware untraceable to me, or to them — plus the finance for my personal operations (which of course they know nothing about). My masters, in the sense of those who hire my services, are getting all the lowdown they could want on a certain rival Company.

204

They are still palming me off with this messenger boy. But there's a possibility that soon I may meet the man who gives the orders. It's been almost a year since I set up surveillance, offered to produce the goods. I had the simple advantage then of easy, undetectable access. My work has proved itself, grown sophisticated since those early, innocent days. And they all trust me, they really do.

My masters are not my masters.

The men who buy my services don't even have my true identity — no one has that. They swallow the story and the proof of it, all of them. Sometimes I marvel at the dumbness of corporate man. It is Born of Greed, the Root of All Evil. Not guessing at the extent of my actions, they've taken advantage of a business opportunity: Bless Them! They're in it up to their eyes, they just don't know yet. They're implicated by association, I would say, in a string of DEATHS like the Persecutor, the Student and the Bitch. Maker — and last night's little problem taken care of.

That's just so far.

It's nice to watch Breakfast Television but this morning I'm a bit pushed, after such a busy night. There's just Time to buy a Decent breakfast, on the way home to sort out the Loft. Freshly baked muffins from down the road and a morning paper. A chat about last night's rain with the woman at the newsagent's, who's feeling her arthritis today. Then briskly home for fifteen minutes, fresh coffee and the two cherry muffins.

Change the tapes, file the old ones For Attention. And set up for the day.

I'd rather avoid the Rush Hour. So to the underground station to catch my train, with newly polished shoes and carrying an umbrella, in case it rains again today.

13

Monday's rush hour: the A406, already sluggish and wet, was solid with trucks and cars. The short drive from home to headquarters allowed plenty of time for previewing the day, the week ahead. From now on I was going to concentrate on business, Mondays to Fridays at least.

Last night had been disappointing. Neither Alison nor I had been too surprised when the journalist failed to show up. Most likely Patricia Abel never had wanted to talk. Why would she, after putting out such devastating, inaccurate vitriol as she had in the 'Unmaking of MakerSeceuro' piece? She had just been trying to get Alison off her back. Now we seemed to have reached a full stop in finding MakerSeceuro's enemy.

I reached the office at five past ten. Everyone was plunging into routine and I was keen to do the same. I greeted Jenny, spoke to Madison and fixed to meet with him at three. At that moment, the call came through from Quest Associates.

'What's it about?' I asked, annoyed because of all those good intentions.

'They're not saying. They're holding. It's
. . . Michael Ash, and he says it's urgent.'

'Suppose I'd better speak to him.' If it
really was urgent, why get an assistant to
make the call? 'Michael. Zoe Maker. What
can I do for you?'

'Good morning. Alison asked me to let
you know that the conference on your case
is being brought forward to this morning.'

I began leafing through the papers waiting
on my desk. 'Please thank Alison. Remind
her that we already discussed it.'

'She asked me to say that she and Jay
Redcliff both think it's imperative that you
attend. Because of what you know — and
because there's been a new development.'

'What development? Can you put me
through to Alison? Or Redcliff, please.'

'I'm sorry, they're both unavailable right
now. There's a lot going on, that's why
I'm calling. The message is: please attend.
And if you can, they'll delay starting the
meeting until eleven. I can tell you the
reason, it's very simple — there's been
another murder.'

★ ★ ★

I took a cab to Regent's Park. First Gill
Tarpont. Then Charlie . . . Now someone

else had been killed, and I didn't know who.

Redcliff met me at Quest reception and we went without speaking to the conference room. Alison was already there, with two investigators who had been working on the case. Michael Ash was a fresh-faced graduate, keen as a sabre. Gwen Farthing I had never met before. She was silver-haired and had a quiet, understated manner. Gwen was the kind of operative Alison loved to use for undercover work. Camouflaged as a granny, she would know how to act invisibly and to dumb down her clear intelligence. People would confide and let things slip, responding to being mothered by this harmless-seeming lady.

After explaining why I was there, Alison went straight to business. 'We've been searching for Mark Jones, the police witness who saw Charlie on the bridge.' She looked grimly around the table. 'At seven forty-five this morning, Mark was found dead.' She checked her notes. 'He was discovered by a street cleaner under the bridges behind King's Cross station — the body was a few feet away from passing traffic. Preliminary examination suggests he was strangled, probably between two and four hours earlier.'

The deep silence in the room was broken

by Michael. 'Was there any sexual element?'

'It's too early to know — but yes, it is a rent boys' patch, and Mark had been sighted in that area before. With other teenage boys. And among the homeless.' Alison glanced at Gwen, before looking at me. 'Mark had changed his mind about talking. Now he never will. Can we be certain this is connected, not some odd coincidence?'

'Does it fit the pattern, carry any of the signature marks?' Redcliff asked. 'He hasn't strangled before. Right? Did Mark's killer use a knife, or take any part of the body?'

'The post-mortem's this afternoon when we'll know for sure. But first indications are there was no knife, nor any evidence of drugs.'

I said slowly, 'They were making sure of his silence. That's why it was less ritualistic, because he was simply in the way.' I thought about Mark, with his cheeky smile in the polaroid. He was almost a child, only one year older than Caro. 'Had he really got into prostitution?'

'Yes, from around King's Cross,' Gwen confirmed. 'We were unlucky to miss finding him last night.'

'Mark did have a home, of sorts,' I put in. 'Never stayed there for long, probably. Didn't get on with his aunt's boyfriend.'

'So let's sum up,' Alison said. 'After getting bail on the burglary charge, Mark was abducted from his aunt's home. He seems to've gone willingly enough, with two men posing as plainclothes officers. They were fake, I can confirm that. But if they killed him, why did they wait until last night? Mark had been on the loose . . . '

Gwen said, 'We had a sighting of him, only two days ago. Near Euston.'

'So why *did* the abductors wait?' Redcliff mused aloud. 'And is there any significance at all that it was made to look like a rent-boy strangling — by the location if nothing else?'

Michael suggested, 'What if Mark was freed, warned off — and disappeared voluntarily? Then he got unfortunate.'

'You're not suggesting this murder could really be unconnected?' I asked. He spread his hands, in a gesture of not knowing. There was a brief pause before Alison spoke again.

'At this stage, it's guesswork. You want my guess? Suppose the abductors and the killer are separate — although with similar interests, perhaps? But operating differently . . . What if each knew that Mark had spoken up? The abductors knew where to find him, so perhaps they were behind his aunt having got the money for bail? She's told us the cash was anonymous, from a well-wisher. No — I'm afraid it's not traceable, Zoe.'

'His aunt put up the bail with a load of cash? She did care about him, then. And wanted him freed. If only she hadn't,' I said. Then paused for a moment. 'So you think the abductors might've warned him off, told him it wouldn't be healthy to remember any more? But Charlie's killer . . . wanted the witness silenced for ever.'

'Enough speculation,' Alison decided. 'We think this is connected, a third murder by the same person or persons, but we don't know yet. The post-mortem and police inquiries will turn up more facts. Meanwhile, let's look at other matters.' She smiled brightly in my direction. 'On Friday, Zoe took a stroll down the canal towpath . . . Over to you. Tell us about it.'

The edge in her voice was slight. I had trespassed on her territory, but had brought home the goods. For the record, for Alison and her two operatives, I carefully began to recount the events of that walk. I described the customer at the Navigator, who had been there at two seventeen on the morning of Charlie's death. 'No one will admit to its existence — their private party. This new witness doesn't want to talk, not to the police or anyone. But he saw Charlie making that phone call to me. And he was injured, with blood down his arm and appearing to be drunk. So he *was* already drugged. The witness also said he was 'helped away' by his mate from the phone . . . ' By now, memories of that night and of Charlie's death were swamping me. I had to stop.

Redcliff stepped in and described the knife attack that followed, on the towpath. Then our discoveries in the abandoned factory. 'All this was reported to DC Quirke — DCI Prentiss being unavailable — and forensic examination is underway. Until now, they've been unable to find where Charlie Maker was held prisoner. If the factory is confirmed as the place, it could provide vital clues leading to the killer.'

I recovered my voice. 'This may or may not be relevant. One of MakerSeceuro's major rivals, the Livesey Group, have premises only yards away from that derelict factory building.'

Michael said at once, 'If Livesey had anything at all to do with the kidnap or death of Charlie Maker, they'd never have chosen that area to take him.'

'Unless it was unplanned,' Gwen suggested. 'But we think the kidnap had been planned, so they do seem very unlikely.'

Redcliff said, 'No one would leave evidence around — unless they wanted it discovered.'

'Or unless they felt it would be unsafe to go back and cover up,' I countered.

Alison intervened: 'Again, this speculation can't take us far — we need the police results. We're working alongside — in addition to — the CID, so remember that. There are ways we can assist. We could also unwittingly obstruct their investigation, and that would be catastrophic.' She gave me a fierce look. 'Don't underestimate Paul Prentiss or his team. A huge manhunt is going on — and the police have leads we can only guess at. And properly so . . . For good reasons, not everything is made public. Or made known to us.'

The meeting moved on, to next steps. Depressingly, these all seemed to involve waiting for the police investigation to provide facts. I could see the case getting relegated by Quest to a bottom drawer, its operatives moved to other investigations. Before Alison could wind up the meeting, I said, 'There's something else I want you to do, and it can be done right now.'

'Fire away then,' she said in her patient tone.

'This won't tread on anyone's toes . . . I've had a lot of time to think my way into his mind — the man who murdered Charlie. We agreed that it was a poorly faked suicide, not really intended to take anyone in. And it was very, very personally aimed. If a couple of joyriders hadn't happened by, I might've killed my own husband . . . What did the killer intend that for? Why the bridge? Why so elaborate, acting out . . . It's like an echo. A form of copycat.'

'What do you mean?' Alison's voice was sharp. 'It was bizarre, and unique. There's been nothing like that — '

'Except a few dozen genuine suicides from that bridge. I want you to look into each one of them. Say, going back one generation? The last twenty-five years. Please.'

There was silence in the room. Redcliff and the others were waiting for her reaction. Alison sounded patient again. 'I can't see what for. With respect, I think it would be a costly waste of time.'

'The cost is down to me. And I can't think why we haven't looked into this before. I'd like details of each case, so we can look for any possible links. It'll be easy enough.'

Redcliff said, 'Yes — it's no problem. He might've been echoing some genuine suicide. Though I can't imagine why.'

Alison looked annoyed that Redcliff was

backing my request. She seemed affronted, even betrayed. For my part, it was hard to see why she had opposed such a simple and obvious line of inquiry. By the time the meeting ended, she was agreeing to it. I wondered if she was on the verge of giving up this investigation. Maybe the DCI, Paul Prentiss, was making sure she had a hard time, since I had blundered into things?

When Redcliff, Michael and Gwen left the room, Alison asked me to wait. She was making a big effort now. 'Zoe, thanks for attending. Sharing the information.'

'It was important to do that. And don't worry. I'm leaving things up to you and the police, now.'

'Are you? You seem to have the support of my partner suddenly. I can only go on investigating Charlie's death if I have your absolute assurance that you won't interfere again. At all.'

I smiled at her. 'I won't interfere again.'

'Because if I find out you've been meddling — '

'Fair enough. I won't. But — Alison? You have got to tell me everything you learn. Everything.'

★ ★ ★

I took a cab back to MakerSeceuro. Could I really rely on Alison? There seemed to be a lot of gaps in the relationship between us, and a lot of question marks. I had spent yesterday evening with her on that fruitless vigil in the pub, yet we hadn't really talked at all. She seemed distracted — and not just by her current lover, whoever he might be. In some wider sense, we were not connecting.

The cab drew up outside the office building. Although it was only lunchtime, the streetlights had come on because the sky was so overcast. The rain had started again, steady and penetrating. As I hurried towards the canopied steps, someone called my name.

A woman was approaching. She had dark hair and fine, bony features. I had never seen her before. There was an intense energy about her, a wired feeling. 'Zoe Maker. I'm glad to've caught you. I want to explain about last night. I'm Patricia Abel.'

A slow anger began to burn through me. 'You're a little late.'

'I went to the Narrow Boat and saw Alison Seely go in. I had a very good reason for turning back.' She paused.

'You want to come into the office?'

'I'd rather . . . Could we?' She gestured towards a blue Mustang at the kerb. She was probably afraid of getting lynched if she ventured into the MakerSeceuro building.

Inside the car, I studied her. She was less hard, less cynical than I had expected. Then I reminded myself, exactly, of the piece she had published — just when everyone thought Charlie was a new suicide. This woman had thrown us all into worse, hurt defence, badly increasing the pain of those days. I kicked off with a pure attack. 'What a thing to print! Let's get one thing clear. I despise and detest your brand of journalism. It was a cheap shot, at an unbelievably bad time.'

Patricia Abel didn't flinch, but her voice got lower. 'I can understand that you're angry — and I'll tell you what happened in a minute. Listen. Your friend was being followed last night. The man who was tailing her parked where she did. He went and waited on the canal bridge to see who would join her in the pub. That's why I didn't go in.'

'Alison, followed? Why on earth would anybody do that?'

'I don't know. And I didn't get much of a sight of him. Tall, about six two or three, and heavily built, wearing dark clothes. You ought to warn her. Cigarette?'

I shook my head and she lit up. 'Of course

218

I'll warn her. And now you tell me — why did you write that article?'

'Because I have a job to do, and I was given certain information. Then — '

'It was inaccurate, misinformation. And that's a huge understatement! You managed to somehow blacken MakerSeceuro with no foundation whatsoever. Then more unfounded innuendo — that the company was in some kind of financial trouble. And implying my husband might've killed himself — for those two, completely fictitious reasons. No facts, no checking — you're lucky we haven't slung the legal book at you! Yet.'

'Right, if you'll stop there for just one minute. Specifically, I do crime — and you can check on my good track record. For my sins I did a short diary piece speculating as to how Gill Tarpont got murdered in her own home. OK? I had received information — documents — on MakerSeceuro's financial projections. And the forecast was grim.'

'But that's not true, not possible. Why didn't you check?'

'But I did — *of course* I did — and they checked out the same.'

'Then those documents were forgeries. Or they were incomplete. Why didn't you come to us? Who was your source?'

'I would never reveal any of my sources,' she said, getting angry now in turn. 'But the point about that diary item — I wasn't the writer, in the end. Yes, it went out under a byline I'd used, just once before. Yes, I'd researched and filed a draft. Then three things happened. I was called away to resume a big assignment. Charlie Maker was found under Suicide Bridge. And that small gossip item became hot and was made the diary lead, reframed around his death.'

'How could you let that happen?'

'How d'you think I felt? I severed my connections with the paper at once. And I've made a complaint.'

Beyond the small, warm car interior, the day was like night, a night in a flood. Lights flashed, streaking over torrenting water. It was like the night I had found him dying.

I turned to her. 'The suicide note in Charlie's pocket — it was quoted in your diary piece. The only people who knew what it contained were the police and the emergency services. And the person who forced him to write it.'

Something flickered in Patricia Abel's eyes. Maybe it was the cigarette smoke. She said slowly, 'I've been out of the country for several weeks — since before your husband died.'

'I've got to know the original source of that story.'

'I'm sorry, that's not possible.' She paused, looking at me. 'But with the way it's all turned out ... If things aren't true, then I'll want to put them straight.'

★ ★ ★

People were drifting back from lunch by the time I finally returned to my office. Among all the questions I had put to the crime reporter, the simplest, the one I had failed to ask, only occurred to me now. Patricia Abel had managed to recognise Alison — without ever meeting her — in the dark and presumably from some distance. She had recognised and waylaid me outside our business address. I supposed she had everything available on file, and had just looked us up. It gave me an odd, exposed feeling.

I put through a call to Alison, then got the information on Peter Doyle from Jenny. All Peter's references had been taken up before he was granted the lease to the flat. The referees painted a glowing picture. Peter had a responsible and honest character, and was a financially careful, hard-working graduate of a Scottish university who had moved south to take a job in London. He was everything MakerSeceuro had wanted in a tenant.

If any ambivalence remained in me, it was not doubt about his background. Our brief conversation about his work and beliefs had preyed on my mind, but not for long. It was easy to put that down to overenthusiasm for his field, together with a lack of experience. I was left with a sense that something might be not entirely right, for Caro, or at least for her at this particular time.

When Madison arrived for our meeting at three, his opening words drove any thoughts about Peter straight out of my mind. 'Have you heard what's happened? The Livesey Group — our ex-MD has joined them.'

14

Madison sat down opposite me. 'We knew Bill would move to a rival camp. Whatever he said, he must've had this lined up before he resigned. Where does it leave us?'

'What's he doing there?'

'Apparently, head of UK operations.'

Given their size, that was indeed a big leap for Bill. He had been offered a prime position and all kinds of reasons began crowding into my mind. How long had this been in the air? How useful might he have proved to them already? Our former MD was a good man, but not spectacularly so. He had grown up well and had lengthy experience. Livesey would go for that, to contain their newer, younger blood. Charlie — with all of us — had trusted Bill over the years.

Don't trust. Not anyone. Promise . . .

'We did all we could, on non-competition and secrecy.' I thought for a minute. 'We should be all right. But the Livesey name does keep coming up, and that's worrying.'

'Especially with my other news.' He paused, frowning. 'We're getting a distinct impression that the rumours haven't stopped — not after our rebuttal of the 'Unmaking of MakerSeceuro' piece, and not since. The target's always the last to hear of these things, but there are signs.'

'What do you mean?'

'New business — it seems to have been flattening out, and we're not attracting accounts the way we were. And our key commercial accounts customers . . . I'll give you an example. Den lunched Tony Morrow, security director of Hexton, last week. We've been chasing a major upgrade across their national outlets. It was lined up — but now they're not committing. It doesn't look good, Zoe — and the change happened too abruptly.'

Although we had always been careful to keep a wide customer base, Hexton, the household goods chain, were very important to us. 'Tony Morrow's new, isn't he? Did he give any reason? Has there been any problem with that account?'

Madison shook his head. 'We've always kept a good relationship. Why would they think of pulling out now? And that's not the only sign of trouble. A couple of other national accounts . . . There's a sense of people wavering. I think someone's been getting to them.'

Madison was level-headed, the least paranoid

of people. If he sensed that someone was acting in a concerted way against us, then he was probably right. 'As a guess . . . do you think this could be down to Livesey — to their PR playing a dirty game, perhaps?'

'Guessing could be a dangerous pastime. I don't know. News of the Goldstar got out prematurely — and we don't know how that happened. It's left us with any number of possible enemies. Companies which normally do very well indeed are suddenly anticipating a big threat from this direction.'

'We need to put out feelers, to suss out who this might be. Maybe talk around it with Livesey's PR? And certainly keep on attending to our own PR.'

He nodded. 'We'll work on that. I think we should also raise your personal profile, with mine.'

'What've you got in mind?'

'The SecureWorld conference, for one thing. We pencilled that out as not a priority. Now I think if you're up for it, we should both be seen to attend.'

'There's nothing like turning to confront the enemy, to confound them, you mean? Yes, let's go to Paris. We'll find out who's going from Livesey. And from A-Zander. Do a whole lot of networking and ferret out who's behind this.'

'Right. Are you in close touch with the CID? You still believe there's a link between Charlie's death, and MakerSeceuro being in the firing line now — that it's the same person or persons unknown?'

'I don't see how they can't be linked.' Getting up, I paced round the office. 'But Paul Prentiss is heading the murder inquiry, Quest Associates are carrying out the private investigation. I'm keeping clear of both, but it's hard. I'm concentrating on MakerSeceuro because in the long run it's probably the best thing I could do for Charlie.'

'A-Zander . . . They've got a new internal security chief. There's someone I wouldn't want to cross. Or bump into on a dark night. Damned if I can remember his name. Has a pretty brutal reputation, personally. He used to work for BOSS — white South Africa's Bureau of State Security — you know?'

'And you think he — '

'I think nothing. Just . . . Kruger, that's his name. He comes to mind as a part of their overall picture.'

'Madison, there is one other thing.' I began to tell him about Patricia Abel and our conversation in her car. His face said it all: this journalist had been the start of all our troubles, and he didn't want to hear about the strange rerouteing of that item she had drafted, appearing altered under one of her occasional bylines. 'Patricia turns out to be a respected crime journalist. She's anxious to put the record straight.'

He was dismissive. 'I don't see how we could possibly trust her. Do you, really?'

'The funny thing is, I think that maybe we can. She's freelance, and if she did something else it would be for a quite different editor. I think she genuinely cares about the truth. And she has another strong motive — she wants information about the murders.'

Madison, who had been expecting to move on to other matters, now leaned back in his chair to consider. 'What exactly are you suggesting?'

'We've everything to gain from having this woman on our side. I think we should try using her, as she wants to be used. If you're sceptical . . . why don't we set up a meeting, and see what you think then?'

* * *

Madison pencilled in a meeting with Patricia Abel and myself for two days' time, but we decided not to involve our directors. We would give the reporter our facts on the company's health, blow open the question of dirty tricks and unfair competition. Provided

Madison was convinced that Patricia was on the level, she might be used to investigate these areas — from our perspective. I knew, or guessed, she was playing for some kind of advantage, wanting to be given the bigger crime story. Patricia had already talked with Alison. She was well known to DCI Paul Prentiss. What she wanted might be negotiable.

When Alison called back, I told her everything that had happened, beginning with the news that she had been followed. 'Why would someone be tailing you?'

She had gone quiet, but now she gave a little laugh. 'Good heavens! Have I attracted some kind of stalker? Did you get any description?'

'Not much.' I told her the little I knew. 'I don't think you should laugh this off. With everything that's happened, you must tell the police at once. They might be able to find out who it was. Aren't you worried?'

'Darling, when you've been in this business as long as I have, nothing much bothers you. It shouldn't be difficult for me to get a look at my stalker — I'll sort it out. So, our Patricia did turn up, and you both survived the encounter? Without the ref.'

I told Alison about the planned meeting,

how we hoped to get Patricia Abel investigating and writing. 'I wish you luck. Be careful.'

'Listen, I know you're in the throes of some wild affair, but — if you find yourself with a free evening . . . '

'Yes. Not in a scruffy little pub, waiting for a no-show journo.'

'At my place, maybe? There's something of Charlie's that I want you to look at.'

'Next weekend, if we can,' she agreed.

By Tuesday morning, Jenny had obtained the updated list of delegates to SecureWorld. It seemed that Bill would not be going to Paris. The Livesey team was to be headed by Christopher Houghton, and we both knew him. There was no difficulty in making contact with Houghton, Madison soon reported. 'He was surprised to hear that we're attending. He's keen to see us, and wants to make it lunch.'

'That seems to suggest he has an agenda. And a positive one — not necessarily what I've been thinking about.'

'He may be being protected from what others are doing to get results. In an organisation that size, the person at the top doesn't always know everything.'

I mulled it over. There was one other rival that Charlie had been in close contact with during the days leading to his death. 'It's time to give A-Zander a call. Ian Darius is on the list.'

'I'll do that, fix for us to see him.' Madison's voice was less than enthusiastic.

'Leave him to me, why not.'

It took until Wednesday afternoon to get through, and that was on his direct line. Ian Darius was busy. He managed to sound surprised by my call, the third I had made to him in twenty-four hours. Since our peculiar exchange in the wine bar, I was not Ian's favourite person and the sweet talk had curdled, grown lumpy. He was pretty booked up for the conference by now, he said. Apart from its second evening, his diary was full. Ian was not a person who suffered overmuch from embarrassment or faint-heartedness, and my antennae were alerted. Soon he was agreeing to have dinner that night.

'You'll be on your own,' Madison pointed out. 'It'll change your plans for getting back that night.'

Dining alone with Darius was not what I'd intended, but it might be useful. 'I'll stop over. It'll give me a good chance to suss him out — they could be behind everything.'

We left the office together to meet with Patricia Abel.

230

★ ★ ★

She was waiting for us in a café in Highbury. Madison, usually the easiest of people to deal with, was not ready to forgive her betrayal of MakerSeceuro during those days following Charlie's death. I had explained the circumstances, but he couldn't believe she'd had no control, especially since he'd learned of her good track record and sound reputation. The first thing he did now was to get under her skin. Sparks flew. She recounted all over again for him exactly what had happened, but I could see her losing patience. We were not the only story in town. Was she about to walk out, lose us this opportunity?

Patricia had studied our statement about the company's finances. 'You were right. The information I'd been given was inaccurate by omission.' She went on to say she was working for one of the national Sunday papers. What she proposed writing would include putting the facts straight.

'That's what we want to hear,' I assured her, with a glance at Madison.

She leaned towards him, her bony face intent. 'Mr Black, d'you want to cooperate on this?'

'Of course we want the record straightened.

231

But I don't see how we can help you now without your revealing to us the source of your original misinformation.'

I began, warningly, 'That isn't — '

'That was confidential,' Patricia cut in sharply. 'And I wouldn't dream of revealing it. Everything you say is either on or off the record. There is no half state.'

'Then I don't see why that can't work the other way around for us,' I suggested. 'Off the record . . . Was it given to you by someone connected with the Livesey Group?'

She pushed away her coffee cup. Her voice was scornful. 'If you expect me to leak a source, how can you possibly expect me to keep integrity in the remainder of this investigation?'

'OK . . . She's right, Madison.'

He was saying nothing, his face dark.

'What makes you think I know their real identity anyway?' Patricia smiled briefly at our obvious surprise. When she went on, her voice was not quite so hard. 'Look, I know about Thwaites's resignation after your husband's death. I know that now he's moved to Livesey. And I think you're barking up the wrong tree there.'

'But there was that leak!' Madison pointed out angrily. 'Of very damaging, lethally timed misinformation. So who else — '

'I'll be dealing with that,' she told him simply. 'If you'll let me know a few other things.'

I decided to wait for Madison. There was a pause. He gave me a glance then said, 'Our security — our strategy — has been breached in other ways.'

The reporter nodded. 'About the Goldstar, for one thing.'

'Is this general knowledge?'

'I do my homework. It's no more than that. I understand that technology is innovative. It's going to revolutionise things a bit in your branch of the industry. That leak's left a lot of people feeling nervous — and not only in the criminal community.'

'We're being targeted. Our reputation, and our customer base.'

'You want me to find out who. And how. To expose them. And then what?'

Madison's response was to look baffled for a moment. I chipped in: 'There are links to the murders — connections are emerging clearly enough. You should talk to Alison Seely at Quest Associates about that. Also to Paul Prentiss, if you haven't already. You know all about the press blackout on this case, and it will be down to him, of course.'

'We have a good relationship,' she assured me. 'We go back a while.'

'I'm pretty sure that as you work on discovering MakerSeceuro's enemy — the one who's orchestrating this attack on us — you'll gain other, useful information. Perhaps an insight into who might've . . . killed Charlie. And Gill Tarpont.'

'There's the boy too,' Patricia said softly. 'The witness on the bridge.' She sat back, looking from Madison to me. 'You'll have to give me all the facts. Every detail. And I want to hear every thought you've ever had about this case.'

I turned to Madison. He nodded, slowly.

I smiled. 'Then let's begin at the beginning.'

★ ★ ★

The week became more routine, except that Madison and I were also preparing to attend next week's conference in Paris. I was talking to Caro on the phone most evenings, concerned especially because she was still suffering from bad dreams, broken nights. Learning of my trip, she seemed slightly riled. Maybe it made hers, already booked to begin the day after my return, feel less special. It was not to be the usual school trek to Morocco. With a few other sixth-formers and a course teacher, she was to spend three days in Strasbourg on a study trip.

She was home for the weekend, of course. 'We should buy you something new to wear,' I suggested. 'Smart but practical. Yes?'

'Oh, Mum,' she groaned, agreeing happily enough. 'OK.'

We spent much of Saturday shopping, pausing at a pizza joint for lunch. In the new clothes we bought her, Caro could have passed for eighteen. It was that classic thing of shedding the old, outgrown skin, or the daily uniform of jeans, tops and trainers. She looked beautiful, and ready for her life.

We arrived back home, footsore and thirsty. Caro tried on everything again, pirouetting in front of the mirror and experimenting with her hair, entranced by revelation. Soon her butterfly clothes were arrayed on hangers, festooning her bedroom with the soft brightness of flowers. She was painting her nails, trying a new way of putting on lipstick. Her bed and dressing table were covered with trophies, displayed nestling in wrapping papers. Underslip and body, silver tunic and smoke-grey leggings, with a scattering of make-up and lotions, hair clips and scrunchies.

Caro was going to a birthday party tonight.

It was Penny's sister, Susan's. 'What time's Peter collecting you?'

'He's coming at seven thirty. But I don't want to get there early.' She sprayed on nail polish drier, admired the effect, then waved a hand in a limp-wristed imitation of languid. 'It's a disco and stuff. Don't worry — midnight curfew, I know. Cinders will be returned home in plenty of time.'

'Make sure you are, sweetheart. Alison's coming at around eight. So you'll see her before you leave.'

'Oh.' Caro didn't sound thrilled. It seemed she was in one of her frequent off-Alison phases. 'Are you guys going out somewhere?'

'I'm sure we will. You'll be introducing Peter to the Harkers — and most of your friends — tonight, then?'

'Yeah. There's no big deal to it.' She danced across the room to put on some music. Blew herself a kiss in the mirror, then winked at me. If I hadn't spent the last twenty hours noticing the shadows under her eyes, I would have thought Caro didn't have a care in the world.

Peter was in good spirits too and quickly caught her mood, seeming easier and more relaxed. 'Hi, Mrs Maker. Nice to see you.'

'And you — but please call me Zoe. Everyone does.'

'Zoe, then.' He grinned, because Caro was tugging him away. 'Hey, not so fast.'

'You can help me wrap Susan's pressie. Come on.' She was towing him, giggling, up to her room.

I decided to shower and change, wondering what venue Alison and I would choose tonight: some smoky basement joint, some nightclub? As it happened, I needn't have bothered. When she showed at a little after eight, she was clearly destined for an evening of resting up on the sofa.

Setting off with Peter for the party, Caro paused in her flight just long enough to distribute kisses. Alison eyed her clothes, then eyed Peter. 'You look great, Caro. 'Bye, kids.'

'We'll be back by twelve.' Marooned in our little group in the hall, Peter seemed suddenly ill at ease again. He spoke to Caro in a stiffly formal voice. 'I'll take you to the party then, if you're ready?'

'You bet I'm ready, babe.' She did her pirouette, waved in a cheeky way. 'Have a fun evening, girls.'

'Caro — your coat,' I protested.

'But it doesn't really go with the look. Oh, all right.'

They finally left. 'The house always feels like a huge, empty barn when Caro's gone out.' I laughed. 'Hey, is that to drink or what?'

Alison looked vaguely at the bottle she was still carrying. 'Oh yes. What a curious young chap,' she said with a frown. 'He's quite pretty, though. Is it true love?'

'I hope not — Caro's way too young. Come on, let's find a couple of glasses. And then — out for a big night on the tiles?'

'*Please*,' Alison protested. 'Can't you see I need some serious recuperation?'

'No Jazz Café, then?'

'Don't. You'll bring on a migraine, I warn you. Listen — about Caro. There's something you ought to know, Zoe. A couple of weeks back, Caro was asking me . . . She was trying to find out — all about your sister.'

15

Shaken, I poured a couple of glasses of wine. My lost sister was emerging over our horizon, finally. After all these years of silence, of not asking anything, Caro wanted to know more about her. It was easy to see why that had happened: because of Charlie, she needed to know about those others, about losing her family before she was born. But she had gone to Alison, not me.

'What did she want to know?'

'Had I ever met her Aunt Astra? And does Astra have any kids of her own? Why hasn't she ever come back from Australia to visit? Why hasn't she ever met her?'

'What did you say?'

'Darling, I know so little about your family affairs that I wasn't much use. But listen, Zoe, why not get in touch now? Oh, I know . . . Charlie said — '

'What did he say?' My voice came out too sharp. 'Astra doesn't want to see me. She hasn't since our parents died. OK?'

'But even — '

'And I don't know where she is.'

There was a silence between us before

Alison changed the subject. 'Look, please don't do a meal — I haven't the energy to watch you cooking. Let's phone out for something. Some kind of convalescent fare . . . And what was it you wanted to show me of Charlie's?'

'That can wait a minute. You need reviving.' I found a menu from a local Thai restaurant and phoned out. Then I began to quiz her. 'So what's all this debilitation about? You keep turning up looking terrible, acting mysterious. And being a tease.'

'Just unsocial hours,' she answered faintly.

'I don't think you mean work.' She smiled but said nothing. It was unlike Alison not to pour out descriptions of her current amour and exciting times. While Charlie was alive, she had always confided. Given the past, maybe those confidences had been a smoke screen, a bid to disarm and to make sure she was liked. Or maybe the person she was seeing now was also someone I knew?

'About work,' she said. 'Let's get that out of the way, shall we? I gather things went well with Patricia Abel.'

'She's been in touch with you?'

Alison nodded. 'I can only give her information if the police agree.'

'She knows that.' I hesitated. It was an evening with Alison I wanted, not to rehash all the things which had come between us. Reluctantly I asked, 'What about the post-mortem?'

She swigged her drink. She really was looking rough. 'Mark was strangled, as they thought. Someone was seen talking to him at King's Cross late that night. There are one or two other leads, and forensics may well come up with useful stuff. There was no sexual contact or violent attack of that kind. And no drug was used, nothing was injected.'

'What's the police line?'

'They're not saying, not to me. Of course, I'm sure it was the same killer. But quite differently done — as you said, not ritualistic. Anything they turn up on this one could help.'

'And those things Redcliff and I found in the disused factory? There must be something new by now.'

'I haven't heard about that. You could always ask Paul Prentiss.'

'It's really nothing to do with me now.' I stood abruptly, refilled our glasses. 'I'm giving away some things of Charlie's and I thought . . . there might be something — anything you'd like, of his?'

'I see.' Alison studied the floor before looking up. 'Well, maybe.'

'Let's do that now. Come on.'

We went through to Charlie's study. 'You've been clearing everything,' she said, an accusation.

'It all has to go. Caro and I can't live in a museum, or a morgue.'

She agreed quickly, 'Of course not,' then looked vaguely around. His office *had* become a kind of museum, stacked with his possessions and clothes, with everything that had not yet been given away or thrown out. It was a violent and ruthless upturning. Alison was looking stricken.

'Hey, Alison.' I took hold of her arm. 'Sorry, how thoughtless. There's no need — '

'No, I appreciate . . . Hell, Zoe, I would like something to remember Charlie by! It was just — seeing it all, like this.'

I gave her a hug. She began to look at things, remembering and questioning. Some of his clothes were here, unmistakably bearing the imprint of their owner. Alison said, 'His little laptop. He always carried that everywhere.'

'For design notes, doodling. Dreaming things up. Prentiss's team just returned it.'

'Could I have that?' She smiled, stroking the worn cover of the computer.

'Of course. If you're sure? All the files

have been transferred and erased. Is there anything else?'

'Nope.' She picked up the laptop. 'Thank you. This was like Charlie's soul, or heart — all his thoughts and hopes went through it.'

The doorbell rang, dinner had arrived. We decanted everything into dishes on the dining tale, then I lit candles, for some reason. 'You really did love him, didn't you?'

'He was my best friend. He was very loyal — and to you, Zoe. And a kind person. When I left the CID, and when my marriage broke down . . . Charlie was like a rock.'

'He didn't make friends easily. He was too preoccupied. And you were always very important to him, I knew that without knowing . . . How often did you use to meet?'

'Quite often.' She sounded guarded. 'For a quick lunch, a chat about things.'

'He never used to mention it. I knew you talked on the phone a lot over the years. Charlie always let me think, when the three of us met up — with or without Caro — that was all there was.'

'And do you mind now?'

I answered slowly, 'He depended on you a lot, didn't he?' On Alison, who had always appeared flightily undependable in her private life. 'I'm not sure . . . It was a good thing that he had you, of course it was. And had you while he and I were living apart.' She laughed, and, after a moment I did too. 'How did you meet him?'

'It was so long ago. I've forgotten now.'

We finished eating in silence. How could anyone forget their first meeting? If you've been lovers, surely that first memory always stays with you. 'I still see him,' I told her conversationally, watching and wondering about that small lie. 'In this house. And around HQ. Every night, I expect him to come home.'

'It'll get better. It will.'

'It's partly guilt. I go on feeling guilty.'

Alison frowned. 'Why on earth? Unless . . . When you left, and took Caro — is that it?' Her baffled expression had turned into avid curiosity. 'Did you — was there someone else then?'

It was my turn to laugh. Alison was back on form. 'Why should I tell you when you're being so secretive. Coffee? Brandy?'

'Yes, and yes please. You're too much of a goody two-shoes.'

'Don't believe everything you hear, sweetheart.'

When I brought the coffee, Alison had put on music. She was drifting slowly around the room in time to the rhythm, in a solitary dance with no one to see. Until she saw me, and stopped.

'You weren't tired. You were hungry.'

'It's been a hectic week. Things always happen in a rush, have to be done by yesterday. If we take on more staff, there's a lull.'

'Is Redcliff becoming more of an asset now?'

'In some ways. But he'll never be passionate about the paperwork.'

'Unlike the rest of us? No, his talents lie elsewhere. And his training. Special forces?'

She sat down, stirred sweetener into her coffee. 'My lips are sealed. Put it this way, Redcliff wasn't in any outfit you'd know much about.'

'I just wondered why he's . . . '

'Redcliff has many virtues. And one real problem — a very hot temper at times.'

'Yes. He seems to be always rushing up to Hereford . . . The very hot temper, has that anything at all to do with why his wife isn't moving to London?'

'Curious, aren't we?' She looked at me with a sudden unfriendly sharpness. So unfriendly that for a crazy moment I wondered if Alison might be having an affair with her partner. The idea was almost ridiculous. Even as a bit of rough, Redcliff, with his manner and background, would not appeal to her. Not even as a novelty to a jaded appetite, I thought, startled by my own sharp attitudes. I shrugged, leaving her to fill the silence.

'Their marriage is on the rocks. Well past its sell-by date. Which doesn't mean he's alone or will ever leave. They're complicated — and she's got the kids.'

'He seems a doting dad, the way he talks about them.'

'Sure. The guy loves his kids. And, just maybe, he hates their mother. Bad news, my friend. I would say, give Redcliff a wide berth on any personal level.'

'Oh, *Alison*. For heaven's sake! I'm not even remotely attracted, he's not my type at all, and anyway — '

'Aren't you, darling? Hm, well. The widow's weeds don't suit you, not as a permanent thing.' She stubbed out her cigarette, placed her hands in her lap for a minute then promptly lit another. I looked at her lighter, which she'd had for as long as I had known her. It was gold, elegantly engraved with her initials. For the first time I wondered who had given her that, whether it had been Charlie.

If she saw me studying it or read my thoughts, she didn't say anything. 'It will be time to return to the human race, the land of the living,' she mused, 'and have some fun. Do you get lonely?'

'After a couple of decades together, what do you think? Who ever had a perfect marriage? I miss him. Of course I do. But Caro's around and things are very busy at work.' I told her about the SecureWorld conference and why I was visiting Paris. 'Madison and I are both going. Business — and to check out one or two people. Then I'll be staying on, because I'm making sure to see your Ian Darius.'

Alison had become closed, wary. 'You're having dinner with Darius?'

'Yes.' I checked her face. 'Why . . . What?'

'Oh, I should think he could be fun in a way. He was on Jersey, I suspect — though you were so cross, you'd rather die than admit it.'

'This isn't for fun. A-Zander were mightily interested in us. And they were in close touch with Charlie just before he died.'

'I know. And I'm sure you'll be careful.'

I sat looking at her, this new change in her mood. Alison had withdrawn again, as surely as if she had left the room. Loneliness? This was it. Carefully I said, 'You and I have known each other a long time. We've come through a lot, and it must

247

mean something. Right from the beginning of the investigation, I've known for certain you were concealing things — important facts — from me. I've waited and kept on trusting that you'll tell me.'

'Don't ask — I wish you wouldn't. Zoe . . . Yes. There are things about the murders that I just can't tell you. Because I swore not to. It could jeopardise the police investigation, the way they're proceeding, if . . . if these things got out.'

'Just to me, Alison? I can keep quiet, I'm safe with secrets.'

'I know you can. But I swore to keep silence.'

'Hell,' I laughed, shakily. 'You're scaring me now. What is this all about?'

★ ★ ★

Alison refused to say any more, and left soon after.

By five past midnight Caro was home, going straight up to get some sleep. I followed, climbing into a bed that was unbearably empty. The evening had stirred a new unease. I was restless and tense, needing touch, missing sex — and love. And there was too much on my mind.

Caro slept in. Around noon, taking her a

cup of tea, I found her groggily reluctant to wake. 'It's PMS,' she groaned. 'And look — my face is covered in spots! I'm ugly. Hideous.'

'Nonsense. You've probably got a bit of a hangover, so drink some tea. How was the party?'

'All right. They had a band, and lots of nice nosh. The Harker relatives were there too, not only friends. I'd like something big like that when I'm eighteen.'

I drew back one of the curtains. The cold winter daylight crept in, unkindly. The purple shadows under Caro's eyes seemed to have doubled in size and all kinds of parental fears stabbed through me. About drugs. About illnesses.

'What?' she asked.

Sitting down on her bed, I began carefully, 'Caro, d'you remember asking Alison, not long ago . . . about Aunt Astra?'

'Oh, that.' She looked away. 'So what?'

'You could've asked me. You can, now. What d'you want to know? You were wondering why — '

'Look, give me a break! You really think I want to discuss your family history? Well I don't.'

'But you did. You asked Alison.'

'It was curiosity, that's all — just a

moment's curiosity. I really don't care. Can we drop it?'

I was silenced, but only for a minute. 'You must've talked about it with Dad as well. Darling, I don't believe your lack of curiosity. When your grandparents both died, Astra decided to emigrate.'

'You quarrelled, then?'

'We lost touch, that's all. People do, you know. But I'm really sorry now. And — '

'Why sorry? She didn't keep in touch with you, the stupid cow. Mum, don't be sorry on *my* account.'

'No?' She didn't answer, and I decided to let it go. 'Caro, you look exhausted.'

She grimaced. 'Didn't get to sleep until eight this morning.'

'But why? Was it the party? You didn't seem to want to talk at all when you got back.'

'I just don't sleep, that's all. And if I do, I keep waking up then can't get back to sleep. It's driving me mad.'

'You've still got those pills the doctor gave — '

'They don't work.'

'Maybe a different kind would. I'll — '

'Nothing works for long, Mum. Only at first. And it's just getting me down. I can't cope, can't study either.'

'Darling. We must do something . . . '

'I get the dreams. Maybe I don't fall asleep because I'm afraid that I might have bad dreams. D'you think?'

'The dreams — about Dad? You're still getting those?'

'Yeah. Dad's alive but . . . you know. Like you see foxes lying there on the side of the road.' Her eyes were bright with tears, in that drawn face. 'And I just don't want to see it any more. So I stay awake.'

'Caro, there's one thing we haven't tried yet. How about it — talking to Rosemary Lomax's friend? You know, the psychiatrist person that she recommended. Might be worth trying just once, d'you think?'

'The mad old fogey?' Caro smiled, wanly. 'I suppose it might be good for a laugh.'

'If he trips over his long white beard, turns a double somersault, d'you mean?'

'Yeah. Kind of thing. If he's mad as a — a shrink! I don't care any more, Mum. If it makes you happy, I will.'

'We can't just leave things the way they are. Poor Caro.'

'OK. I'll talk to him just once. And then see. All right?'

'I'll call Rosemary tomorrow. It might help a bit. Anything that helps . . . Now, are you going to get up and have some brunch?'

She had been so set against trying counselling, until now. Her new willingness must be some indication of how rough things had become. I hated the idea of her returning to school, but she was easy about that. The A level syllabus was well under way, her school research trip about to happen, and she liked the people she was studying with.

We walked on Hampstead Heath that afternoon, then watched a video. On the drive to Waterloo Station, Caro turned to me and said, 'This'll make you happy, Mum. I've been going off him, quite a bit.'

'D'you mean Peter?'

'Uh-huh. Now you'll ask why.'

Peter had not been mentioned all day and had loomed large by omission. The change seemed very sudden. 'Why, then?'

'Don't really know. It's . . . When it's just us, he acts one way. Then it's the way he seems when there's other people. Sounds daft? I can't really explain. Anyway, I know you don't like him.'

'There are one or two things about him . . . Didn't he get on with your friends?'

'Not really. He didn't seem to be acting — acting real. Not with you either, when I brought him home. Then last night. He kind of seizes up, and gets all banal.'

'I know what you mean. That's possibly

shyness, d'you think?'

'You defending him? You want me to — elope with him?'

'No thanks! And I didn't really take to him, you knew that. It's just, if people seize up, as you put it, they're probably shy.'

'At his age? Pathetic! Plus he's got no sense at all of — you know, how to enjoy things. Bloody *hell*! Anyone who can't dance is just a boring stick. Not sure what I saw in him.'

So that was it: he couldn't dance. 'You're not planning to see him again?' I asked cautiously, trying to keep my voice neutral. Feeling massively relieved that the infatuation might be over.

'Don't know — but I can't see what for. You can breathe again, Mommy dearest.'

Caro seemed cheerful as her train prepared for departure. 'You've got this trip to look forward to,' I told her. 'So enjoy Strasbourg. Then we'll compare notes on the state of Europe.'

'Yeah, you have nice times too.'

The next day, Rosemary Lomax put me in touch with her neighbour. She had so stressed the variety of Dr Tyrone's work and his celebrity, I was surprised at getting through quickly. He seemed accessible and, when he learned of Caro's bad nights, interested in seeing her as soon as possible. First he wanted to talk with me — but not as much as I wanted the chance to check him out. If anyone was about to meddle with Caro's mind, they needed to be the best possible person.

'Tomorrow I'm working in west London,' he said. 'Any chance you could come to see me — around eleven?'

'I'm on a train to Paris just after ten. Then away for two days.'

'We could make it seven thirty-five,' he suggested.

'Fine. Thank you.'

He gave some fairly complicated instructions for finding the way to his address, then through entry systems to his waiting room. By now I was beginning to feel more nervous for Caro. Perhaps if she could see him in Sussex, as Rosemary had suggested, it might make things less daunting for her.

After packing that evening, I soaked in the bath and tried to imagine what the trip would be like. Charlie had flown the MakerSeceuro flag at the larger events abroad, while I had only attended a couple of conferences in London. In recent years, Bill Thwaites had gone with him. It seemed unlikely that our ex-MD would turn up at the last minute, representing Livesey this time, at SecureWorld.

The phone rang. It was Alison, sounding abrupt. 'Where are you? There's an echo effect, are you in the bath? I can hear water.'

'You're not a private dick for nothing.' Then I registered the anxiety in her voice. 'What is it? Something's happened.'

She paused. 'What our friend said — it turns out to be true, and more. That shit who's following me around.'

'Alison. You're sure, then, and — '

'I haven't nailed him yet, but I will . . . I hope you're listening to us, shit head! Or maybe I've found everything. I had a sweep done at my home office. Found a couple of gadgets. He's enthusiastic, I'll give him that.'

'You were being bugged? Your phone — '

'The works. That isn't why I called, though. Just thought I'd mention it. No . . . That little something else, which I didn't tell you last night.'

'My heart began to beat faster. 'Yes?'

'You free at all tomorrow?'

'Paris,' I reminded her. 'Sorry.'

Alison swore loudly. 'Before you leave — that any good?'

'I'm leaving at seven. Could see you on

Thursday, though. I get in around noon.'

There was a rustle of pages, then she cursed again. 'The earliest I could make it on Thursday would be . . . six?'

We arranged to meet at a wine bar in Primrose Hill. She wouldn't say anything else on the phone, except to shout again more angrily, 'Are you listening, shit head?'

'You have told Paul Prentiss and his team about this? Alison?' She was silent. I found myself shouting now. 'Why ever not? You're breaking all your own rules! Get professional, will you. Call the murder squad right now — or else I will. You want me to?'

She promised that she would ring them right away.

★ ★ ★

At seven thirty the next morning a cab dropped me at Simon Tyrone's London address. It was a quiet, tree-lined street tucked away behind Brompton Road. The house was late nineteenth century, of mellowed brick. Standing on the pavement, I looked up at the third-floor apartment and saw someone hanging on to a windowsill there. A dark-haired man in a green jacket, he was actually leaning perilously far out of a window, towards the branch of a plane tree.

Was this a potential suicide, a cat burglar or a lunatic?

It was Dr Tyrone, of course. From inside the porch I rang the bell, saw him disappear hastily through the window: this was Caro's mad old fogey. I took the lift, and at his door keyed in numbers as instructed. A narrow corridor was revealed, its red walls almost completely covered by Edwardian drawings and etchings. It led to a small waiting room with button leather sofa, magazines and a coffee machine. Almost immediately, the inner door opened and Simon Tyrone appeared. He had ascetic features, at odds with a wide and generous mouth. His hair and smile were dishevelled, the Barbour had gone and the suit was expensive.

We shook hands. 'Like a coffee? And d'you want to order a taxi for eight?'

'I already have. And yes please.'

There was no couch in the consulting room, just a battered-looking Parker Knoll and a tall-backed rocking chair. The latter overlooked the street and I saw what he had been doing. A bird feeder was attached to the branch, within view of the chair where he worked. 'So we're here to talk about Caro.'

'May I ask you a few questions first?'

'Certainly you may.'

'Rosemary Lomax referred us to you. She

tells me that you worked with someone else from the school. But I don't think you specialise in counselling children, do you?'

'No, I don't. But if Caro's sixteen, then she's not a child. I've almost retired from clinical work. Generally I don't take on new clients these days.'

'If it's a favour, to Rosemary . . . ' I fumbled for words, because he didn't say anything. 'It's just . . . I recognise your name — and face now. From newspaper features. And there was a radio show. You seem to do a lot of media comment. How would this fit in, talking to a teenager about losing her father? It certainly doesn't seem to.'

He glanced out at the plane tree, then looked back at me, thoughtfully. 'There's no favour involved. My fees will set you back if Caro and I do take each other on. I'm interested because, from the facts I've been told, this is an area where I'm particularly good.'

'Bereavement counselling?'

'And working with young adults.' He nodded. 'Quite a specialist field — and you're right to ask plenty of questions. What has Caro heard about me?'

'I suppose Rosemary may've told her the same kind of thing. The other areas you've worked in.'

Seeming to reach a decision, he said, 'Rosemary won't have mentioned at least one of those, because she's not aware of it. In recent years my workload's included some criminal profiling for the police.' I must have looked as taken aback as I felt, because his expression changed to an intent concern. 'Does that worry you?'

'I'm not sure why you're mentioning it. Did you . . . Have you had anything to do with — this case? With the murder of Caro's father?'

'If I had, would that worry you a lot?' Then, as I didn't answer, 'To the extent, perhaps, that you'd prefer Caro not to talk to me?'

Confused, slightly angry, I thought about Caro pouring out her experiences. Her thoughts might then be relayed, for all we knew, to Prentiss and his superiors. Or was this just some game being played?

Dr Tyrone broke into my thoughts. 'If I had worked on that case,' he said firmly, 'then I assure you, there would be absolutely no crossover. Client confidentiality is total. My work for the CID is also confidential.' He looked at the clock on the windowsill. 'We've ten minutes left. Tell me about Caro, and what you feel she needs. Why you think she could benefit from talking to me.'

I began to tell him about Caro's present troubled state, how she had learned of her father's death and what she knew now. Small promptings led to an outpouring of fears. He wanted to know details of her relationship with Charlie, even about that early break while we had lived apart so long ago. I described the way she had suddenly started lying, going out with someone older she had just met — then, as it seemed from yesterday, losing interest in that relationship. I wanted her home, returning to day school if the infatuation was over, but Caro seemed to feel more settled where she was. 'She's been through so much. One minute she seems OK, open about everything. The next, she's acting like a hostile stranger. Is this going to affect her — I mean, in any lasting way?'

He glanced at the clock again. It was just before eight. 'This will always affect her. Our experiences always do. The question is — in what ways? Caro's coping with events few people ever have to cope with, at any age. The nature of her relationship with her father, that will be crucial. Also how she gets to see it all — what she makes of it. There I may be able to help her . . . We have to stop. Would you like to think this over, discuss it with Caro again?'

'She wants to see you. Actually, I

think she's getting so desperate about not sleeping . . . ' I stopped, embarrassed.

Warmth had come into his eyes. He had us down as sceptics all right, but it seemed to amuse him. There was a ring on the doorbell and he peered down into the street. 'Your taxi.'

'Will you see her?'

Dr Tyrone smiled and shook my hand. 'Thanks for talking to me. I'll give Caro a call.'

16

I took the train to Paris and met up with Madison.

The SecureWorld conference was being held in parallel with a trade fair boasting all the new developments. From over thirty different countries, four hundred companies and organisations had exhibition stalls. There were thousands of visitors daily. The giants were here, rubbing shoulders with manufacturers, specifiers and installers from every field. The event had the buzz of a boom industry.

With the Goldstar protected by patent, we would launch our new technology at global fairs like this one. Next year, SecureWorld would be truly for us. We would be on the map.

There was groundwork to be done. We had a full schedule and many of our contacts were new. In this context, it was no bad thing that word had got out prematurely. MakerSeceuro was interesting, we were in the air. By the second day's lunch with Livesey's chairman, Madison and I were wondering if he was the best investment of our time.

I had visited that morning's conference session, which was about developments in intruder and perimeter protection. It had thrown up nothing to touch our new baby. Livesey's head of research and development had also attended, taking up points with the Swiss and German presenters before we broke for lunch.

Together with Charlie, I had last met Christopher Houghton five years ago at a London event. MakerSeceuro had been quite small fry. I had been truly a paper nobody in Houghton's eyes — not only a woman but also a wife — and was treated with a show of respect plus total disregard. His attitude had been symptomatic, normal in our industry, and it left me seething. That was part of the reason I had kept the business, to show them all and to change things.

With his round figure and red face, Houghton only needed a Santa Claus outfit to complete the persona. His avuncular manner made me hope he would not try to pat my hand. 'Charlie was a highly respected innovator, Zoe. We miss him — he was always at events, we often got together.'

'Yes, he was. Madison and I are taking things onwards now.'

'Onwards and upwards, I'm sure you are.'

'We were rather expecting to see Bill,' Madison said. 'Isn't he here?'

'Bill's got a lot of settling in to do. We were surprised when you allowed him to depart. With his track record we became very interested, very quickly, in the fact that he was free.'

He began talking solely to Madison, and once again it was as if I didn't exist. Either Houghton didn't understand MakerSeceuro, or he was just so used to dealing only with men that the assumptions were too ingrained. It didn't take him long to reach the subject of our plans for Charlie's last innovation. 'As you probably know, he and I had been talking, on an informal basis. If Charlie had lived, bless him, I believe we would've moved things forward successfully . . . We have the structure in place, at Livesey, and could do things nicely.'

I tried to take in what he had just been saying. 'Interesting,' Madison said. 'This was never mentioned, was it, Zoe?'

'Absolutely correctly,' Houghton put in swiftly. 'We had chatted a few times, one to one, about possibilities. About our structure being already in place for maximum exploitation. Your founder was a brilliant man. But if you'll forgive me for saying so, his greatest strength lay in his technical, inventive brilliance.'

'This is retrospective. It doesn't reflect the current position,' I said.

Houghton took off his thick spectacles and polished them vigorously as he talked. His eyes were revealed, sharp and darting. Perhaps what he was saying did explain some of Charlie's calls in the days before he died — but if it was true, why hadn't Houghton come forward during the past few weeks to tell Madison or me about it?

Charlie had been too much of a go-it-alone man to be interested in the type of deal that was being sketched out. While Houghton was blindly absorbed, Madison and I exchanged a glance which said everything. 'To our mutual benefit,' Houghton was finishing, 'if you'll forgive the expression, we could make sweet music in bed together.'

I removed my hand from the lunch table, in case Livesey's chairman did actually pat it. 'What you're suggesting might've applied to MakerSeceuro while Charlie was at the helm,' I agreed, easily. 'His breakthrough technology will benefit this branch of the industry worldwide. It can be of benefit to everyone who uses intruder security. Our plans for market exploitation are firm.'

'Very recently they were not. I'm sorry to

hear it, because that isn't what Charlie and I were discussing.'

'But there's no record of discussion,' Madison said. 'Not on our side.'

Houghton conceded, 'We hoped to explore the best way forward — but it didn't get that far. A pity, then. I was a great admirer of your husband, Zoe.'

After lunch was over, Madison asked me, 'What did you make of Houghton?'

'He showed some intelligence but not much style.' I shrugged. 'Seriously? Nice try.'

Whatever the unjustified rumours circulating back in London, they seemed not to have penetrated across the Channel, and that was a great relief. Without having to dispel any cloud over colleagues' or customers' perceptions, we were free to move swiftly through our own agenda.

These companies wanted to share the breakthrough of the Goldstar technology, that was clear. But would anyone have tried to sabotage MakerSeceuro for their own advantage? Would anyone really have wanted to harm Charlie? Someone, somewhere had killed him — throwing the company into real disarray. That could have turned us into easy meat, open to offers, as Ian Darius had expected or hoped. Even so . . .

'Madison? Have I been sheltered from reality — or are we sheltered here, among the camaraderie? Look around you. Have we been mistaken about what might've been going on?'

An edge of cynicism lined Madison's pleasant features. 'Just because the wolf smiles at you, vowing he's your friend, it doesn't mean he wouldn't gladly gobble you up.'

'But . . . *Charlie?*'

'Keep an open mind.'

'Perhaps you're right.'

'And talk to A-Zander tonight. Gauge Darius's reactions to us now. Wish I could be there.'

* * *

A message was waiting in my hotel that morning from Ian Darius. He was obliged to cancel our dinner — but perhaps I might join him instead at a restaurant by his hotel? Since this was very close to my own hotel and the exhibition centre, he believed I would find it convenient.

I was annoyed at the *fait accompli*, the lack of discussion or explanation. His assumption of control put me less in charge of the evening. Had he sensed what I was about and decided to wrongfoot me, or was there a more innocent reason?

I dressed for dinner, thinking about the mixed dislike and attraction between us. Ian had been fired with enthusiasm for acquiring MakerSeceuro. The rejection of his plans might have left a bitter determination to succeed. Now I had to judge whether he was capable of acting covertly to damage us, and whether he had done so. If it was him, somehow I would need to learn just how far he had gone.

Arriving at the restaurant, I was surprised to be shown through the main dining area to a small side room. In this were seated four Japanese businessmen — plus Ian Darius, at the head of their table. I seemed to be the only woman.

Ian came to greet me with a welcoming smile. I must have looked as disconcerted as I felt, and he was clearly amused. 'We're so glad you were able to join us. This is a little celebration.' His other guests had risen to their feet to form a polite audience. As we went round the table with introductions, I wondered what they were making of my presence here. These men were international bankers, it quickly emerged. A-Zander appeared to have done good business with them.

The company was charming, the food and wine were excellent. The evening was a show of strength as well as a punishment. Frustrated in my purpose, I fumed secretly. Unwillingly I recognised that Ian had gone up in my estimation, even while I disliked and suspected him more than ever. It was almost funny. I had been invited here to be thwarted, to decorate the opposite end of his table and to witness some triumph I could only guess at. They were a jolly group and I sat small-talking on the sidelines, in a pointless end to a good two days.

A couple of hours later the Japanese bankers left. They were flying to London tonight. I was about to return thankfully to my hotel, but Ian seemed suddenly reluctant to let me go. 'Let's have a drink. I believe there was something you wanted to discuss?' By now, my reasons for seeing him would be difficult even to hint at. I said nothing, as he spoke to the waiter then turned back to me. 'I remember what you like, from our evening together on Jersey.'

'That seems a long time back.'

'Have you forgiven me, Zoe, for altering our plans tonight? It was rude and I apologise. I had a good fair, extremely good. And you?'

'Yes, it was very successful. Madison and

I covered a lot of ground.'

'I saw you with Madison Black, of course.' He paused, thoughtful. I was about to mention our internal security — to watch for his reaction — when Ian went on quickly, as if he had read my mind: 'This was a nice idea of yours, to see each other. Why don't we meet up in London? But nothing to do with business now. Just for pleasure?'

Certain he was deliberately evading me tonight, I nodded. We would meet back at home and I would catch him unawares, catch him out. I was trying to ignore the attraction singing through my body. Ian was an enemy, he wanted MakerSeceuro and he would certainly damage us to obtain what he wanted. All I had to do was get proof of his involvement in any of the bad stuff that had happened.

Like Charlie's death? Too unlikely, too horrific. Quickly I banished the idea.

In his pleasant, persuasive way Ian Darius was asking, 'D'you happen to like flying, Zoe? Messing about in planes?'

I stared at him. There was nothing I hated more but I wasn't going to admit to terror, not to the thumping of my heart nor the way my hands were starting to shake just at the very idea. 'Have you ever flown?' he asked innocently. 'In light aircraft, new or old?'

270

I shrugged carelessly. Did he know somehow about my phobia? 'Once upon a time . . . You do?'

'I adore it. I happen to be a real enthusiast.' The waiter came and spoke some message into his ear. Ian murmured a reply. I watched as he signed for his party.

'Do you have a plane, Ian?'

'I suppose it's eccentric. I have a tiny vintage plane — a Tiger Moth. It's the most enormous fun, hopping around in it.'

'Where do you keep that?' I asked, idly now as we were preparing to leave the restaurant.

'In Hertfordshire, at a small private airfield. I asked you because it really is such fun — you must come out for a spin some time. Shall we go?'

Walking the short distance to my hotel, he took my arm. This was someone I profoundly distrusted — could hate deeply — for what he might possibly have done. Outside the foyer, I stepped back and away from him. 'Goodnight, Ian. Thanks for a very nice dinner.'

His thin lips curved into a smile. 'Yes, goodnight. I must rejoin my party. We're flying back tonight.'

I still hadn't found out what he had been

up to, if anything. 'Let's be in touch, in London.'

★ ★ ★

I was coming out of the Eurostar terminal at Waterloo next morning when Madison called urgently. A crisis had broken — he didn't want to be specific. He needed to brief me on what had happened this morning: he was arranging emergency financial meetings. Could I come to HQ right away?

The lunchtime traffic was heavy on the North Circular, the cab crawled. I spoke again briefly to Madison, then to Stuart. By the time I reached MakerSeceuro, it was after two. By then I had a better idea of what the problem was. Our investors had shown signs of nervousness, suddenly threatening to withdraw finance. At first this was thought to be the result of the rumours and false innuendo, hitting home where it hurt.

Things turned out to be potentially even more serious. A confidential document had gone AWOL, in the worst leak yet. Ironically it was a piece of paper we could have done without, an internal memo depicting a worst-case scenario and only drawn up to balance our projections. We were confident about our planned expansion: this memo was a caution against overoptimism. Somehow it had arrived at the headquarters of our investment bank.

'Stuart's car was broken into yesterday,' Madison explained grimly. 'His briefcase was stolen — we think that's how they were given the information.'

Reassuring the bank should have been simple, but now it seemed the rumours about MakerSeceuro had been filtering through. Filtering too steadily, too relentlessly to be anything but a deliberate feed, we felt sure. To the bank it looked like increasing signs of foundation cracks and instability.

For several hours that afternoon, in a succession of meetings, we attempted to repair the damage. With the accountants, Whyte Majors, we produced every piece of evidence we possessed of MakerSeceuro's good health. By six that evening, the investment bank's serious upset with us appeared to have turned into a willingness to study all the facts and figures. There was still talk of getting an independent auditor.

We finished up back at the office, still worried and angry. The bank would come to their senses but that wasn't really the point now. Who could have done this, and what else might we be in for? Irritable and exhausted, we were about to split for the night when Den produced a small missile.

'I'd better mention this now. The Hexton chain, who were dragging their feet — we haven't got the upgrade, they didn't renew. And guess who it turns out they've moved to? Only A-Zander.'

Fiercely I turned to Madison, 'You're not going to tell me that's coincidence?'

Den was insisting, 'It could be, though. They decided not to come back to us — why not A-Zander?'

'We need proof of something illegal in practice,' I agreed.

Madison clapped a hand on my shoulder. 'Zoe, we're all knackered. We should sleep on this, let it go until tomorrow.'

I picked up my travel bag and headed for home, the day's events lying leaden on my mind. The finance was essential. The way things were looking right now, it might even not be replaceable. What we were up against was a threat to our survival.

At home I hoped for a message from Alison. We had missed our meeting at six, after Jenny had tried to get hold of her all afternoon. Alison was out of the office on some job, with her mobile switched off. There was nothing from her now. Perhaps she was out on surveillance work? Calling her home, I couldn't get through.

Among the messages was one from Caro. It made me smile and I replayed the tape. 'You'll want to hear this — I saw Simon, the old fogey, ha ha. Twice actually, because he's got this sort of *ranch*, with wonderful horses. So am I enamoured! Got to go now, and conquer Europe. Catch you later.' Her voice was cheerful and confident. Things seemed to be working out with Dr Tyrone faster than we had dared to hope. 'Simon', indeed.

I showered and changed, unpacked then fretted, microwaved supper. A slothful evening beckoned but I couldn't get into it. Why hadn't Alison rung? It had been hours.

Uneasily I thought back to our last phone call. She had been insistent, needing to talk — and angry, frightened. Someone was stalking her and bugging the office at her home. In Paris and during today's dire events, I had almost forgotten how she had been.

She had promised to tell DCI Prentiss. She had promised and I had just assumed the police were taking care of her.

Suppose she hadn't told them?

Pacing the house, I tried to imagine any reason why she wouldn't seek protection. A conflict of professional interests, perhaps? Pigheadedness? She often preferred to operate alone. It gave her the thrill she sought. But on an investigation this big, involving both Quest and her own personal safety . . .

Alison would have told somebody — about being watched, and whatever it was she had decided to tell me.

I had a sweep done . . .

Someone had helped her. Perhaps Redcliff. I didn't have any phone number for him.

What if she had caught the person who had been following her? She had learned who they were, or who was hiring them, and . . .

Were they to do with some other case of hers, or were they connected with what had happened to Charlie?

Feeling cold, I glanced at my watch. It was a little after ten. I dialled the number of her mobile, found it was still switched off, then called her home again, expecting the machine to answer.

Instead the ringing stopped abruptly: someone had picked up. 'Alison? Are you there?'

Silence.

My skin was beginning to crawl. I could hear — or sense — the listener on the other end. If it was Alison, she would speak. Instead, that terrible silence echoed on the open line. Memory rushed through me.

'Alison? It's Zoe.'

In the quietness came a tiny cracking sound. The line went dead.

Without stopping to think, I grabbed keys and mobile. It was a gusting, squally night and I drove faster than was safe, covering the short distance south, circling the dark mass of Hampstead Heath. I turned up Fitzroy Lane. Between the wintry tops of trees, house lights sparkled.

Except from Alison's house. At the end of the road, her home lay in a peculiar swath of darkness. She never left it dark. We had installed automatic lighting there.

I braked abruptly, got out of the car. I didn't need to touch the gate; it was swinging open in the wind.

★ ★ ★

For a moment I paused, staring up at the building. What was behind those blind windows, the darkness? Was Alison inside, or someone else?

There was a flashlight in the car. Taking it, I went quietly through the gate and up the path. The front door was locked and the windows were firm. Around the back, the french windows stood wide open to the night. For another moment I hesitated, feeling the mobile in my pocket. Superstition, deeply buried, surfaced through my dread. I wished so desperately that this might turn out to be only a burglar. Somehow a thief had gained access, with Alison not here . . . I don't know where it came from, that fear — to name this as an emergency might turn things worse, might even doom her.

Inside that perfect, architect-designed house, everything seemed in order at first. In the kitchen, the flashlight picked out gleaming, almost empty surfaces. An unused wine glass stood, solitary, on the table near the vase of silk rosebuds. A tap was dripping at the sink, disquieting. Absentmindedly, against all the rules at a break-in scene, I reached across and turned it off. Silence, then.

Silently, jumpily, I followed the spiky light beam. Lobby and cloakroom, utility room . . . Whoever had got in could perhaps still be hiding somewhere. The large, open living space looked undisturbed. Her office seemed to bear the usual amount of scattered papers, used coffee mugs.

Under the stairs, a cupboard door hung open. The mains was switched off. There was a fuse missing . . . a back-up battery had been removed.

Quieting fear, it was a couple of minutes before I went on, silently, up the curved staircase. Something tall and pale was looming. It was only a long taupe frock on a hanger suspended from a door.

Her bedroom was empty, undisturbed. In the dressing room beyond, the wardrobe doors were closed. Clothes lay bundled for washing in a corner. The spare bedroom looked undisturbed, the bathroom its usual muddle of cosmetics, bath towel lying on the floor. No steam, no warmth.

A chill was creeping over the house. Had it been cool before, when I arrived? Hot and cold with fear, I hadn't noticed.

I had searched too thoroughly to have missed anyone. The house was empty now. Thinking this, without any logic I began to shout Alison's name. Yelling it out, then listening, just in case.

Nothing. What had I expected? She wasn't here.

Now I could call the police. I should have felt relief. Instead, something was nagging . . .

Something about the tap. The sink.

Silent again, back down the stairs. In the kitchen I paused, unwilling. Something I had not quite seen. That was glimpsed, subliminal? Or that hadn't meant anything at first glance? That I didn't want to see.

It was the bit of dark shadow, a slight streaking of darkness, around the inside of the sink. Not quite washed away.

I shone the flashlight now. In the sink, under the tap, it was lying there. Alison's best French kitchen knife. It was not quite clean around the haft. Something dark . . .

Blood. Her knife. With her own knife.

The dressing room . . .

On rubbery legs, I crept back up the stairs, drifted weirdly through to Alison's bedroom, into the small room beyond.

The wall of clothes cupboards . . . Those closed doors. After a moment, grabbing, flinging them wide open, I shone the light in. The smell hit me, then the sight — blood, awash with blood . . . And the something pale suspended there, a face disfigured, the body naked. Disembowelled . . .

Kneeling. On the floor, the world swam by as ages passed. Beneath splayed fingers, cold and spongy wetness. It was everywhere, everywhere.

That rhythmic noise. Charlie calling? Ringing and ringing. Obedient then, doing what I could. Fumbling, dropping the mobile and everything unclear. Sound and vision were underwater, out of grasp.

The familiar sound of Alison's voice, that I had longed to hear? With the illogic of nightmare, I expected her to be speaking now.

This was a man's voice. ' . . . *Zoe?*'

Charlie, then? Unable to speak, I made no sound. 'That you? What the bollocks is going on?'

Redcliff's voice.

17

THE DAY OF JUDGMENT.

I have an eye for an eye.

Her time had come — I Pre-Dated her planned Check-Out, bringing it forward, this execution of the Guilty. The cow was about to break my rules, spill a crucial bean and spoil My Game. I am well schooled in the virtues of flexibility: adapt or die. He did school me.

Always surviving, the rituals must be adhered to, must be. I've read a little on this subject, too. Throughout History, execution has always been dignified where possible, when preplanned, by important ritual. This is only human and I bow, I obey.

Bathed in Blood, washed in the Precious. Now the cleansing, consigning matter to the flames.

My boat is solidly built, modest by others' standards perhaps. Since inheriting her, I've done a little research. She was a Dutch cargo vessel designed for canals. Her hull is now reinforced with steel and she has been soundproofed — a useful, even essential feature as it turned out. She has all the advantages of mobility, with the attendant degree of anonymity. Boats have their connotations of summertime and pleasure.

By an almost Sinfully early hour, I am stepping back on to dry land. Driving with a suitcase, back to my flat. From inside the case, unpacking mementoes and expensive gifts. There are several disks. And, of course, the laptop computer. That should come very expensive. It should ensure a meeting with Mr Big, and will not leave my Hands for less than it is worth. Why am I interested in meeting him? I don't like it, it doesn't amuse me, this being palmed off with a messenger boy.

Personal Souvenirs: the Precious Blood, the Eye. Temporarily unpacking his — before packing hers, too, in the freezer — I am struck by how different they are. His and hers, the persecutor and the cow. In life — IN EVIL PURSUIT — they were an ill-matched pair, not fitting at all and they knew not what they did. Individually, singly now, I can see that each has an iris of a quite different colour and formation. His cornea has clouded, making this an imperfect specimen. Her iris has an interesting circle of yellow, merging into the blue.

Perceptions, perceptions.

It's time for a little shut-eye.

THAT EVIL PURSUIT

I read that Wolves, being a most intelligent species, pit their Wits in packs or pairs or Lone to isolate the 'creature of their choice'. An outrunning follows, a merciless wearing down over a great deal of Time, before they Devour it Alive. There is no nicety, no quick despatch.

I have taken them on, my 'Mission in Life'. Testing their intelligence, I am frequently disappointed. The cow was easy to pick off. Are they only frightened and cowardly, the Guilty?

I only relearned, at His knee. Already I had inherited His mantle, Me.

The Persecutors reappeared, theirs were the lies that were told to Me. Mine is the simple truth of proof. I spit in the eye of Authority, I quench Political Lies! This is the true secret of Eternity, unravelled to our Gaze.

★ ★ ★

Nothing on the news yet. Nothing surprises Me any more.

Detective Chief Inspector Paul Spencer Prentiss. An odd fish, even for a Mr Plod.

He should be in trouble with his superiors by now. How will they describe it this time, the butchering of the cow? I would like to place a bet. It was only a touch of self-harm, just a little self-inflicted Death. A suicide, ha ha.

With a Melton Mowbray pork pie and can of NRG, up to the Loft.

Nothing is happening at Cedar Court, the widow hasn't returned and the housekeeper is in. It is always a tick to my handiwork when Mary dusts unsuspectingly — over the pinhole lense in the light, across the TV's microcamera. She thought I was the Electricity Man. So did the cow, once upon a moon. Nice, simple jobs. And Check-Out time.

The housekeeper is leaving now. At CC, the screens are blank. She is away . . .

We are meant to be — United and together for ever. She and He that's Me: Mine.

Since Maker went to meet his.

The she-DEVIL wears two faces, unaware she is being watched. I see, hear everything: no place to hide, then.

You have no place to hide from Me.

18

Prentiss's bony face leaned closer. 'What did you do after finding the body?'

He was sickly pale. It must be the greyness of dawn seeping through the tiny window of the interview room, or the fluorescent striplighting, stark overhead. 'Some time passed and my mobile was ringing. It was Jay Redcliff.'

'You stayed in the room, in that small space?' Prentiss's new DC, Ned Shaw, spoke with a broad East End accent and looked like a fledgling stockbroker: sharp eyes in a fleshy face, sharp suit, gelled hair. Sarah Quirke didn't seem to be around.

'I crawled out then, and answered. Redcliff must've been nearby. He arrived soon after. He . . . I waited in the bedroom while . . . he checked the house.' Redcliff had been interviewed, they had his statement but I didn't know how he had described those next few minutes. 'He wanted to check the killer wasn't still around.'

'He did this while you were in her bedroom?'

'Yes.'

'Her car was in the garage — did he go there?'

'I don't know.'

'How long did he search before calling us?'

'Five minutes? Maybe less. Everything seemed to be happening very slowly, we were both so shocked. He was making sure it was safe to stay at the scene. Then he came back up to where I was, and phoned.'

'No reason to hurry,' Shaw said speculatively. 'While you were in the house, did you move anything or take anything?'

I shook my head. The dark vision of her dead body — that glimpse of it — kept swimming before me. 'The tap. The wardrobe door. You know about.' He had gouged out an eye, eviscerated her. Like Gill Tarpont, almost the same . . . How could we have let this happen, to Alison of all people? 'Are you going to let people know?' I was shouting at Prentiss, at his bland, watchful silence. 'This is a serial killer and no one's safe until he's been caught!'

The DCI leaned back with an abrupt movement. His voice took on a sarcastic courtesy. 'You believe that no one's safe? You think Alison Seely was an arbitrary choice of victim? Given her investigation into two other murders, and her closeness to your husband?'

'Of course not. I'd asked her to investigate. This is my fault.' I stared at Prentiss's yellow-stained fingers, laid out tensely on the table top. 'The public has a right to know, and . . . She was about to tell me something she'd been keeping secret — I think on your orders. She was being followed and her home was bugged. Alison knew she was some kind of target, and she was scared . . . '

'But neither you nor she reported this!' We glared at each other. His unspoken words hung in the mean, heated air: she could still be alive if you had . . .

'I believed that she had reported it.' I cleared my throat. 'We were due to meet at a wine bar in Primrose Hill — '

'Where she never showed. Either she'd got your messages cancelling — or, by six, she couldn't get there.'

'How long . . . When did she die?'

Shaw glanced at his notebook, then swiftly at Prentiss. 'We think about half an hour before you discovered the body. If getting there did take around fifteen minutes, the victim was already dead when you last called her — when someone answered the phone at her house, but didn't speak.'

'What he did to her,' I whispered. 'Was

that the same as — to Gill Tarpont?'

Neither answered. The silence stretched until it was as if I had never spoken. Until Prentiss broke it. 'Alison used a computer at home. Was it still there when you looked into her office, before going upstairs?'

'It's hard to remember. There was only the flashlight . . . My impression was, things were much as usual.'

'What about the laptop which had belonged to your husband? Did you see that?'

'I didn't notice that. But it's small. It could've been anywhere in the house.' Prentiss and Shaw exchanged a look. 'Why? Has it been stolen?'

'So far as we can ascertain, the laptop and Miss Seely's computer were both stolen. Some disks may be missing also. What was on the laptop, anything new?'

'There was nothing on it since it came back from you, only software. His design files were all deleted. Alison wanted it purely as a memento of her friendship with Charlie. Did the killer take it thinking it contained something useful? Like research and design secrets from MakerSeceuro?' Prentiss didn't answer. 'Chief Inspector, we had another leak from HQ. An internal memo — turning up at a bank. That must've been sabotage, to frighten investors . . . MakerSeceuro's enemy and the murderer — since he stole those computers — they must be the same person.'

'Tell us more about the problems at MakerSeceuro,' Prentiss said. 'You told us before that the board suspected some kind of campaign was operating against your company.'

I told them everything. When I talked about the meetings with Patricia Abel, they showed no surprise: she must have been in touch with Prentiss already. 'Our MD resigned immediately after Charlie's death — and quickly joined the Livesey Group. Now there are signs of our key customers leaving, and A-Zander Security seems to be getting them. Both those companies, Charlie had contacted — '

'We know,' Prentiss cut in, then paused. 'Your technical director . . . '

'Keith Naylor?'

He nodded, turned to Shaw. 'Let's have another talk. And with the present MD.'

'They're both sound. Loyal. Madison Black's been with us for some years.'

'I'm sure they are. Make it Monday.'

Shaw made a note. I shoved a coffee mug across the table between us, furious. 'You'd ordered Alison Seely to keep quiet about something. It seems clear she got killed because of what she knew. If Alison was at risk, why wasn't she protected?'

Prentiss's brows shot into one straight line. He thundered back, 'Ms Maker, why the hell should we inform *you* of any surveillance operations? We ask the questions. You worked on her — persuading her — didn't you? She was about to reveal something she had absolutely no right to reveal. Just maybe that put her at risk from someone intent on saving his skin. How dare you interfere?'

Yes, how dare I? Alison had lost her life. While the police had been busy investigating . . . Was Prentiss implying that the surveillance on her might have been part of the CID operation? Then how could they have let the killer slip through their net? He was making that up, misleading me.

Alison. If I had never persuaded her to investigate Charlie's death, then would she still be alive?

But if she had died because of the investigation, then how could I possibly leave things as they were? Prentiss hadn't turned up Charlie's murderer — or Gill's. He was saying anything to keep me at arm's length from what was really happening. Why would the CID have bugged Alison's home, or her phone? That didn't make sense.

It hadn't been them.

I stared back at Prentiss, equally angry. 'Tell me something else. In the factory by the canal, I found bloodstains — '

'Animal blood, probably a rabbit. The chain had dog hairs attached. The fire was made by some dosser — recently. Want to know how we know that? Following normal procedure, the entire area was combed immediately after Charlie Maker's death.'

I frowned. 'Sarah Quirke was — '

'DC Quirke is no longer here.' DCI Prentiss smiled. It was an unpleasant smile. 'Interfere again, Ms Maker, and you will be prosecuted. Wasting police time, obstruction, messing with evidence — you name it.' He rapped the table. 'Do we understand each other?'

I spread my hands. 'We seem to.'

He shot me a look, not quite sure whether he'd had the desired effect. A knock sounded at the door and it swung open. Shaw, then Prentiss, conferred urgently with someone just outside.

'DC Shaw will take your statement.' Prentiss was showing something, a slip of paper, to Ned Shaw. 'See she gets driven home.'

'Will do.'

Prentiss was out of the door.

Shaw intoned, 'Eight sixteen, DCI Prentiss called away from interview.' He looked at me and raised his eyebrows, then switched off the recording. 'Need a break? Or d'you want to continue?'

'Let's get this finished.'

★ ★ ★

Twenty minutes later, after signing a statement, I was being whisked down a corridor by DC Shaw. 'I'll get one of the lads to run you home.'

'That won't be necessary. I'm taking her.' It was Redcliff, uncannily materialising from out of nowhere. I felt a rush of relief that he was there. Then I saw how he looked — like death. Steering us out of the building, he grasped my hand and we headed towards his car. 'Fucking *hours*! What was he doing, grilling you for breakfast?' I laughed. 'You want to go home, or where?'

I shook my head, because I didn't care what happened next. Redcliff began to drive as if on automatic pilot, through north London's anonymous, tree-lined streets. People were walking, getting on with their lives . . . The stuff I was feeling must have been going on all the time with him too. A few minutes later he stopped, parked at the side of some quiet road. He punched the dash, over and over.

Alison. Everything I had been holding on to cracked. *Alison.* The most alive of people, vibrant with the sheer adventure of living dangerously. Redcliff had slumped, his anger gone. When I reached out to hold him, his arms went round me quickly. He was so solid, warm — I could feel a pulse in his neck, could hear his heart thudding. I felt the wetness on his face. We were alive, after all, and our friend was dead.

He drew back and we looked at each other. 'We need to talk,' he said. 'You're all in. I'll take you home.'

I thought of Cedar Court. Charlie's ghost, resurrected by Alison's murder, was stalking again through my skull. 'To your place, then. I'd prefer it.'

'Right. My flat.' He looked quizzical. 'It's a real dump.'

'I expect a real dump, Redcliff.'

He laughed.

It was a basement apartment in St John's Wood. Inside was just as advertised: it was pretty desperate. Those walls had forgotten what paint was. A photo of his children stood on a shelf in the living room. There were toys in a corner, with a small shiny bicycle. Tough-guy kit — mountain boots, outdoor gear and what looked like a pickaxe — spilled out from a bedroom door.

'Not quite what you're used to,' he said with some satisfaction. 'I doss here, Monday through Friday. Coffee? And you need a drink — something in it.'

'Charlie and I built a life, and a company. But before that we had nothing at all.'

He looked at me swiftly, questioningly. We had taken a night trip to hell together and that had left some intimacy — with this aggressive, bullying thug. How had I ever seen Redcliff in that way? Right now, he could not have seemed more different.

Charlie's name hung in the air, with all that we needed to talk about. Redcliff brought coffee. He said, 'Prentiss went apeshit, you know that? Going into Alison's house — on your own, no backup. He thinks you're crazy, a dangerous lady.' He smiled, briefly.

'Sarah Quirke was . . . Is she off this case?'

'She's resigned.'

'Are you sure?' I was surprised, then disappointed. 'She was a good contact. Is it because . . . Is that part of why? Did she get pushed?'

Redcliff shrugged. 'I think the disenchantment was mutual. I know where to find her.'

I stared. He wasn't going to explain. 'If

she was already off the case, she wouldn't know anything about . . . ' Then I couldn't speak it, couldn't say Alison's name aloud. The spectre — that glimpse of the horrifying thing that had been her — flashed into my mind's eye then, as it had across the hours, mugging my consciousness.

' . . . about Alison,' Redcliff finished. His voice was harsh. It was harsh against himself, as he went on. 'Alison was out of contact all yesterday afternoon. At Quest we knew that but we didn't begin to suss the reason.' He spun round, eyes blazing. 'Then this morning, I learn she'd been under surveillance at home . . . She never told me that! Who did she get to do her sweep? It wasn't Quest. Why would she go to another outfit for something like that? Why?'

'I should've told you. Should've called Prentiss too, as soon as . . . Redcliff, did I kill her then?'

He leaned forward, grim-faced. 'Listen. Alison was a great lady. She loved a risk. She couldn't resist stepping into danger. That killed her, you could say. Or else,' he added urgently, 'if we don't believe that, you and I will both go out of our skulls. Think I'm feeling great? Alison was my partner and it was my task, my job to protect her. I could not have failed any worse.'

'She didn't give you any chance.'

'Maybe. You're right . . . I can't believe it that she's dead. Less than a year, I knew her — that was all. But doing our kind of work — I thought she and I trusted each other.'

I hugged him, we stayed close. It was getting difficult to move apart. Was this some kind of hostage syndrome? I laughed, drunk from a cocktail of adrenaline with exhaustion. Were we both hostages — or had one of us captured the other? 'Of course she trusted you, Redcliff. She relied on you completely. Only she had some secrecy deal going with the police.'

He was thoughtful, suddenly alert. 'That was her background, CID.'

'Yes. Charlie met Alison a year or two before she left the force . . . And they were lovers,' I added slowly. He looked surprised. 'But that explains nothing. I don't understand. First Gill Tarpont . . . Why Charlie, then Alison? They knew each other but . . . What possible reason could there be — unless for what she'd found out.'

'He left all of his trademarks, the signature.' Redcliff got up from where we were sitting. He was restless. 'The killer wanted it known for sure that she was one of his victims.'

I pushed away that image, the spectre. 'He

did the same to her . . . '

'Just the same. They'll find that drug at the post-mortem today. This was an almost exact copy of the Tarpont murder.'

I lurched to my feet and the room swayed. 'I keep remembering her.'

'Yeah . . . Zoe. You're all in,' he said again. His breath was exhaling, warm — nearly hot — on to the top of my head. 'Come and lie down, catch up on some rest. There's something I've got to do, right here in the flat. A job that'll take maybe an hour. So catch up on some sleep.'

★ ★ ★

It was icy cold. It was dark and panic swelled through me. Alison's body hung suspended. Charlie lay . . . He was dying before my eyes.

Her eye. One — staring straight at me, above the gag. The other a bloody socket. Madness.

Madness always has a logic to it.

Where had I heard that?

'Zoe?' Redcliff. His silhouette was in the doorway, moving towards the bed. Light was shining through from the kitchen across the hallway. 'You all right?'

'Cold,' I said through chattering teeth.

Never more glad to see another human being.

'It's a furnace in here. Delayed shock. Hey — move over.'

He got into bed and lay cradling my body. I clung to him as if he was life itself. His warmth crept slowly through my limbs, melting the horror. I sank into the wholeness, the safety of our flesh. A while later, and consciousness had become a tolerable thing. The sun had set but only on another day. A bad day . . .

Alive, we were alive. Not to be alone — that was all I had wanted.

Redcliff moved away, rolled over and switched on a bedside lamp. He studied my expression. 'You knew her a long time. A lot happened between you. She was your link with Charlie. The closest link after Caro.'

'She was like a sister. A surrogate sister.'

We talked — or I did, mostly — about her. It got easier. Death had to become real. It had to be made a fact, ordinary. I was getting to be an expert after all. First Charlie, then Alison. Take a look at the common link, Zoe. Was I some kind of a worst-luck carrier, a Jonah? Then who would be next?

'Give you a penny for all those thoughts. Forget them, yeah? You slept. I checked on you a few times.'

I looked into Redcliff's eyes, near to mine, and saw a gentleness I had never expected to see. We were quiet for a while. When he stirred, I felt a current passing between our bodies. We were both tense with desire.

Why not?

There were only a dozen reasons why not. Under his loose open-necked shirt, I saw the taut skin of a muscled shoulder. Slowly I drew back. Reading each other, we let go and I slid out of bed. Redcliff was out of the door in one movement. I found the bathroom and stuck my head under the tap.

He went into the kitchen and was there for a while. In the living room, my gaze was drawn automatically to the photo of Lisa and Danny. I went to see what Redcliff was doing and found him making coffee. There was a computer set up on the kitchen table; it looked as if he had been working on it. From the doorway I watched him move about, register my presence then return to what he was doing. A thought struck me. 'It's the weekend, isn't it?'

'I called and talked with the kids,' he answered. 'I'm not expected. Is that what you meant?'

I nodded. He must have seen everything in my face. It was quite some pretence we were keeping up.

'What about Caro?' he asked. 'Even if they censor the story, something's bound to be reported. She'll find out. She and Alison were good mates. Right?'

'Caro's out of the country until Sunday. She can't just find out — I must go and break this to her. In many ways she worshipped Alison. And it's going to bring back everything about her father.'

He touched my shoulder briefly, then turned away. Looking past him, I felt a jarring of surprise. The computer on Redcliff's kitchen table was Alison's. It bore the blues band logo that she had stuck on to the side.

It had been stolen by the killer, Prentiss had said.

* * *

I sat down at the keyboard. I remembered borrowing the computer from her once, remembered Alison and shivered involuntarily. 'Damn it,' I said through the lump in my throat and the springing tears. 'Damn this way that the dead are everywhere. You stole it? While you pretended to look around the house, before you called the police?'

He regarded me. 'This is Quest property. And so are the files that Alison had on it.'

'Yes, but — Redcliff! And if Prentiss finds out . . . Did you steal Charlie's, too?'

'I did not. Whoever murdered Alison stole Charlie's design laptop . . . The other thing he did was erase all her files from this one. There's nothing on it. Of course,' he went on softly, almost to himself, 'there's a chance that Alison wiped them herself.'

'But it was just her personal computer, her stuff. And when she worked from home, that's . . . Why would anyone delete the files?'

'Good question. I don't know for sure.'

'Why on earth did you take it? Prentiss will — '

'Prentiss won't know,' Redcliff cut in with an edge of sharpness. 'Zoe . . . Alison was obsessed about Charlie's murder. And Tarpont's. She never really let any of us close. Those conferences? Load of bullshit. Your investigation? That was only a front, keeping you quiet.' I was silenced, waiting. 'Most recent thing was, you asked us to look into recent cases of suicide from that bridge.'

'And you came up with nothing.'

'Alison came up with nothing. Yes. She'd insisted on it, taking that little task for herself.'

'Whatever for? You think she did find

something that linked in?'

'If she did, it's not at Quest.' And he tapped the monitor, thoughtfully. 'But it might've been on this little lady.'

'Then we'll do the same job. Find and follow the track she was on. And hope we find — and recognise — whatever it was she'd found.'

'My guess is, Alison was carrying out her own, very private investigation. For her own reasons, whatever those were. And whatever she'd learned, or worked out for herself, was all on here.'

Her computer stared mutely back at us. 'That is only a guess.' I got up, impatient. 'If all her data's been erased, then we'll never know. But we can start ourselves — from scratch.'

'Sure we can. You hungry, by any chance?' Suddenly aware of being starving, I nodded. 'There's nothing in the place, I never eat here. Shall we go and eat, then I'll take you home?'

On the drive, we were silent. We zipped past cars, pedestrian couples going out for the evening, all the disorientating normality. Rows of terraced houses were flashing by, each prettily lit, humming with ordinariness. Shops and pubs, restaurants. 'Pasta joint?' he suggested. 'That do OK?'

'Fine,' I agreed. Now we were right inside it, that ordinariness. Among the tables full of couples and groups of friends, devouring plates of tagliatelle. It was warm and comforting. Relaxing, still we scarcely spoke.

Inside the car, our proximity had taken on giant proportions again, distorting the narrow space between Redcliff and myself. If we denied what was happening, would it go away?

We left the car in the driveway at Cedar Court. I hesitated as we went in. It was as if I was listening for something, trying to sense the emptiness and make sure of it. Then I went briskly through the hall, Redcliff following close behind. 'Like a drink? Or coffee?' In the kitchen, I caught him looking around quickly, as if he was checking. 'What is it?'

'Zoe, I'm going to take a swift look over the whole of your place, OK?'

I went cold. What did he mean, check for someone — the killer — lying hidden, waiting for . . . ? But that was stupid. Before I could frame a question, Redcliff was gone.

After ten minutes, he came whistling through the hall, breezing back in. 'Everything seems to be just fine and dandy.'

'What were you expecting to find?'

'Nothing. I was expecting to find nothing
. . . Hey.'

'What?'

'I've spooked you.'

Suddenly I was grinning at him across
the table. 'For a moment there . . . For
a moment, I thought you meant to spook
me.'

For a split second he hesitated. Not for
long, though. 'Why would I? Would I want
you too spooked to spend the night alone?'
He laughed. 'Would I?'

Laughter was stronger than fear, stronger
than logic. It broke every resolve. He was
across the kitchen, close.

Redcliff stayed that night.

19

He stayed the next day.

My body craved for him the way you ache for oxygen after being underwater. When we weren't connected, I hurt.

In other circumstances, could it have been different? Who was I fooling? In other circumstances, Redcliff and I would have remained two people who couldn't exchange two words without a fight. After what we had just been through, we both knew this was time out. We were grasping for oblivion, demanding proof from each other that we were alive, every moment.

He was the first man since Charlie. My marriage had revealed no glimmerings of this kind of sexual need. It felt like some regression into adolescent passion.

If all of my body was intently his, throughout those almost twenty-four hours part of my mind kept remembering Caro. She was due to return to the UK and would travel, with her classmates, directly to her school in the morning. There would be news reports, if they had not already appeared, and they would have no reason not to name Alison.

'Hey.' Green eyes, disturbed-looking, questioning. 'You keep flying far away. Feeling hungry, by any chance?'

When I forgot what had happened, I was. 'Famished, and you must be.' Gliding my hand over that strong, muscled back, stroking down over his haunches, reluctantly I let him go. 'We should find lunch. Or how about dinner?'

It was dark again, seven in the evening. By eight we were showered, dressed and eating at the table as if this was a normal evening. As if it could ever be normal for Redcliff and me to be domestically paired. We ate duck, from freezer to microwave, and he helped himself to a third plateful. When I looked at him, I wanted sex again. If I touched him we would never resurface, not for hours.

'In the morning, Caro flies back . . . She'll be going straight to her school.'

'That's in Sussex? And she'll need to be told.'

'Yes. I must do that.'

'We ought to see what they're saying. What kind of reports there are.' He was refusing to meet my eye, suddenly.

There was nothing in that morning's paper and, being a weekend, the evening news on TV was short, with only a brief report. Alison was named, they showed a photo of her but gave no details of the murder. There was no mention of the killer's method or possible motive, there were no police theories. Incredibly, to a casual viewer the reports would suggest no connection to any previous murder victim. Not to Gill Tarpont, nor Charlie.

'Caro could see it. She could see a paper, in the morning. Alison was . . . Sometimes Caro seemed to idolise her, but then she could be very critical.' Now I wondered about the reason. When Caro was a little girl, Charlie and Alison were having an affair — did she remember something of that time? 'Redcliff, I'm scared for Caro. Did I tell you she started seeing a counsellor, a psychiatrist? I'm afraid of what Alison's death might do to her.'

'Caro needs you, not some shrink. She'll need you to tell her, and spend time with her.'

'I must drive down there early, catch her as she gets back. She mustn't hear this in a casual way.'

'You want me to come?' He read my pleased reaction, followed by uncertainty. 'While you two are chewing the fat, I can bugger off. Caro would sense things. She'd figure us out right away.'

'She would. She's smart.' Hungrily, I

studied him. The piece of ground we were standing on together was pretty small. It was strange to us and would look incomprehensible to Caro or anyone else. How long could we stay right where we were, surrounded by minefields? At least we had tonight.

Pushing away all thoughts of the morning, wordlessly we started up the stairs. The phone rang and suddenly I thought that it could be Caro: she might have heard something. I answered.

It was Simon Tyrone, the psychiatrist. 'Hope I'm not disturbing you? It's rather late to call.'

I pulled a face towards Redcliff: you go on up. 'That's all right. I was going to try to contact you in the morning — but I don't have your weekend number. Maybe you're telepathic.'

'That would be a big advantage in my job.' He laughed briefly, then became serious. 'What did you want to speak about?'

'Caro gets back to school in the morning. I'm driving down to see her, early. A close friend of ours . . . has just been killed.' I waited, but he said nothing. 'Caro knows that Charlie was murdered, of course she does. And now Alison . . . So I must tell her.'

'Yes, that would be best,' he answered, after a moment.

'How do I go about it, what would you say?' What could anyone say? I thought in a rush of helpless anger. You're sixteen years old, the world is an evil and unsafe place, your parent, people around you are being murdered and we don't know why. We can't explain this to you at all . . .

'I think you'll know what to say. Just be there, whatever her initial reaction is. Caro and I have an appointment at two tomorrow. Will you be able to come with her?'

'Yes, of course. Well, that's good. Where do we go?'

'Caro knows where I am. She's been here before.' He paused, as if waiting, before saying goodbye.

Slightly puzzled by Simon Tyrone's call, and especially by its timing, I went to find Redcliff. He was sitting on the edge of the bed, looking through a travel book. From the doorway I watched him reading, unconscious of being watched, or so I innocently thought. It was oddly piquant, coming upon him there on Charlie's side of the bed. His body, looked at from a distance for almost the first time, was the most perfect mean machine I had ever seen.

'Coming to bed now?' he asked in a soft, amused way.

I was behind him and had made no sound, cast no shadow. There was no mirror to reflect my presence. I don't know how he knew that I had appeared at the door. For one startled instant, my earlier view of him surfaced, like a warning. He was a sinister thug, always in the wrong place at the wrong time, always with an explanation.

Putting down the book, he turned and smiled. 'OK — the phone? It wasn't Caro.'

'It was her counsellor, the psychiatrist.' I went to him, looked into his face and saw trust, with affection.

Redcliff, in his easy, vulnerable nakedness, held my fully clothed body in his arms. 'That was a bit opportune. Unless you'd rung him?'

It was, as he said, opportune. It was also slightly puzzling. I was distracted from worrying about it because Redcliff, with a fine air of purpose, was beginning to unfasten my clothes. 'Or — unless he saw the news. Did what we don't think anyone could do, and put two and two together.' The news report flashed into my mind again, and I shut my eyes tightly. 'Unless he's telepathic.' I pulled Redcliff against me, crushed his hands on to my bare skin. 'Don't let me think, don't let me see.'

'I'm telepathic. I know exactly what you want.'

* * *

That insistent sound . . . Ringing, in the darkness. A voice. Something terrible, something wrong.

Drenched in sweat, out of my depth, I swam up into consciousness, into cool night air. Against something hard, the bed or wall. A light went on. It was Redcliff's hand, he was there. Redcliff's voice. He had stopped cursing, switched on his mobile. That's all it was.

Suddenly his voice was furious. 'What d'you mean?' I pulled the cover round me, shivering. When he spoke again, it was a different octave. 'What're you saying? . . . I got that. When did it . . . ? *Damn* it! . . . OK, let's get calm — I'm not . . . Listen, I'm sorry. On my way. Tell her I'm coming . . . *Shit!*' Throwing the mobile on to the bed, he reached out abruptly, briefly. 'Lisa's in the hospital.'

He was fumbling around for clothes, and I switched on the other light. He was in a panic, stumbling.

'What happened?' I was finding his jacket,

keys, wallet. 'You're still half asleep. Let me — '

'I've got to go — right away. She has asthma. I wasn't there and she gets these attacks when I'm not around. Why *is* that?'

'Calm down if you're going to drive. Is it in Hereford?'

'I'll be all right once I'm on the road.' He was lucid, quieter. 'Zoe, don't stay here. You could go to Sussex. I'll call you. You've got my mobile number?'

We were down the stairs, kissing quickly on the doorstep. 'Lisa will be all right. You be careful.'

He was gone.

I locked and bolted the front door. I had never seen Redcliff afraid like that before. The way he had screamed at the phone, at his wife. *The guy loves his kids. And just maybe he hates their mother.*

Alison's words. It seemed a lifetime ago.

I wasn't going to spare too many thoughts about that. It was four in the morning, with hours to go before the dawn. I didn't want to set off for Sussex as he had suggested; there wasn't any point. I climbed back into the empty bed, cold, still wearing my dressing gown. Troubled, listening to the silence all around, some time later I must have drifted off to sleep.

Alison and I were walking through Regent's Park. Alive, intangible as people are in dreams, she was younger and looked different. Still I knew she was Alison, and was talking about her business partner. I told her how I had been wrong about him, then she turned to answer. 'A dream machine? No, darling. He's a killing machine.' She smiled, in a wistful way that Alison never did. 'Zoe, darling. You know it all already.'

I woke, full of fear, to the morning light. Quickly I got up and did sensible things like showering and eating breakfast, dressing in warm country clothes. I put on the radio, avoiding news programmes — there was nothing I could do if Caro found out before I got to see her — then finding a nonstop music station. I worried about Redcliff's daughter, imagined him with his family, the kids he loved and the wife whose name I didn't even know. I set off for Sussex.

Through London and out on the clear road, those final words of the dream resurfaced. Alison's words again, as if she had spoken from some other world. Was my subconscious using her voice, trying to draw my attention to something I knew but couldn't quite recall, or recognise?

Zoe, darling, you know it all already.

Grimacing — Dr Tyrone, it's Caro's

mother who needs the psychiatrist now — I found the music station again. The phone rang and I pulled into a layby. 'Redcliff? What's happening?'

He sounded tired, but otherwise OK. 'She's stabilised. She's all right, but they're keeping her in.'

'Thank God she's come through. Are you still at the hospital?'

'Yes. I'm staying here until this evening, if all's well. Did you get straight down to Sussex?'

'I'm on the road now. It didn't seem worth leaving so early.' Briefly my dream came back, with its strangeness, the sense of warning.

'I want to ask you something.' He was hesitating, as if trying to find the right words. 'D'you get HQ swept for covert surveillance? Professionally?'

'Yes. There's someone who does a sweep for us now and then. The boardroom, directors' offices.'

Redcliff's voice was level, relentless. 'And they've never found stuff? You ever think of trying another outfit, Zoe?'

'You think I should?'

'I think that would be a good idea, yes. Will you let me fix to do that, with Quest?'

'OK. Why not?'

'We might find nothing. But I'll fix it, try for tomorrow.' There was a pause. 'You spending today with Caro, then?'

'Yes. I'll be back tonight.'

'I'm missing you.' His voice was soft. 'Catch you later?'

'Yes.' Later, sooner. Whenever.

★ ★ ★

The school minibus came up the drive to Mayhall, and I was waiting for it. One glance at Caro told me she didn't know yet.

'Hey, surprise!' Dropping her luggage on to the ground, she came over and we hugged.

'Nice surprise? You look in good shape. How about lunch at the Dog and Duck, you can tell me all about it?'

I was firing off words too quickly, hoping she wouldn't tune in yet to the way her happy mood was about to be shattered.

I gave her until after lunch, listening to all her news. In terms of belonging to her new gang, the trip had been a wild success. It had possibly been useful to her political studies too, but that concern was less pressing. Caro had an increased enthusiasm not for politics but for street life and European cafés at night, I thought, and said so.

Her smile faded. 'You've come down here for a reason, Mum. What is it?'

This was it. We went out from that cheerful, noisy place and walked through the pub car park. When we got to the car, I told her that something terrible had happened. Alison was dead.

Caro didn't react at all at first. 'I see.' She leaned against the car, her breath puffing out into the frosty air, then stared up at a row of bare elms. 'How did it happen, then?'

I began. 'This is hard to say — '

'Oh, you mean she got herself killed. Right?' Caro's voice, brittle as eggshells, had a scathing, scratching edge to it. I said nothing for a minute. Her hands were in her pockets. The trees still held her full attention. 'The silly cow.'

'Caro — '

'Oh, shut up, Mum!' She turned away, abruptly tugging at the car door. 'She was always on line for it, wasn't she. If you mean she was murdered, that is?' Glancing briefly, tightly into my face, she must have seen the answer there. 'That stupid cow! You know she was always picking up strangers and — '

'It's cold. Let's get in the car.'

She slammed the passenger door on us, violently. 'Fuck her! Why did she do it? I

317

hated Alison, you know that? Of course you know. So fucking insincere, and — '

Just be there, whatever her reaction, Dr Tyrone had said. So I had steeled myself for shocked disbelief or torrents of tears — for the entire rerun that might happen of her terrible emotion when Charlie had died. But this sudden detachment and cold rage of rejection, how to deal with this? It felt jarring, unreal. She was refusing to connect what had happened with her father's death, and refusing to care about Alison.

Just be there. Her counsellor had meant don't try to interfere. It was twenty to two and I drove us to his house. On the way, Caro and I scarcely spoke.

Tyrone's weekend home was not, as she had described it, a ranch, but a modest Sussex farmhouse built with red brick. What had been the yard was now grassed over and there were stables. I parked, glancing across at her. Seeming composed, Caro hopped out of the car at once.

'There's Simon.' She waved. He had appeared at the door, informal in old corduroy trousers and a jumper. 'Hi, Simon.' Caro was sparkling, somewhere between a social hostess and a favourite niece. 'You've met Zoe, haven't you? Mum's here because a friend of hers went and died. Corny, isn't it?

318

Too much of a recent trend! Hey, remember what you promised?'

He smiled at her, watchful. 'Hello, Caro. Mrs Maker, come in.'

We went through a narrow hall, cluttered with a kindling basket, rags and tins of soap for cleaning tack. At the back of the farmhouse, a living room looked out over the garden to a field with woods beyond. A dark-haired woman, friendly but quiet, brought mugs of tea. By then, Caro had curled up in the depths of a comfy old sofa, for all the world as if she had only come for a nap.

'Time for our appointment, Caro,' he reminded, ignoring her quick glare. 'Will you be all right here?' he asked me. 'Magazines, TV — or feel free to wander around outside.'

Caro must have started hoping that somehow she could avoid this particular session. She had reckoned without Dr Tyrone. He insisted, quietly but with all the firmness Caro needed, that they were going to keep to their agreement. When she trailed bleakly after him, I recognised how much I had been letting her down. Since Charlie's death, I had been putty in her hands and I was feeling for her now, too close, too involved to be of any real use. Poor Caro, she had been hoping to hold off the pain of this second bereavement.

Fifty minutes later, they were back. Caro had clearly been crying but she looked better — more alive and more relaxed. She had been promised a bit of riding on one of the two horses kept there. 'It'll start getting dark in an hour, can we go now? Going to come and watch, Zoe?'

The dark-haired woman Gwyneth — who must be Tyrone's wife, I thought — went with Caro to the stables to saddle up. 'It's really muddy after all that rain. Let's find you some wellies,' he suggested to me. 'There are plenty of spares around.' The back lobby was stuffed with boots and coats, bits of tackle and a family's muddle. He fished around, producing one mud-caked wellington. 'This might fit you, if we can find the other . . . What?' he asked, because I couldn't suppress a smile.

'You're not as I imagined a psychiatrist would be.'

'What did you imagine?'

'Well . . . somebody tidy, more in control.'

He pounced, producing the second wellie. 'Chaos and confusion are the twin guardians of truth,' he said firmly, sounding as if it might be a quote.

Putting on coats, we trudged through the cold, grey afternoon to a paddock beyond the stables. Two bay mares — a handsome hunter and a friendly-looking cob — were being led out. Caro, obviously by some prior and canny negotiation, got the hunter.

'She's a good rider. Harmony's taken a liking to her.'

We watched the two riders, side by side, circling the paddock then crossing between the jumps. 'Is Caro going to be all right?'

'In a nutshell? I can't say. What d'you mean by all right?' Flummoxed, I didn't answer. 'Who is *all right*?' he asked rhetorically, considering.

'I mean . . . Will she get by?'

'This close friend who's died? Alison Seely. She was a friend of your husband, as well as Caro and yourself.'

'Yes. Why?'

By now I had stopped expecting any answers from him, to anything I asked. If eels could speak, they would converse like Dr Tyrone — in slippery half-circles. To my great surprise, he gave an answer. 'Because I need to get the picture — Caro's picture. By any chance, was Alison Seely the woman your husband had a close relationship with when Caro was an infant?'

I stared at him, and felt suddenly angry. 'Yes,' I said shortly. 'I'm not sure whether Caro knows or remembers how close they were — I only found out recently.'

'Thank you. That alters the picture, and complicates things for Caro. Of course she knew. We always know. You did.'

Because it was true — on some level, I had known about them — I asked, 'Complicate in what way? She's always had very, very mixed feelings towards Alison. Worshipping. Despising.' Betrayed, I thought. Caro, Charlie and Alison: that triangle.

'Interesting, isn't it?'

'Interesting? That isn't the word I'd use for what's happened.'

He started to say something in answer, but my mobile rang. 'Excuse me.' I grabbed the phone quickly. It was Redcliff and I turned away to talk, as if that could bring him closer. I was devouring his hunger.

'Where are you?'

'Still in Sussex. And you?'

'I miss you.' He was low-voiced, urgent.

'Yes. I miss you too.' I could hear his breathing.

'What're you wearing?'

I grinned. 'A heavy coat. Old wellingtons.'

'Where the hell are you?'

'Standing in the middle of a cold, muddy field. Crazy? I'll be leaving in an hour. How soon can you get back?'

'Don't know yet.' There was a loudspeaker system in the background. He was still at the hospital. 'Shall I come to your place?'

'I'll be there. Wherever. Redcliff — '

'*Damn*. Look, got to go.' His voice dipped. 'Can't talk now, I'll catch you later.'

Like someone reminded of their addiction, I felt him then all through my body. The muddy field, rooks cawing, the horses trotting out of the paddock. Dazed, I was only half aware of it all.

'Caro and Gwyneth are going for a hack around the woods before it gets dark.' It was Simon Tyrone, quizzical. 'Are you freezing? So am I. How about a quick walk . . . Or shall we go back in?'

I shrugged, not caring which, and he took that to mean I wanted to walk. He set off with an energetic enthusiasm that belied those scholarly features. We were following Caro and Gwyneth up a cart track of deep, ridged mud. Their clear voices, with the churning of the horses' hoofs, soon dwindled ahead of us. A mile or so later, they sped off and vanished into the distance.

'Do you know,' asked Simon Tyrone, 'just how angry you are with your husband?'

Aware of his look, I shrugged again. Agreeing cheerfully, because I had Redcliff, had my revenge. 'Yes. I'm all over the place.'

'That too. Of course you are.' He paused at a stile. 'Let's cut down across the field, back home. There's too much of an icy wind up here. Two of your closest relationships, then? I'm guessing.'

Hunched against the wind, we started down towards the house. 'And Caro, what about her?'

'This hasn't quite hit her, I think, not yet. I'm not pushing her and I'd like you not to. Let her shut down. People can only take so much at any one time. Until today, we were dealing with Charlie's death . . . Working on grief is very painful. It takes time.'

'Right. I will let her.' I stopped, so that he had to. 'Now you tell me something. About Alison Seely's death. You were obviously not the least surprised when I told you what had happened. You knew all about her, and the murder. That's why you rang me last night.'

'That's true,' he agreed, after a moment.

So you are working with the police, I thought. You are profiling this case for them. You are somebody who has their facts about the killer.

I decided at once not to let him know that I had guessed. Simon Tyrone had knowledge of the facts, with details that Redcliff and I might well need.

'You had watched yesterday's news,' I said.

He didn't answer.

20

Caro returned with Gwyneth, seeming as if nothing had ever been wrong. 'We had a fantastic time! We jumped the stream twice, and went all through the woods.'

They had come back in the dark. The horses' hoofs rang out in the lane beyond the farmhouse, then we heard them in the yard. The two mares tossed their heads, bridles jangling, as the riders dismounted. 'Harmony's a dream,' Caro said.

The hunter snickered softly in greeting as Simon approached. Gwyneth took the horses' reins. 'She needed a good ride. Caro's a fine horsewoman — they took to each other.'

'I can see Harmony was in good hands. She's not always easy. Well done, Caro.'

Enlivened by the ride, she glowed at Simon's praise. It was kind of him and his wife to show such interest. It went beyond what anyone would expect. That would make it easier to get what I wanted: to check with him again about Caro's progress and at the same time find out anything possible about the CID's facts.

Caro was reluctant to leave. As if she

blamed me for something, she was growing cool and distant. Gwyneth was already busy in the kitchen, starting to prepare their evening meal, when I chivvied Caro out to the car. Her counsellor came to see her off, reminded her of their next meeting. He stepped back from the car and saw me waiting there. 'I liked our icy walk. Have you recovered?'

'It was quite enjoyable. Dr Tyrone, thank you so much for all your time, and care.'

'It's a pleasure. Caro is a special young woman.' He looked questioning. 'What?'

'May I call you about her?'

He considered. 'Why don't we meet in London? I'll tell you what's happening with Caro.'

He had made it so easy. Rather too avidly I agreed, before setting off back to the school with Caro. 'Was it OK, the session?'

She turned away from my glance, stared out at the dark countryside as it passed by. 'Just let me get on with it.'

'I only want you to be happy,' I told her, with a pang. 'That is quite something, Dr Tyrone letting you loose on his best mare. Don't you think?' We were back at Mayhall, winding up the long lane to the courtyard between the houses. I pulled up there and she pecked me on the cheek.

'Thanks for the lift, Mum.'

'Take care of yourself. Let's talk in a day or two.' I watched her walk slowly across to her house and up the steps. She looked very young, and so alone.

She will be all right, she's seeing the right person, I told myself on the drive back to London: he will make sure she comes through this.

There had been no word from Redcliff. At eight, back at Cedar Court, I rang his mobile. Sounding distracted, as if he had just been interrupted, he asked, 'Where are you?'

'Just got home. And you?'

'The hospital. How was Caro standing up to things?'

I described her ride with Gwyneth. 'It's almost as if she's found a second family there. They couldn't be sweeter towards her. She's still very shaken up, though. It's hit her hard, I think.'

'Poor lass. You're really all she's got. Are you OK?'

'Yes, but ... Why're you still at the hospital? What's happening?'

'Problems about getting back to town tonight. Zoe, sorry. I thought it would be possible.'

I swallowed the disappointment. 'She needs you. Yes?'

'They both do — Lisa and Danny. He's only two and all this has been disturbing. It's best if I'm here for them both in the morning.'

'When d'you think you will get back?'

'Tomorrow — I have to. Quest is in turmoil, everything. I hold the strings to most of it.'

I tried to imagine what it would be like at Quest now. Alison had controlled everything, Redcliff had joined her only last year. 'I'll miss you tonight,' I said softly. The words could not have been more of an understatement. I needed him, a lot.

His voice was full of feeling. 'Me too. We'll get together tomorrow. I'll even try and get to HQ in the afternoon, see to that sweep. Will you be OK tonight?'

We were spinning things out, wanting to stay connected. I told him about Dr Tyrone, how he sometimes worked for the police — and the notion that he might be their profiler on this case. 'He sort of raised the possibility, was more or less sounding me out about it, right from the beginning. I don't see how else he could've known about Alison, or her connection to Charlie and me, when he called last night.'

Redcliff's voice grew keen. 'If he is . . . Hell, Zoe. He will know all kinds of stuff!'

'Exactly. We're going to meet again soon. I'll find out whatever I can.'

'He'll have the information. As Charlie's widow, you can ask. If he's any sense of decency — '

'But Tyrone never answers questions directly. And I'll have to be careful — these things are strictly confidential.'

'Yeah, sure you will.' There was silence between us. We were talking again about the events that had thrown us together. All I wanted tonight was Redcliff, his physical presence. We finished talking and I put down the phone.

There was no escaping then. The house closed in, emptily. My mind filled with Alison and I thought of the terror she must have suffered. It was not bearable even to think of the pain. My mind skipped on. Prentiss had said that her car was found in the garage. Some time that afternoon, she must have returned to her house, and probably the killer was already with her, holding her at the end of a gun. She must have been forced to enter her house and to take him in with her. She would have kept doing what she was told to do — still hoping to avoid death somehow.

Alison must have been so much on her guard already. If it had happened like that, how had she been overpowered? Was she simply caught, or was the murderer someone she knew and had no reason to suspect?

Late that night, with a bottle of Jack Daniels dulling my thoughts, I crawled into bed and prayed for unconsciousness. But the way she had been, that final glimpse of Alison, could not be erased. The image echoed, it haunted.

It was like having words on the tip of your tongue and almost there to be said: somewhere I had another memory — a vital, connecting link to what was happening — and it was hovering right on the edge of recall.

★ ★ ★

Before the weekend, Madison and I had been due to discuss our marketing plans. Events had overtaken if not flattened us and the meeting was scheduled for Monday afternoon. I was in the office before nine that morning, together with a kingsize hangover. By soon after eleven, the MD and I were in urgent conference.

Alison's death was terrible *déjà vu*,

repeating Charlie's loss, even if it did appear less personal to MakerSeceuro. Whatever facts the police might choose to withhold temporarily to protect the methods of their investigation, to the outside world this was still the second murder of a customer. No matter that Alison's security system had been irrelevant when she was killed. That had made little difference to the reporting before, about Gill Tarpont.

Part of me was too saddened and sickened to care any more, but part of me was still fighting. Madison recognised that, he latched on to it.

'Charlie wouldn't want to take the ship down with him. People are afraid they'll be murdered in their own homes. Our name's got connected up with that fear, Zoe. And the scare stories? They'll escalate, because that's what happens.'

'How can we check it, prevent it from starting this time? The rumours. The leaks.' A small voice was saying inside: so long as the killer is still at large, the problem for MakerSeceuro is not going to go away.

'The new PR consultant can help us to issue a statement immediately. Then decide what else is needed. There's the bank, our customers. The media. Whatever we put out . . . DCI Prentiss is on his way here. You've already been interviewed about Alison Seely? They said you found her.' I nodded, and Madison grimaced. He went on, 'Prentiss wants to talk to Den and Stuart, as well as me, about what's been happening here at the company.'

'Shall I join you?'

'You won't be allowed to — they want separate interviews, apparently. Fishing for connections, aren't they? And Quest are doing a sweep here, at one. We've been with the same company for years for anti-surveillance checks.'

'This is an extra precaution. Madison, you do agree that it's necessary?'

Impatiently he nodded. 'We've been wide open. Of course it's a good precaution.'

'I want a word with Prentiss while he's here.'

'I suspect he'll be wanting a word, too. Zoe, you look . . . '

'Terrible?' I smiled grimly. 'Let's just get through today.'

We concentrated on damage limitation until Madison was called away. An hour or so later, Prentiss and Shaw showed up in my office. Since our interview at the end of that dreadful night, the DCI had become human again. I wouldn't want his job, I thought. We shook hands and he asked how things were.

'OK. Have you finished talking to people here?'

Paul Prentiss nodded. 'Madison Black said you had something for us, Zoe.'

'Only a thought, I'm afraid. You found Alison's car in her garage. So had she driven home?'

'At some point that day, she or someone else had returned her car.'

'So she could've been taken prisoner, escorted home. Or she returned for some reason — then the killer came to the door? I mean that it's quite possible he was someone she knew. And that she didn't suspect, until too late.'

'We're getting forensic results on the car. At this stage it looks as if Alison drove herself home — but somebody could've been with her. He may've been someone she knew, that's one hypothesis we're looking at.'

I sat back at my desk. 'There's one other thing. In our press statement, we need to repeat that neither Gill Tarpont nor Alison had any security system in use when the killer entered the building. He was not an intruder, he was allowed in. You do agree?'

'I've approved the statement.' Prentiss looked embarrassed. I bit back a retort about their earlier handling of this. 'I understand your position, believe me. What hasn't been released to the public has been kept back for important reasons. Up to now.'

I didn't answer and he didn't elaborate.

Ned Shaw said, 'We are going to get him, Mrs Maker. There are new leads and developments every day. Anything else that occurs, or especially anything that you remember — just give us a bell.'

'Right. I'm sure you're doing everything possible.'

They stood up to leave. Prentiss was searching for words. 'This pattern that's emerging. It's put you right in the centre of these killings.'

The pattern had not escaped my attention. No wonder Prentiss was sounding careful. I agreed, almost calmly. 'Whoever he is, he's close to home.'

'So long as you appreciate the fact. We're relying on you being vigilant, extremely careful — d'you understand? Take no risks. None at all. Any cause for concern, or any more thoughts, come straight to us.'

As the detectives left, two anti-surveillance experts arrived. There was no Redcliff and no word from him since last night. Had he even made it back to London? The operatives would sweep our executive offices, beginning with the boardroom.

Leaving HQ for a couple of hours, I

returned there to be confronted by the MD.

* * *

I had never seen Madison more angry, nor so triumphant. 'We've nailed the rats, we've raked in all their hardware and it's quite a haul! I'm surprised the newspapers weren't printing the colour of our underwear.'

The devices, micro-sized, had been ripped out of light fittings, mirrors, pictures and telephones. There were bugs and covert cameras with pinhole lenses. Somehow they had been expertly installed, invisibly concealed in Madison's office, mine and three of the directors' — Den, Stuart and Keith. The key functionings of the business — finance, technical, national customers — had been wide open. I felt sickened, and unsurprised. In the aftermath of Charlie's death we should have questioned our own security arrangements. We had not, and our secrets had been transmitted on a regular basis. The only hard information we lacked now was the identity of our enemy.

We went into my office. Somebody had been listening to every word that was spoken in here. They were unlikely to be among our immediate staff, but Madison was closing the door in a cautious way. 'This feels like wartime,' I said. 'Careless talk . . . '

I went to my desk. He was still too furious even to sit down. 'You didn't mention the boardroom.'

'They found nothing in there. About the only place.'

'Isn't that odd? The most useful place to any spy. Why is that, d'you think?'

'Maybe the bastards who did this couldn't get access there. Perhaps it was trickier. I don't know.'

'But how did they get access to our offices? Whoever installed those . . . Do we begin suspecting our staff?'

'You tell me, Zoe. Do we need to install covert cameras in our own HQ, to spy on our own people? I'd rather not live to see the day.' Madison shook his head angrily, sat down at last. 'This could've been done by any casual labour. Cleaning, or maintenance. Temps. Someone doing an installation in the building. The caretaker? No . . . Somebody coming in, it must've been. Surely.'

We were silent. I thought of that could of suspicion lying over everyone, perhaps, until the culprit had been caught. 'Yes, surely. When you think about how easy that could be . . . But we've had the place checked before. Charlie had begun to . . . So why didn't our regular anti-surveillance people find the things? When did they last do a check?'

'Three months ago — that was not an ongoing contract.' Madison groaned, hitting himself. 'I'd only assumed it was.'

'Madison, these have not been normal times. We made a mistake. It's that recent then — since we became aware of the leaks.'

'Our plans, the forecasts. I can't believe the damage that's been done, the sabotage. They've known exactly when and where, how to strike. Now we'll get them.'

'Quest needs to do a full report and that must go straight to the police. Get on to Patricia Abel, make sure she sees it.'

Madison said flatly, 'We know who's behind this.'

'It could be any rival, surely. Anyone who's stood to benefit. OK, Livesey or . . . You don't think . . . ?'

'I'm not sure this is Bill Thwaites's style. Unless I never knew him, perhaps. But Zoe, my money is on A-Zander.'

'Why? We don't have any kind of proof.'

'There's one way to get proof. We just do the same to them.'

'We might find out we were bugging the wrong outfit.' But if Madison felt so sure — and that added on to my own instincts — then why was I hesitating? I stared out of the window at the streams of traffic emerging, disappearing through the overcast afternoon. Red taillights and white headlamps, like trails of blood constituents and flowing almost endlessly.

Turning back, I saw the expression of pure revenge on Madison's face. 'This is war.'

'Yes, it is. How would we get into A-Zander's London offices?'

He came to the window, looked out at the streams of blood below. 'We'll find a way. We could start by asking Jay Redcliff.'

★ ★ ★

Since last night, Redcliff had been out of touch, and now Quest revealed he hadn't been in today. I assumed he was still at the hospital. Had some new crisis overtaken him? It was too complicated, talking when he was surrounded by his family, so I decided to wait for his call.

He rang soon after six; he was about to set off for London. There had been no relapse, Lisa was back at home but he had spent the day with her and Danny. He needed to head straight for Quest and start catching up tonight. He would be working very late.

OK, I thought, hopes plummeting. Was it over between us? 'Well, thanks for arranging the sweep. Did you hear what they found?'

'The report's right here with me. Explains everything, doesn't it? All this high-quality stuff! Who d'you think's responsible?'

'Madison's convinced it must be Ian Darius's company, A-Zander. And he wants to return the compliment.'

'Sounds a good idea. After all, you were pretty convinced before.'

'If someone can just walk into our building, install all those devices and leave them undiscovered . . . It must be possible.'

'We need to meet tomorrow anyway.' He paused but I didn't answer. 'We've something to show you — at Quest. Could you make a meeting, first thing?'

'I'm needed at HQ, so not before eleven.'

'Eleven, then. Zoe . . . '

I swallowed my pride. 'You couldn't come by this evening, on your way?'

He was silent again for a minute. 'It would be tricky to do that.'

I let the silence go on but he didn't explain. 'Well then, tomorrow.'

'I do miss you.'

'Yes.'

'Hell, Zoe. You've gone cool on me?'

'Isn't it the other way round?'

'Listen, we've both got too much to handle.'

'You get back to town, Redcliff. And sort things out.'

We left it like that. I could feel that he wanted to meet tonight, that it wasn't just me. I would let him think about it.

When I called Caro, she had gone to see a film but her house-father said she seemed fine. I gave him a message that I would ring her tomorrow. I tried Simon Tyrone and spoke to Gwyneth. He would be in London from tomorrow night.

By eight that evening, I had convinced myself that Redcliff would come by. He would be unable to resist a chance of our meeting. That was why, when someone buzzed from the road, I let them through, then hurried to the door without checking who it was. Heart pounding, I threw the front door open.

It wasn't Redcliff.

Peter Doyle's big body was hunched against the rain, his hands thrust into pockets against the cold. From the drive Caro's boyfriend, or ex, looked up expectantly.

21

'Peter. What's wrong?'

'I need to talk . . . to you, Zoe.'

'Whatever is it? You're all wet. Come in.'

Leaving his raincoat to dry in the hall, we went through to the kitchen. There I put the kettle on, feeling cross because he wasn't Redcliff. Peter sat forlornly at the table. His fringe, lank from the rain, fell over his glasses and dripped on to his face. Resisting a temptation to mop him up, I thrust the kitchen towel into his hands as he looked up suddenly, alert. 'I couldn't stop thinking. I've been walking and walking.'

'Thinking about what? You can tell me.'

'I can, can't I? She didn't want to see me — Caro. All weekend. You didn't have anything to do with that, did you, Zoe?'

'Peter, Caro wasn't even in London. You know she had that trip to Strasbourg? Then something terrible happened. She had some very bad news about a friend.'

I was waiting for him to ask, what news? He didn't. 'Then she should be needing me.' There was more than a trace of petulance in his voice. 'Why doesn't she want to see me?'

'Listen, Peter. We had an agreement, remember? OK, it's hard — I know you're very fond of her, but Caro's life is at school in Sussex. And . . . ' I spread my hands, wondering if it would be best to tell him to forget her.

'You mean she's suddenly too busy to see me. You mean something's gone completely wrong.'

Why didn't I feel sorry for Peter? Maybe it was the demanding, dissatisfied note that was creeping into his voice as if he had some kind of rights over Caro. I answered sharply, 'You know she's too young to get involved. We talked it through. And this is a bad time, after losing her father.'

Peter looked down at the mug in front of him. It seemed a long time before he spoke again. 'Doesn't it worry you, Zoe? Being alone in the house with me? After all, you don't know me very well.' He caught my surprised look and drank some coffee, which was much too hot. 'Do you find — compensations, or d'you miss him — your husband?'

'Of course I miss him. How can you ask?' Suddenly Peter seemed very young, less mature than I had thought at our first meeting. His questions were coming across like some weird provocation, when they were only gauche. He was disappointed about Caro and I was impatient at his presence. 'I still grieve for Charlie most of the time.'

'Don't you ever feel you'd want to die for him, though?'

'That's a very strange question. Sometimes there are thoughts about suicide, but those pass. It all passes, truly it does.' I leaned across the table towards him, trying to re-establish sympathy or understanding between us. 'This may be hard to believe, but — if it is over, with Caro — a few months from now and it won't hurt any more. Your life will have moved on.'

He laughed. 'Is that a fact? You do crease me up sometimes.'

The buzzer sounded, distracting us both from a conversation which seemed to have gone suddenly, inexplicably wrong. This time it had to be him and I stood up quickly with a rush of relief. Peter didn't move but seemed quite frozen in his chair.

'Excuse me a moment.' I hurried out.

Seconds later, Redcliff was pushing in from that wild, wet night and grasping my hand. Then we were in the hall, holding each other tightly. 'Hey,' he said. We had moved apart a bit. 'How're things? Just had to call by.'

So he wasn't planning to stay around tonight. I felt a desire to make it very difficult for him to leave. We kissed, both breathless, before I stood back. 'Things are just fine now. Come through for a minute.'

'But I can't stay,' he began to explain, warning. I led him towards the kitchen.

'I want you to meet someone.' Then opening the door, I saw that the kitchen was empty. 'Peter. Where are you?'

'Talking to imaginary people, Zoe?' Redcliff laughed. 'There's a word for that.'

'I had a visitor, he seems to've disappeared.' I tried the back door but it was still locked from the inside.

'Peter Pan — and he flew away? Who was he?'

'He can't have vanished into thin air.' I glanced distractedly at Redcliff's broad grin. 'You think I made this up. Do you? To get you into the place, or what?'

'And then what?' We were kissing again, more urgently, our hands seeking out each other's bodies through our clothes, inside his heavy coat, the thin shirt I wore. 'Damn it,' he breathed. 'And I have to go. Can't stay . . . because — '

I stopped his words with my mouth. He pushed me up against the wall, his hand searching under my skirt, up my thigh. We were lost for minutes.

The front door banged shut.

We had closed it, coming in. I froze in Redcliff's arms.

'What was that?' His voice sounded muffled, distant.

'My invention, our Peter Pan?' I looked at Redcliff, at the naked desire in his eyes. Straightening my clothes, I turned away. 'Unless . . . It can't have been somebody coming in? We should check.'

Redcliff's attention flew away, tangibly towards security. He went out to the hall and I followed. Peter Doyle's mac had gone and there was no one in the house. He must have fled, first via the downstairs cloakroom or utility room, then out through the hall once we were in the kitchen. He must have felt embarrassed — as I did now, wondering how much he could have heard, or seen. 'That was Caro's ex. He came for a shoulder to cry on.' Peter's questions about Charlie — and about compensations — stuck uneasily in my mind.

'Not too hot on saying goodbyes,' Redcliff remarked. He seemed in a hurry to go now. 'Hey, Zoe. I never meant to come in. Got young Danny asleep in the car outside.'

I recoiled, from surprise. 'You brought

your little boy with you? Left him alone in the car?'

'Chrissakes, he's not alone! Would I do that?' He paused, getting a grip. 'Theresa's with him. My sister-in-law.'

'You'd better go then.'

'Hell, I just came by to . . . You wanted me to.'

'That's fine. But you'd better go, Redcliff.'

We stared at each other, it seemed from a great distance, then he stepped back. 'They'll be staying at my place. It was the only way I could get back to work straightaway. Zoe, it's important you do get to the meeting tomorrow. At eleven, at Quest. What Alison was working on, her case data? We've been recovering that — and it's only turned the whole damn show upside down.'

He wouldn't say any more.

★ ★ ★

It was what we were really about, the most important thing. So I tried to put Redcliff out of my mind and somehow to banish him, for now. He was a man with a complicated family life. There could be no escape from his situation.

There was no escaping either from a sense of the darkness gathering about each of us. The dark destroys relatedness, it soon separates. We are born connected but we die alone — and now death was all around. I didn't want to visit Quest at all, didn't want to feel the loss of Alison any more by going there. Yet it had to be done.

Something else had to be done next morning, before I left for that case conference. An idea had been taking shape for a way we might trap Ian Darius. It would mean meeting him alone, and if possible, at his home. On his own ground, I might be able to beat Ian at his own game. It seemed clear that if bugs were planted at his office, they were too likely to be discovered. A-Zander, if they were the guilty party, would be careful about their own regular anti-surveillance.

This morning, like magic, Ian was Mr Available.

'I was going to call *you*,' his voice purred, caressing. 'I heard the terrible news about Alison Seely. It's — so shocking. I'm so sorry, because I know she was a friend of yours.'

'She was a friend of yours too. Wasn't she?' He didn't answer, so I went on: 'It's such a shock to anyone who knew her. Alison could not have been a more alive person.'

'These are frightening times. Zoe, what can I do? We were going to meet, remember? Are you going to let me show off a little and take you flying? Leave your troubles far behind. Do come!'

I shuddered involuntarily, and was glad that he couldn't see. The image of leaving the earth — to become airborne and fragile, in a tiny plane — seeing the ground in a shrinking perspective far below . . . That filled me with so much horror, it took a minute to be able to speak. Then my voice came out breathless, almost faint. 'Maybe sometime . . . But we were thinking of having dinner, weren't we? A chance for you to tell me all about it, perhaps.'

'Excellent. At the weekend? And this time we won't be talking business. Is that agreed?'

It was easily agreed. We didn't need to talk business, because he had been right all along. Everything between Ian and myself was personal, just as he had always implied. The deaths of Charlie and now Alison, the threats to MakerSeceuro. Without understanding Ian's connection to all of this, I felt now that our relationship was and always would be somehow deeply personal.

★ ★ ★

The difference at Quest was subtle, full of reminders. There was that similar air of

349

shock in the background, of people operating on automatic pilot as they had throughout MakerSeceuro HQ after Charlie died.

Gwen came to reception and explained she couldn't be present, too many staff were off sick. She took me through to the meeting. It was being held not in the conference room, nor in Alison's prestige office, but in a narrow, almost windowless cupboard of a room lined with banks of shelving, computers and technical equipment.

This was where Michael Ash worked, it seemed. Redcliff and Michael were there, already deep in conference. Both looked in need of a shave, as well as a good night's sleep, as if they had tumbled out of a red-eye after delays. The small space felt airless. It stank from old cigarette smoke and stale sweat. 'Strong coffee,' Gwen said as she left.

I yanked open the tiny window and two tired faces looked up, registering surprise at the sudden flow of fresh air. Moving a heap of files to the floor, I sat down. They were working at Alison's computer, which didn't seem to make much sense. 'OK. What's happening, what've you got? I thought you said all the data had been erased from that?'

'It was,' Redcliff said. 'Either by Alison,

or the person who killed her, while he was in her house.'

'Then how . . . ?' Baffled, I looked at the busy screen. Michael was scrolling through bits of files. 'Is that her work?'

'Yes. Whoever deleted the files probably didn't know they could be retrieved from the computer's memory.'

'I don't understand.'

Redcliff said, 'When you ask a computer to erase files, the only thing it actually erases are the access links. The text is still on the hard disk, but no longer recallable — not by normal means. The file remains, still existing in fragments, until its spaces are filled over with new entries. And no one had entered anything new to cover Alison's data.'

'Then how did you recall it?'

'By using a new program,' Michael said, 'to show exactly what is actually there on the disk. The material comes out very fragmented, because that's the way computers work, using whatever spaces are to hand. They add their own signposting to make any document appear to be a continuous text.'

Gwen brought coffee, then went off again.

'How fragmented?' Looking at their intent faces, riveted towards the text on the screen, I sensed their excitement. 'Is it decipherable, what she was working on?'

Redcliff swivelled round towards me. 'We can give you the gist of what we've discovered so far.' His voice had become sober. He hesitated as if wondering where to begin. 'It seems that Alison was working on links with another case. Maybe you remember it? Some years back. There was a serial killer, his name was Eric Sutter.'

The name jarred, touching some nearly forgotten memory. I frowned, trying to force a better recall. 'Sutter. Wasn't he the Essex murderer? He — killed several women. He was caught.'

Redcliff nodded. 'Sutter seems to've been Alison's last case for the CID before she quit.'

'When she was a DS? I didn't know she'd been involved in that. She never talked about it, or even mentioned Sutter's name ... He was horrendous. That case was truly a nightmare, wasn't it.' As I spoke, Sarah Quirke's words were echoing inside my head. *Whoever murdered Gill Tarpont was a real sicko — a psychopath.* Fighting a wave of revulsion, I saw Alison's body. Crucified, eviscerated ... 'Just how connected are these?'

Redcliff's voice was flat, toneless. 'He killed four women. Those murders were sexually motivated. The victims were raped and knifed, dismembered, then buried in his garden. That was his undoing — because a neighbour got suspicious.'

'Yes. I remember now.' The case had been given a high profile in the national press, the trial's revelations were everyday news for weeks. Struggling with a marriage in difficulties, coping alone with a young child, I'd noticed those headlines but avoided learning any details.

'Here's a link we would've discovered — except for Alison deciding to take on that little job herself,' Redcliff said. 'Sutter's victims were drifters, homeless young women who'd run away to London. He killed them at his house in Essex, and there was some conjecture as to how they got lured there. Suspicion fell on his wife, Irene — that she might've procured them for him. That she at least knew what was going on, and kept quiet. But there was no evidence found against Irene, before she committed suicide.'

'And guess where?'

'On the A1 . . . Suicide Bridge?'

'When Irene jumped, she died instantly.' Michael looked up. 'Her body was full of the drug temazepam. She'd taken an overdose — orally, just before leaping. I guess it was to make things easier.'

There was a silence in that cramped cubicle of a room.

'Is he still in prison?' I asked.

'He's dead too,' Redcliff said.

I got up and stretched, trying to release an unbearable tension. This was too weird. Where was it taking us? 'Alison knew this much, but said nothing to anyone?'

'We were all kept in the dark. Until we've reassembled and collated everything she was doing, we can't be too sure — but it does look as if all this information was intended to be kept from us. And from you.'

'That doesn't make sense. You mean, the investigation Alison was doing for me? That really was a complete sham? It was some kind of cover, to keep me off her back. Or off Prentiss's back. And what about him? Was she keeping the CID in the dark about anything she learned?'

'We don't know. Possibly not. That should become clearer too.'

'But they must know anyway. Prentiss and his team will have made all these connections ages ago. Since Gill Tarpont even? Certainly since Charlie died . . . '

Redcliff nodded. 'They'll have made the connections, and gagged the press.'

'Was Sarah Quirke sacked because of this?'

Unexpectedly, his face broke up into a broad smile. For that moment, the tension in the room dispersed. 'I think Sarah herself decided she wasn't right for the Criminal Investigation Department. I believe she wasn't pushed, but jumped.' Then, abruptly, his grin faded. 'We don't understand why Charlie was killed. Why him? And — it's too elaborately staged, this copycat.'

'There's a taunting element,' Michael agreed. 'There are things which don't add up, and other facts which do add up almost too well.'

'What are the links?' I asked. 'Charlie's faked suicide, to resemble Irene's real one. But — why?'

'Yes, why kill Charlie? And two women, murdered in a similar way to the pattern which Sutter had established. But with differences in the manner of it — the killer's signature. Also, big differences in the choice of victim.'

I sat down again. We all stared at a jumble of text pieces on the computer's screen. 'Alison must've been instrumental in catching and convicting Eric Sutter. And that suggests a grudge, a revenge killer. But Gill Tarpont had nothing to do with — '

'Michael cut in: 'You're wrong there. Another fact we've just learned, courtesy of the ghost in the computer. The way she and Alison first met, and the reason Gill got murdered, for sure. Gill Tarpont, all those years ago, lived in that same small town in Essex. She was Eric and Irene Sutter's next-door neighbour in those days. It was Gill's observation and evidence which led to Sutter being caught.'

Again we were silent. Gill's courage, in coming forward and in testifying, had brought about her death. Alison's professionalism and dedication had doomed her. This had been her last case after several years in the CID. How it must have sickened and terrified her, unnerving her for such grim work. So much so that she felt she had no choice but to resign, leaving a promising career to make a fresh start.

Until the past, in some still unfathomable way, had caught up with her.

My words came out as almost a whisper. 'I dragged Alison back into all this. Pressured her into finding out, and learning too much.'

'That can't be true, Zoe. Because — '

'She would've left things up to the police when Charlie died if I hadn't — '

Redcliff interrupted, harsh: 'She never left it up to anyone! She couldn't. Because of the dates we're getting — dates when she was working on these facts, putting it together and linking the Sutters to Tarpont, to Charlie.'

Michael explained, 'Alison started working on this the day after Tarpont was murdered. She was that quick off the mark.'

'It was before Charlie died, and long before you asked for her help,' Redcliff underlined. 'So forget the guilt.' He grasped my hand. I don't think either of us cared what Michael Ash made of it. I thought about Redcliff's sense of guilt, believing he had failed to protect his partner. Guilt had flung us together; it held us like flies trapped on glue, wings flailing. I longed to hold Redcliff, to comfort us both.

'We'll know more,' Michael said, 'when I've had time to work through all this properly, to put it more together. Everything's an impression so far.'

'How soon can you do that?' I withdrew my hand from Redcliff's.

'How long is a piece of string? Or in this case, thousands of pieces of string.'

'Maybe we could meet again, the three of us, in a day or two. Let's say Thursday,' Redcliff suggested. 'We should have more by then.'

'OK . . . ' I was remembering the last conversation with Alison. 'She'd been sworn to secrecy on the link to Sutter. Alison died because she was about to tell me what she knew — we'd arranged to meet that evening, and the killer must've been aware of it. She was under surveillance.'

There was a brief silence. Redcliff said, 'Once Tarpont was killed, Alison must've suspected she was in danger. She kept going right ahead.'

'Who is he? Who's doing this?' Michael muttered. He stared exhaustedly at the screen, as if that might suddenly produce an identity, a name.

I decided that tonight would be a good time to call Simon Tyrone, after his session with Caro. 'I'll be talking to a psychiatrist who's probably working on this. If he is profiling, I'll try to get something useful.'

Michael scrolled on, his eyes glazed. 'By Thursday would be good.'

Why didn't I mention the evening with Ian Darius, arranged for next weekend? To achieve the purpose of that meeting, I was going to need Quest's help. Something was holding me back for now, and it had to do with Redcliff's drawn and weary face, with bad timing. We had set it up as a dinner date and now I was trying to find a cooler way of describing it, a way that didn't suggest me as bait and which might get Redcliff's backing.

Michael interrupted my thoughts. 'So it looks this way. For some reason, the police haven't wanted the public to know enough about the new cases to connect them. Right?'

'If they did throw it open, release the details now — since Alison . . . Then everyone would remember Sutter, fast.' Redcliff leaned back in his chair, away from the monitor. 'Why doesn't Prentiss want him remembered?'

'It could be a strategic decision,' I suggested. 'Look how much this killer wants attention — he's a dedicated copycat. All the details have been so carefully planned. And, except for Charlie . . . he's been picking off each of the people who was involved. It's revenge of a truly fanatical kind.'

22

There is one thing you do right and that is be afraid. Remember the rosy crucifixion. Blood colours everything, bonds and sticks. Bone fragments. Me and the I.

Be afraid because your Time Will come. It Will.

'The Cow is mad at you, I will learn you,' He said, and He did. The carcasses were hanging, caves of flesh, and the cold was intense. I was in training, learning to be strong. Rank cold, stench of blood, the dark. Dead skin brushing my skin. Entrails under a groping hand. No one to hear. No one to see . . . Screaming. Shameful tears. Wet my pants. Released . . . Grabbed.

THE EYE. 'Eat of My Flesh, and Be Mine.' It's hard to chew, the viscous ink of it is bitter and I AM SO SICK.

But I survive. I can survive and get away with anything, anything! Acting for Him, disproving the official line. Meat is tender, love's tough. The Giant and All Powerful, He did the lessons daily all to tenderise, to toughen and to make Me strong. My path led onward, Blood to Blood and dust to dust.

After the Guilty had done their worst . . .

Then, don't we all need a sense of Purpose? Enlightenment! Be afraid and tremble for Man has a short Time to live. You never forget the first Time they say and it's True. Every detail stays fresh as a daisy in the Memory. The first is special. My Initiation he was, the Breakthrough, and it served Me well. I have this Really Useful Souvenir — the passport to another life.

* * *

They have summoned Me — they rate Me now, I am getting Respect. My request or demand for a meeting with Mr Big has met with favour since they're hoping I Will bring True Business Nirvana. They like the news of the laptop computer, although naturally I have avoided being too specific. They are lapping up this promise of milk and honey money, in the form of Maker's posthumous Portable Brain and plans, ideas. Mr Mastermind Big is Mine for the meeting. I AM assured.

I hold an Ace and Aces have their price. I have a Hold over My 'masters', it would appear, and also I know what they've been up to. Now I have to consider one other question — how much of a Hold do they have over Me? If they knew more, theirs would be the Hold of a boa constrictor.

But are they Truly Innocent? It's just like the game of Happy Families! I Will See.

It is very annoying. My favourite Subjects getting wise. Now I may only listen to boardroom shenanigans and how very boring those meetings are.

Still, My Target is not too wise. I have CC.

* * *

Up to the Loft with NRG. I like to be close. I prefer not to be Seen.

She is there. She knows by now, they all know and Will soon be closing in. I cannot stand to be thought erroneous or ignorant — by the cow, the wholly holy she-DEVIL, the widow — for all I reveal is Purposeful and is a part of My Mission! The cow is always telephoning men, I have pictures of her taped with the man there in unspeakable FILTH! Maker scarcely Cold, his disgusting WHORE was writhing and moaning, Filthy with wicked Abominations in the bed of Sin — may Fire now Consume THE DAMNED! This WHORE in fornicating Carnal Knowledge! It is personal with the widow, it is worthy *of My True Attentions.*

But she is off the scent now.

Soon the net will close right in on Me but also on her. Practising caution, at all Times I will carry My Gun. Time once more to move the boat and I think, towards My Hide.

A full circle, life, isn't it?

23

'Caro won't talk to me now. If I ask about anything, she gets furious. Is she doing OK?'

'She is — or will be. I think so, yes.' Simon Tyrone placed both hands on the table between us, as if to soothe. They were flexible hands, with long, narrow fingers, looking out of place on formica. When he had suggested the zoo for lunch, I'd laughed. It turned out not to be a joke. Seriously, he wanted to visit the zoo.

We were sitting in the restaurant with plates of cod, chips and peas, surrounded by families. The sounds were like an animal house and our window displayed *Homo sapiens* at play. Simon's choice was beginning to seem less odd but my sense of dislocation was making it hard to focus. He was watching my expression. 'You're Mum, so you get the fallout,' he said. 'She's hurting, so you get the rage about that. There could be some rough times ahead.'

'If she just gets through this time . . . ' Realising I had mirrored his gesture, hands on the table, I picked up my fork again.

'Good fish and chips?'

'Not bad. She must need to talk. I hope she is, to you?'

He nodded. 'Yes, she is. I think we're doing fine.'

'You're important to her, Caro likes you a lot. We never thought . . . '

'I'm very important to her at the moment, yes. For a while. Youth has a resilience to it, remember. Don't drive yourself into the ground too much, Zoe.'

'We always talked. I thought that we were close.'

A small boy zoomed past our table, pretending to be something that flew and shrieked. As Simon Tyrone looked after the boy, his mouth curved into a smile. 'I miss my sons. Although we do manage to see each other quite often. They're grown up, and both live in America now.'

'Oh. I'm sorry.' The sudden personal revelation was surprising, and so was the fact that he had adult children. He looked too young.

'There are degrees of loss,' he said. 'Bereavement is third degree, I always think. But we don't really ever lose our children.'

I gave up the attempt to eat. It wasn't the food, it was everything else. 'They aren't ours, they don't belong to us.'

'They're the sons and daughters of life's longing for itself.' Simon smiled again, and it made him attractive. 'When did you read Khalil Gibran?'

'As a teenager. And you?'

'Every now and then. You're not very hungry, and I've finished. Shall we have a look around?'

We went out into the chill afternoon, past a cage full of birds of prey. Overhead the vultures perched, obscenely bunched, observing from invisible eyes. Small rodents lay still and bloodied on the ground. They nudged me back to a sense of purpose. 'Maybe you can explain,' I began, 'whether there are natural-born killers? Or is it nurture and circumstance?'

'A debate that's alive and well.'

'But changing. We were all getting into liberal theories, then along came the geneticists. Super-liberal, in a way. Has Caro told you about her ex-boyfriend?'

'Yes, she has.'

'He works in genetic research, apparently. He has no doubts — we're entirely programmed, from before birth, in every way.'

Simon gave me a swift glance. 'Rather an extreme view. You don't have to be a behaviourist to allow for the influence of learning experiences. Surely it's obvious that we're a mixture — what we're born with, what we learn to be.'

We were walking between monkey cages, barred windows and mesh, concrete and tile with patches of garden. 'Charlie and I used to bring Caro here, years ago, until she decided it was cruel. She loved watching the gibbons.' A pair of gibbons were at play, swinging on Tarzan ropes, dominating every corner of their space, staring down at us, at the pushchairs and darting children as they began their strange, whooping screech. Was it play, or fiercely territorial?

'It's probably cruel that we keep ourselves in cities,' he said. 'But perhaps we've built them so we can survive in the future, as a species? I don't know. It's interesting to see the different ways we respond to containment.'

I blurted it out then. 'I need to understand, Simon. About the person who killed Charlie, and Alison. I need to.'

Another swift glance. 'I'm sure that's true.'

The spider monkeys were gliding along, handsome in their glossy, feathery fur, like tentacled shadows. They seemed gracefully oblivious to their surroundings, the tourists and flash cameras. 'You must've read about the case, and gained an understanding. What kind of person killed my husband? I need to know.'

He didn't answer for so long that I thought the question, like other questions in the past, was going to be ignored. We came to a cage full of chimpanzees. They were preoccupied with fruit and with intricate social relationships. It was easy to see which was dominant or submissive, the group comedian, the outcast or the carer. It all looked obvious and so human, I began to laugh.

Maybe it was the laugh that convinced Simon Tyrone that my questions were only personal and not really significant. He began to speak, quietly: 'From the few details that were released just recently . . . '

'Yes?'

'OK. I think he's young, probably early twenties. He has a deep desire to be known or recognised — and an equally deep-seated fear of being seen.'

Alison's eye. Suddenly I was nauseated, remembering. Simon went on: 'I suggest he has a real, phobic horror of being looked at. If so, the phobic reactions may be a trigger, although the attacks are carefully prepared and the motives appear complex.'

'Is this why the police aren't giving him the exposure he craves? I mean, if they've reached the same conclusion as you,' I added quickly, and ploughed on. 'And why does he inject his victims with a drug every time? Is that to make it easier to control them?'

'Not necessarily. Injecting the drug is part of the ritualistic aspect. That could be a key to his thinking, and his motives . . . Don't let's join the crowd around that sad gorilla. Come on.'

The sad gorilla, clasping its knees in a foetal position, was rocking slowly from side to side. I pursued Simon's wandering attention. 'A detective working on the case used the term psychopath.'

'As people do. Our killer has delusions, and that would be atypical of psychopathy.' He sounded impatient.

'What kind of delusions?'

Abruptly he said, 'You found Alison Seely's body. Saw the position of it. What did that remind you of?'

Alison was there before me. Crucified, eviscerated. I grasped at cage bars, lurching forward. 'She was crucified,' I whispered. 'You mean he has religious delusions.'

'Zoe, why are you asking these things?'

'Because I can't live with this. With not understanding.' It was both the truth and misleading. A lie. What I wanted was more information to tell Redcliff and his team, later this afternoon. 'The way Alison . . . It's been reminding me of . . . D'you remember — twelve, fourteen years ago? A serial killer called Eric Sutter — remember that case? Don't you think it's rather similar?'

At once he closed down. Simon Tyrone had guessed what I was about: either that, or he was suddenly bored by the subject. A fine rain was beginning to blur the chill grey afternoon and the zoo was clearing of visitors. 'Let's go this way,' he suggested, pointing.

It seemed a strange occupation for two adults, but there was an hour before the meeting at Quest. 'All right.'

I followed him down a ramp and he waited to allow me to catch up. 'You're not being entirely frank with me, Zoe Maker. And I've said too much. Now, let's go somewhere warm.'

'I just want to understand.'

'That subject is closed now. Come on.'

We went into the small mammals house, then down into the zoo's moonlight world. It was warm and semi-dark. Lemurs with enormous eyes were peering shyly out from refuges, while the bushbabies seemed to fly between branches. Marmosets and mongooses, rat-kangaroos and rats: they were busy and purposeful, scurrying through the simulated night. Caro had loved these tiny creatures. 'I expect you used to come here with your sons?'

'We did, now and then. We were all living in Sussex most of the time.'

'Your sons went to Mayhall?'

'Yes. Were you raised in London?' As I nodded, he fired off questions. 'Siblings? Parents still alive?'

'No. I did have one sister. She settled in Sydney.'

'You still have a sister, then. Do you ever meet? Don't you keep in touch?'

'Not now, since our parents died. Because . . . we have totally separate lives, on opposite sides of the world. We don't need each other.'

'Really?' he said, after a moment. 'Since Charlie's death, haven't you wanted to contact her? Does she know, even?'

I shrugged. 'Astra and I didn't get along. There's no reason for her to know what happened. I've no idea whether she married or has children by now either. You think that's odd? It's not so unusual.'

'It is unusual.' His eyes were warm, sympathetic. 'Unless there's a very good reason.'

There was the best reason in the world why Astra and I would never contact each other again — but why would I want to tell him about it? These things had been settled years ago. She had not been on my mind very much until recently. 'I'm quite sure Astra never even thinks about me. Why on earth would she?'

'So you lost touch when you married,' he said.

'It was a bit later.'

'What else did you lose touch with?' he asked, friendly. 'In marrying a man who was quite a bit older — and much immersed in technology and in business, I think? Caro was born when you were very young. Something else was lost, or given up, wasn't it?'

'I don't know what you mean. You're very inquisitive.'

'Like you — about the killer. That was all for a reason, which I happen to be uncomfortable about.'

'Sorry.'

'This obsession . . . with digging into danger. That is what you're doing?' I didn't answer, and he went on: 'Think carefully about it — about what you're doing, please. Think about Caro as well.'

'I do, all the time.'

Simon Tyrone turned to glance at his watch. 'It's almost four.'

'Then I'm late and must go. It's been . . . '

'What?'

'You want to know, really? Coming here with you — has been one of the most eccentric afternoons I've ever spent.'

He laughed. 'And how are you feeling now?'

'Better,' I admitted. 'Thanks.'

★ ★ ★

That feeling better did not last very long.

Refusing a lift from Simon, I decided to run the short distance round Regent's Park to Quest Associates HQ. Dusk was beginning to fall with a bitter cold, and the rain came sheeting down, bouncing off the tarmac. Streetlamps and headlights had turned the city into instant, vibrant night. I arrived ten minutes late, very wet but exhilarated.

With sudden reluctance, I followed Michael from reception to the meeting. It was like returning to some dark tunnel, a closed world of fear and pain. *Think about Caro*, Simon had said: *Think carefully about what you're doing, please.*

Redcliff's office looked like a burglary scene, with a jumble of papers obscuring every surface. He sat perched casually on his desk. Kneeling on the floor, marooned in the muddle, Gwen was sorting out photos and press cuttings. As Michael began clearing a couple of chairs, I felt a wave of anger. Without Alison and her bright presence, the agency that she'd built up did not look destined for continuing health. Redcliff was a slob. He lacked any finesse. He would alienate Quest's corporate clients and lead her business into decline. In the end, did it matter? Alison was dead. She was not here to speak out.

'You're damn late. We nearly started without you.' Redcliff was wired with irritation.

'What a dump!' I burst out. 'You think Alison would ever have allowed things to go downhill like this? Her clients — what would they think? You might look after the business for her!'

Jumping off the desk, Redcliff took a step across the room, then stopped. His voice grew an edge of cool reasonableness, making my outburst more ridiculous. 'We're reorganising. The physical reorganisation — including the filing space — has to be completed today.' He paused. 'Maybe we could start this meeting now?'

Humbled and annoyed, I found a chair. 'Of course, you're reorganising.'

'Let's call our new operative.' He nodded at Gwen, who went to the connecting door and knocked.

Sarah Quirke came through, smiling. Quest's new operative?

This was a happier Sarah, loping across the minefield of Redcliff's office with a spurt of liberated energy. 'Hi, Zoe.' She laughed, turning back to him, her curly red hair wilder than before. 'You hadn't told her? This is only my second day working here.'

'Sarah, it's really good to see you. Whose brainwave was this?' She would make a brilliant private investigator, especially with the CID training. Sarah knew the rules but possessed her own, infamous independence. The next moment I thought: Sarah knows every detail about the police investigation.

'It was Redcliff's idea.'

'She kind of approached me for it,' he said, appraisingly.

'You're ideal,' I told her. 'Alison would approve.'

She looked swiftly at Redcliff. He sat down again, on the desk. 'Sarah can't participate in this. But she'll sit in on our meeting. She's not able to divulge police information about the investigation into these murders. However, we do have a lot of new information ourselves, from our work — Michael's work — with Alison's computer data.' A small smile was playing round his usually set features while he said all this. That smile, the careful words and tone were explanation enough.

We got down to it.

'Let's begin with DCI Brian Mayhew.' Redcliff was consulting some notes. 'In thinking that there'd been three victims now, we were wrong. There've been at least four. Mayhew was the senior investigating officer on the Sutter case — Alison's superior. Eighteen months ago, he was found hanged in Epping Forest. At the time, there was no clear link with the Sutter murders.'

'He'd been injected with the drug,' Michael said. 'This was the first time it was used that we know of. Also, the killer took an eye, the right eye, from the body.'

'The killer has a thing about eyes,' I put in quickly, then hesitated. Although Sarah had left the force, it might be better for Simon Tyrone if his name was not mentioned. 'It's as if he's afraid of being looked at, of being seen.'

There was a little pause in the room. Sarah was looking pleased, and as innocent as she knew how. Gwen spoke first. 'So he removes the possibility — while taking a trophy? As if that could remove the fear.'

'Interesting notion.' Redcliff, sounding unconvinced, went on: 'Sutter had been found hanged in his prison cell soon after conviction — a suicide. But when DCI Mayhew was murdered, that could've been connected to any number of hard cases that he'd dealt with. Drug rings, professional crime . . . It only connected to Sutter the moment Gill Tarpont's body was seen.'

'But Alison must've felt under threat when she heard Mayhew had been killed,' I said. 'She must've felt or suspected something, that early.'

'And what about the other trademarks? What he's been doing — to the women?' Michael asked, in a quiet voice. 'There's a lot of inside knowledge about Sutter in the details. But it is different, what he's done. Like the way the victims were placed, and bound.'

'They were crucified,' I said. 'Weren't they? He might have religious delusions, do you think?'

'Could be true,' Sarah said encouragingly, as if she had never heard this before.

'In the Sutter case,' Redcliff pointed out, 'the wrists were found to've been tied together. Another big difference is the sexual element. Or rather, in the present cases, apparently an absence of it. Eric Sutter was a sexual sadistic murderer. This killer has never raped. He used a knife — genital mutilation. The victims were gutted . . . rather like animal carcasses. But there was no attempt at dismemberment, and no disposal. This one makes no attempt to conceal his crimes.'

The room had grown heavy, silent until Michael spoke again. 'Eric Sutter was a butcher, quite literally. He kept a shop in a town in Essex.'

'It's as if he's still alive,' I said, my voice grown small. 'And stalking . . . every person who worked at bringing him to justice.'

Sarah cleared her throat. 'Sutter's dead. So is his wife. And we don't believe in ghosts.'

I looked round at them all. 'What about Charlie? Where does he fit into all this? Charlie had nothing to do with the Sutter case. Do we still think it was the same killer?'

'There was one small connection,' Redcliff said. 'Show Zoe the picture.'

Gwen picked up the papers she had been sorting, shuffled through, then passed them across. Everything was from the Sutter case: pictures and press reports about the bodies being found, police statements and the news of Irene Sutter's suicide jump, long reports of the trial itself . . . And there it was, neatly filed in place by Gwen. One photograph, among a whole lot of others taken by a tabloid. One photo of Charlie, leaving the court with Alison. My heart gave a lurch.

'They were friends,' I said. 'It must've been difficult for her, giving police evidence in that horrific murder trial. Charlie must've been supporting her by going along there with her.'

He appeared so young in the photo. He looked carefree: the camera does lie. Charlie was being a friend, as well as her lover, and Alison would have felt glad of his presence. Had he really died because of this, because of one photograph?

I looked up at Redcliff. 'Was this picture printed in a newspaper?' He shook his head. 'Then who could've seen it?'

'Anybody,' Sarah answered for him. 'Anyone at all who looked in the newspaper archives. That doesn't narrow the field, I'm afraid.'

'The killer must've thought he was more involved. Perhaps even that he was another witness for the prosecution,' Michael said. 'Relying on this photo — it suggests a degree of ignorance about the trial itself.'

'Then he could be almost anyone. But *why*? Is Eric Sutter a kind of role model to some stray weirdo out there? Is that all it is? Or did he have a relative, a brother or cousin maybe?'

'Neither,' Michael said, with a glance at Sarah. 'He was an only child of an only child. Sutter himself was sterile, unable to father any children.'

'He seems to've had great significance for somebody. You sure there are no blood relatives surviving?'

'There are no blood relatives,' Redcliff confirmed.

★ ★ ★

The meeting broke up soon after six, with no more revelations. I told Redcliff I needed to talk with him and not at the office. Ten minutes later we were out of the Quest building.

We set off on foot. Cars cut through the dark, leaving trails of oily vapour. The wet, blind rush hour was full of British bad temper, with a blend of stoic endurance and sheer bloody-mindedness. Walking was impossible, so we wound up in a seedy café on Parkway, and were lucky to get half a table. The place was pure Tex Mex, with bad cover versions played at volume, eighties menu, rag-rolled walls and plastic cacti. A crowd of kids about Caro's age were draped round the bar, looking wrecked and smoking their heads off.

'We don't have to do this,' he said.

'There's a couple of things I need to say, and to ask. And they can't wait.'

'Can't they wait half an hour? You want your lungs kippered? We could go to your place.'

That did not seem like a good idea. We would be at each other's throats again — either fighting, or tumbling back into some kind of sexual addiction that didn't make any sense. Whatever it was that we'd shared together, it had got to be over. I didn't want to think about Redcliff and me, on a personal level, right now.

'This'll do fine.' I leaned in close, against the noise. 'Listen. When the killer stole Charlie's computer from Alison . . . We don't know who's got it, but we do believe there's a business link. They'll get Charlie's design secrets off the hard disk.'

Redcliff nodded. 'I've spoken to your journo mate, Patricia Abel. The upshot is, she agrees with us. We need to go in and find evidence against A-Zander. Like, by setting up audio surveillance in their HQ.'

'Madison would back you there. But if Darius's company is behind the dirty tricks, just imagine how cautious they'll be acting now. We'd have no chance — '

'Gwen Farthing's an expert on setting up

covert surveillance. She'll go in as a temp, and do her harmless granny.'

'Not for me she won't. For God's sake! They'll do sweeps — anything she did plant would be discovered in five minutes. I've a better idea. Instead of bugging his office, we bug Ian Darius.'

Redcliff scarcely considered this. 'No chance, and anyway — '

'Easy. I'm having dinner with him in a couple of days. I can get access to his home, and I can get close contact with him. All that's needed now is the hardware, and the backup. I'm going to do it.'

24

Redcliff sat back, arms folded. 'The hell you are. That's not an option.'

'He won't suspect anything. Not on a date, and not at home. And if he is behind the dirty tricks, we'll find out fast.'

His voice was full of ridicule. 'I've heard some crazy ideas, but this one beats the lot.'

'Just think about — '

'There's fuck all to think about. We do the counter campaign, Zoe, as I've planned — '

'We haven't got time — '

'I'll use Gwen. There's a frequency they won't easily detect in any sweep. We'll get results.'

I shook my head. 'They're on red alert. It would take too long. I'm seeing him on Friday, and I'll get to the heart of it.'

'It's too big a chance to take. We don't know enough about Darius, or what he's capable of.' Redcliff paused. He looked set, determined to make me drop the idea. 'I can't help you. Not with this.'

'All right,' I agreed. 'We won't talk about it any more. I would've felt easier if you were nearby — if it was you receiving. But I'll hire another company's services. That's no problem. Goodnight.'

Pushing out through the crowded bar, I walked towards the high street. The rain was still falling. The pavements were slightly less full now. I wove between late shoppers and the lurking druggies, and stopped at a corner. Several taxis passed, all taken. When someone grabbed my arm, I wrenched away. It was Redcliff and he looked furious. 'Don't be so bloody stupid!'

'There's nothing for us to talk about. I should never've asked you.'

'You won't get a cab, not for hours. I'm parked five minutes away from here.' We stood looking at each other, jostled by pedestrians. 'Let me run you home, OK?'

I nodded. We set off, arm in arm against the night and the crowds, as if we were in some way together. Reaching his car, we tumbled into its refuge. Redcliff started up, then with an exasperated sound he turned off the ignition again. 'I'm too mad. I can't believe you'd try this!'

'It's the obvious thing to do. I'll be fine. We're only having dinner. I'll go back to his place, for a drink — '

'It's a honeytrap.'

I smiled slightly, in the half-dark. 'But if

you were nearby, picking up any signals, then there'd be no risk.'

Redcliff gave me a really filthy look, then started the engine again. He set off north, towards Finchley, in silence.

'You don't want to do this, and I'm not going to pressure you,' I said after a few minutes. 'Let's drop it. How are things? Your family, your little girl?'

'Lisa's doing good.' He nodded to himself, then glanced across at me again. 'They're all staying with me in town. That's better for the kids right now.'

It's not better for you, I thought, studying him as he drove. Unwillingly I felt a softening, that pull of attraction which had never lessened. What went on in Redcliff's life — or under his skin? I wouldn't ask, didn't want to find out if the on/off marriage was on again. I knew nothing, beyond the misogyny he seemed to carry and the few things Alison had said. The pressures since her murder, and from taking over at Quest, those I could understand. Redcliff was thirty but the last couple of weeks had added years.

We reached my house and went in, without speaking. Being here with him brought everything back: I wanted to stop all this, to stop the clock and have him close again. I poured Jack Daniels into two tumblers and we sat on separate sofas. Then I just waited, not helping at all.

'You'd need a receiver van,' he said finally, defeated. 'For some of those kinds of transmitters, we'd have to park close by. Where does Darius live?'

'In Mount Street.' I tried to sound nonchalant and not to jump up, fling my arms round his neck in gratitude.

'We would be just outside. I'd be in the van, with a couple of others. If there was any sign of trouble, you'd alert us and I'd come in.'

'Yes, of course. The transmitters . . . They'll have to be very simple and quick to install. Invisible. Is there anything that I could plant on him, or among the things he carries around?'

'That's difficult. Unless . . . Does he use a lighter?'

'He doesn't seem to smoke.'

'A pocket calculator?' I shrugged, not knowing. 'You happen to've seen what kind of pen he uses?'

I thought for a moment, remembering: Ian Darius in the Paris restaurant, signing for the bill. 'It's a ballpoint using black ink. A Parker, black with gold, classic. Why?'

'I could get a copy made up,' he said, with satisfaction. 'It'd have a transmitter with a range of one to two hundred metres. You'd have to switch it with his.'

'That might be possible. During the evening sometime.'

'It'll be voice-activated. There's a tiny pinhole microphone. People never notice.'

'And what about the phone?'

'You ever been to his place before?'

I shook my head. 'I've no idea what's there.'

'I can get standard small devices. A telephone socket, looks exactly like an ordinary one — you just swap them over. And what looks like a normal power plug to go in the wall. You'll need to get enough time on your own, in the living room or wherever he keeps a desk and the phone.'

'That shouldn't be a problem. Redcliff, thanks for doing this.'

'If anything goes wrong . . . ' He paused, becoming practical.

'If anything looks like it could go wrong, you press redial on your mobile. You'll have called me in the van just before you go to meet him. And if I do get that signal from you, I'll be there within two minutes.'

'Right. I've got a strong feeling about this. We're going to learn what he's up to.'

'For Chrissakes, don't let Darius know what you're doing.'

'I'll lay on the charm, he won't suspect anything. And the biter will be bitten.' I smiled. Redcliff, watching me in a careful way, did not smile back. Maybe he was wondering just how far I was prepared to go to get the proof we needed. I had been thinking about that too.

'I must be crazy, getting drawn in,' he said suddenly, cold and angry. 'If Prentiss knew, what would he say to this?'

If he breathed a word to Prentiss, then it was all off. I got up quickly and went to sit next to Redcliff. We we so close, not touching. 'You wouldn't . . . ?' He didn't answer. I said, 'You and I, we were always about working together on all of this. We always were . . . I can never forget Charlie.'

'We made a mistake,' he said sharply. 'That's what you mean. Yeah, of course we did.'

'I don't regret it.' We sat looking at each other. Redcliff didn't answer, he wasn't going to agree or disagree about that. He got up and went to fetch his coat. It was still soaking wet. 'Can you get these things to me by Friday?'

'Probably, if I get on to it right away. If it's what you do really want to try?' He was distant and brusque, and I was aching.

I nodded. 'In that case, I'll get on to it tonight.'

'Thanks.'

We went to the front door. Redcliff turned back on the doorstep and touched my cheek. I wished he had not.

'I sort of miss you being around,' I told him. 'God knows why.'

'God knows why.'

'Look . . . Stop imagining — bad stuff. This is going to go well. It'll get us what we need.'

He smiled at last, in a sickly way. 'Turn off the paranoia, you mean?'

'And take it easy.'

I watched him driving away, too fast down that quiet avenue.

★ ★ ★

Paranoia was alive and well, as Simon Tyrone might have phrased things. Perhaps it was from the prospect of danger, or maybe that strange afternoon had started me thinking. With a couple of casual questions, Caro's counsellor had stirred up the distant past. Now that old dust refused to settle again. The next two days were full of introspection, with troubled memories that I'd rather have forgotten.

It was all about trusting, or a lack of trust. In their own ways, neither Alison nor the CID had been honest with me — not about Charlie's death, not about the tangled knot they were really trying to unravel. Perhaps those deceptions had been justified. My own nature, for a long time quashed and mummified by a not-so-good marriage, was beginning to reassert itself. It was a nature born to seek out trouble.

Astra: my long-lost, no-love-lost younger sister. She would have said that I was born to create trouble. Astra said that was why I chose someone like Charlie, with immersion in routine, domesticity and the dulling minutiae of business. Astra believed that was an attempt to avoid any more of my own destructiveness — to try and sidestep it somehow. Maybe that's what lay behind all the guilt now, because Charlie's death was the third, before Alison . . . Because I seemed linked to disaster for other people, for people who were close. Being the albatross, I was trapped in futile attempts to change that role, to change my species.

My sister had sailed away, and sailed so far that she had escaped the orbit of my flight. She had succeeded where others had failed. Alison Seely, sister elect and substitute, had been a lot less lucky. I had a lot of debts to repay.

If anything happened to me, what would become of Caro now?

Calling her on Friday lunchtime, I caught her just before a class. It was our first conversation for several days, since before I'd talked with Simon Tyrone, and I wanted to know when to expect her. 'You are coming home for your study week? Tonight, or tomorrow?'

'It's not awfully convenient, Mum,' she answered in her distant voice. 'Trekking all the way up to London. I've got things to do with my work group.'

'But surely everyone's going home for the week? And half of them live in town.'

'Yeah, but I'd get more done if I'm here. There's things to catch up on, that's all.'

'Caro . . . not for the whole week, surely?'

'Don't know. Look, I can't talk long.'

'I've been looking forward to it. Don't you want to . . . What's wrong?'

'Nothing. Honestly! I'm just busy.'

'You are still seeing Dr Tyrone?'

'Yeh, yeh. Look, gotta go, Mum. I'll call you tomorrow, OK?'

'Please do. Please take care of yourself, all right?'

She rang off, too abruptly. I was left with the uneasy feeling that she wasn't being straight with me, that something could be wrong. This sudden enthusiasm for her studies just didn't ring true. Maybe she was growing closer to people in her year? Some of them had parents living abroad, so they might be staying at Mayhall for the entire week. Perhaps that was it. When Caro called, I would suggest she invite friends home to stay with her.

That afternoon, Redcliff came to my office at HQ. He brought with him two small white electrical fittings and the Parker ballpoint. They all looked utterly ordinary, indistinguishable from the usual thing. I picked up the pen, weighing it in my hand. Suppose I had misremembered, made some mistake about the design? Could we really hope to get away with planting these devices? Perhaps it was a hare-brained scheme, as Redcliff had thought. It was too late to back out now.

'They look so innocent,' I said.

'Any one of them could give us the hard proof we need.'

'If the pen works on a battery, how long does that last?'

'Fifteen hours.'

'We'd be lucky to get anything useful in

that time — especially over a weekend, I'd have thought.'

'The phone and mains transmitters can just keep going, so give them priority. Zoe? You must only go ahead if you're really certain of not being caught.' I nodded agreement. 'There are other ways — remember that. Gwen's ready to go into their HQ, she could do it in a week.'

'I'll remember.'

'When's he picking you up?'

'Seven thirty. I don't know where we're going, he hasn't said.'

'I'll be in the van with a couple of blokes, down Eldon Avenue. We'll follow you, wait outside the restaurant. If you do go on to his place in Mount Street, we'll follow and wait outside again. Remember to dial from your mobile before he collects you tonight, then don't use it again.' Redcliff paused. He was ready to leave. 'How're you feeling?'

'Nervous as hell.'

With an edge of malice he said, 'Why not enjoy the date?'

★ ★ ★

I showered, and dressed with care for the evening, in sheer stockings, high heels and a short black dress. I chose red nail polish, a couple of pieces of jewellery. This was a honeytrap, as Redcliff had said. This was the sleek businesswoman of recent weeks, out for an evening's playtime. She was not me, but it was easy by now, slipping into her pampered skin, her brittle shell. I put on the manner with the clothes, hid the bugging devices in my bag beneath a scarf, then waited.

Arriving ten minutes late, Ian Darius seemed different, almost ill at ease at first. He was subdued, and if I hadn't known him better by now, I might have imagined that he too was nervous. He was well known in the trade for his activities, dating a string of women and this was just another date to him. It was Friday night and maybe he was still preoccupied with business. Needing to be taken back to his place, I set out to cajole him from his mood.

There was no sign of Quest's receiver van as we drove to a small restaurant in Dover Street. By now, Ian was recovering some of his former flirtatious self. We had quickly banned business as a topic and got on to the subject of holidays and how we liked to spend weekends. Ian had never married and had no children. Now he asked about Caro with a warmth that sounded genuine. 'I often think about her, and that evening on

Jersey. She must've been putting on such a brave face.'

'Yes, she was. But you provided a big distraction from her grief. Which was part of the idea, wasn't it?'

'I'm good at doing that,' he agreed with a small, wry smile. 'Providing distraction, as and when required. Some would say I have it down to an art form.'

'That sounds almost . . . '

'Cast as the Fool, but yearning to play centre stage? Not at all. If I'm a passable companion to my friends, then that's enough.'

I found myself touching his hand across the table. 'Is that really enough?'

'I believe the word means an accompaniment. I accompany those I like. Like you, Zoe. You're a puzzle, never what you seem to be. For some reason, I do find myself trusting you. Even respecting most of the decisions you've made. I was a great admirer of Charlie, of everything he built up.'

'I know you were. Charlie sometimes talked about you too. He saw you as belonging naturally in the major league — while secretly seeing himself as almost a beginner still.'

'Really?' He sounded astonished. 'Such delusions. You seem to be coping well. And the weekends, are they still devoted to Caro?'

'Not always. Sometimes she prefers to stay at school.'

'No reason to return — that is, beyond yourself? She doesn't have a boyfriend? I found last weekend — rather slow. Until recently, I was much involved with someone.' He must have seen my surprise as he went on quickly: 'Oh yes. Now, I love to fly, but find myself without a partner.'

How could Ian know the dread he inspired just by the mention of flying? My palms had begun to sweat, it was difficult to breathe. Coward, I told myself. The best way to find out all about Ian . . . You should be jumping at the chance. He was talking about his plane, in the excluding monologue of the enthusiast. It was an original Tiger Moth, such a prize, and he kept it as close as he could, in that small airfield in Hertfordshire. Caged there like a monster, just waiting to pounce, to fly.

I managed to speak at last. 'You go up in the winter months?'

'Sometimes, weather permitting. It would be a thrilling adventure, and somehow I think you love adventures. I'm very experienced, I've been flying this baby for years. Zoe, how about it?'

He must have been misinterpreting my glazed expression, the fixed stare. Perhaps he thought that I couldn't wait to be hundreds of feet up in the sky — with him as pilot. I felt sick, about to faint. I felt as bad as we feel when we've just learned about the loss of someone we love. I licked my dry lips, to speak. 'It sounds very exciting.'

'It's truly magic, I promise. We will go up then. The first mild weekend.'

I dragged my mind back to a problem more urgent than how to get out of a flying trip — how to plant three bugging devices which were hidden in my bag. Had I been wildly overoptimistic, thinking this would be possible? Ian kept his pen in the inside pocket of his jacket, along with his wallet. Suddenly access to that looked too unlikely. And suppose we never went back to his home?

Then it could not have been easier. 'Shall we have coffee?' he asked, as the waiter cleared the dessert plates.

'I've never seen where you live, Ian. Perhaps we could go back and have coffee there?'

He paused for a second, then agreed, sounding unsurprised. He signed for the meal — and that identical Parker ballpoint went straight back into his pocket. Then we drove the short distance to Mount Street. There was still no sign of Quest's receiver van. Perhaps it had lost us already.

Ian lived in a mansion block and, of course, his home had to be the penthouse. It was only five storeys up, but phobia hit the minute we were off the ground; we might as well have been soaring into space. Fear turned my legs into needles, then into rags. I leaned against him for support. He probably misinterpreted that as well. Then we were stopping, coming out into a small foyer. His flat was boldly designer-decorated in jade with black and ivory, and the blinds were mercifully all closed. Ian loosened his tie. He took off his jacket, draping it over a chair in his living room. That was like an open invitation, which could be read two ways. Did he know?

He took my coat, as I looked around. 'What a marvellous room. Who designed it?'

'Not me. Drink?' I nodded. 'It is a good room. It takes up most of the apartment.' As he went to a drinks cupboard, I quickly studied the layout. The living room was L-shaped. The office area, taking up one corner, looked as if he did some business here. As large as many executive rooms, it held a desk, with the phone and other equipment, and extra seating.

He handed me a whisky, with a quizzical smile. 'Make yourself comfortable while I make coffee.'

I had an eerie feeling then that Ian might know exactly what I was going to do, that he might be about to trap me. The only way to find out was to go ahead. I looked after him as he crossed the hall to a kitchen at the end. Taking the pen from my bag, I fumbled to find the one he kept in his jacket. Was the bugging device slightly heavier, or was that my guilty imagination? I couldn't tell, and would have to take the chance. I slid the device into his inside pocket, then accidentally dropped his pen. It rolled under a chair and I scrambled to find it. Then I stepped gingerly to the door to check on Ian.

The reassuring hum of the coffee grinder, sounding like music. He would be busy for a couple of minutes. I looked swiftly around, scanning the electric plugs. By the small office sofa, a table lamp was plugged in close enough to pick up conversations. The plug adaptor that Redcliff had supplied seemed awkward but it went in and looked identical. There was a soft chinking, the sound that china makes. I stood up just in time to make a show of examining a cabinet nearby, as Ian came back in. I indicated the antique carved ivory displayed there. 'Beautiful, isn't it?'

Ian set down the coffee tray. I had done it. Or done two thirds of the job. It would be most important to bug the phone. Then I saw that his quizzical smile was back. Maybe I ought to forget about doing the phone. Except that might prove to be the one small manoeuvre that could catch him out, so I had to try.

We were settled, chatting on the sofa and seeming for all the world like two people relaxing at the end of an evening before going our separate ways, or before going to bed. Ian was describing how he had bought the Tiger Moth, a *fait accompli* involving a Saudi Arabian deal at the end of the eighties. I was praising and preening, keeping up every kind of pretence. Then saying I'd like to freshen up.

'The bathroom's the second door on your left.'

Ian's bedroom was the third on the left. I pushed the door half closed, having located the telephone by the bed. Sixty seconds later, the bugged phone socket was sliding into place.

Easy I thought, straightening up.

Then I saw it.

On the door hung her dressing gown, familiar as if I had last seen her wearing it yesterday. A white kimono with an orchid pattern finely printed on the silk. It was so very Alison.

25

This was her big secret, the one she had refused to name, preferring to be mysterious. He was behind all that secrecy, all those lost nights, her crashing hangovers — and perhaps her growing fears.

Alison's last lover before she died was Ian Darius. After that first shock, there was no surprise. My mind ran in circles.

Was it purely attraction? I would have believed that, for both of them, except there was too much else involved. Had part of it really been about Alison investigating A-Zander — or had Ian been attempting to use her to gain inside information about us? She surely would not have fallen for it. But then she had seemed besotted during that final affair, pretty well out of control.

Ian had been seeing her secretly — and then she was killed. When were they last together, was he behind her death? Was he connected with the murders?

'Whatever are you doing in here?' He had pushed open the bedroom door and switched on the dimmer.

Automatic small laugh, slight pretend

tipsiness. 'I thought it was through this way.'

Of course Ian was not taken in. 'What an interesting way to stray. What should we read into it, I wonder?'

The reality of my situation hit home. The bed, with its corner angled between him and me, was where he and Alison had spent nights together, making love and whispering whatever in their pillow talk. Then he could have killed her. Ian stood between me and the door.

I said, slowly, 'You and I need to talk.'

'Absolutely we do. That's what we're here for. Shall we do our talking in a more normal kind of comfort, a more ordinary setting? Or do you prefer my bedroom?' he said, with some mischief.

I followed him across the hall. The bag over my shoulder held my mobile; it would be easy to make the prearranged signal for help. I remembered that now but felt a reluctance. I could be right on the brink of learning something important.

'I saw her dressing gown,' I said, as we were going back into the living room. 'You were in a relationship with Alison. It was her.'

He was taken aback. There was a slight jarring in his move towards the cafetière, before he grasped hold of its handle. 'D'you

402

prefer black or white?'

'Black, please. No sugar. I wonder why you never mentioned that.'

'Some things are private, to both people.'

If I hadn't known better I would have been lulled by his warmth, by that new tone of voice which suggested a loss, and real sadness. He did sound genuine. 'I want to ask you some things.'

'That goes both ways. There are one or two things I want to ask you.'

'About Alison,' I said, sharply. He waited. From everything I might have said next, I chose the most peripheral, because if he had killed her, this was so inexplicably careless. 'Why did you leave it there on the door? Her dressing gown?'

Before Ian could answer, my mobile rang. We both looked down at the bag on the floor, surprised by this interruption from the outside world. I didn't move and it went on ringing.

'I kept it because I was crazy about her. My gorgeous Alison . . . Surely you understand?' The phone still hadn't stopped. 'Why don't you answer that?'

Reluctantly, I did. It was Redcliff. 'Zoe?' The bugs were operating then. He had probably heard every word we were saying. 'I'm busy,' I told him.

'What we agreed — '

'I don't want to do that.'

Redcliff swore, fervently. 'We're coming in.'

The line went dead. I looked up to see Ian Darius watching me. He had quickly recovered his equilibrium. 'There's a problem at the response centre,' I told him. 'The director's unavailable. It looks as if I'll have to go.'

'That's a shame.' Unmistakably sardonic now.

I said quickly, 'It's you that doesn't understand, Ian. I do want to talk about Alison. I do want to know.'

He stood up, and I did too. We were close, then touching. 'In that case, I promise you'll hear all there is to know. After all, we both cared about Alison so much. But we're both such busy people . . . When we go on our flight together — I'll tell you then. Where else can we remain undisturbed but up in the skies?' He saw me to the door. 'If the weather's all right, why don't we make it Sunday? Yes?'

* * *

I met Redcliff as he was approaching the apartment block. He had brought Michael Ash, so they must have expected trouble in picking me up. I was angry with Redcliff's interference. I hadn't asked for help and hadn't wanted it. And he was furious with me for that — I recognised all the signs. Either he was making a big effort to wait before saying anything, or he was just too angry to speak, as I was.

We walked to the end of Mount Street. The surveillance vehicle, an anonymous grey trade van, was parked just round the corner. Redcliff talked quietly to Michael, then sent him to rejoin Gwen, who was operating in the van. He and I, still bound by uneasy silence, headed towards the underground NCP where he'd left his car. We seemed to be forever fighting, and usually on the inside of his filthy BMW.

'Right,' he said. 'What was all that about Alison?'

'I was just going to find out about her. When you lost your nerve, I suppose, gatecrashing the party.'

'What was it,' he repeated, ominously calm, 'about Alison?'

'Her dressing gown was in Ian's bedroom. When I went in there to bug the phone. I planted them — all three, by the way — if you're still remotely interested.'

'I heard, yes. You're saying that she and Ian Darius — '

'They were having an affair in the weeks before she died. He admits that, says . . . You heard.'

'Then it could've been Darius — when she was being followed. Had her under surveillance. Murdered her . . . for all we know! Those sweet sentiments? Grow up!'

'If you hadn't interfered, I would've found out — '

'You would've been fucking dead.' He looked at me like a stranger. 'We had an agreement. Then you didn't give the signal.'

'It was too good a chance to pass up. You wouldn't — '

'The moment you knew that Alison had been with him, you needed to get out. Agree?'

'Maybe. But you would've stayed!'

'Listen, I'll say this only once. I will never trust your word — or plain common sense — again. I will never help you again.'

I looked at the set of his face, inside the shadows of that car, under the cold striplights of that parking place. There was no point in arguing with his decision. I knew Redcliff well enough. And I knew he wouldn't give up his investigation now into Alison's murder.

'OK.' I nodded. 'That's fair.' If anything came up again, like another chance to move things forward, I would be on my own with it.

Redcliff dropped me off at Finchley, after fixing to meet for another case conference at Quest. Neither of us had mentioned the flying trip with Ian Darius. Perhaps he had missed that part of the conversation, or perhaps he had decided that, crazy as I was, nobody would be quite crazy enough to go. At the time, that was what I thought too. I expected just to get out of it.

★ ★ ★

That night, I was falling through space with no landmarks, nothing to grab hold of. Alison appeared, and she was hanging on to the wing of a plane. I was divided from her, clinging tightly to the opposite wing, when she turned into a mass of darkness. Looking across the metal body, I saw she had become Astra — that was Astra's face, from when we were girls growing up together. The plane stopped flying and was veering in circles, the circles decreasing, smaller and tighter. My arms ached, numb with weakness. My hands were slipping. The plane separated from me and glided away through the night, taking Astra.

Waking up to grey skies and emptiness,

my face was wet with tears. I was falling to bits.

Caro did not come home. Instead, we quarrelled over the phone. Like lots of rows, it began as a discussion. Did she want to bring someone home to stay? The short answer was no. Somehow, in avoiding the two-letter word, she and I got mired in history and tangled up in old feelings. How had we got on to this?

'You left Dad. When you started that business course? You took me away from him, didn't you? Poor Dad was all alone.'

'I don't feel great about it. But we were going through a bad time then. Probably I was too young when we got together. Charlie — '

'You left him, Zoe! And I didn't have any choice. What was I, three at most? And d'you think Dad ever felt that he could rely on having a family after that? Or did I?' she said bitterly, getting to the crunch point. 'I don't really feel that I've had any family. Or if I ever did, then where are they now?' *I'm stuck with just you*, she didn't say. *If only you'd died, instead of my dad. It's him I want . . .*

Guilt made me angry too — guilt and loss, and my own huge sense of being unvalued. 'Nothing could be enough for you! I went back to him, or doesn't that count? We were still a family.'

'But you never *wanted* to go back. I often think you never even wanted to have me!'

'What's going on here really?' There was a pause. 'Is this because of the bad nights?'

'No,' she said, shortly. 'It's not — and they're better anyway. Maybe I'm just getting older and thinking for myself.'

'D'you talk about all this with Simon Tyrone? You are still having sessions, over study week?'

'Yeh, yeh.' The bored tone. 'Look, Zoe, sorry if you're upset. Just don't try to live your life through me now that he's dead. You got rid of him at last. Because I'm not available, I've got other people in my life.'

'Of course you have.' I hesitated, then decided to ask anyway. 'But something's wrong, Caro. There's a lot you want to say. And phones are — they're impossible, really.'

'I'm busy all weekend. We're doing our projects.'

Another silence. 'Well, you can call me any time. You can come back any time,' I said. We left it like that and she rang off quickly as she had before. It's just teenage angst, I told myself, plus bereavement. Things are getting stirred up by the counselling sessions, because Charlie and Alison are dead. It'll pass. I told myself this, then went up to Caro's bedroom and sat there for a while, looking at all the stuff of her childhood years, the things that never seemed to get too much less, no matter how many were taken to Sussex.

Or maybe her childhood was not such an infinite pool of content as I had assumed. She had clearly been insecure. Maybe she had been truly unhappy? 'Or is this about *my* bad nights?' I said aloud, and went to call Simon Tyrone.

Calm and untroubled, he listened until I had finished pouring out my fears. 'Let's meet up, shall we?' I could hear a page of his diary turning. 'Perhaps we could make it for lunch again.'

'Could we possibly make it breakfast?'

He thought for a minute, then suggested a hotel that was more or less equidistant between our homes. I thanked him and put down the phone. It rang.

Redcliff's voice. 'Zoe? Looks like we may've got something on one of the recordings.'

'From Ian Darius . . . What do we have?'

'Best if you could get over here and listen.'

410

Gwen ran a section of the recording. It was almost indecipherable, with Ian Darius's angry voice just recognisable above a muffling interference. On a second hearing, a few words and phrases emerged. *Time to get clear . . . for our security, too sensitive . . . Will he agree?* . . . Another voice, heavily accented but more clearly recorded, was saying he would arrange the meeting, and fix things. The blizzard of interference took over again.

'This is terrible quality. What's the accent, is that South African? Was it a phone call?'

'It's Kruger, his security chief. He arrived at Darius's place — we were watching. They went off to a club, we followed but missed seeing if they met someone there.'

'This was from the little Parker ballpoint?'

'Not surprisingly, it wasn't receiving too well.'

'Anything from the other bugs?'

Redcliff looked at me in a level, careful way. 'They both stopped operating soon after Kruger got to the flat. We think he must've found them. Perhaps he'd even been called over to search for bugs. Darius must know it was you who planted those.'

'Not necessarily.' I felt a lot less confident

411

than I sounded. 'There's nothing he could do about it anyway. He probably did the same to us, at MakerSeceuro HQ. If only this tape was . . . Can't you get someone to make it more audible?'

'We're going to work on it. The part you heard sounds promising, there might be a lot more to that.'

'It seems to suggest something. But we need proof that he's behind the dirty tricks — and to know who else is involved. It might be who they were discussing. D'you think there's some kind of inside spy?' Suppose they were from our own HQ? An employee . . . or even, possibly, a board member? It could be someone in a position of trust, and close.

Redcliff said, 'Sarah thinks we should get this tape straight to the police — or a copy of it. I think so too.'

'Why the police? You'd have to explain how we obtained it.'

'There are ways around that,' Gwen intervened, 'and I agree with them. The CID are getting very close now. This recording might prove A-Zander's part in what's been going on at MakerSeceuro. And it could be relevant to the CID's murder investigation.'

'You mean . . . because he was with Alison? You think Ian Darius . . . that he knows something?'

'We should arrange for Prentiss to receive a copy of this recording,' Gwen repeated after a moment's pause. She turned to Redcliff. 'You must tell Zoe now. About Patricia Abel's story — and the Sutter boy.'

What Sutter boy? I looked from Gwen to Redcliff.

'Right,' he said. 'Let's go to my office.'

We walked down the corridor, the three of us, from the technical room. Redcliff was giving himself time, perhaps. It seemed a lot had been happening and he was clearly in two minds about telling me any of it. I was being very careful now, demanding nothing from him. Gwen and I sat down in his office which had been magically cleared and looked almost like a working space. Redcliff stood, back to the window, choosing his words.

'The police are working with that journalist, the one you and Alison brought into this. Patricia Abel.'

'She was going to do an exposé on the dirty tricks,' I reminded them because he had stopped.

'Patricia was hoping to get to the murder story ahead of any other reporters,' Redcliff went on. 'I've been keeping in close touch with Paul Prentiss on this. It seems the CID have decided to use Abel to give the

413

murderer a bit of choice publicity at last. The publicity he seems to want so badly.'

'This way,' Gwen put in, 'it can be carefully monitored, and timed.'

'She's going to do a sort of profile piece about a man the police are looking for. A man they want to interview in connection with five murders.'

'In other words, they're planning to blow the whole thing out of the water.'

'In a controlled explosion,' Redcliff agreed. 'There are big risks — but there are also big risks to keeping the information quiet. As we've seen. Anyone who's been connected with Sutter's case, or with the present investigation, is a probable target. That includes all of us, Sarah and Michael, the police team.'

'Who is it?' I asked. 'There's a prime suspect . . . someone they want to interview.' I was trying to sound calm, to seem detached and as if I couldn't care less whether Redcliff did tell me or not.

What Sutter boy?

Infuriatingly, he was taking his time. 'The piece Patricia's writing . . . It's not an easy decision to do that. It could escalate events. Or change their direction. The result's unpredictable.'

'But most importantly, it could lead to

public help,' Gwen said. 'You see, the person they're profiling — Eric Sutter's ghost, if you like — is presumed dead.'

'Are you saying that he did have a child? A boy?'

Redcliff sat down on his desk. 'No. Like we said, Eric Sutter was sterile and unable to have any kids. The boy was his wife's. No one knows who the father was. Irene gave birth to Donald — to Don Sutter, as he became known later — a few months before she met Eric. The baby was farmed out before and during her marriage with him.'

They had a prime suspect, and that changed everything. Don Sutter . . . 'So what d'you mean, he's presumed dead?'

Redcliff was still going at his own pace, measuring the information as if it was a drip feed. 'The young Don was passed from pillar to post, it seems. Temporary foster homes. The occasional short, troubled stay with his mother and stepfather. Until he was ten and Eric Sutter was arrested, accused of the murders of several young women.'

Gwen said, 'Imagine — having him for a stepfather all those years.'

'Soon as the murders were discovered, Don was fostered out again. Raised in Scotland by a couple, they belonged to a religious sect. Redemption through punishment, all that kind of idea . . . The child was probably branded as a real original sinner — virtually the devil, by that reckoning. Imagine.'

It all added up. 'Anyone feel like telling me now? Why Don Sutter is presumed to be dead?'

'He *is* dead,' Redcliff stated, 'Officially. Has been for four years now.'

'It was a boating accident, on a loch,' Gwen added. 'He was with another twenty-year-old and there was a squall, the sailing dinghy capsized. Out in the middle of those deep waters, there was no way either of them could possibly have survived. He was dead.'

'It can't be him then. Can it?' I said.

'The only thing is, Donald Sutter's body never was found.'

26

This is it, My Sanctuary. This, My Path. Here the Trunk is broken, split by the Head, the weight of the head as it hangs down, all the way down right to the Earth. They call it the weeping tree and say: Its leaves are big tears, or little boats.

There are no leaves. I AM in Winter.

We all Need somewhere to play. This was it, the Hide — I came here a lot, unseen. Here I did secret daily Survival Training Practice. Survive the cold, survive the water's falling at the weir, survive them the grown-ups and all authority — hey presto, the Man is sorted from the Boy!

I AM the Elite and Chosen One. In Force I WILL SURVIVE.

Survive anything, anything, ME! Survive Water that cleanses Man, of Life! Eternal Fire that Purifies!

The stove is lit, the boat is berthed in secrecy, in waiting for the Final Time. Ice on the River's stagnant pools, in its corners, on Thin Ice. Water deaths are freely releasing — a mercy, out from the mirage of Life's Travails, of human sin. It is a better place

417

To Be. They did Lie to Me. To each one comes the Just deserving, IN ACTION is the Proof. ME I AM the bearer of tidings of . . . That Uttered Preciousness of Blood.

I am beyond their messenger boys — because they know something of what I have got, Me. I have gone too Far Ahead, they can't keep up. Must now be full of querying, about My sudden shyness, Me the Innocent, performing pet and Evading the masters. I DO BELIEVE he is almost a madman nearly a psychopath — My Mr Big's right hand of Darkness baring the light fantastic, dance of dealing and dying, High Noon! They must Believe that I Will keep to it, keep that appointment soon with 'Mr Henchman and Mr Big' or I am done for — they would get to Me too fast, My Mission abort . . .

MOTHERS: I CAN TELL YOU A THING OR TWO!

The Widow Meddler, Maker has it taped, got it all taped up — she so fondly believes that. The DIRTY STINKING WHORE! I SEE the Net, the Noose, nearer to Me but nearer to her . . . <u>Be a Man and fight, Mother's Boy, Boys don't cry</u> . . . The watcher Watched, the taper done for, nearer to her I like to be, to be or not to be up close, up close to do it.

Keep it close now the gun as everything

changes then. *The base, the job. All is changing as I Have Prophesied.*

I will unveil the secrets and Initiate. No Time to lose for the High Priestess. Be prepared, be readied for My Final Act.

Now.

27

Simon Tyrone was unfolding a pink linen napkin to reveal a nest of croissants. He held out the basket across the breakfast table. 'Families,' he said, with a sympathetic emphasis. 'The family cauldron — stir it at your peril. But if you don't ever stir it, then what happens? It can all too easily settle into a form of poison.'

The croissants were warm and buttery, comforting. There was jam — strawberry, apricot — and a silver pot of coffee. I poured from it now. This was an improvement on the zoo.

'You're stirring things, Simon. Our family, or what remains of it. Caro's still rejecting me.'

'And it hurts. Try to see it as a process, leading to a better understanding.'

'We fight every time we talk.' He nodded. 'She seems to hate me. But she does talk about her father.'

'That's very good, isn't it?'

'She seems to have only good memories now of Charlie. He's become . . . idealised. She so longs to have him back, her dad.

As if — wanting to get rid of me . . . '
I hesitated, then struggled on. 'To destroy
me, almost . . . as if that could bring back
her father. Like making a deal . . . '

'The kind of deal a small child might
dream up — as preferable. But not actually
want.' I shook my head, not knowing. 'Have
some breakfast,' he suggested. 'You look
exhausted.'

'Caro's nightmares are better, I expect
she's told you? She sees you as . . . You're
in Charlie's place, for her, aren't you?'

'I don't think it's quite like that. It's
temporary. Eat, Zoe.'

I pulled a croissant apart, took a spoonful
of jam. 'Does she see Gwyneth as her
mother, d'you think?'

Simon looked startled. 'I can't imagine
why — ' Stopping abruptly, he gave me a
questioning look. 'My two sons — they're
really my stepsons. I married a widow;
Donna had been left with them aged only
ten and twelve. You've probably worked it
out, she was older than me.' He looked
down at his coffee cup. 'I don't consider
the marriage has failed — does that sound
odd? Arrogant, perhaps? We raised the two
boys before moving apart. They taught me
so much. I love them all. Rob and Tommy
are flesh and blood to me.'

Why was he recounting this? His openness made me feel ashamed that I'd been so secretive before. 'I assumed you and Gwyneth . . . '

'Did you think we were a couple?' He smiled suddenly. 'She's my housekeeper. Gwyneth would be very amused — or appalled, I should think.'

He went on smiling to himself at the idea. I watched him. I felt not just liking — there was a gentle attraction between us. I hadn't allowed myself to feel it before. Then I remembered Astra. We were flesh and blood but divided, held suspended in two halves by that silver body, that blade or knife of an aeroplane. The unconscious is not very subtle. It's pretty literal sometimes. An urge was forming inside me, and growing. It was a need to give something back to Simon, and to let him know me. Perhaps it was the simple urge to confess.

The way we had talked before had left Astra indelibly on my mind. 'Simon. Now Caro sleeps well, I'm the one full of bad dreams. About . . . Like — the murderer, perhaps. I have a phobia.'

'Do you, indeed. It's certainly not the same. What is it?'

'Being in high places, any high place . . . And I can't fly.'

'You can't fly?' He waited, then asked lightly, 'What's it feel like?'

'Total panic. Nausea. Fainting — my breathing goes crazy for one thing. There's a label, isn't there? Acrophobia. And fear of flying? What would Freud say . . . I'm sure he said it about everything.'

'And sometimes a cigar is just a cigar. Yes, the fear of high places, that's acrophobia. D'you know how it started?'

'Yes,' I began slowly, carefully. 'And I did give up something — a lot, really — but never from choice. When I was a girl, there was a family friend of my mother who was a pilot — he flew small planes. I adored flying, couldn't wait to learn. My father stopped me going up any more — he was afraid for my safety. The pilot, Rory, he was a big risk-taker. That was the thrill, the excitement.'

'It does sound exciting,' Simon agreed. I didn't go on, suddenly I didn't want to tell him. 'What else happened?'

'Later . . . I was twenty, married, newly pregnant but that hadn't been confirmed. My father couldn't tell me what to do now. I went up with Rory again in a little Cessna with twin controls — he was flying it, of course. It was the most thrilling experience of my life, I do still remember that.' And I stopped again, feeling sick.

'It wasn't an accident? You wouldn't be here today if — '

'It was an accident. I was defying Charlie, marriage — and Dad. Of course I took over the controls from Rory, but only for a minute. Dad would've guessed . . . He and my mother, they were on their way to meet us. They were driving along the A3 outside Guildford, near the airfield. We were going to meet at Astra's home. Dad knew I was in that little plane, buzzing stupidly low. He crashed the car.'

'And what happened?'

I am the devil, I thought. I dragged the words out. 'The car went under a lorry. Mum's neck was broken, she went into a coma. It was forty-six days later when she died.'

'And your father?'

'Dad's heart was broken. He lived another five and a half months. Astra and I, we sorted things out — their home, their things. But we never spoke of how it had happened, we couldn't possibly have done. She took a job in Sydney — we never contacted each other again. And Caro was born.'

We didn't speak for quite a while. I thought I knew what he was thinking. He said at last, 'Zoe. Every year, a lot of people are killed on the roads.'

'Oh, please! One self-indulgent, destructive twenty-year-old, behaving without a thought for anybody. Take her out of the picture, then the others would all still be alive. Still be a family.'

'He was driving, and his wife died. Have you invented yourself as a cause?'

'I was doing what he'd forbidden me to do, and — '

'When you were a girl,' he interrupted. 'But by then you were an adult. A wife yourself. Soon to become a mother.'

I laughed aloud at that. 'Some adult, yes? Allowing Rory to buzz the woods near the road. I'd even known they were driving to Astra's place. I knew they were nearby.'

'If you imagine you caused their deaths, then you *want* that guilt. You've been carrying it around for a decade and a half, so it's nice and familiar. Who am I to argue with that?'

'I don't want it. Phobias are — crippling. You asked where it came from. It's pretty cut and dried, you can't alter that.'

'Why would I wish to alter anything?' Simon asked. 'You're not my client. We're having breakfast together. Can we have a fresh pot of coffee?' he asked the waiter.

'My daughter's your client. Did she ever

tell you this bit of history?' He made no response. 'She and Charlie must've talked about it together. Most kids . . . they grow up with some extended family around. Grandparents, aunts. Caro lost out before she was even born.'

'Maybe.'

'Is that all you're going to say? She's never met Astra. And she misses having a family — especially now. She's blaming me, underneath, isn't she?'

'Of course she is — but that's because you blame yourself.'

'I wiped them out. An entire family,'

'What happened wasn't your fault. An accident happened. It caused a chain of fatal consequences. But your sister — she's still alive.'

'Astra's made it clear what she thinks.'

'Try the apricot jam. It's good. And just how disabling is it — the acrophobia, and the aerophobia?'

'It gets worse.'

'You've avoided flying? That's reinforced the fear and made it stronger. It's probably extended into other areas too. You retreated into a sheltered life. Now that's been blown, for good.'

I tried the apricot jam. Looking at Simon, I knew he had more to say. 'So what're you suggesting?' I asked, and then, as he shrugged disinterest, 'What should I do? Somebody's invited me to go up — in a Tiger Moth, of all the crazy things! A tiny rattletrap two-seater, for doing sharp manoeuvres in. With no lid to it either, of course.'

He laughed: my expression must have said everything. 'Sounds ideal, doesn't it! The person who's flying, do they know you're phobic?'

'Possibly. I'm honestly not sure.'

'They'd need to hear about it, and to know how desensitisation works. But even then it could be highly dangerous.'

It would be more dangerous than he could ever suspect. Idly I asked, 'How does it work?'

'What we're talking about is called flooding. If a person chooses to swamp themselves with their fears, the fear can retreat. But the anxiety level can be unacceptable, far too risky. I'm certainly not suggesting or recommending it.'

'I'd die,' I said, dismissing the notion, to Simon's visible relief.

'The sensible next step would be a systematic, gradual desensitisation.' Conversationally he went on, 'As a choice, given your drive to seek out danger now . . . It would be better to tackle the phobia, with proper help — and to give up searching for Charlie's murderer.'

'You've got the wrong person,' I lied, getting my breath back from the surprise, the way he had sprung it. 'I'm just a mother. An ordinary businesswoman. Where did you get that idea?'

Simon continued thoughtfully, as if I hadn't spoken: 'It would be better to tackle the sense of injustice in your life — by talking with Astra, don't you think? Stop trying to channel it, wanting to pursue a highly dangerous course. You've no chance of bringing the killer to justice yourself.' I opened my mouth to deny it again, then could not. 'It isn't your job. You could get killed, like Alison Seely.'

'And I'm all that Caro's got. Of course. Listen, Simon. There's two investigations — and one of them's private, on my behalf. That's enough. I've stopped getting mixed up in it. Anyway, isn't it true that the police do have a suspect?'

'You hear too much.'

I sat back. 'There are two killers — him, and me. And phobia does cause illogical responses, and actions that are illogical. This unknown man and I . . . We both happen to

428

be phobics. Charlie and Alison's killer, and me. I find that — '

'So long as you think that way, feeling linked at all, you're — rather like a lethal weapon. Aimed against your own life, as well as the people around you. Give it up. Just let it go. The serial killer the police are hunting is a criminally insane individual. You are perfectly sane and no madder than the rest of humanity. There is no connection.'

'I suppose that's true. Of course you're right,' I agreed, after pretending to consider. 'Coincidence is no real connection, is it?' And isn't it odd, all this sense of guilt is only recent. I was simply getting on with life before.'

'When you do eventually fly again, or just go in a high elevator — without those faulty responses attached — you'll realise something. The sensations we get from fear and excitement, they're exactly the same. It's a matter of degree and interpretation. The brain can get the signals mixed up.'

'Fear can be pure illusion then. Is that what you're saying?'

'It can be, yes.'

'I'll remember that.'

Simon asked, 'What're you doing today, you and Caro? Are you having a day together?' Then he must have registered my shock. 'What did I say?'

My heart skipped a beat. 'Caro's in Sussex, staying there. She's at school now. Isn't she?'

He shook his head, catching my anxiety. 'I don't think so. That's not what she said. Caro told me she was spending time in London with you.'

★ ★ ★

I rang home. No one answered. Calling the school, I caught Caro's house-father. 'She told us she was going home after all. Isn't she with you?'

'No, she isn't. And it's the first I've heard of any plan to come back.'

'Then where's she got to?' His voice was worried now. 'I know the lass has a project meeting — it's with some of her study group, tomorrow morning. Said she wanted a day or two in London before that. Hang on, can you.' There was a consultation, against a background of rock music. Someone was calling, 'I'm off now!' He came back to the phone. 'Caro did leave here, yesterday afternoon. Sheila took her to the station, put her on the train to Waterloo.'

'I'll go home and check now, in case she's turned up.'

430

'We assumed she'd told you, and arrived back. We'd better tell Rosemary Lomax.'

'Give me half an hour, Bob. There might've been some misunderstanding. I'll call you back.' Putting away the mobile, I turned to Simon. 'They put her on a train to London yesterday. I'll go back to the house. In case she's called in, left a note saying where she is.'

'I'd like to come with you. If she's missing . . . It seems Caro may've lied to me, as well.'

On the way, in the car, I turned to him. 'She did this kind of thing before. When she started seeing Peter, she fibbed about where she was staying.'

Relief crossed Simon's face. 'That's probably where she'll be, then. With her boyfriend. But why didn't she say?'

'But she's not still seeing him. Is she?' I stared. 'She doesn't like Peter, she found him — odd. After that first infatuation. Or has she . . . What's she told you?'

He answered carefully: 'She doesn't like to talk about him. But I think it's just possible she could be with Peter Doyle now.'

'I can't believe she'd do this again. The last time, I didn't even know of his existence. Caro'd said she was stopping over at friends' houses when all the time . . . she must've

431

been sleeping with him, right next door to headquarters. He's one of our tenants, he has one of the flats in the building.'

Simon looked troubled. 'How long did that go on? Caro fibbing to you?'

'Two or three weeks . . . possibly longer. It was just the weekends. She'd come home, then make up these stories about going to parties or whatever. Well, at least if she's gone back to Peter, we know where to find her.'

'This could be nothing to do with him. There might be another explanation. If only she'd called you.'

I remembered our last phone call, how rejecting she had been. 'It seemed the last thing she wanted was to be around me. She was staying at school.'

We drove to Cedar Court. Simon parked in front of the house and followed me in. The place was empty, I knew that straight away but still called out to her. I shouted up the stairs, then went to look in her room. I had only been out of the house a couple of hours, and Caro hadn't been back. There was no note left on the kitchen table. Why would there be?

'There's a message on your answer machine,' Simon noticed.

I hurried to the phone, but it was only

Ian Darius's silky voice. Intensely irritating, he seemed to go on for ever while I scarcely listened. 'You're up and out bright and early! Thought I might catch you in the shower.' He paused. 'Not there? Just confirming our trip this morning. High adventure begins today, we can do a modest flight. The weather outlook is surprisingly good! We'll have lunch somewhere. I'll pick you up at eleven — your house, unless I hear from you. *Ciao.*'

There was nothing else. No word from Caro, nothing at all. I rang Penny's home. She wasn't there and hadn't been in touch. I was fending off a sense of terror. Caro had gone missing before, so it would be all right this time too. I found Peter Doyle's phone number and dialled. There was no answer. I looked up, saw Simon pacing distractedly around.

'There's no one at his flat.' I hung up.

'They might not be answering.'

'Well, there's an easy way to find out. If she's there, or if she was there last night. He's our tenant, so the key's at the office.' Whether he was home or not, I wanted a look inside the flat. Suddenly I felt sure Peter must have had a hand in deceiving me the first time around. I could not have said why, it was nothing specific. Now I just wanted him out, right out of our lives.

'Where's the office? Let's go.'

We drove the short distance along the North Circular to MakerSeceuro's car park. I looked up at Peter Doyle's flat, at the top of the fire escape. There was no sign of him, nor of Caro. 'He won't be there,' I said, 'but I'll go and see if things are OK. I'll fetch the key.' I hesitated. Simon seemed quiet and abstracted, as if he was mentally somewhere else. 'D'you want to go? I expect there're things you need to be doing.'

'They can probably wait,' he said, looking unsure.

'There's no need. I can call you later, Simon. Caro's bound to turn up, she could even be back at school by this time. Why don't you get on now?'

Five minutes later, I had collected the key and was knocking on the door of Peter Doyle's flat. There was no answer, so I went in.

28

'Hello, anyone here?'

Peter and Caro could be here, not answering.

The flat smelled sour, as if the windows had never been opened. There was something else to that staleness, a rancid scent which did not belong to the building. The rooms looked clean but unlived in, squalid and cold with clinical neglect. The plain white walls carried no pictures. No ornaments or personal possessions were lying about and the blank, unrelieved daylight felt depressing.

'Peter?' I went to the bedroom and looked in. His bed was neatly made. A full rucksack was propped against it, buckled up. There was nothing else at all in there, or in the bathroom. If this was tidiness, Peter Doyle was more than obsessive. Not even his razor was on the shelf, no toothbrush or comb. Did he keep everything inside the mirror cabinet, with its doors so firmly closed? It was tempting to look.

I had no right to be snooping around, no right to be here without first letting our tenant know.

I went into the kitchen, though. It was just as I expected by now. It looked like a laboratory, clean and orderly but unused, with no food, no cooking pans in sight. There was none of the stuff of living, yet the smell seemed to come from in here. Rotting food? Unlikely, with such a fanatical hygienist. My gaze travelled over scrubbed formica, a pristine sink, the outdated but serviceable cooker and the tall fridge-freezer, which I guessed might be empty.

Caro had not been in Peter's flat, I felt sure. The place looked almost as if he was planning to leave, and I hoped he was. Going out through the hall, I saw the ugly aluminium extension ladder which led to the loft. Fixed at the top, it was usually kept pushed up out of sight. Why was Peter using the loft? I stepped towards the ladder. Then stopped.

Someone was opening the front door.

The key turned quietly, the door swung open. Peter Doyle was coming in. Not with Caro, then. He stopped abruptly. His face was white, a dark-red stain of anger beginning to suffuse across it. He put both his hands in his pockets and I thought it was a way of staying calm, or trying to appear calm.

I held up the master key, as unlikely

excuses went tumbling through my mind. 'Peter, I'm glad you've come back. I've been calling you for ages, and began to think something might be wrong.' He was standing there still, in the open doorway. 'I startled you.'

'Not at all, Mrs Maker.' He cleared his throat. 'What was it you wanted?'

'We think there might be something wrong with the drains. Have you noticed they're beginning to smell? We wondered if they're getting blocked up.'

'Where, exactly? You've been taking a look.' Peter came in, edging past me in the narrow hall. 'I haven't noticed a problem. Is the plumber here?'

'Perhaps it's our cloakroom then, next to the boardroom. We didn't want to ring maintenance until I'd spoken to you.'

'How thoughtful.'

I wished Peter would take his hands out of his pockets. There was nothing relaxed or casual about his body language. I had intruded on his space and the shy scientist was incensed, trying not to show it. I had been staring at him and he looked away, nervous as the first time Caro had brought him home.

'There's another reason I'm here. I'm looking for Caro.'

Peter smiled. 'Now you're talking.'

'Zoe, is everything all right?'

Peter and I looked round, startled. Simon was in the doorway and I felt a huge, inexplicable relief at the sight of him. 'Peter's come back,' I said quickly. 'We were just talking about the drains. I think it must be next door after all. Because there's no problem here.'

Simon asked, 'You're Caro's boyfriend, aren't you — Peter Doyle? I'm Dr Tyrone. I think Caro spent last night with you, didn't she. Do you know where she is?'

'Of course,' Peter answered unexpectedly. He seemed suddenly at ease. 'She came up to London yesterday because she wanted to see me. I've just dropped her off at your house, Mrs Maker. A few minutes ago.' The left hand came out of his pocket at last, in a gesture of understanding. 'She didn't go and do it again? Not telling you where she was . . . So that's it.'

There were a lot of things I could have said then, about our past agreement — our understanding. I was stopped by the simple fact that Caro had chosen to see Peter again, and this appalled me. Knowing what my reaction would be, she must have pretended all along. Yet none of this seemed to quite fit together . . . I loathed him instinctively, now. I distrusted him, but why?

Glancing across at me, Simon asked, 'D'you want to find Caro?'

'Yes. Let's go.'

Peter came to the door. 'She's only picking up some clothes, then she has to get a train back to school. If you're quick, you might just catch her.'

* * *

'What did you make of Peter Doyle?'

'Nice young man? Too nice, that's the thing. He's extremely tense. Beyond that . . . ' Simon shrugged as he pulled away from a traffic light. 'I think we're right to be concerned. Can't put my finger on why, exactly. I'd like to talk some more with him, if we could find a way.'

'I wish he would just disappear.'

'That doesn't look very likely.'

'Well, he's begun to spook me in a big way . . . You decided to wait then? You must've seen him come in.'

'I was going to keep an appointment. Decided to cancel it instead. Then I spotted him going up the fire escape.' Turning into Eldon Avenue, his voice lightened. 'Look. There's Caro.'

Caro, swinging moodily along on the

439

other side of the road, was going in the opposite direction from us and towards the underground. She was carrying a heavy tote bag over her shoulder, gazing at the ground and scuffing her trainers as she walked, thoughtful and unhurried.

Simon slowed, pulling up beside her. When Caro glanced across and saw him, she looked amazed. Her pleasure outweighed any dawning apprehension as she came over to talk. 'What're you doing here . . . ? Oh, hi Mum.' She must've begun to realise then that we had both been out searching for her.

'Caro,' said Simon, 'I'm so glad to see you. Let's go back to your house, yes? Hop in.'

Caro protested, briefly. She had been on her way to catch a train and needed to get back to Mayhall. That wouldn't do, not now. She got in and we returned, each of us for the second time in that short morning, to the house. 'Are you all right?' I asked.

'Why wouldn't I be?' She was beginning to feel victimised. 'Oh, I get it now. You've been checking up on me again.'

'Caro . . . ' I was trying to put things in a way she could respond to. 'You did say only yesterday you were staying at school. And you told me you'd stopped seeing Peter.'

'You haven't gone and talked to him! Whose life is it anyway?' Then she shrugged, lowering her voice. 'Just changed my mind, OK? Or isn't that allowed? I changed my mind about coming up to town as well. Got to get back, though.'

We were in the living room by now, Caro sprawled on a sofa and me hovering. Simon sat by the window, keeping out of it. I decided to tackle what was bothering me.

'Caro. You said some time ago you didn't like Peter. Now it seems you just spent the night with him, somewhere or other, and . . . Why?'

'He stayed around,' she answered, sitting up straight. 'So maybe I feel wanted. Anyway, he's just a friend — like when you laid down the law about it, remember that? If you really want to know, we were on his boat.'

'What boat? Where?'

'He owns this funny-looking boat. It's really rather hideous, I do think he ought to paint it. It's moored on a river.' She shrugged again. 'Somewhere in the country. So we decided to sleep on the boat last night. Where nobody could get at us. Sounds romantic? He's not my boyfriend, Mum. Honestly!'

Caro looked towards Simon, rolling her eyes at the magnitude of all this fuss. He spoke at last. 'One of the things that's troubling Zoe troubles me too. Why didn't you let her know, and let the school know where you'd be?'

'People have secrets, OK? Nobody owns us. If Peter asks me to keep a secret,' she added pointedly, 'then I do. Friends do. It was fun going to the river.'

She didn't look as if it had been fun, somehow. She was looking tired, even oppressed, and that wasn't only from this confrontation. There was something downcast about her this morning, despite all the spirited self-defence that was on display.

Suddenly she laughed, glancing from him to me and back again. '*Mea culpa*.' She was beating her chest and batting her eyelashes at the same time. The two actions combined into a comical charm offensive. It more or less worked too. But why had she deceived us all, to stay with someone she felt ambivalent about? Whatever her feelings were for Peter, I sensed there was little affection. It was something else — not love, and not real friendship. 'Gotta go,' she was saying casually, getting up.

'You could stay. Surely?'

'Doing our project meeting first thing tomorrow — and I'm not nearly ready! All my stuff's back there.'

Simon stood. 'I must go too. If you're

heading for Waterloo station, Caro, I could give you a ride.'

Caro jumped at the offer. I thought Simon wanted a chance to talk to her. I went to the door with them and it felt odd, saying goodbye after seeing her so briefly.

'Listen, Caro — please take care.'

She hugged me, then our eyes met. 'You're looking knackered, Mum. A fortnight in the Bahamas, perhaps?'

I smiled, 'Why not?' and she swung out to the car.

On the doorstep Simon turned back. 'Shall I call you later?'

'Please. It's Peter . . . I think there's something wrong,' I said softly.

He nodded. 'Yes, that's possible.' Then he looked awkward, hesitant. 'One other thing, Zoe . . . I overheard, this morning when we were here. That phone message.'

I couldn't think what he was talking about. 'What phone message?'

'You've forgotten, then. I'm very glad to hear it.'

'Oh, you mean . . . '

'About going flying, yes. You wouldn't be so crazy as to go then,' he said, with obvious relief.

'Of course I wouldn't.'

We are bound to what we resist, it seems. I was being drawn towards what could kill me.

Fear can kill. If the flight didn't, Darius would. This was beyond crazy but I needed to do it, since everything had got mixed up together. The past, with its tragedy, guilt and misunderstandings, had welded itself on to recent loss, present terror. Two keys existed for understanding and unlocking both. One key was Ian Darius. The other was fear.

The airstrip covered a small rise overlooking the gentle Hertfordshire countryside. It was perfect weather, clear and almost mild, with a soft breeze whispering over the grass. The little Tiger Moth, painted bright yellow, stood outside its hangar. It was being groomed for flight by an engineer.

Someone else was with us on the strip, watching these preparations.

I had never met him before but recognised his accent from the tape. This was Ian's security chief. Kruger's voice had the sound of concrete, of sharp chunks twisting off and colliding. Built like a bullet, he had a shiny cap of scalp and pale, heavy-lidded eyes. This was a man who had chosen to provide the enforcement of an oppressive regime. One look at him told me everything. Ian had employed a killing machine, experienced and without a conscience. Why had he? And why was Kruger here?

There was one thing I had to make sure of. I had to fake it, at least while we were on the ground, and pretend to myself up to the last moment that this was not really going to happen. We were admiring the plane. Maybe if we kept on admiring it long enough, we might leave it at that and drive somewhere sensible for lunch. I laughed aloud, sounding slightly hysterical. Ian glanced across.

'You never spelled it out that you had an original. Not a rebuild, either.'

'She's a real British warbird. This beauty took years of loving restoration. Most of it's original, including the propeller. Flies like a pussycat.'

'I'm sure she does. How's the forecast?'

'We'll be heading west. I'm planning to drop in on Land's End, for lunch in a local pub. OK?'

It sounded tame enough. 'Fine.'

Ian, in leather flying jacket and layer of fleece, was ready to go. Feet still firmly on the ground, I watched him talk with his engineer before he and Kruger went into conference. With his dark, hunky good looks, Ian was inscrutable as ever. We were about to take a joyride together, a small flight to — in the end — I did not know where. I would be completely in his hands. The only comfort was that he could do nothing to harm me, while we were up in the skies, without killing himself as well. Or could he? My harness could easily have been sabotaged and Ian might go in for daredevil tricks, just like Rory had. Spinning a loop and flying upside down, way above the earth, I would stand no chance of survival. I could still get out of this somehow.

But I had to know what Ian knew. Had he had a hand in Alison's death? In Charlie's, too? It was as if he was daring me to find out.

Now I was being handed into the second cockpit, strapped inside. Ian was in. I put on the old leather flying helmet with goggles. A minute later, the engineer was pulling away the chocks and, with a vigorous swing, starting up the propeller's whir . . .

It looked as if I was really going through with this. Why?

The plane seemed remote, beginning to taxi, as if it was some great distance away. I was beginning to scream, but silently, deep inside, as my body was seized by a massive panic attack. Heart racing in leaps and jumps, I was swimming in sweat, my skin electrified and lungs hyperventilating, unable to function. The sky and ground were a sickly blur. We had stopped. We had started again, I couldn't look but felt in waves of nausea the vertigo of speed, the protesting of the wind, vibration, noise . . .

We were off the ground. Ian gave a whoop. 'How you doing there?' Without looking, I could feel the pressure of climbing up the air, defying what was natural or safe. Death was all around, inside me and outside. There was nothing else.

He was talking again, his voice intimate through the headset. 'I know all about you. The blood on your hands. I know that you're really terrified. And I wonder what it is you want — so very much.'

I didn't answer. Scared to death, I blacked out.

29

Opening my eyes, for the first time I could look.

It seemed a very long time later. We were simply in the air, just cruising along. The little Tiger Moth, with her yellow wings, flew steadfastly through the pale-blue sky, and it was as if we were carried by the sun. Below were tiny towns and villages, roads through fields, a sweep of moors and a grey blur of sea.

I smiled, remembering Simon and what he had said about the flooding technique.

'Still there,' Ian asked, 'and in one piece?'

'Yes, I'm good.'

It was weird and wonderful, this feeling of calm. My clothes were still clinging against my skin, a chill reminder of all the years of fear I had just miraculously left behind. In the end, all it had taken was facing the beast. I was beginning to remember what life had been like before the long nightmare had begun. Life had been about freedom. A casual, taken-for-granted sense of being free.

'We're approaching Land's End. Hold

tight, and hone your appetite.' Ian was cheerful as a party host, taking us gently down. The ground flew up like a pair of wings, soft, bearing us. The flight was over — too soon, I felt now — and we were clambering out of the plane, finally confronting each other.

'That was wonderful! Thanks.'

'You came through, then.' He laughed. 'That's good. The seafood is famous here, no point in missing out.'

He had booked a window table in the restaurant of a local pub. Outside lay the sea, basking under a weak sun.

'You knew I was phobic. You know about my family. How?'

'Common knowledge, my dear. There are no secrets in our world.'

'Not true, it seems, if your name is Ian Darius — or Alison Seely.'

'Not wasting any time then,' he retorted, sounding annoyed. We ordered lunch.

I waited until we were alone again, safely alone with forty strangers around. 'We came to talk about her. Remember?'

'So we did.'

'It was some achievement, keeping your affair hidden. You promised to tell me, Ian. All about her.'

'What d'you want to know? Alison . . . '

His voice softened momentarily. 'I was beginning to care deeply, I was falling in love with her.' His face had become blank, expressionless, as he looked across the table at me. 'It's been devastating, quite simply. Well, you know. Better than I.'

I began to believe him then, because I recognised the blankness in his eyes. I believed he was genuine but still I felt ruthless. Abandoning caution, knowing I was adding to the hurt, I was insisting on more answers. 'Why did you decide the relationship needed to be secret? Whose idea was that?'

'Alison's,' he said. 'We'd been aware of each other for a long time, without ever becoming friends. We'd both been unlucky in love, we felt. There was a certain reputation held, perhaps, on both sides.'

'For playing the field? Is that what you mean?'

'When things changed between us, it was quite sudden. We were more than close, it felt intense. Perhaps this would turn out better, we thought, if people didn't get hold of it and — ' He stopped. 'If we had been more open, if Alison had been more *with* me . . . Would she still be alive?'

'The night before she was killed, did you see her?'

Ian nodded. 'She was at my apartment.'

'Did you talk business together?' He looked surprised, shook his head. 'Did you have a fight?'

'What on earth about?'

'They say most murders are committed by a person known to the victim, and close.' I took a deep breath. 'If you'd had a motive, you could've made it look like the others.'

There was a loud burst of laughter from nearby, crashing out from behind one or other of us. It bounced off the walls like gunfire. An expression of shock had crossed Ian's face. I sat back. He looked every bit as offended as he had a right to be, and just as angry. I gave him the best shaky smile that I could muster. 'Bad taste, yes. Don't . . . I have to — to make light of things. Because she haunts me. They both do.'

'You found the body,' he said, white-faced. 'Some animal. Insane . . . She haunts me too, more than I can say.'

Ian was warm and open, plausible. The idea that he had genuine feelings for Alison was taking root and growing. It foxed me for a while. His response had been real, and that seemed to tell me all I needed to know. If he had nothing to do with Alison's murder, he would know nothing about Charlie, or Gill.

One question remained, and it could not

be left. Warning him off was the main reason for spending this day with Ian Darius. There had been no more news of our own illicit tape, and it could still prove to be innocent. Bugging Ian's home had scarcely been an innocent act on my part, and he almost certainly knew what I had done. If I was wrong — if Patricia and Madison were also wrong in their suspicions — Ian would add to his sense of outrage.

These thoughts flitted through my mind as we ate a three-course lunch. I was going to have to tread very carefully but allow him to know, quite casually, that we had all marked A-Zander Security's card. So we talked about anything else, everything under the sun except business or the recent nightmare events.

Eventually I suggested, 'Shall we go and look at the sea?'

'Let's do that. Can't be long, though.'

Walking to the very end of the peninsula, we talked of the landscape, Cornwall and Jersey, the Normandy coast where Ian often landed for a day. The sun had gone in but visibility was still good. From the mass of Land's End, I looked down at the rocks and the milling ocean below, feeling no fear and still surprised by its absence.

It was easy to guide our conversation back

to the subject of secrecy, company security. 'We seem to've been wide open,' I said. 'Confidential documents. False information, directed to where it would do the most calculated damage. Madison and I do recognise it's a concerted campaign. By one rival, we think.'

'Good heavens. You're quite sure? How long's that been going on?'

'Since the time that Charlie died. So much was happening, it took a while . . . When we did a sweep at HQ,' I glanced at him, 'we found the whole place had been bugged.'

'This is very serious. I thought Quest Associates . . . Don't they work on your behalf?'

'Yes.' I paused but he didn't say anything more. 'Naturally, we informed the police. They're analysing one or two things . . . It can't be ruled out that there's a possible link with the murders.'

He touched my hand. 'I wonder you can sleep at night.' Then, abruptly, he broke the contact. 'Oddly enough, I've also been a target. Our head of security, Mr Kruger — you met him this morning? He found little devices — of an ordinary type, in my home. Funnily enough, two days ago. Not funny, though.'

Bluffing it out, I felt convinced he had

just been doing the same thing. 'In your home? How . . . invasive that must've felt. And whatever for?'

'I can't imagine, if you can't. There seems to've been something of a plague of bugs,' he added, almost jovially.

His phone rang. Ian, with a murmured apology, stepped a little distance away and talked for several minutes, quiet and intent. With a glance in my direction, he spoke again then finished his call. 'There's a bit of weather, could just touch us. We must be off. Back to the airfield . . . and home.'

Was this all we had come for? It seemed the subject of mutual suspicion was closed, none too soon. We were walking across the Land's End airfield when Ian spoke again, as if he could not quite leave things alone. 'I feel we know each other a little better. Don't you?'

'Perhaps.'

'I've had nothing to do with any of what's happened.' He stopped, so I paused too, waiting. 'What if I had? Supposing I had done that terrible thing . . . If you thought so, why would you be here with me?'

I said nothing.

'Believe it, Zoe Maker.' He stared into my eyes and his own were compelling, cold. 'You had better believe it.'

Suddenly he smiled broadly. What had sounded for a second like a threat was turned into just a joke.

* * *

At six that evening, Ian dropped me off outside the house. Eldon Avenue's familiar lights shone out, illuminating the clipped yew hedge, slender branches. The quince tree was in small, tightly furled bud. I felt disorientated seeing that neat promise, sensing a mild stillness in the air. The long, torturous winter was breaking at last. And something else lay ahead.

I went through the gate and started up the drive, still buoyed by the lightness that comes when fears have been shed. The fear of flying. Fear of Ian Darius, who was surely no more a killer than I. Perhaps that sense of release was the reason why I didn't even notice, at first.

The house lay in darkness, and that was not right.

There should have been lights, automatically switched on at dusk. Noticing now, I faltered, then kept on walking like a machine. I let myself into the house, not stopping to think and not remembering too much, not yet. I was meant to come in. The darkness was an invitation. The memories were just beginning, revving up, like an overture.

The house was empty, I could feel that. There was no glimmer of light, not anywhere. The electricity had been turned off. I went to the cupboard in the hall and switched the mains back on. So calm, so logical.

Then the fear began.

Flooding the hall and stairs with light, I staggered up to the landing, like someone dead drunk. Stopped there, leaning against the banister. The house was huge, the distances grown infinite. Space and time, all perception depended on the next breath and the next small, impossible step. Over a carpet bought somewhere mundane and trodden a thousand times. If he had got her and I was too late. Stupid, stupid, not to see! Her room lay a million small steps away. No sign that anyone had been in here? Just like before . . . Caro's wardrobe. A floor-to-ceiling affair, proudly installed and solidly built, right for a young woman exploring her life, exploring excitement and pleasure, all her years of living that were stretching ahead. A voice praying aloud, how odd: my voice. And the smell . . . That was odd, too, unexpected.

On the floor, clothes. Bundled as if for washing.

Her wardrobe. Rolling back the doors. And

there it was, glistening wet and dark red. No body, though. I was on my knees, thinking: no body.

And that wrong smell.

It was paint? Crawling forward. On my hands, it was clear. It was bright-red glossy paint, fresh and scarcely dried at all. Splashed everywhere inside, and fallen into pools. Laughter was ringing out round the room. Abruptly I stopped laughing.

It was a warning, then. A terrible warning . . . And a worst-taste joke.

Ian Darius. He had kept me away from town, uselessly occupied all afternoon.

I stumbled out to the landing to pick up the phone. Bob answered, at last.

'It's Zoe Maker, Is Caro there?'

'No, she hasn't been back.' His voice rose. 'D'you mean she isn't with you?'

I disconnected the number, to ring the murder squad.

★ ★ ★

While Prentiss's team were on their way to the house, I called Redcliff. His mobile was switched off. Finding the number of his St John's Wood flat, I dialled again. A soft-voiced woman answered: Redcliff's sister-in-law. 'He's out with the children.

Can I take a message?'

'Please. Tell him . . . just that — it seems Caro has been taken.'

'Caro has been taken?'

'Yes.'

I rang off. Five minutes later the place was crawling with police, then forensics. Prentiss and I went into Charlie's study.

'Did you touch anything?'

'Door handles, switches. He's got her, hasn't he?' A shadow touched the DCI's face, then it was gone. 'Why Caro? *Why her?*'

DC Shaw was in the room. 'There's a message on your machine from Simon Tyrone. Says he put Caro on the train to Haslemere.'

'Then she *did* get on the train to school.'

'Not necessarily. He could've dropped her off at the station.'

I gave them a number for the head at Mayhall. 'She never arrived, not at the school. She didn't let them know to pick her up at Haslemere. Neither did I . . . '

'Zoe, it's just possible there's some other explanation why she hasn't arrived yet. This warning — taunting — could be just that.'

Another willing, unscheduled visit to Peter Doyle? For some reason, that idea was making me feel worse. Much worse. Simon had been anxious about Peter too, about something not right . . . There was a confusion in my head, the residue of shock. We had got to find Caro . . . Who else were we looking for?

Donald Sutter?

'Are you still trying to find the Sutter boy? What's Patricia Abel written about him?'

Prentiss unfurled a paper and passed it across. The CID had broken their cautious near-silence with a lead piece in the news review section of a national. Here it all was, the details of the murders and their emerging similarities to the Eric Sutter serial killings. Not just copycat, these victims were picked for revenge . . . Police were anxious to trace Donald Sutter, who disappeared four years ago.

There was a picture.

He was a quiet-looking boy, ordinary-seeming and probably just into his teens. The dark hair was neatly clipped and his features were scarcely formed, not yet adult.

I had never seen his eyes; they were always hidden behind heavy glasses. Still, it was the eyes that gave him away. Even as the camera had searched into them, they had been somehow subtly withdrawn. They succeeded in expressing nothing at all. There was nobody behind them.

'I know who this is.'

30

They have quit stalling, then. My Role is His-Story, achieved and almost done, the True Inheritor: 'a clever imitator, cunning and accurate', 'Hand of the Past' . . .

SUCCESS!

Now You know it! AM The One, The One and Only YOURS! Those lies, the lies are wiped away, the Truth Admitted — VICTORY!

<u>I can do anything, anything!</u>

They hunted Him, they Will hound Me now for sacrifice.

On the road. She is snug in the back of My new van.

When the Final Plan is, the Plan of Action is with Caro Mine. Maker's widow, then and It must Be fitting, My Triumph, My blaze of Glory abetted, served by She. Wife of Mine.

'There have been Times of Blood, a fitting — always fitting — Tidal Flow of Tribute. Many of these . . . I could show You things, I almost showed You souvenirs but the World You Live in is all wrong. It wouldn't jell. You'll see the Truth in all

My Actions. You'll soon See.'

She has grown quiet now and Her eyes are closed. Darkness I Do Not Wish to See. Such ignorance. Women never know what they Want, You've got to Teach them He said. And they Spake and said unto Us, the Women are Fallen. She can't Know how She Wants it with Me. I shine the Light of My Path, for Shackled in Darkness I Do Not Wish to See.

I Wanted Her in the boat but they Will seek it now. Taking the boat beyond the Hide, it Will be safe.

No problem, arriving now. How Wanted AM I? No one's about.

Taking the van up the bumpy track, pulling the old gate to behind us. Spread weeds and debris again across its lowest bar, looking undisturbed. Driving on a thick carpet of plantain, never on the tell-tale mud: a little Time is what I Want. Turning off into woodland, scrubby and untended, that borders on the Tributary. Leave it here. Camouflage work To Be Done, in case of the uninvited visitor. Carrying gear to the boat. Carrying Her, the Bride to the Chamber.

Still not Understanding, struggling again . . .

'Don't cry. Lucky I got to You, isn't it?

We are meant To Be. I do not like doing this to You. You will get the she-devil, See, Witness Me, when I kill the influence. Assist Me now, Sweet. Don't You understand yet? You are Mine . . . '

31

'The flat's empty, he's gone.' DC Ned Shaw came nearer, his face closed against my question. 'No sign of your daughter, not yet.'

'He's got her.' Why was he standing there uselessly? 'He'll . . . She's next, then. Find her!'

He was sitting down, a strand of gelled hair falling forward. His voice grated, a protesting machine. 'We've launched a manhunt, a huge search for both of them. We'll find her. We need your information.'

'They stayed on a boat last night — a boat he has. On a river.'

'What river?'

'Somewhere in the country, Caro said. An odd-looking boat, hideous, she said. For one night — and they were back early this morning. So it must be — not far away.'

'We'll get to the boat. What else?'

'You know about his job?'

'Yes. Anywhere else you can think of at all they might've gone to?' I shook my head. 'He's her boyfriend. You think she's gone willingly with him, then?'

I stared. What were they making out of Caro's disappearance? 'You don't understand! He . . . seemed a lot older, to her — it was just after her father died. They dated for a few weeks. Then she disliked him, she stopped seeing him. Until last night . . . He seems to've had some hold over Caro . . . Fear. She's been afraid of him.' Unable to quite break free but caught, held paralysed by fear. Why hadn't I understood before? 'He's taken her. You don't believe me?'

'We'll keep open minds, cover all possibilities.'

'You think . . . ' Did they really believe she was some kind of accomplice? Under his spell?

'Whatever Caro's position, our priority is her safety and public safety.'

'You've got proof of who he is, what he's done?'

'We've got proof. Yes.'

'What're you doing, where are you searching?'

Without answering, he stood up. The sharp suit was as crumpled as litter in the street. 'We're placing you in protective custody, Zoe.'

★ ★ ★

I had to play their game and appear to be willing. It was the only way out. There was a chance to pack a few things, so I took some business papers and slipped the mobile into a pocket. Then they drove me to a safe house. I wanted to go there, wanted to be locked in securely — that's what they believed. They thought I didn't care where it was located. It was at the end of a road behind West Hendon Broadway.

Now there was nothing to do but wait.

Caro. The sense of her warm, living flesh and the scent of her skin, like no one else in the world. That sense of her since babyhood, just after her birth. They always say that if you drown or fall to earth, scenes from your past will flash through your memory. That reeling in of a struggling life, before being landed on a strange shore.

Through the early hours of the night, I was falling, falling, but it was Caro's life unreeling through me.

★ ★ ★

Time passed so slowly. Maybe he never would get in touch. Maybe she . . .

There was nothing at all that I could do.

It seemed a long time later: Sarah Quirke walked into that shuttered, timeless capsule

465

of a suburban living room. At first I thought I was dreaming. Then I realised the baby-sitters had just changed shifts.

She was still DC Sarah Quirke then. For some reason, the surprise didn't last long. I got up from the sofa where I had been lying, and switched on a lamp. 'Sarah . . . Moonlighting?'

She pushed a hand through that tangle of red curls. 'I've been on leave for a while. Yes — moonlighting, if you like. I never told you I left the force, did I? . . . You can't sleep?'

'What d'you think? Could you?' I stared at her. Sarah had been working undercover at Quest. *She kind of approached me for it*, Redcliff had said. So Prentiss, wisely, had distrusted everyone — he knew Redcliff had taken Alison's computer. Prentiss had sent Sarah in to check on everything Alison had found out before she was killed.

Sarah crossed the room and sat down on the sofa. 'Look, we will find her. The DCI wants to know if you've remembered anything else about him, about Don Sutter.'

'I met him — a handful of times. I quizzed him a lot . . . Peter Doyle.' Why hadn't I trusted my instincts? How could I have let it happen? 'He told me his family comes from just outside Edinburgh, his father's a lecturer and — '

466

'That family belonged to the real Peter Doyle, who disappeared.'

'And the genetics research job?'

'Don and Peter knew each other slightly, as boys. Don studied genetics at only a very basic level — at school. Peter became a graduate in genetics and immunology.'

'Then how — '

'The real Peter Doyle was given a job at the lab, but he disappeared before taking it up. Don took his place, pretended he'd had a breakdown — so he could work at the lab in a caretaking position.'

'Then he's not a scientist at all? But he's obsessed with genetics. That first time we met . . . More importantly, he's obsessed with inheritance, then.'

'Yes. Don's father is unknown. He seems to've been trying to prove he was Eric Sutter's son.'

'You think he killed the real Peter Doyle — to take his place?'

'It looks that way.'

Where was Caro now? What was happening to her? In a panic I said, 'He does all this ritual. The places that he goes to . . . The women have been killed in their homes. There's the canal, that whole area. And the bridge. His mother, Irene, died there. And then — Charlie . . . '

She nodded. 'If he's returned anywhere, then we've got him. His van — the van he kept Charlie in? We found that — in a Kent reservoir. It had been there for a bit. It was registered under another alias. Forensics are at it now.'

'And at the flat . . . ?'

'Covert surveillance, from the loft. High-tech stuff.'

'He was spying on Alison, and on MakerSeceuro HQ?'

'Yes. And on you.'

I looked at her in astonishment. That had never occurred to any of us. 'But why? Because . . . was he spying on Caro?' Sarah shrugged. 'Was it sound, or cameras? Where?'

'Both. And they were everywhere, Zoe. Everywhere.'

I still didn't understand. 'He's criminally insane, and I didn't — ever realise. I went to the flat to search for them — for Caro. All this time, I've had a key! And the loft ladder was down, I was going to look up there when he — Peter, Don . . . came back. And — there was a smell. In the kitchen. Something rotting.'

She was silent for a moment. 'The fridge-freezer. It had broken down.'

'And inside . . . ?'

'Inside, we found human remains,' she said, her voice gone flat. 'We found human parts.'

We sat without speaking. It had all been there — every marker, every clue to him. By simply not joining it all together, I had failed her. 'He has nothing to lose now. Has he?' Sarah didn't answer. 'Did this happen because of Patricia's piece in the newspaper? He saw his picture and the story broken, his real name in print. Yesterday . . . And then he took Caro?'

'That's possibly why,' she said.

A few minutes passed and something else jumped into my mind. 'How pricey was it? The equipment he'd got set up in the loft?'

'It was pricey.'

'He was being funded then. It isn't just Don Sutter, is it?' She didn't answer and gave no sign of listening, particularly. I went on fast, desperately: 'Why was he spying on our HQ? How could one individual have done all that? How did he escape you for so long? Sarah, did you know Alison was involved with Ian Darius? A-Zander Security's chief executive — he was with her the night before she was murdered.' Sarah smiled faintly, in a patient way. 'Darius took me out of town yesterday afternoon. And somebody got into the house and . . . '

She stood up, ready to go. 'Zoe, we've analysed the tape. The one from that little Parker pen . . . Look, I've got to go now. Why don't you try to sleep?'

What did any of it matter? None of the facts would bring her back safely. Where was Caro?

I went into the bedroom, lay down on the bed and pretended to sleep, pretended to be a willing prisoner. The bodyguard was downstairs, keeping an eye on monitors of the house exterior. A WPC was sitting in a chair near the bedroom door.

Some time later, he rang my mobile.

★ ★ ★

'*You got my message then. It won't be paint next time.*'

I recognised his voice at once. I couldn't speak.

'*If you make one sign to the police, you'll never see her again — I'll kill her.*'

Sitting up in bed, I saw the WPC looking in round the bedroom door. I closed my eyes, willing forward that other self — the calm, the cooperative, the cool. 'We can take steps to save this,' I said carefully. The businesswoman. I reached for my briefcase

470

and opened it. 'What kind of approach are you thinking of?'

Don Sutter was silent, the line hummed with tension. *'You'll come here, to her.'*

'Yes. Of course.'

'Now. On your own. One sign to them — if they suspect, if they follow you — then she dies, immediately.'

'There won't be any problem on that score. Luckily I've got the papers with me. It's one thirty in the morning here ... I'll look at how to get free from this situation. Can you call me back in an hour?' There was no answer. 'Is that all right, Harvey?'

He had rung off, cutting the lifeline.

The police constable was watching. I tried to get up off the bed slowly, reluctantly. 'That was New York, a crisis.' I glanced at her. 'It's a major deal. We've nearly pushed it through. Perhaps it'll take my mind off things.'

'Perhaps it will.' She couldn't disguise the contempt in her voice.

I put on my shoes and checked my pockets casually, put the mobile back in. I paused. 'Is there any news?' The WPC shook her head, and I went out to the landing. 'I'm still asleep — going to make coffee, take a bath.'

One minute later, locked in the bathroom,

I was checking the physical security at the window. It was basic. The safe house had been designed for protection, to keep people out. No one had imagined they would be trying to keep someone in.

⋆ ⋆ ⋆

Out.

In some street, keeping still in the night's shadows . . .

'*Listen. You want to see her alive?*'

'Don't touch her. Please just tell me what to do.'

'*Bitch, listen carefully. Are you alone now?*'

'Yes, I'm alone.'

'*How do I know that, bitch? You could be surrounded by accomplices!*'

'I'm out on the street and on my own.' A police siren was sounding faintly in the distance. Would he hear it and jump to conclusions? What if they found me? Was the siren getting nearer? It was going . . . 'Listen, nobody knows that you've made any contact. I've got out and I'm here alone. Now tell me where — '

'*I don't trust you. How do I know you aren't lying to me?*'

'I'll do anything you want. Just tell me

what you want me to do . . . Let me speak to her.'

Silence. The lifeline cut again. Would he call back or not?

I was standing at the end of a cul-de-sac. A narrow passageway ran through to the main road, arterial route, stations and taxis. Lifeblood of the city, ebbing low. There were very few people around.

Waiting, I dialled Redcliff's mobile and found it was switched on. I told him what was happening and where I was. I rang off quickly, in case Don Sutter might be trying to get through.

It was ages before he called again.

'*Are you alone?*'

'Yes.'

'*Listen very carefully. Do exactly what I say.*'

32

'*I'm watching you. I can see everything you do.*'

It was only a whisper in my ear, close in the darkness of the small hours.

'Then you can see I've come here alone.'

'*And you can't see me, not at all. Can you?*'

'No. I can't see you.'

Not a river. Dark sky, black water pointing straight ahead, coffined in concrete, through invisible country. A city-to-city motorway from the past, an industrial canal. London's aura lay still in the sky: purple. In the ghost light jutted cutouts of trees, cutouts of warehouse blocks, striding in a line. Miles from anywhere or anyone, deserted.

'I've come on my own and nobody knows. No one knows that you made contact. Peter . . . '

'*You know better than that, Widow Maker! You know who I am.*'

'Where is she? You said if I came to you, I could see her.'

A long silence. Then the mobile went dead. He was somewhere nearby. Did that mean Caro was close too?

Water sounds, small wild creatures and the wind, brushing branches. Waiting. He rang again.

'*All right. You can see her. Go to your left, on to the path . . . Now walk forward, about ten paces . . . A bit further than that. Down in the water. Undo the rope, and step down into it.*'

There was a small rowing boat, fastened to a ring at the path's edge. I untied the mooring, then slid down off the concrete wall. Below ground level, the blackness grew suddenly dense. The canal, sharp with its own echoes, bit cold and its water stank, rotting and swollen. He hissed down the phone.

'*Go on, then. Get away from the bank, and out into the middle of the canal. Then pull the starter chain on the outboard motor. Going to take a trip and say hello to her?*'

Pushing off from the bank. Drifting out, into the centre of the long hell pit. Finding the ring on the motor: couldn't get it started, it choked and spluttered and died. Then again.

He had rung off. Nothing. Suppose he had left?

A stretch of derelict waterway, an old industrial estate ahead. Marshes and fields, factories and drainage works, underground reservoirs . . . and she could be anywhere at all. Held somewhere . . . *Charlie never came out of this alive* . . . Was she still alive?

He was the only person in the world who knew where she was.

The outboard turned over, struggled into weak life. Quickly I took hold of the rudder. Where was he? I yelled, splitting the night into rage and fear. 'Where d'you want me to go?' A waterbird crashed into the skies and was gone. There was nothing else. The small boat chugged slowly. I was steering it up the water duct the way I'd been heading, towards those factory buildings, keeping to the middle of the water. He could see I was alone, it was so empty. The banks on each side and the fields beyond — all so empty. Couldn't he see?

On. Living things, weed and rushes were dying away, giving up to the scum of old industrial waste. Mooring bollards and posts, a slipway holed by rot. Tall, dark walls approached, beginning to narrow, to close in. Mute weaponry stood. Erect black necks of cranes, hushed, still as museum exhibits and watching. Something spanning the sky overhead. A bridge? A steel walkway. A filigree arc, drawn tall across the water between the loading bays.

Buildings gaping. Light at the end, open country again. No further — she had to be here. I cut the engine and listened. Nobody. I screamed out again, 'Where d'you want me to go?'

The echo died.

From somewhere nearby, he said, 'Throw it out into the water. The phone. Do it now!'

He was very close. I didn't look round, but picked up the mobile and threw it over the side. A small, dull splash. The lifeline gone. 'Where is she? You promised.'

He laughed. 'How naive . . . You want to say goodbye?'

'Why don't you come out? And face me?'

A pause. 'Don't you want to know where Caro is?'

'Yes.'

'She's at the island, Mrs Maker.'

What island? I stared through the darkness. 'Where? Where is that?'

'Widow Maker, I've got a gun — and it's pointing directly at you. See me? Start the engine. Then keep going, straight ahead . . . You'll see.'

The motor started quickly this time and the boat puttered forward, parting a jam of debris. I had glimpsed him now: a man standing on the canal path, only ten yards off. He was in the shadows of a warehouse. He was holding a gun.

The aisle of water was splitting, parting. There it stood, at the end of the industrial estate: a small island with a few trees, dropped there into the middle. It was a nesting place . . . a mooring place. I could just see her now, under a willow. A grey boat, tied there, an odd-looking boat . . . narrow and long, cased in steel, ugly as a weapon. I cut the engine as I got close, then drifted up.

'Going to have a look?' His voice spread cool across the flat water. 'Take a last look at her, Mrs M. But go very, very carefully . . . '

Approaching the narrow boat, that was when I saw Redcliff. At first he was just a shadow under the water, in the shallows of the island's banks . . . Was that him, or was I just imagining things? I'd been hoping so desperately that Redcliff had found me before I'd moved on. That he was following, and I'd been leading him to Caro.

I saw him again when he reached the bank, behind the boat. Redcliff had raised his head, just enough to breathe and hear . . . Would Don Sutter see him?

I splashed the oars, a clumsy amateur. Grappled noisily to retrieve them. Then called back, 'Why carefully? What've you done to her?'

'To my one? It is what *you* would do to her . . . What you have done.'

Beginning to paddle, I paused. No one. Redcliff had let me see him, then he had vanished again.

Softly and silently now, drifting in towards the steel cradle.

'Tell me what you mean.' Closer, closer. No sign of life . . . 'Can I go in?'

Silence. I touched the boat, its cold metal skin.

'You can step on the side and look in — but no, don't go any nearer. If you try to go in — if you touch the deck, or the cockpit — then there'll be a very big bang, Mrs Maker. Then you'll both be dead . . . The deck has been wired up, you see. To kill. You understand me?'

I withdrew my hand. He had boobytrapped the boat? Then there was no way of Redcliff getting to her . . . Or was he bluffing? Maybe Caro wasn't even in there.

'Why would I believe you?'

'You'd better believe me! Don't you want to look? Don't you want to say goodbye to her?'

Goodbye? Gently I placed one foot on the gunwale, then drew myself up. I looked in through one of those long canalboat windows.

Caro was inside, in the cabin. That was true. She was behind glass that had been dulled by weather, but I could see her lying on a bunk. Her face was turned towards me. She was awake and could see. I watched her eyes widening. Her lips parted but the cry had no sound. Involuntarily, I reached out to her.

A shot rang out. I felt the bullet sear past, it was so close to my hand.

★ ★ ★

'The next bullet! That one's for setting it all off — the big bang! The next is meant to be for *you*!' He was angry, screaming and ranting. 'What's your choice? State your preference as a consumer. I'd be sorry if she went first. She's meant to go last, she's meant to be with me!'

I do believe him. He would do this, of course he would. This is Don Sutter . . . And Redcliff needs time. 'Don. What is it you want?'

'Can't you guess by now?'

'Tell me.'

'She died for him. My mother. She followed faithful to the grave. Haven't you

480

learned anything yet?'

'The bridge . . . ?'

'You can come across and get out now, on this side. And walk back with me. We're on our own, Widow Maker.'

That boat was a silver tomb, a tightly welded chrysalis. It carried her life or death inside. Turning my back on Caro now. I had to trust her survival to Redcliff.

Every bit of me protesting, I got back into the dinghy. Started off, away from the island. Going with the killer . . . Keep talking, asking questions. Distract him. What to say? My mind was numb, in a funk.

Paddling softly to the canal's edge. Keeping breathing. Not so clumsy, not so fearful . . . Panic breeds panic. He's already used the gun.

Tying the dinghy, I clambered awkwardly on to the bank. Sutter was still hiding in the shadows. I saw only a faint gleam when he moved. By the water's seam, I stood on the towpath. At its edge there towered the warehouse buildings, derelict. The path led by like a narrow funnel towards the bridge.

'Start walking.'

Edging slowly backwards, keeping his eyes on me . . . Behind him lay the island with its willow trees, the boat . . .

Redcliff . . . I was praying, frantic inside. I

said, 'Don. Will you let me understand now? I want to learn . . . Did you keep Charlie on the boat? What happened to him?'

Sutter didn't answer. I heard it then — the dulled splintering of glass. Heard the instant of its happening and knew that Redcliff was going into the boat to get her . . . Instinctively I'd scuffed the ground, tripped and fallen noisily. He had the gun trained on me. 'Get up!'

Scrambling up. Keep his attention fixed. How?

'Keep walking.'

Edging back away from them, from whatever was happening on the island. On the boat. It could blow up — sky high. It could do that . . .

The bridge was growing nearer. Glancing round, I saw its steel legs spanning the darkness of the sky.

Sutter laughed. 'Curiosity killed the cat, they say. Yes, we had a long conversation on my boat . . . A little hiccup when Charlie Maker escaped in transit — but not for long, only a few minutes.'

'Why did you kill Charlie? Why him?'

'They were thick as thieves, in it together — him and the cow.'

'Charlie and — you mean Alison? Because you saw a photo of them . . . outside the court? But he had nothing to do with it — the trial. Nothing!'

'You won't pull the wool over my eyes. He was guilty and he died!'

'Guilty of what? Of finding out?'

'My masters had it in for him. His death would be a happy event.'

'A happy event? Who were your masters, Don?' He didn't answer. 'Charlie suspected you, didn't he — of murdering Gill Tarpont?'

'That one? The bitch conspired with all the persecutors!'

Behind him on the shore of the little island, someone was moving. Two people, running away from the boat. Caro! Redcliff was getting her clear, and all I had to do was keep on talking.

Sutter had been ranting: suddenly he stopped. Did he suspect something? I went on fast. 'You did that — to Charlie . . . Then leaked the 'suicide' note — you'd dictated it, hadn't you . . . And the documents? Was it easy, living next to MakerSeceuro? Next to our boardroom. You must've had a lot to offer when you first went to them. Was it that way round — you made them an offer they couldn't refuse? Tell me who they are, Don . . . Shall I guess?'

'You know nothing, Widow Maker. Go on now — to the bridge!'

'I'll give you a guess — it was Ian Darius. A-Zander were buying your information, weren't they?'

He didn't answer. I was feeling the way as I edged slowly backwards, step by step. Must be nearing the bridge, I thought, not wanting to look round or see it again.

Sutter was still keeping to the shadows.

There was no sign of anyone now. They must have gone. She must be safe by now . . . Where was he taking her? Would Redcliff help me? Surely he must have alerted the police — why weren't they here?

Keep on talking. Redcliff might come. 'Why the bridge, Don? She chose to jump, Irene did. No one made her do that.'

'*Shut up*! You all made her, all the death-makers, the *guilty* . . . Just walk.'

'And it wasn't this bridge — '

'But you're going to find out what happened. You're going there. It's the same place in the end — I didn't think that, for a while. She was faithful . . . *dirty stinking whore, I saw you doing it in the bed he shared, I was watching you*!'

The bridge, yawning and hungry: it was here now. Right at the edge of the shadows before it, I turned to face him. Don Sutter had stepped out on to the path, not speaking at first.

It came as a whisper. '*Be very, very careful, whore . . .* '

'Irene was your mother and she's dead. But your father? You know he's alive, Don.'

'He lives through me!'

'No. You've never met him, you don't know who he is. Irene took that secret with her — you'll never know who he is.'

'*I knew him, bitch*! My giant and my god, he tested me as his — I survived and *I survived*! Yes, they lied to me. It was easier for them to farm me out in Scotland if they said I wasn't his, he was not mine. Haven't I proved it enough? The truth is *in here*.'

'The truth is in Eric Sutter's grave. He was nothing to do with you. If you'd got the courage — if you believed what you're saying and trying to prove — then you'd just have got a DNA test by now. Wouldn't you?'

Silence. I expected it then — death, oblivion — *what happened to Charlie . . .*

Instead he answered with words. 'You are making it very bad for yourself. Step on to the bridge.'

'What for, when it makes no difference to me?'

He took another step forward, towards the edge of the shadows. 'The power is in here . . . My DNA. *Divine — natural — authority*! Say it to me.'

485

'Why would I, what for?'

A pause. 'Who is the widow maker, Zoe? You or me? Who is the orphan maker? I was — *am* an orphan too — like she is now. Caro will be.'

'You were born months before Irene ever met him. Eric only became your stepfather. You don't want us to see who you are. But I'm watching you, Don. Everyone's been watching you. *I can see who you really are.*'

He raised the gun and aimed at me.

I heard two shots, and the world exploded.

33

Missiles were hurtling through the sky. They were spinning with flame, falling as jagged bones of black. Fragments. Bits of structure? The silver boat . . . It was a fireball, a blazing beacon lighting the trees. And Sutter had gone but I couldn't move. Something was dragging at me, clawing my leg. It was a hand. I stumbled and fell, falling into an embrace.

I was lying in the arms of Don Sutter, and he was dying. He was dead: part of his head had been shot away. And the blood . . . Gargling it, spewing like a gargoyle. Then his hand slid down. He had rolled away to face the sky.

The gleam of his eyes. I had never seen them before.

But he couldn't see me. I knew he couldn't see me.

'*Stay exactly where you are, Zoe!*'

Don Sutter was dead and somebody else was out there in the night. I shrank back in the shadows.

'Stay exactly where you are!'

Behind the concrete foot of the bridge,

something was lying on the ground. It was black and metallic. His gun. I sank to my knees, crawled forward. I had hold of it now.

'Drop the gun! Get up. Slowly.'

It was Kruger's voice. He was just behind me, very close. I let go of the gun. Slowly I stood up.

'Now turn round. And kick it towards me.'

I turned. He was standing on the path. I looked into the open mouth of his gun. Behind him cinders were drifting, black confetti over grey smog.

'Your daughter is dead, Zoe Maker! you all found out too much. Now — kick the gun towards me!'

Kruger thought he had killed Caro. Did he want to shoot me now, with Sutter's gun? That would leave things neat . . . I would be Sutter's final victim after all.

He stepped nearer. What could I do, try again to get more time? 'Tell me — '

I heard a laugh, disembodied. I recognised Darius. 'What do you want to know? Whatever could be *that* important, Zoe?'

The voice had come from above. I looked up. It took a moment to see him there, encased in the frame of a window: he was in one of the warehouses, in a loading bay overhead. Ian Darius ... The past long weeks had been leading up to this: he knew better than to get any closer now. Darius's security chief — his hired gun — had just executed Sutter. That said everything about Ian. Everything except what he would do with me.

He was lounging up there over the windowsill, almost elegantly. 'Zoe Maker, troublemaker. Tell you what, that's so very important? Please don't be shy.'

They would have to kill me too now. I licked my lips. 'I want to know about Charlie.'

'When you came flying with me, why didn't you ask me then? I would've told you all about him.' He paused. 'Don't you really know — not at all?'

'You wanted his secret ... that badly?'

'The Goldstar ... Yes, that was the beginning of the end, for him.'

'Was it just — for *that*?'

He didn't answer. I waited, then went on, 'Why did you let Sutter get away with it? With having killed Charlie? You must surely have known? If not then, soon afterwards. Was it only — '

His voice cut coolly down. 'I did not like Charlie Maker. We all have fantasies, don't we, of the people we would like not to be

489

around any more. People we'd prefer not to be alive . . . Don't we?'

'I don't understand.'

'I despised him. I detested the man!'

'But why?'

'Oh, it was only a small thing, perhaps. He never even . . . To Maker, I was a non-person.'

'But — what did he do?'

'He pretended . . . never to recognise me. We had met before. It was after I left college. I was young. I wrote and asked — almost begged — to work with him. I had admired him so much. I really did! He saw me. Turned me down flat, for someone else.'

'But why — '

'I don't know. But this is what I could not forgive . . . When we met again much later, he cold-shouldered me. Pretended not to know me. I can't describe my contempt for that man, or how it grew! There were other things between us, after that. I set him tests, and every time, Maker failed.'

'Didn't you know that Charlie had memory lapses? Especially about people he'd met — Charlie's head was deeply inside his inventions. He would never have pretended not to know you! That was not deliberate.'

'Of course it was. Well — I became rather a success, as it turned out. Many years passed. During those years I had entered the marketplace. And turned myself into a major player. I had even become quite a threat, to Mr Unmaker.'

A pricked professional ego, then. A small grievance, swollen by misunderstanding, as years, a decade and more had passed? Festering.

'He just had a bad memory,' I said.

'I would see him, see both of you at functions. I never stopped watching him. You both preyed on my mind. When I learned he was dead, I danced. I danced so much, I failed to register one or two important links at first. And then things did get out of hand, I admit it. That was my mistake. There won't be any more of those.'

'Hiring your spy was a big mistake.'

'The young man was useful, so we paid him. Eventually, we did finance his operations. It was such an opportunity to know what was happening. Business is all about opportunity, Zoe.'

'Didn't you know who he really was? Surely — '

'We checked on him, of course. But he had put up such a good cover. Why should we have suspected anything? He'd picked us out. He drew us in. When we found out he was Don Sutter — and his real agenda — by then it was too late.'

'Alison,' I said, dully. 'That was when you knew.'

'Yes. He'd got her by then.'

'And you'd been using Alison for information.' I paused, because Darius said nothing. 'Is that all it was? The reason you were seeing her?'

Something changed in him, just for a moment. He answered at last: 'It began that way . . . Against my better judgement, I became involved. Alison . . . Was she gathering information for you, sleeping with me? I assumed she was.'

'Did you love her?' Again he was silent. 'Alison cared about you. Did you know that?' He said nothing, impassive. Kruger was waiting, still covering me. If only I could pick up Sutter's gun, there might be some chance. 'Why don't you come down and face me?' I said.

'Why would I wish to?'

'You were taken in by Sutter for quite a long time — for months. Or was it longer than that . . . ?'

'He was a clever operator. The insane can be highly intelligent, it appears. Intelligent, and normal-seeming. If it hadn't been me, he would've found the finance elsewhere for tracking his future victims.'

'You're telling me a lot, Ian.'

'You've no proof of any involvement on my part.'

'That's where you're wrong. And if anything happens to me, the police will know exactly what your involvement was. How you became an accessory to murder.'

'You'd say anything right now.' His voice was sneering.

'Your Mr Kruger found and disabled two of the bugs.' I looked at the gunman: he was suddenly alert. 'But you missed the third — it was your ballpoint pen.'

'She's lying,' Darius said.

'It uses a different frequency. And it recorded enough for us. The police are on to you, Ian. They've got the tape. You and Kruger were talking about Don Sutter that evening. Don't you remember the conversation? You had decided to get rid of him — because of your involvement in the murders.'

There was a pause, then Kruger spoke. 'She's bluffing . . . The gun — to me! You are about to kill Don Sutter. He is about to kill you.'

I glanced fleetingly up at the loading bay. Ian was silent.

Kruger said again, 'Kick the gun over — now!'

493

There was the sound of a shot. He crumpled and fell. I heard someone shouting, '*Run, Zoe!*'

It was Redcliff's voice.

In a second I had grabbed up Sutter's gun from the ground, and raced away down the path.

★ ★ ★

More shots rang out behind me, turned into a heavy exchange of fire.

I ran hurtling down the river path, blindly into the near dark. The gunshots had stopped: nothing now. Loud in the silence, my breath jagged out. Heart drumming, feet stumbling over uneven ground. On . . . I saw a gleam of mesh, running alongside. The path was fenced off and a solid white wall loomed ahead. Dead end. Trapped like a rabbit, I looked back. Darkness.

Trying to still my breathing, to listen. Nobody. At the top of the fence, spikes shone lancing down. The wall, then. I stuck the gun into a jeans pocket, tried to get a hold on the bricks. Trying to scramble up, slithering down. Anti-climb paint. Not a chance.

Listening again. Nothing.

I pulled off my jacket and threw it to

494

cover the top of the fence. Climbed the wire, then drew myself over. On the other side were buildings, beyond them the open countryside. I dropped down on to tarmac, paused a moment, then stumbled through an obstacle course. Swings and a climbing frame. It was the playground of a school.

Tall dark brick walls. A passageway led between the buildings, like a tunnel. I blundered into something — a wooden crate. It dragged scraping across the asphalt. I crouched by the wall, quieting my breathing.

Before me lay a gate, and beyond were dark fields with a faint aureole, the first beginnings of dawn. I must have got clear of Darius, I thought. Perhaps Redcliff had got him, or the police: the gun battle had been a number of people. I would hide here and wait for daylight.

I sat down on the crate and rested my head against the wall. My racing heart began to slow. I began to feel safer, just not quite safe enough to come out. Had the police picked up Ian Darius? He had planned to kill Sutter, had known what he'd done and hidden the facts. I shivered in the cold. Maybe it was all over now. Perhaps I would be home with Caro very soon.

Something was at the back of my neck,

icy cold and hard, pressing. Someone there
. . . Illogically, in a surge of fear, I said,
'Redcliff?'

The words came very quietly. 'Don't move,
Zoe Maker. If you move or scream, I'll
kill you.'

Ian Darius's voice, and a gun barrel
twisting against my neck. I whispered, stupid
from shock, 'Why?'

His voice was full of hatred. 'Your friend
can't help you now.'

'What have you done?'

'You and I are going for a walk together.
A very quiet walk. There's a surprise waiting.
Get up.'

I stood up, with the gun still riveted in my
neck. He pushed me forward. In that early
dawn light, the fields and woods stretched
flatly, for miles. We were over the gate. He
put an arm around me, pulled me tight,
clamped against him. Across a track, into
grass. Stumbling, circling. He was using me
as a shield. 'Why?' I gasped.

'Shut up. Keep moving.'

A macabre dance. He was expecting to get
shot. We circled, fell into a muddy ditch.
And Sutter's gun — my gun — dug into my
hip. He didn't know I still had that . . . He
had pulled me on top, we were a parody of
lovers. I was there to shield him from bullets.

'They're here,' I hissed to him. 'You were firing at them and now they're all around. You know they are! How can you hope to — '

'Shut up or I'll kill you.'

'And have no cover? Go ahead!'

He was listening, but not to me. There was a faint throbbing, a whirring in the sky. It was a helicopter, still some distance off. And a scream rang out, deafening. He'd been hit, somehow? It was him — the scream of a cornered animal. But they didn't know that.

Light split the sky, killing the dawn. White beams of light were stalking through. Twin giants dwarfing the landscape, pinning us there. They thought *I* had screamed? I saw his face, fixed like death. He was beyond all reason, desperate. He was hunted, prey. Immobilised and held by that light, we waited. The gun was at my head, pressed to my skull.

A voice, sounding amplified over the open ground.

'You are completely surrounded! Lay down your gun — come out with your hands above your head!'

Then he was yelling, shrieking curses into the emptiness. I grabbed his arm and tried to urge him back to reason. 'Do what they say! Ian, you stand no chance!'

'Call off the pilot! Get rid of the lights! Let me go — or I'll kill her!'

For a minute there was no response. Then, as suddenly as they had appeared, the lights went out, leaving it somehow darker than dawn. Seconds later, the circling drone of the helicopter began to fade.

Now there was silence, with nothing to see but grey fields and trees, flat as paper. The emptiness was not real, he must have known that: they were all around, guns trained and waiting.

He yelled again, 'Leave! Let me go!' The words echoed and drained away.

'Ian,' I said urgently. 'Where d'you think you're going, what're you trying to do?'

'Shut up. Start crawling.'

We crawled along a ditch, through mud and water, battling undergrowth . . . We emerged cautiously, much further on. It was almost daylight now. I saw at last where he'd been heading.

It lay like the sun before us, golden, perched on the curving brow of a field. Yellow wings at rest, waiting. All around lay the sodden earth, a far from empty countryside, in silence that felt sinister. They were watching every move he made, watching us.

'Ian,' I urged again. 'Where can you go? Where can you hope to hide? Give yourself up.'

'On your feet,' he said. 'Hands behind your head. To the plane.'

He grasped me close again, grotesque. We circled, moths towards the sun. Into the sun . . . 'Shield me!'

He was starting the plane when I tried to break free. The Tiger Moth had coughed into life but we were still struggling, grounded there. He was trying to drag me along but I was fighting hard. I grabbed hold of his arm and he couldn't escape, he couldn't even fire at me. I clawed at his face. He punched my throat. Winded, I fell. Then saw him aim at me.

I felt the bullet's impact in my leg. There was no pain. It was all wrong, I couldn't function, couldn't move. He was in the plane and revving, speeding over bumpy ground. Shots rang out across the fields. I had dragged out the gun, I had it trained. My blood was seeping into the ground. The metal sun was rising as I fired. I saw it falling, falling.

34

'Mum?'

It was Caro, her face peeking round the door. I reached out a hand and she came cautiously into the room. She looked unharmed, just like they'd told me. 'Come here.'

She smiled. 'I shouldn't talk too much, they said.'

'What nonsense. Talking's the best thing.' I glanced around but there didn't seem to be any chairs. 'Typical hospital. Why don't you sit on the bed.'

She perched beside my uninjured leg and I studied her. She was still pale from the shock of everything that had happened, but she seemed OK.

'They said you lost a lot of blood, Mum. You do look a bit ghastly.'

'Well, thanks! I'm fine, and the leg only needs time to heal. Caro, I was so afraid I might never see you again.'

We hugged. Every fear came back to me then. Because she was all right, I could relive it all.

'When I saw you, Mum — looking in

the boat . . . I had no idea what was going on, not for ages.' That was just as well, I thought. She was snuggling into the bedcovers. 'Redcliff was ace — real commando stuff — he saved my life, Mum.'

'Yes, he did. I saw some of that.' Redcliff had been shot in the shoulder by Darius, they'd said. 'Is he in hospital or — '

'You *are* joking, Mother dearest? Last heard of — six hours after being left for dead in the river — Redcliff was back working at Quest. Probably hot on the trail of someone or other.'

'Yes, he probably is.'

'This was supposed to be my study week, remember?' And she laughed.

'So it was . . . Caro?'

'What?'

'When he kidnapped you, Sutter — Peter . . . '

'Mum, he didn't do anything to me. That's what you mean? He didn't harm me. He'd got the idea that — he had to kill you.'

'I know. And it's so clear now. Simon had already told me everything, really — what to look for, every clue. But when you think you know someone, you never suspect for a moment . . . '

We were silent. 'At least I was right about the greaseball,' she said. 'Wasn't I?'

'Ian Darius? Absolutely, you were. Darius

501

is more than an accessory. He'll go down for a long time.' I looked at her. Was she going to be able to trust her own judgement in the future? 'Your instincts were right about Doyle too, once you'd had a chance to start getting to know him. But then he wouldn't let go.'

'I'd got afraid of him. At the start, it seemed sort of creamy. But you know, I just needed someone . . . I was missing Dad. I always will.'

'Of course. We always will.' I held her, and remembered the night it had all begun. I thought about Charlie — and it felt as if they were both with us then. Charlie, and Alison. 'Nobody can ever be replaced,' I said. 'He'll always be special to us . . . '

'But life has to go on. That's what you mean?'

'Something like that. Yes.'

We were quiet for a minute. 'The police came to question me,' she said. 'It was all right — Simon's staying around until you come out of hospital.'

'Good. You told them what you know?'

She nodded. 'Redcliff says they were on to things early, but . . . They didn't know it was *him*, of course. Hadn't any way of sussing *that*! Then they had to act, even though it could precipitate stuff — make him even worse. So they did that page in the newspaper.'

'I should've told them where I was going, at the end. I should've, but I was so terrified for you. Thought I could bargain with Sutter.'

'You almost got killed, Mum.'

'But I did tell Redcliff. Then the police were all around but they couldn't storm in. They had to play a waiting game.'

'They'll tell you off,' she said sternly. 'And quite right too.'

I tried to stop thinking. The memories were too recent and there would be time enough, as much time as we wanted in the future.

Caro smiled. 'Simon's nice, Mum.'

'Yes, he is.'

She looked mischievous. 'He's downstairs in the cafeteria. He wanted to see you, but they said I'd be more than enough right now. You look disappointed. I'll tell him.'

'You'll do no such thing, Caro. I'll be out of here in a few days. And whenever you feel ready, you can get back to school. Yes?'

'On one condition, Mum. That we take a holiday. A proper one?'

'Good idea. Soon as I'm better? Why not. Where d'you want to go?'

'Australia,' she answered at once. 'I'd like

to go and stay in Sydney . . . Now you're giving me an old-fashioned look.'

'*Well*,' I began. 'Why Sydney, exactly?'

Caro took a deep breath. 'Mum, just hear me out — '

'What've you been up to?'

'Nothing! Only . . . Yeh, we've been invited to stay with my Aunt Astra. Any time. For as long as we like.'

I was too surprised to say anything, at first. 'You've heard from her then?'

'And d'you want to know something? The last fifteen years, she hasn't known where we were! And her letters got sent back by the mail, Mum.'

'But — '

'Must've been about the time you and Dad moved, and started MakerSeceuro?' Caro interrupted, rushing on. 'Anyway, she's really, really nice and she's got two kids and she and her husband are teachers and . . . We can go, can't we?'

Caro was looking guilty, somehow. And I just couldn't take in what she was saying, not for ages. 'You've talked to her?'

'Yeh, that's right. Mum, she knows that Dad died and . . . You've missed each other, you and her. Don't be cross with me.'

'Why would I be cross? So you found her.'

'Actually, Simon did. But only because I *begged* him to. He contacted the embassy, and they were awfully quick ... Mum? You're *crying*?'

'Not really. It's just ... '

'You're not cross with Simon?'

Out of all the bad things that had happened, it looked as if Astra and I had found each other. She'd tried to stay in touch, she wanted to see me. I realised just now how much I was longing to see her again. Nothing could make up for the loss of Charlie — nor Alison, or the others who had died. But this was so unexpected — so haphazard an outcome to all the months of pain and fear — that we should finally have my sister back.

Caro was watching my expression closely. I said, sounding rather stern, 'I think you'd better go and fetch Simon. Right now. There are one or two things I need to say to him.'

As she hurried out of the room, I began to laugh.

We do hope that you have enjoyed reading this large print book.

Did you know that all of our titles are available for purchase?

We publish a wide range of high quality large print books including:
Romances, Mysteries, Classics
General Fiction
Non Fiction and Westerns

Special interest titles available in large print are:
The Little Oxford Dictionary
Music Book
Song Book
Hymn Book
Service Book

Also available from us courtesy of Oxford University Press:
Young Readers' Dictionary
(large print edition)
Young Readers' Thesaurus
(large print edition)

For further information or a free brochure, please contact us at:
Ulverscroft Large Print Books Ltd.,
The Green, Bradgate Road, Anstey,
Leicester, LE7 7FU, England.
Tel: (00 44) 0116 236 4325
Fax: (00 44) 0116 234 0205

Other books in the
Ulverscroft Large Print Series:

THIS MORTAL COIL

Ann Quinton

'PETS. Exits arranged. Professionally. Effectively. Terminally. Apply: The Coil Shuffler.' Thus reads the business card of a professional assassin. When physio-therapist and lay reader Rachel Morland stumbles across one of these cards on the body of a frail parishioner, her suspicions are at once aroused, not least because she has seen it before — when her beloved husband apparently committed suicide. Policeman Mike Croft, a friend of Rachel's, also realises the significance of the calling-card and, together with his former boss, Nick Holroyd, sets out to track down the killer . . .

GRIANAN

Alexandra Raife

Abandoning her life in England after a broken engagement, Sally flees to Grianan, the beloved Scottish home of her childhood. Running Aunt Janey's remote country house hotel will be a complete break. Sally's brief encounter with Mike — gentle, loving but unavailable — cures the pain of her broken engagement, but leaves a deeper ache in its place. Caught up in the concerns of Grianan, Sally begins to heal. And when fate brings Mike into her life again, tragically altered, she has the strength and faith to hope that Grianan may help him too.

AN INCONSIDERATE DEATH

Betty Rowlands

In the sleepy Gloucestershire village of Marsdean, Lorraine Chant, wife of a wealthy businessman, is found strangled. But why, when both the Chants' safes had been discovered, was nothing stolen? What was Lorraine's relationship with Hugo Bayliss — a man with a dubious background and a penchant for attractive married women? How did Bayliss come to meet Sukey, police photographer and scene of crime officer, before the investigation became public? Then, in a cruel twist of fate, Sukey unwittingly plays into the hands of Lorraine's murderer . . .

THE SIMPLE LIFE

Lauren Wells

Lawrence Langland has had enough of corporate politics and fifteen-hour days. He wants out, to a simpler life. Isobel, his wife, whose gold-plated keyring says 'Born to Shop', has her own reasons for wanting to escape. Fortunately for Jacob, their eight-year-old son, it means leaving his horrible boarding school, although his elder sister Dory needs more persuading. And so the Langlands become 'downshifters', exchanging a comfortable house in suburbia for a small cottage in the countryside. Making the decision was the easy part — but can they cope with the reality?